"Everyone knows that bayou men are just born with that irresistibility gene," Aaron drawled.

"Irresistibility?" Fleur couldn't help but laugh, but then she shook her head at his hopelessness. "Don't waste your time on me. I'm practically a nun."

"I thought they kicked you out."

"They did not kick me out. I'm merely taking a sabbatical. And I'll still be helping with the rescue missions."

Fleur had gotten to know Aaron fairly well over the past year as he flew them on some of their rescue missions. She tried to stop thinking about him and looked out the window of the plane. They were circling over the bayou region. For the first time in like forever, she felt a tug at her heartstrings, as if she were coming home.

So where did Aaron LeDeux fit in?

By Sandra Hill

Cajun Series
CAJUN PERSUASION • CAJUN CRAZY
THE CAJUN DOCTOR
THE LOVE POTION

Deadly Angels Series
GOOD VAMPIRES GO TO HEAVEN
THE ANGEL WORE FANGS
EVEN VAMPIRES GET THE BLUES
VAMPIRE IN PARADISE
CHRISTMAS IN TRANSYLVANIA
KISS OF WRATH • KISS OF TEMPTATION
KISS OF SURRENDER • KISS OF PRIDE

Viking Series I
THE PIRATE BRIDE
THE NORSE KING'S DAUGHTER
THE VIKING TAKES A KNIGHT • VIKING IN LOVE
A TALE OF TWO VIKINGS
THE VIKING'S CAPTIVE (formerly MY FAIR VIKING)
THE BLUE VIKING • THE BEWITCHED VIKING
THE TARNISHED LADY • THE OUTLAW VIKING
THE RELUCTANT VIKING

Viking Series II
HOT & HEAVY • WET & WILD
THE VERY VIRILE VIKING
TRULY, MADLY VIKING • THE LAST VIKING

Creole-Time Travel Series
SWEETER SAVAGE LOVE • FRANKLY, MY DEAR...

Others
LOVE ME TENDER • DESPERADO

CAJUN
PERSUASION

*A Cajun
Novel*

SANDRA
HILL

AVONBOOKS

An Imprint of HarperCollinsPublishers

Excerpt from *The Love Potion* copyright © 2012 by Sandra Hill.

CAJUN PERSUASION. Copyright © 2018 by Sandra Hill. All rights reserved. Printed in the United States of America. No part of this book may be used or reproduced in any manner whatsoever without written permission except in the case of brief quotations embodied in critical articles and reviews. For information, address HarperCollins Publishers, 195 Broadway, New York, NY 10007.

First Avon Books mass market printing: July 2018

Print Edition ISBN: 978-0-06-256653-9
Digital Edition ISBN: 978-0-06-256640-9

Cover design by Nadine Badalaty
Cover photographs © InnervisionArt/Shutterstock (face/neck);
© Pinkypills/Getty Images (body); © Kjell Leknes/Shutterstock(hair);
© tj-rabbit/Shutterstock (sky); © buzzbuzzer/Getty Images (plane/
airfield); © Nadya/Shutterstock (roses); © Nemeziya/Shutterstock
(foreground)

Avon, Avon & logo, and Avon Books & logo are registered trademarks of HarperCollins Publishers in the United States of America and other countries.

HarperCollins is a registered trademark of HarperCollins Publishers in the United States of America and other countries.

FIRST EDITION

18 19 20 21 22   QGM   10 9 8 7 6 5 4 3 2 1

This book is dedicated to all the victims of human trafficking around the world, especially to the children who are sold into the slave trade. The statistics are shocking. Even here in the United States, the land of the free, there are literally hundreds of thousands of victims. God be with them, and with those who attempt to rescue them.

Prologue

(ONE YEAR AGO)

A girl's gotta do what a girl's gotta do . . .

Fleur Gaudet, whose name tag read Doris Jones, stood in the dressing room of the Silver Stud Club in New Orleans, using a long-handled dust pan and broom to sweep along the edges of the tiled floor, all the while keeping an alert eye on her surroundings. Although she wore a blonde wig to hide her identity and a rather demure black nylon uniform with a white apron, as befitted her new job on the club's cleaning staff, unlike the scantily clad women around her, she was still outside her comfort zone. Way outside!

She decided to offer up the discomfort as a penance for past—and future—sins. Mortifying the flesh, so to speak. Like that self-flagellating albino monk in *The Da Vinci Code*. You had to be Catholic to understand the logic of suffering in silence and offering it up as a heavenly gift.

But then, Fleur *was* a nun!

An honest-to-God, hope-and-pray nun.

Like Mother Teresa.

Well, not really like that holier-than-holy nun, bless her heart, who had lived, by choice, in abject poverty in Calcutta. In the old days, Mother Teresa would probably have worked in a leper colony.

On the other hand, a strip club was somewhat like a leper colony, wasn't it?

Truth to tell, Fleur wasn't really a nun yet. More like a nun-in-training, with the Sisters of Magdalene religious order. The Magdas had originated in Spain, but expanded into satellite convents throughout the world. Like the one in Mexico, with which she was affiliated, that had in recent years joined forces with the rogue order, St. Jude's Street Apostles, in Dallas. Their mission: to rescue girls kidnapped into the sex trade. Which was why she and some of her partners were in this sleazy club tonight.

There were other females in the dressing room, but mostly they kept to themselves as they lounged or touched up make-up. None of them were the young, frightened teens they hoped to rescue, though. Not that they were old, exactly. In fact, Peaches Galore, the girl in front of her, was no more than twenty-two years old, wearing a sheer black bustier and a G-string and heels high enough to give a person a nosebleed.

Peaches was on her cell phone, presumably talking to one of her three children, all under the age of eight, that she'd told Fleur about a short time ago. "No, you cannot make a frozen pizza, Henry. You know the stove is off-limits. The microwave, too. Did Jimmy say his prayers before you put him to bed? He skipped Auntie Priss?" Peaches laughed, and murmured something under her breath about how she would skip the old bat, too. "Did you change Elisa Mae's diaper? I don't care if it stinks, do as you're told. I know, sweetie. I'm sorry I yelled. Be a good boy, and tomorrow we'll go to the park with your remote control airplane."

It was sad, really. But the Magdas couldn't rescue everyone. And not everyone working in this club wanted or needed rescuing.

Just then, the door flew open as a group of strippers, waitresses, lap dancers, and bar maids trooped in, laughing, cursing, talking, many of them pulling five-, ten-, and twenty-dollar bills from their G-strings or thigh-high fishnet stockings. The pounding beat of that old Mötley Crüe song "Girls, Girls, Girls" could be heard through the open door, coming from the DJ station.

Also, through the open doorway, she could see the raised circular stage with its spokes leading out into the crowd, up close and personal. At any one time, a dozen girls were dancing. Another dozen would be doing lap dances in semi-private alcoves.

A regular meat factory! Ironically, that's just what this former warehouse had been . . . a huge meat packing plant.

And none of these activities included those upstairs, which was why Fleur and her "posse" of nuns were here tonight with the Rogues.

"Gentlemen, let's give a warm—no, hot—welcome to the next round of ladies," the DJ yelled out. The door hadn't closed tightly. "Chocolate Cream. Bubble Icious. Fanny Bigguns. Ms. Demeanor. Moana Bigona."

Yep, this was a high-class place, all right.

Fleur rolled her eyes as the air compressor door finally swooshed shut, muting the club noise. Just then, she noticed one of her religious cohorts, Sister Carlotta, leaning her forehead against the wall, muttering something. Lottie was working as a waitress, not a topless one in the bar, but a regularly dressed one in the coffee shop. Her uniform was similar to Fleur's, except shorter, and she wore the proverbial high heels. She wore a wig, too, but hers was black and cut into a straight bob. Attractive, actually.

Fleur went up to her and whispered, "Lottie, are you all right?"

Lottie nodded, then turned to face her. "I was praying. This place just gets to me. How disgusting! And sad!"

"I know what you mean."

Carlotta waved the ten-dollar bill in front of Fleur and said, "A man stuck this in my blouse, then had the nerve to ask if I had five dollars in change. This place feels like hell."

Or a leper colony. Fleur barely stifled a laugh. Carlotta wasn't that old—about twenty-five—but she'd been in a conventional Spanish convent since she was thirteen. The philosopher John Milton's "cloistered virtue" personified.

Carlotta, like many other humble nuns who cherished the insular life of prayer and meditation inside the walls of an abbey, was a victim of the upheaval in all the flagging religious orders, male and female, throughout the world. The old ways no longer worked.

Nunneries and monasteries were now forced to open their doors to deal with modern issues. Prayer was fine, prayer with action was better.

A strip joint wasn't what the papal decree on reformation of religious vocations intended, of course, but in this instance "needs must," the Magdas were told by their Mother Superior when outlining this mission. Mother Jacinta, who was noted for her dry sense of humor, had said, "Some nuns go to jungles to convert the natives. You will be going to another kind of jungle, to bring just retribution to the natives who harm these young girls."

And so there were five nuns here at the Silver Stud jungle this week, including herself, working undercover. To say they were all outside their comfort zone would be the understatement of the century, but some more so than others. Like Carlotta.

Now, if they could only make their connection with Brian Malone, the former Air Force pilot who was now a priest with the St. Jude's Street Apostles, this show could get on the road. Literally. Well, the skies, not the road. Brother Brian had a plane waiting for their getaway.

Speaking—rather, thinking—of Brother Brian . . . she took Carlotta by the arm and led her toward the back of the room. "This isn't your usual time for a break. Has Brother Brian made his connection with you yet, or anyone else?"

"That's why I came to get you," Carlotta said, dabbing at her eyes with a tissue. "No one has seen him since early this evening, and there was some kind of ruckus out in the alley a little while ago. I saw several bouncers rush toward the back exit doors."

"Oh no!" Fleur bit her bottom lip with dismay. "Well, perhaps Plan B needs to kick in now. You go back to the coffee shop and wait for the signal. I'll make my way upstairs."

Carlotta exchanged a worried glance with Fleur, then left.

Fleur inhaled sharply, straightened her shoulders, and picked up her long-handled dust pan and broom, preparing to go out into the jungle . . . uh, leper colony. Like Daniel going into the lion's den, or the Christians entering the coliseum to be food for the lions and tigers and such. If worst came to worst, she could always use these tools of her cleaning trade as weapons, she joked to herself.

But then, she reminded herself, nuns eschewed violence.

On the other hand, she shrugged, she wasn't yet a nun.

Was it irony, or celestial humor, that the loud song assaulting her eardrums when she entered the arena was "Eye of the Tiger"?

Snakes are alive and well in Louisiana . . .

Aaron LeDeux was in his *garçonniére*, or separate bachelor quarters, on Bayou Rose Plantation outside Houma, Louisiana, when he got the phone call that changed his life. Not that there hadn't been a lot of changes in Aaron's life already.

He and his twin brother, Daniel, had been born and raised in Alaska by their Cajun-born mother, Claire Doucet. After her death a few years ago, they'd come to Louisiana to discover their roots. Hah! Those roots were more like tentacles. It was supposed to have been a temporary visit, but with one thing and another, including Tante Lulu, that outrageous busybody aunt (or whatever she was of theirs), they were still here.

Dan, a pediatric oncologist (*Try saying that three times real fast!*), had gotten married last year to the former Samantha Starr of the Starr Supermarket chain. Although Aaron and Dan owned the plantation jointly (*Don't ask!*), the married couple lived in the main house, an arrangement perfectly agreeable to Aaron, who'd gotten tired of all the love sounds the newlyweds were making, *in every frickin' room of the mansion, at every frickin' time of the night, or day*, and, yeah, he was probably a little jealous.

Dan was finally settled, to everyone's relief, most especially his twin brother (*that would be me*) who'd been worried about him for so long. Aaron, on the other hand, a pilot, was still trying to find himself, or his place, in this crazy world. Maybe it was time to move on.

He'd just emerged from the shower and hadn't yet decided what to do on this Saturday night when his cell phone rang in his bedroom. He caught it on the fourth ring, just before it went to voice mail.

Maybe it was Babette, the new nurse at Dan's medical center. She'd told him that she might be able to trade shifts with another nurse.

Or maybe it was Remy LeDeux, his half brother. Even though Aaron had been part owner of his own air shipping company in Alaska, he worked for Remy's company here in Louisiana, running copters back and forth to the oil rigs. Eventually (praise God and pass the grits, as Tante Lulu would say), he would form his own business here. Or not. Decisions, decisions.

If it was Tante Lulu wanting him to do her yet another "teeny tiny" favor, he was not going to answer.
Not on a Saturday night. Since he was the only one of
her "nephews" who was unmarried, she figured he was
free all the time.

To come kill the raft of fire ants in her toilet, for
example.

"Why not just flush them away?" he'd told her at the
time.

"Because they'll swim back up, fool!"

Turned out the fire ants had just been rust flecks that
had loosened and backed up from her ancient septic
pipes.

Or the time she wanted him to row her pirogue out
to a gator nest in the swamps to gather gator eggs.

As if!

But, no, it was a caller he'd never expected to hear
from. Brian Malone, an old Air Force friend, better
known by his nickname "Snake," for obvious reasons
when he went commando. "Is this Aaron LeDeux I'm
speakin' with?" He pronounced LeDeux like Lay-
dough, rather than La-doo.

"Snake! I'd recognize that blarney voice of yours
anywhere."

"How are you, lad?" he asked Aaron in a deep Irish
brogue that sounded more like "Ha ware ya, laddie?"

Even though he'd been living in Michigan for
twenty-some years, Brian still retained the musical dialect of the "old country" he'd emigrated from as a
teenager with his parents. When drunk off his ass, the
Irish proverbs that spewed from his mouth with an
elongated Irish burr had amused all of the flight squad-
ron. "As ye slide down the bannister of life, may the

splinters be goin' the wrong way." Or Aaron's favorite, "May all your ups and downs be under the sheets."

"Still doin' somersaults above the clouds, are ye, Ace?" Snake asked now.

"Snake? Where the hell you been, dude? I haven't heard from you in ten years. Yes, I'm still flying. Copters at the moment. What's up?"

"You wouldn't believe it if I had the time to tell you."

"How'd you know my number?"

"Ways and means, me boy. Ways and means. Actually, I've had it for a while now. Got it from your aunt up in Alaska. Been meanin' to call."

"You married? Any kids? Weren't you engaged or something to that girl from your hometown . . . Jillian, no, Julie?"

"No engagement. No marriage. No children," Snake said. "I'm a priest."

Aaron dropped his phone and had to scurry to pick it up off the floor, from under the bed, where it had slid. He could hear Snake laughing when he put the device to his ear again.

"You're shittin' me."

"No. I really am a priest. I work with St. Jude's Street Apostles in Dallas."

"Huh? I never heard of . . . wait. Aren't those the yahoos that rode motorcycles into a cult campground last year and rescued a bunch of teenagers? And I saw something on CNN recently about them liberating some American girls who joined ISIS?"

"Um," Snake said. "I'm not so sure about the yahoo part, but, yeah, we're sort of a rogue gang . . . uh, brother-hood."

"What do I call you? Father Brian?"

"You can call me whatever you want, buddy. But most folks call us Brothers . . . Brother Brian, Brother Samuel, Brother Chuck. No, I'm not kidding. There is a priest named Chuck. Used to be a member of Hell's Angels. Some of us in the Street Apostles are ordained priests, some are monks who haven't taken vows. Just easier for all of us to go by the Brother tag."

All this was more than Aaron could take in. "Let's get together and catch up. Are Brothers allowed to drink a beer or two?"

"Bite your tongue, me lad. An Irishman always has room for a beer," Snake—rather, Brother Brian—declared. "But that's not why I called, my friend."

Uh-oh. That "my friend" sounded ominous.

"I need a favor. A big favor."

"Sure."

"Can you come to the Silver Stud in New Orleans?"

"A strip club?" Aaron laughed. "I don't know, Snake. I'm not really into the club scene anymore. How 'bout tomorrow? You can come out here to—"

Suddenly, Aaron could hear shouting over the phone, and then some popping noises that might be gunfire.

"Holy shit, Snake, what kind of trouble are you in?"

"Big trouble. The deadly kind."

Snake had saved Aaron's ass on more than one occasion when they'd served in Afghanistan. Aaron owed him. "It will probably take me an hour to get there."

"Thanks. Gotta go."

"Wait. Where should we meet?"

"The alley out back. I really appreciate this, good buddy."

"Maybe you should call the police."

"No police. And no weapons."

"Are you sure? I have a small pistol that I can hide—"

"No. Nonviolence is essential for our order. We rely on unconventional warfare of a different sort. Disguise and creativity are our tools."

"How's that working for you?"

Snake laughed. "Sometimes we get the bear, sometimes the bear gets us."

"That's just great. We have a lot of grizzlies in Louisiana. Not!"

"Hold on a minute," Snake said. He appeared to be speaking to someone in a whisper. When he came back on the line, he told Aaron, "If I'm not here . . . or I'm . . . uh, incapacitated . . . go inside and find Fleur. The password is 'lug nut' tonight."

"Floor? What floor?"

"Not that kind of floor. Fleur, like a flower. F-L-E-U-R."

"Okaay," Aaron said dumbly, chilled at Snake's mention of being incapacitated. "Is this Fleur a stripper?"

Snake laughed. "She's a nun."

"You mean she's dressed like a nun? Remember the time we went to that German nightclub, and the nun came out on stage—"

"No. Fleur *is* a nun."

Oh boy!

Then the line went dead.

Who can explain the things that turn a guy on? . . .

Aaron wended his way gingerly through the crowd, asking occasionally if anyone knew where he could find a woman named Fleur. He'd already cased the alley behind the private club with no luck. No Snake. In fact, no people at all. However, there had been an ominous pool of fluid that might have been blood. But then, the lighting had been dim, and, besides, the back alley of a strip club . . . ? It could have been anything.

Once inside, after having slipped the doorman a twenty, he glanced right and left, scanning the joint. Even though he was no stranger to male entertainment establishments, at this stage in his life—the wrong side of thirty-five—it was not an appealing sight. Too much noise. Too much booze. Too much smoke. Too much fleshy exposure.

People considered him wild and, yeah, he'd done some outrageous things in his sorry life, but this scene wasn't wild. It was . . . well, sad.

Good Lord! I must have grown up along the way without realizing it. My brother will be so pleased . . . if I'm ever dumb enough to tell him. Of course, Dan will be quick to point out that I came to this realization inside a strip club.

If it wasn't for his concern over Snake, Aaron would skip this rodeo and stop at the Swamp Shack for a beer before calling it an early night. This was not his scene.

That was, until he spotted the blonde bombshell sitting on a high stool outside one of the lap dance alcoves. She wore some kind of see-through, black blouse thingee, or maybe it was underwear. Who knew today! A scrap of red fabric barely covered her crotch. Her long, bare legs were crossed at the knee with glittery red fuck-me-please high heels dangling from both feet. She couldn't have looked more bored if she'd been chewing gum and blowing bubbles.

Maybe we could be bored together.

No, no, no, that is not why I'm here.

Still, he paused and asked, "Don't suppose you know some woman here by the name of Fleur?"

"Cain't say ah do, sugah," she drawled in an exaggerated southern twang. "Won't ah do?" She licked her crimson lips and made a kissy noise at him.

He was just about to respond when he felt something smack against the back of his calves. He turned to see a cleaning lady with a raised broom. With her straggly blonde hair and a skinny body in a shapeless uniform, she looked like a bag lady.

"Oops," the woman said and grinned, showing him a dark space where one of her front teeth should be. The grin told him, without words, that that swat with the broom had been deliberate. And, oddly, peering closer, he could swear it was just black gum on her one front tooth. Whatever! He started to turn back to the lap dancer, figuring he could stand around here and look for his contact as easily as prowling the joint aimlessly.

Another poke in the back. This time, the broom, handle end now, was prodding his shoulder.

He was getting annoyed now. "I beg your pardon . . . Doris," he said after checking out her name tag.

"Were you asking for Fleur?"

"Yeah," he said. "Do you know Fleur?"

"I might," she said.

"Get lost, Doris," the lap dancer ordered. "Yer interferin' with mah business."

Yeah, he wanted to agree, but wait a testosterone minute. Was the cleaning lady surreptitiously beckoning him to follow her with a forefinger held near her one hip.

He tilted his head to the side in question.

She cast a suddenly frightened glance out toward the bar where an employee was taking note of the lap dancer waving for him. The guy was built like a Greyhound bus.

He had no time for this shit. Taking the cleaning lady by the forearm, he frog-marched her toward a side corridor. "Are you Fleur?"

"Um. Who wants to know?" she asked, shrugging out of his hold and rubbing her arm as if he'd hurt her.

He hadn't. At least he hoped not.

"Snake asked me to look for someone named Fleur if I couldn't find him outside in the alley."

"Snake?"

"Brian Malone."

"Do you mean Brother Malone? Brother Brian?"

"Yeah. I guess."

"Why would he ask you to come here?"

"Maybe because I'm a pilot. Snake and I served in the Air Force together."

"Aaah!" she said, as if now she understood.

He wished he did.

"Well, Brother Brian must be in trouble then," she concluded. "This is bad. Really bad. I need to get out of here and check with one of my team members. Mother Jacinta should know what's up." She stared at him kind of funny then. "If Brother Brian is . . . um, incapacitated, I guess you'll have to take over."

"Take over what?"

"The escape plan. Getting the girls out and flying them to Dallas. From there to Mexico."

"What? Who? I'm not going to friggin' Mexico, with or without some girls."

"Didn't Brother Brian tell you anything?"

"Not much."

"I'm with the Sisters of Magdalene convent in Mexico. We have six girls upstairs who've been kidnapped. All part of the sex trafficking ring being run out of this dive. Mexican Mafia working with the Dixie Mafia."

"So, a bunch of crackpot nuns are going to crack a dangerous human trafficking operation? Seriously? What are you? Special forces nuns?"

"We're not here to crack any operation. That's up to the government and law enforcement who aren't doing a very good job, by the way. No, we just need to get these six girls on a plane to the Street Apostles' refuge outside Dallas."

"That's all?" he said with another dose of sarcasm. "And you expect me to get involved . . . why?"

"Your friend, Brother Brian, must have expected you to."

He swore under his breath. He shouldn't have to remind himself that his buddy was in trouble, might at this very moment be wounded or worse. "You mentioned your team members. Are you a cop, or with the feds?"

"Hardly." She laughed. "I already told you. I'm a nun. Sort of."

He had no time to ask her what a "sort of nun" was. "That's right. Snake told me you were a nun. Would you rather I call you Sister Fleur?"

"Whatever. Just Fleur will do."

A nun who says "Whatever!" Who is on some asinine mission in a strip club? She's the damnedest nun I ever met. Aaron shook his head to clear it. "I've gotta find Snake, *now*," he said.

"We have to get the girls out, *now*," she said at the same time.

But just then the guard who resembled a bus, the one who'd been signaled by the lap dancer, came stomping toward them. "What the hell are you doing out on the floor, Doris? Aren't you supposed to be cleaning the urinals in the VIP men's room?"

"Oh, I forgot."

The Bus rolled his eyes and muttered, "She forgot." He glanced at Aaron and made a twirling motion with a forefinger near his head to indicate that the cleaning lady was a few bricks short of a full load.

"We were just talking," Aaron said, which was a big mistake.

Fleur looked at him as if he was the one missing a few bricks.

Now suspicious, the bouncer asked, "About what?"

"Um, it's like this, Mister"—Aaron paused to check out the guy's name tag—"Albertson. I have this thing about cleaning ladies. The first time I got laid it was with a cleaning lady. I was only fourteen, and well, it was pretty amazing." He shrugged and pretended to be embarrassed. Actually, he *was* embarrassed. *How do I come up with this crap? Oh hell, it's the best I could do on short notice.*

Albertson pocketed the twenty that Aaron slipped him, then glanced between Aaron and the clearly unattractive cleaning lady. "With all the hot babes here, you want *this*? I don't believe it. Is this some kind of *Candid Camera* or *Punk'd* or something?"

Aaron passed the smirking guy another twenty and said, "Actually, I was wondering if Doris and I could go upstairs."

"Are you frickin' serious?" Albertson let out a hoot of laughter.

But Aaron noticed that he pocketed this twenty, too.

"I've heard of guys going for some pretty weird kinks, but cleaning ladies? That's a new one." When he was finally able to get his laughter under control, Albertson asked Fleur, "Are you willing?"

She was startled at first and indignant.

Aaron kept winking to alert her to his ploy to get them upstairs and hopefully find out what happened to Snake.

When The Bus went off to ask his boss if it was all right for the cleaning lady to take a trick, Aaron hissed at her, "Get with the program. You said the girls to be rescued are upstairs."

"Oh."

"Didn't you see me winking?"

"I thought you had a nervous tic."

He put his face in his hands for a moment and hoped that when he looked back up, this would all be a bad dream. But, no, The Bus was back. "Fifty bucks!" he announced.

"What?" Aaron and Fleur both exclaimed, he because he thought it was a rip-off, she because she probably thought she was undervalued. But then, they both said, "Sure!" at the same time, too.

Following the big bruiser as he made a pathway through the crowd, then up the stairs, Aaron and Fleur exchanged several whispered remarks.

"Our mission goes down at eleven p.m. sharp," she informed him.

Once again, this woman sounded more military than nun-like. When most nuns talked about a mission, they usually meant a religious vocation in some foreign land, bringing Christianity to the natives. When he was a kid, they were always asked to save their pennies for the poor missions. But that was neither here nor there. "Eleven! It's ten-thirty now!"

And there was another difference between this cleaning lady and the average nun. Her body. As he followed her up the stairs, and her uniform cupped her bottom with each lift of her legs, he couldn't help but notice a nicely shaped ass.

She glanced back at him over her shoulder and made a disgusted sound.

Busted!

"It's a short time frame on purpose, to get the girls out the second-floor fire exit and down to the van in the alley. The longer we have them out of their locked rooms, the greater the chance of discovery."

"There is no van in the alley," he noted. "I already told you that, didn't I? I was just there."

"There will be. Sister Evangeline will be driving. Did you bring a vehicle?"

He nodded. "A pickup truck."

"We might have to use that, too."

"Nice of you to ask." He was beginning to think this was a big mistake, friend or no friend.

"It's for a good cause."

"The Cancer Society is a good cause. Wounded Warriors is a good cause. Hookers for Jesus is not a good cause."

"Stop being an ass," Fleur said.

"A potty mouth on a nun? Really?"

"Shhh!"

"Just out of curiosity, does your religious order do strip clubs all the time?"

"This is a one-time thing. Hopefully. We usually work in jungles, or on city streets."

"Aren't I the lucky one?"

"Shhh!" she hissed again.

They came to a desk in the wide second-floor corridor where a woman who looked almost as big and muscular as The Bus sat, not topless or in some sexy hooker attire, thankfully, considering her size and gray-threaded brown hair, but wearing a T-shirt with the Silver Stud logo and black slacks. There was a list of services on a laminated cardboard table poster. He handed over his fifty bucks.

"Room thirteen, end of the hall, fifteen minutes," Ms. Bus said.

"Fifteen minutes!" he complained. "It takes me fifteen minutes to get my boots off."

"Here's a news flash, Forrest Gump," The Bus said with a smirk, already heading back downstairs. "You don't need bare feet for a blow job."

Once The Bus was gone, Fleur whispered to Aaron, "This is Sister Mary Michael."

Of course, she was a nun. Why hadn't he realized that? In his defense, it was the first time he'd seen a nun who looked like a bouncer.

Then Fleur told Ms. Bus, "This is . . ." She glanced at him and raised her eyebrows.

He realized that he hadn't yet given her his name. "Aaron LeDeux," he said.

"Aaron LeDeux," Sister Mary Michael repeated with a smile. "Thank God! We were expecting you."

"You were?" Aaron asked dumbly. This was a day, rather night, for dumbness on his part.

"Brother Brian said he called you to come help."

"Ah," he said.

Sister Mary Michael glanced right and left to make sure she was not overheard. "Brother Brian got himself shot. He's in the back of the van. Mother Jacinta is caring for him, but he's lost a lot of blood."

"Whaaat? Snake is injured. Call 911." Aaron pulled out his phone.

"Shhh. No, no, no! No police or ambulances," Fleur cautioned. "There's a doctor at the ranch headquarters in Dallas."

He was afraid to ask who would be taking Snake there. He knew.

"At least I'm dressed for a ranch," he quipped.

"It's not that kind of ranch."

Fleur took him by the hand and yanked him along with her, down the hall, to room thirteen, which was next to the exit door. To his surprise, Sister Mary Michael followed after them. She was about the same height as he was and fifty pounds heavier.

When Fleur opened the door, Aaron was taken aback. Literally. Huddled about the small room, which held a single bed and not much more, were six obviously frightened girls of various ages and nationalities, mostly under sixteen, he would guess. Also in the room was a woman in a nun outfit. A real nun, or a nun stripper? he wondered.

The nun acknowledged Fleur's entrance with a nod of her head, and his presence with a raised eyebrow, but then she said, "Let's all pray until we get the cue to run."

"What cue?" he asked.

All the nuns dropped to their knees and began to pray the "Our Father." The girls stared at them as if they were crazy, not believing yet that they were about to be rescued, but then they, too, dropped to the floor.

He stood. Not that he was against prayer, but couldn't they pray as they ran?

Just then, there was an explosion somewhere below, followed by several others. They sounded distant, like maybe in the basement, or the far side of the club's main floor.

"What the hell?" he exclaimed. "Snake emphasized nonviolence."

"Firecrackers," Fleur explained.

Organized chaos ensued as the group was herded out the door by Sister Mary Michael, along the hall, around the corner to the exit door, and down the metal fire escape to the alley. More explosions could be heard popping and sirens sounded in the distance. Just before they entered the sliding door of the van, which had miraculously arrived, Fleur announced, "By the way, when I heard your last name, LeDeux, I realized that we share a mutual acquaintance."

"Yeah, I know. Snake?"

"No. Tante Lulu."

Why was he not surprised?

Chapter One

Oh, brother! . . .

On a lazy Sunday afternoon in late August, Aaron LeDeux sat on the upper verandah of Bayou Rose Plantation with his brother Daniel. The plantation was named for its once famous rose garden, not because it was on Bayou Rose. It was, in fact, on Bayou Black. Why they hadn't named it Bayou Black Plantation was anyone's guess.

Cajuns! Who could ever figure them out!

Beside Dan's chair sat Emily, a small potbellied pig, one of the few animals remaining from Samantha's old animal rescue days. Emily had been depressed (*Yeah, I know, a depressed pig!*) before becoming attached to Dan. Every once in a while, Dan's hand would extend down and scratch behind her ears.

On Aaron's side lay Samantha's elderly German shepherd, Axel, snoozing in the sun. Sometimes he would snore, other times he growled at something happening in his dreams, or else he let loose with the most noxious farts. Samantha's big Savannah cat, Maddie, which resembled a cheetah, was probably off chasing snakes, along with the two "normal" cats, Felix and Garfield. From inside the house, there was the occasional "Holy shit!" coming from Clarence, Samantha's foul-mouthed cockatoo.

Ah, life on Bayou Rose Plantation! Good thing Samantha had gotten pregnant, diverting her attention in another direction. Otherwise, who knew how many animals they would have here? Or what kind. Goats, horses, peacocks, ducks, and gerbils came to mind.

Both men had longneck bottles of Dixie beer in hand, their legs crossed and propped on the balcony rail, Aaron's in worn denims and scruffy cowboy boots, Dan's in more conservative khakis with sockless loafers.

They were twins, bonded from birth, but from a young age, they'd moved to a different beat, deliberately seeking their own identities, especially in physical appearance. Aaron, a pilot, kept his brown hair longish and had a reputation for being a bit wild. Dan, a pediatric oncologist, kept his hair business professional short and his lifestyle conservative.

Despite outward appearances, having recently passed their mid-thirties, they were still connected by that extrasensory twin-thread that allowed them to sense the other's feelings, even when far apart. They loved each other deeply.

For once the Louisiana temperature was mild and

balmy. Even so, a sharp contrast to Alaska, where they'd grown up. A day of serenity.

But then Dan asked the question that had been a constant refrain of late. "What the hell are you doing every night, Aaron?" Dan shook his head as he stared him down. "I've been getting a bad vibe lately."

"Um," Aaron said, taking a draw on the cold brew, giving himself time to think of a suitable answer. The longer he kept his family and friends in the dark about his activities, the more they could claim ignorance as a defense if everything suddenly blew up. Literally.

What had started as a favor more than a year ago had turned into a lark and then a bloody mission. How he'd gotten suckered into continuing work with street monks and psycho nuns was a case for some psychiatrist's couch. Sucker Syndrome.

"Gone almost every night from dusk till dawn. No explanation. Hardly any sleep when you're off to fly copters for Remy's company." Remy was one of their many newly discovered "kinfolk" here on the bayou. "You could be spending the night with three twelve-dollar hookers and look more rested. It's a wonder you don't zone out and crash going back and forth over the Gulf to the oil rigs with so little rest."

"Holy crap! You sound like my mother, not my brother."

They both went silent at that last, having suffered the loss of their mother in Alaska a few years back. They still grieved.

To break that somber note, Dan poked him in the arm with his beer bottle. "You know what people think, don't you?"

Aaron grinned. Yeah, he did.

"Some folks think you're dating a stripper who's only available late at night. That gets my vote."

Aaron shrugged, giving nothing away. His first exposure to the nutcase nuns at a strip joint would take too long to explain.

"Others think you're stripping yourself."

"I don't dance that well."

"Still others speculate that you're running drugs."

"You know better than that."

"How about our neighbor, Delilah? You been shagging the alligator farmer?"

"Nah. She smells kinda swampy, dontcha think?"

Dan arched his brows at him, as if a little *eau de swamp* would matter when the heat was on. Besides, Delilah was a beautiful woman, even if she did wrestle gators on occasion. Every red-blooded male who met her had to wonder how she would be wrestling . . . well, bed partners. Naked, of course.

But that was beside the point.

"What is it then, Aaron? You know how it is with us twins. Sometimes we sense what our other half is experiencing."

"What? You're not getting your rocks off, secondhand-like?" he tried to joke.

"Not even firsthand," Dan quipped. "With Samantha lumbering around like a grumpy hippo, all I have to do is glance at her with sexual intent and she gives me The Look. You know, the one that says, 'Touch me and you are dead meat.' Why do women always blame men for getting them pregnant? Like they had nothing to do with it!"

Dan and Samantha had been married more than a year now, and their twins—gender not identified—

were due in a few weeks. Aaron, almost as excited as Dan about the impending births, hoped he would be around at the time.

He and Dan, along with everyone else in the family, amused themselves by making baby name suggestions to Samantha: Adam and Eve. Mutt and Jeff. Abbott and Costello. Tom and Jerry. Ben and Jerry. Bert and Ernie. Bonnie and Clyde (his favorite). Hansel and Gretel. Thelma and Louise. Scarlett and Rhett. Tarzan and Jane.

To these proposed names, Samantha usually just shook her head at them and pronounced, "Dumb and Dumber."

But to Dan's question about women blaming men for pregnancy, Aaron answered, "You're asking me? I'm the single guy here. One bit of advice, though. You better not let Samantha hear you refer to her as a hippo if you want sex again in this lifetime."

"That's for sure. Actually, Aaron, I love my wife's hippo shape. You should see how she looks when she's naked with all those freckles covering her belly. When she's in a good mood, she lets me connect the dots with washable markers. I draw a great anatomically correct teddy bear."

Samantha was one of those redheads—auburn hair, she was always quick to correct—whose creamy skin was covered with freckles, head to toe. Some folks, including Samantha, thought they were unattractive. Not his brother. From the get-go, Dan had considered her freckles sexy. Go figure!

"TMI, brother. Way too much information," Aaron remarked at his brother's description of a naked and very pregnant Samantha.

They grinned at each other, and clinked bottles.

But then, Dan turned serious. "Cut the crap, Aaron. No more diversions. No more evading my questions. What have you gotten into?"

Aaron set his bottle down carefully and turned to his brother. The time had come for him to reveal all. In fact, it might very well blow up in the news media any time now. "I'm working for a group of monks . . . on a mission."

The shocked expression on his brother's face was priceless. "A mission? Monks? You've become a missionary?"

Hmm. A person who works on a mission . . . that person could be called a missionary, I suppose. Although I wouldn't want to be the one to tell a group of rowdy SEALs on a mission over in Iraq that they're doing God's work, instead of Uncle Sam's. Whatever. It's all semantics. He chose the easy answer. "Sort of."

Dan burst out with laughter. "What? You? A missionary. Next you'll be telling me you want to join the priesthood."

Aaron shrugged, as if that wasn't totally out of the question. Which was a stretch. He wasn't that sinless or noble. Just a sucker.

"Seriously?"

"Seriously. You could say I've got a good news/bad news situation here."

"This ought to be good."

Aaron sighed. "Bottom line . . . the good news is I've become practically a saint with all my extracurricular work lately."

"And the bad news?"

"I'm probably going to prison."

"Oh. My. God!"

"And I'm halfway, maybe sixty percent, in love with a nun, who considers me an effin' moron."

Take this job and love it . . . or leave it . . .

"I'm being dumped from nunhood?" Fleur asked incredulously as she saved the computer document she'd been working on and gave her full attention to her superior, who stood in the open doorway of her much larger, adjoining office.

"No," Mother Jacinta said, her lips twitching at Fleur's choice of words. "I merely suggested that after this upcoming mission with the street monks, you take a break. Live in the real world. Perhaps go back to your roots, the place where all your . . . um, problems began. Seriously, Fleur, you need to find out what you really want."

"But, Mother, I know what I want."

Mother arched her brows, which was a feat with the stiff, white linen wimple which pressed against her forehead, around her face, and under her jaw, giving her a double chin. When back in the convent in the remote Mexican hills, many of the Magda nuns reverted, by choice, to the old-time religious habits . . . full-length black gowns, scapulars and white half-circle breast cloths, wimples and veils.

Fleur wore religious garb, too, but as an aspiring nun, hers was knee-length and minus the torturous wimple. Plus, it was white to denote her place in the hierarchy of the order: aspirant, postulant, novitiate, sister/white, light brown, light blue, black.

The older nuns, and even some of the younger ones,

claimed that the "uniform" gave them a sense of identity and a peacefulness after returning from their lay work outside the church. Especially after such sordid forays as they'd experienced last year in New Orleans.

"You've been with our community for ten years now, and have yet to take your final vows. Not even novice vows." Mother held up a halting hand before Fleur could protest and added, "That is not a criticism, my child. Merely an observation."

Calling Fleur "child" was one of Mother Jacinta's quirks, a form of endearment. She was only ten or so years older than Fleur, who was almost thirty. In fact, Mother had been known to reference some of the elderly nuns back at the motherhouse in Spain the same way.

Panic was beginning to set in with Fleur, though. Child or no child "endearment," what would she do out in the "real world"? No, that could not happen. "I feel safe here."

Mother shook her head sadly. "A ship in the harbor is safe, but that is not what ships are made for."

"Some ships are," Fleur argued. "I'll take the postulant vows tomorrow, if you want. In fact, I'd take final vows right now, if I could skip all the steps."

"A vocation cannot be forced. Come," she said then, motioning toward the open French doors which led out into the gardens. "Let's get some air."

Mother was about the same height as Fleur but very thin, giving the appearance of being taller. While surprisingly well versed in the modern world, she claimed to have wanted to be a nun since she was five years old and so became a postulant by age twelve.

Whereas Fleur had been running wild in the bayous at that young age. Her only religious calling had been to attend Sunday Mass, and the calling had come from her mother, who threatened a switch on the back of her skinny legs if she didn't put on her church dress (the only dress she owned, two sizes too big, a hand-me-down from her older sister Gloria) and stop dawdling.

Happy times! Not! With eight siblings, two parents, and a half-demented grandmother all living in a three-bedroom cottage (shack) along the bayou, it was no wonder Fleur had rebelled.

At first, Fleur and Mother Jacinta just walked in silence. Mother was probably praying the large wooden beads that hung from her cloth belt.

It was a lovely setting with well-worn slate pathways among the flowers and trees. The warm air was redolent of rich floral scents, as well as citrus from the orange and lemon trees, and pungent herbs.

Sister Mary Michael, one of the twenty-two sisters, three postulants, and two novices who resided here, was on her hands and knees working the soil around a rose bush. Not an easy position for a woman who was six feet tall and big-boned. Amazon Nun, she sometimes laughingly called herself.

The gardens had been laid out long ago by some famed landscape architect, a woman who'd entered the convent after her husband and four children had been killed in a fire. Some of the rose bushes here were more than a hundred years old and still flourishing. Sister Mary Michael claimed the secret was donkey dung. *Try buying that from the Home Depot garden department. Or the Internet.*

Another nun, who wore an apron over her habit, was sitting on a bench outside the kitchen where she'd just baked the morning bread. Sister Seraphina was reading from a ragged cloth Bible, probably in Spanish.

Sister Carlotta sat on a grassy patch, talking softly with three young girls, no more than fourteen years old, recent rescues from a Tijuana brothel. Wounded birds, that's what the Magdas called them, these victims of sex trafficking.

The motherhouse of the Sisters of Magdalene was in Spain, where it had first been established almost two hundred years ago, but there were eight satellite convents, like this one, in various countries throughout the world. At one time, pre-Vatican II, there had been twenty. They had always been an active ministry, working outside with the poor and oppressed, as compared to more contemplative religious orders that spent all their time cloistered to pray and meditate. The Magdas followed Saint Paul's directive to "pray without ceasing," but they believed that prayer could take many forms, including rescue and rehabilitation of "wounded birds."

Like Fleur had been.

Mother Jacinta's mind must have been traveling the same path because she said, "That dark-haired one reminds me of you when you first came here. See how she sets herself apart. The others weep or cringe, but she is stiff as a board, holding in all her pain."

Fleur studied the girl in question. She was a plump little thing who barely spoke, but her chin was raised stubbornly. Taken from a French village—in fact, sold by her parents into sexual slavery—the girl had to have been only eleven or twelve when first introduced to the dark side of life.

Fleur had been fourteen.

"But I wasn't a child when I was rescued. I was twenty. I had already been a prostitute for six years . . . a lifetime."

Mother nodded and took Fleur's hand, holding tight as they walked. "You stayed with us for two years before you broke down and began to heal. Then you became an aspirant. The whole process of becoming a nun usually takes no more than three years." She turned her head to stare at Fleur. "Not ten years."

Fleur felt her face heat with embarrassment but still she argued, "I work hard. I am not dead weight here." Fleur was an expert computer programmer, self-trained, handling all of the convent's outside communication and organization. And she was active in the rescue operations. In fact, the sex traffickers who'd kidnapped her off the streets of New Orleans were still in operation, except bigger and in more countries. She had a dog in this fight, so to speak.

Mother squeezed the hand she still held. "Oh, child! You are invaluable to us, but I'm not sure we are what's best for you. I suspect that while the convent is a refuge for you, it has also become a crutch. You need to walk on your own before deciding that this is the life for you."

"But—"

"Even your resistance now is a sign that you are not ready for the life of a nun. Total obedience to the will of God sometimes means doing that which is distasteful, or uncomfortable. Yes, you enjoy working for us, but can you honestly say that you enjoy sitting quietly and praying for extended periods of time, as we do sometimes?"

That was true, unfortunately. But Fleur could learn to be more patient. To fit in better. She could!

"Besides, my child, you can always come back when you are sure."

Tears filled Fleur's eyes. "But what can I do?"

"It's never too late to be what you might have been." Fleur wasn't so sure about that. "Where would I go?"

"Louisiana," Mother answered. "You already know Louise Rivard from when you were a child. She is a great benefactress of our work. She has offered to help you."

"Oh no! Tante Lulu! That old busybody!" She immediately regretted her words, but it was too late.

Mother tsked her opinion.

Fleur should have known that Tante Lulu had something to do with this. Fleur might not have lived on the bayou for sixteen years now, but she heard things. Usually it was the old lady's extended LeDeux family that reaped the "benefits" of her meddlesome ways. Something occurred to Fleur then. "Does this have anything to do with Aaron LeDeux? I swear, that man is driving me crazy."

Mother just smiled.

"What?" It was probably her language. As hard as she tried, she often reverted to street vernacular. At least she hadn't said "bat-shit crazy," which she would have in her former life.

"Well, this man—Aaron LeDeux—seems to prompt such a strong response in you. Perhaps that is another reason why a religious calling is not for you."

It took Fleur a moment to understand. "Mother! I have no interest in men that way. After my experience with sex? No way!" And that was the truth. Any sexual desires Fleur might have had as a promiscuous teen had been hammered out of her as a prostitute. "And least of all that Aaron LeDeux, who thinks he's God's gift to the female race," she added.

"Your very vehemence is telling, my child."

"It is not!" She inhaled and exhaled for patience.

"Maybe. But I think you judge him too harshly. He has done much to help our mission this past year, you have to admit."

"He only agreed as a way to help his friend, Brother Brian, while he recuperated."

Mother shrugged. "Perhaps at first."

"How is Brother Brian, by the way?"

"Better, but he's not yet fully recovered."

"I still think that Aaron LeDeux has ulterior motives for being involved in our missions."

"Like what?"

"I don't know. I just don't trust him."

They passed a grotto that held statues of Mary, the mother of God, along with Mary Magdalene. Two nuns were scrubbing the marble kneelers there and saying the "Hail Mary" aloud as they worked.

"Do you still harbor a hatred for all men?"

"No. I realize that all men are not as evil as those I experienced in my early years, or those we witness these days in the sex trade." Fleur saw that she wasn't making any headway and asked, "What does Tante Lulu have to do with all this?"

"She has agreed to have you come live with her for a while. A temporary arrangement."

At that little cottage on Bayou Black? Less than a mile from where I once lived? And probably not so far from where Aaron LeDeux lives, too. Oh no! Oh no, no, no! She started to refuse, but saw the look of determination on Mother Jacinta's face. So, a decision had already been made regarding her fate. Fleur sighed with surrender. "What would I do there? Get a job? I have no formal education. And I would need a car. The old lady lives on the bayou, far from town. And clothes.

I would need at least a minimal wardrobe, I suppose. Oh, Mother, wouldn't it be easier to just have me take vows and stay here?"

"Ms. Rivard has a car you can use."

Fleur had seen that vehicle, if it was still the same one. An oversize, vintage lavender convertible. In a million years, she couldn't imagine herself—a nun, or almost-nun, or ex-nun—tooling down the highway in such an eye-catcher.

"As for work, there are many possibilities. You could even go to college."

"At my age?"

"Child, there are many returning adult students in college today. But, actually, Ms. Rivard has a job for you, initially. Take a laptop with you. She wants to organize all her folk remedies. And she's thinking about writing her memoir."

"Are you sure this isn't some penance for past misdeeds?"

"More like a new beginning."

The beginning of what, Fleur had to wonder.

She wondered even more the next week when she was sitting next to Aaron in a small Piper Aztec plane as he flew toward a private airfield in Houma, Louisiana.

He wore his usual T-shirt and jeans with cowboy boots. Okay, she had to admit, he was a handsome man with overlong, dark brown hair and whiskey-colored eyes. Even wearing those denims and cowboy boots which enhanced his tall, lean frame. The man oozed sex appeal.

Good thing she was impervious.

"Stop grinning," she told him.

"Why?"

"Because there's nothing to grin about."

"Can't a guy just be happy, *chère*?"

"*Chère?* I heard you were born and raised in Alaska. Suddenly you're getting all Cajuny?" She paused at his raised eyebrows, then admitted, "That was snarky and uncalled for. Sorry."

"Apology accepted," he said. "I've always been Cajun. Cajun isn't a matter of address. My mother was born right here on Bayou Black. Of course, I didn't know I was Cajun until after her death." He glanced her way and grinned some more. "It's just taken me a while to develop the accent."

"Why bother?"

"Because Cajun men are irresistible, dontcha know?" He winked at her.

Which caused a tiny flutter in her belly. Probably disgust-induced nausea. "Says who?"

"All my LeDeux half brothers."

She couldn't help but laugh.

"Hey, a few years back when the oil riggers were streaming into Louisiana from Texas and Canada, they noticed how the Cajun men seemed to get all the women. When asked, they admitted that their virility came from eating so much mudbug fat. Those dumb outsiders began scarfing up that orange crap in the heads and tails of the crawfish, like it was some kind of Viagra caviar. Yuck! Meanwhile, the Cajun men just laughed their asses off. They knew that bayou men are just born with that irresistibility gene."

"Irresistibility?" She shook her head at his hopelessness. "Don't waste your time on me. I'm practically a nun."

"I thought they kicked you out."

"They did not kick me out. I'm merely taking a

sabbatical. And I'll still be helping with the rescue missions."

Fleur had gotten to know Aaron fairly well over the past year as he flew them on some of their rescue missions. There was no repeat of a strip club rescue, but they had gone into several brothels in Mexico, the United States, Guatemala, Panama. Twice, they'd gone into jungles where terrorists were holding some kidnapped girls that they did not want any longer, or would rather have cash for than their services. And often they just swooped them up off the streets.

She looked out the window of the plane now and noticed that they were circling over the bayou region. What a sight that was! Like a lace tablecloth, or a spiderweb, the brown streams of varying width twisted and turned on themselves forming ever-changing patterns through the emerald land mass. For the first time in like forever, she felt a tug at her heartstrings, as if she were coming home.

"Do you think that's a good idea? Continuing to work against sex traffickers as a layperson? Could be dangerous. I mean, you had some protection behind the convent walls if the traffickers suspected the Magdas' involvement. But you'll have zippo now, except for a senior citizen roommate who may, or may not, have a license to carry," Aaron remarked.

"You should talk. I hear you're having troubles of your own. Legal ones."

He nodded. "The FAA is pissed about my crossing US borders. Sorry. Is *pissed* a word that offends nuns?"

She ignored his teasing. "And . . . ?"

"Some lunatics at the FBI think I'm the one involved in sex trafficking."

"Why would they think that?"

"I've been seen with young girls getting in my plane."

"Can't you just tell them what you're doing?"

He shook his head. "Steps on too many toes. It looks like I—we—are saying that the feds and local police aren't doing their jobs."

"They're not. At least not enough. Or fast enough. Too much bureaucracy. There's enough work for all of us."

He nodded. "During the year I've been involved, seventy kidnapped girls have been rescued. That's not even a dent in the huge number unrescued, but I figure those are seventy girls who might have been lost in the underbelly of several countries by the time officials slogged along regular channels. Let law enforcement go after the source of all these kidnappings. Like you said, there's enough work for everyone."

She nodded. "Still . . . you take a risk every time you take off with new 'cargo.' Are you worried about being arrested?"

"No. Well, a little. But my half brother Luc is covering my back. He's a lawyer."

"I know who Lucien LeDeux is. Everyone in the South has heard of his courtroom antics. Don't they call him the Swamp Solicitor?"

"They do. He's that good."

"You're grinning at me again."

"I can't help it. I keep picturing you and Tante Lulu as roomies."

Fleur had spent the past week reconciling herself to this exile from the convent. She figured a few months spent helping the old lady organize her folk healing recipes, perhaps even collating them into book format, would occupy her time. And taking notes on her supposedly outrageous history might even be interesting. After that, Fleur could return to the convent. Piece of cake!

"It won't be that bad," she told Aaron.

He grinned some more. "Wanna bet?"

As the plane landed, then rolled at an increasingly slower rate down the runway, then to a full stop, she saw her welcoming committee standing beside a vintage lavender convertible. A little old lady wobbled back and forth on wedge sandals as she used both hands to hold on to what looked like a Farrah Fawcett wig, which almost blew off in the wind. Her tiny body, with a surprisingly curvaceous, probably fake bootie, was stuffed into tight pink spandex shorts. On top was a T-shirt with cleavage (probably also fake) that proclaimed in glittery letters, "Bayou Bimbo."

Standing next to her was a real bimbo. Well, the self-proclaimed "bimbo with class." It was Charmaine LeDeux-Lanier, Tante Lulu's niece or something, who owned a chain of beauty salons. She often dressed like a hooker and made deals like a Wall Street guru, according to an Internet business magazine article Fleur had once read. In fact, as a kid, Fleur had idolized Charmaine when she'd won the Miss Louisiana pageant. At forty-something, Charmaine was still hotter than Louisiana asphalt in a body-hugging, sleeveless red jumpsuit, with a baby bump the size of a watermelon.

Aaron didn't say anything. He didn't have to.

Chapter Two

S̶he took networking to a whole new level . . .

After handing Fleur off to Tante Lulu and Char-maine, Aaron headed directly for his lawyer's office in downtown Houma.

He was still grinning over the stunned expression on Fleur's face as she'd crawled into the back seat of Lillian, the name given to the old lady's big honking pale purple 1960s convertible. Everyone on the bayou recognized the vehicle when it came barreling (or crawling) down the highway, especially when the notorious Tante Lulu could be seen propped up on several pillows behind the steering wheel.

"Hey, Aaron, glad you could stop by," Luc said when he entered the office, which was located on the ground floor of an old Victorian-style building. Luc's secretary, Mildred Guidry, who was on the phone, had waved him through.

"Any news?" Aaron asked.

"I have some meetings set up for next week. Most important, with the FAA for Wednesday at eleven a.m. in their Nawleans office. They want you to bring a list of every flight you've taken in the past five years, whether on your own, for Remy's company, or for the company you owned back in Alaska."

"Easy enough to get the Alaska records. Aunt Mel put those in storage. She's here at the plantation waiting for the twins to be born, but I can ask a friend to go into the unit to find them."

Aunt Mel was Melanie Yutu. She'd been his mother's longtime partner, as in gay couple, and his business partner, as well, in Alaska Air Shipping.

"Great. It's always good to bury them in paperwork. To some of these desk jockeys, paper is still king."

"And Remy keeps meticulous files. So, I know those will be easily accessible, too. On computer. Hell, I can print those out, too, if necessary."

Remy's claim to fame, according to women of the bayou, anyhow, was his exceedingly good looks. His shame (in his eyes, only) was that he'd been badly burned in an explosion during Desert Storm when he'd been flying Chinooks over enemy territory. The burn scars covered one side of his body only, head to toe. People who knew him hardly noticed, but Remy was self-conscious, even after all this time.

Aaron had been in the Air Force, too, but a few years later than his half brother, being quite a bit younger. Aaron had been working for Remy the past couple years, until he could decide what he wanted to

do, exactly. Unfortunately, or fortunately, Aaron had
been distracted from those goals this past year by his
outside activities with the Street Judes.

"Is Remy still pissed at you?" Luc asked, calling
him back from his rambling thoughts.

"Not so much since I explained the situation. He
was more upset that I didn't tell him ahead of time so
he could help. And, actually, his main concern these
days is Rachel and their upcoming new baby."

"Pff! Don't I know it? Sylvie is waddling around
like an oversize duck with all her excess weight, alternately cursing me, the doctor who did my vasectomy,
and Tante Lulu."

Aaron couldn't help but smile. All the LeDeux men
had become suddenly virile about eight months ago
when Tante Lulu had put a curse on them all. Well, not a
curse because, of course, a baby could never be a curse,
but a St. Jude wish of hers. Everyone on the bayou—
hell, everyone in Louisiana—knew that St. Jude, the
patron of hopeless cases, was Tante Lulu's favorite saint.
Supposedly, she'd been praying one day and happened
to mention to the saint, "Wouldn't it be nice if there were
more babies in the family?" And, voilà! Mass pregnan-
cies. A classic case of be careful what you wish for.

The odd thing was, everyone thought the "curse"
had worked last summer. But then it turned out the
next month that the LeDeux women weren't pregnant,
after all. The following month they were. Next month
they weren't. By Christmas, though, it was a done deal.
Tante Lulu claimed it was Saint Jude having a bit of
fun with them. Everyone blamed her.

"Speaking of Tante Lulu, I saw her a little while
ago. She came to the airport with Charmaine to pick
up Fleur."

"Speaking of which," Luc began, "who is this girl that Tante Lulu is taking in? I don't like the idea of some stranger just moving in."

"First of all, Fleur Gaudet is a woman, not a girl. About thirty years old, I would guess. And—"

Luc raised his brows at that. "A thirty-year-old novice nun?"

"Not anymore."

"That's another thing. Kicked out of the nunnery? For what?"

"She was never a nun, exactly. More like an aspiring nun. And she wasn't exactly kicked out. She's just taking a break." *A permanent one, if I have any say in the matter.*

"'A shady lady, bless her heart, who's not shady anymore.' That's how Tante Lulu described her. You can see why I have questions. I don't want this person turning my aunt's cottage into a cathouse."

Aaron burst out laughing. Their "aunt" did have a way with words. And, in fact, Louise Rivard wasn't really an aunt to any of them. A great-aunt or something to Luc, Remy, and René through her great-niece Adèle, their mother, but more like an honorary aunt to the rest of them: him and Dan, John, Charmaine, Simone, and a whole slew of other LeDeuxs. The common element being their horndog father, Valcour LeDeux.

"Don't worry about Fleur turning Tante Lulu's cottage into a brothel. She hates men." *Me, in particular. But not for long, if I have any say in the matter.* "I'm not sure about Tante Lulu's 'shady lady' reference, anyhow. Maybe by 'shady' she's referring to one of the Judes/Magdas missions that took place in a strip joint. No, I am not going to elaborate."

Luc didn't look convinced. "Still . . . what do we know about her?"

"Trust me, the old lady is safe with Fleur. It's more a question of whether Fleur is safe with Tante Lulu. Back to Wednesday's meeting. The list of my flights related to the sex traffickers . . . should I be totally honest, or fudge, or go all 'I refuse to answer on the grounds, etc.'?"

"Make an honest list, for me. Then let's sit down and lay out a plan."

"It might be easier if I just join the priesthood, an official member of St. Jude's Street Apostles, and claim religious immunity. If there is such a thing."

Luc leaned back in his chair and grinned. "Are you ready for celibacy?"

"Hell, no!"

"That wouldn't work anyhow. No way you could become a priest in less than a week. And, by the way, you've got to lie low for the next couple months, while you're in the feds' crosshairs. No more unregistered flights."

Aaron nodded, but he wasn't so sure he could avoid involvement with the Street Judes. There was an upcoming "shipment" of girls coming into Mexico from Syria, of all places, that he might not be able to ignore. Snake wasn't always available to fly.

Thankfully, Luc was off on another tangent, saving him having to give an actual promise. "But here's another thought. Why not talk it over with Tante Lulu?"

"Are you crazy?"

"Really. The old lady knows everyone. Maybe she could pull a few strings. She's a friend, or a friend of a friend, of some really powerful people."

"As powerful as the FAA?"

"Hah! Higher than that."

Later that day Aaron was driving his new silver pickup truck home, a replacement for his previous truck which had been mangled by a hit-and-run driver outside the Swamp Shack one night. As he drove along, he watched the Saint Jude bobblehead do its thing over the bumpy rural road. Half in jest, he said, out loud, "So, Saint Jude, think you could help me get out from Uncle Sam's radar?"

He could swear he heard a voice in his head answer, *As you wish.*

So, in for a penny, in for a pound, he added, "And I could use a little help with a certain lady."

The voice in his head was silent.

Some memoirs might best be left unwritten . . .

Fleur was settling in at Tante Lulu's little two-bedroom cottage on Bayou Black. She'd even made peace with the old lady's pet alligator, Useless, by feeding it a favorite treat, Cheez Doodles. Maybe this "sabbatical" from the convent wouldn't be too bad.

Crushed shells filled the driveway and the neat flower beds of the dwelling, which was painted a cheerful yellow with green shutters and a green metal roof. It had originally been built in the old Cajun style of bousillage, according to Tante Lulu, which meant half logs with a chinking of fuzzy mud, a mixture of clay, Spanish moss, and crushed clam shells. The Cajuns did love their clam shells. Later, the structure had been stuccoed over and painted.

A stretch of lawn led down from the back porch, with its three rocking chairs, to the slow-moving, narrow stream. Midway, there was a fig-laden tree and a Saint Jude birdbath statue. Off to one side was a vegetable garden enclosed by wire mesh fencing to keep out the bayou critters. On the other side of the house was a detached garage, which seemed hardly big enough for Tante Lulu's monster car.

Inside the cottage it was almost as if there were a third person present. Saint Jude. Every room was graced with some sign of Tante Lulu's favorite saint. Saint Jude pictures on the walls and Saint Jude statues on practically every side table. In the kitchen, a Saint Jude tablecloth and napkins, fridge magnets, and mugs. A Saint Jude night light in the hall. A Saint Jude crocheted toilet paper holder in the bathroom. (*I kid you not!*) There was even a Saint Jude wind chime out on the porch, which would probably drive Fleur crazy at night with the bayou breezes.

Tante Lulu had insisted on feeding her right off, after Charmaine left for the ranch where her husband was planning a barbecue for that evening. Besides, he worried about her being so far from home when she was so far advanced in her pregnancy, Charmaine told them.

While Fleur had chowed down on the most delicious gumbo and the lightest biscuits and a glass of iced sweet tea in a kitchen fitted out with a vintage chrome and Formica dinette set with vinyl-covered chairs, Tante Lulu asked, "Didja ever meet Charmaine's husband, Rusty Lanier?"

Fleur had shaken her head, her mouth full.

"Whoo-ee! That boy is so handsome he cain't even

walk down the street without women doin' a double take. 'Course he's a cowboy. And a Cajun. A double whammy."

Fleur had thought of Aaron then, who was Cajun, and dressed like a cowboy. And, yeah, he had the "Whoo-ee!" factor down pat. Not that any of that mattered to her. At least, it hadn't for a long, long time. Not that she would mention any of that to Tante Lulu, who fancied herself some kind of celestial matchmaker.

Now Fleur was in a room off the kitchen, the pantry, which had been converted into Tante Lulu's work space for her *traiteur* business. A *traiteur* was a folk healer in Cajun land. A butcher-block table in the center held a mortar and pestle. Labeled bottles and jars and baskets filled all the floor-to-ceiling shelving units around the room. Everything from recognizable herbs, like rosemary or thyme or St. John's Wort, to animal parts floating in murky liquids. Frog tongues, gator teeth, pigeon livers, snake hearts, bull bollocks, porcupine quills.

Fascinated, Fleur asked, "How did you get involved in folk healing?"

"I learned at my MawMaw and my mother's knees. In the old days, nothin' was written down. Jist passed down amongst the women in the family. Later, some receipts—thass what they called 'em back then—were kept, 'cept it was hard ta tell what some of the measurements meant. Like, how much is a passel of swamp grass, or a dollop of skunk oil? I've been tryin' fer years ta organize it all inta book form. I've had help, but never quite finished. Somethin' allus comes up."

"Well, I can certainly help with that. Do you have any notes?"

Tante Lulu handed her a bulging old rent receipt book with loose sheets hanging out and a shoebox overflowing with scraps of paper. Fleur glanced at what was written on the back of a Boudreaux's General Store receipt. "Heat Rash. Boil pig brain. Mix rendered fat w/ground gator tongue and mashed okra. Grated lemon peel to hide stink."

Okaaay, looks like I have my work cut out for me. But that's okay. It might be interesting. "I think all these remedies would be enhanced if you had a provenance with them."

"Prava-what?"

"Provenance. The history of a recipe. Where you got it from. Perhaps a funny story about gathering the ingredients. That kind of thing."

"I get it. Like the time my MawMaw and my Aunt Tildy almost drowned in the swamp when their pirogue was overturned by a gator. The mama gator dint want them harvestin' any of her eggs fer their hemorrhoid salve."

"Exactly," Fleur said with a hidden roll of her eyes.

"And, by the way, yer not the first nun, or ex-nun, or almost-nun, I've been associated with. I'll hafta introduce ya to my friend Grace O'Brien who lived here with me fer a spell. She's an ex-nun who also happened ta be a professional poker player and a treasure hunter. She was helpin' me ta organize my herbs, too, but then she met Angel Sabato, and the Thunderbolt of Love hit her, and wham! Now, she's busy raising babies. I 'spect you two will have a lot in common."

Listening to Tante Lulu was like trying to catch popcorn as it popped in an open pot. She was all over the place. Fleur blinked several times, waiting for her to elaborate. When she didn't, Fleur brought up another subject. "I understand you'd like me to write your memoir, too. I'm not sure I'm the right person to do that. I don't have any background as a writer."

"'Course you're the right person. You have 'zackly the right background ta suit me."

Fleur waited for the old lady to elaborate, again.

"I used to be a Shady Lady myself, jist like you." The old lady winked at her, as if they shared a secret.

At first, Fleur didn't understand. But then she exclaimed, "Tante Lulu! You were a prostitute? No way!"

"Yes, I was. Well, not a prostitute precisely, but, fer a while there, I did open my legs fer every man with a hankerin'. I lost count after twenty. Did you ever keep count? No. Well, I kin understand that. My Fall From Grace came right after my Big Grief. Are you writing this down?"

Fleur put her face in her hands. What insane person had decided that her sojourn here on Bayou Black would be a retreat? It was more like the Black Hole of Bayou Madness.

For just a second, she glanced up and saw the image of St. Jude staring at her from the medallion at the end of the ceiling light's chain pull. And she could swear she heard laughter in her head.

Shrine that! . . .

Since it was a Saturday and he didn't have to work, Aaron decided to spend the rest of the day helping with the never-ending renovations around the plantation. Quickly tearing off the clothes he'd worn for the flight

to and from Mexico and the ride into town to meet with
Luc, he pulled on his go-to cargo shorts. The ones with
all those pockets for nails and stuff, no need for a tool
belt.

Although . . . maybe a tool belt would melt Fleur's ice.

*Then again, maybe not. If I can't impress her with my
Hot Pilot Persona, which usually works with women,
I'm not gonna do it with Handyman Hunkiness.*

He opted for no shirt. It was about ninety in the shade.

*Maybe Fleur would be turned on by my bare chest.
I'm in pretty good shape.*

Then again, maybe not.

Despite the heat, he laced up a pair of heavy, steel-
toed boots, having learned his lesson the hard way by
accidentally nail-gunning one of a favorite pair of
Lucchese cowboy boots last year. While he was in
them! Shot that bugger right through to the floor.
Good thing he'd missed a toe. *Good thing he had a
doctor on the premises,* Dan had observed with a
laugh at the time.

He raced down the steps of his *garçonnière* apartment, and practically barreled into his brother as he
opened the door. "Whoa! I thought we had a workday
scheduled."

Dan was dressed like he did for work, his real work.
Belted khakis, a dress shirt and tie, loafers, no jacket.
He usually exchanged those for scrubs or one of those
white doctor coats when he got to the medical center.

"Sorry. I was just coming to tell you that I got an
emergency call. A little girl having a bad reaction to
chemo. I shouldn't be long."

What could he say to that? "That's okay. I'll just relax
by the pool till you get back. Wait a minute. We don't
have a pool. Darn!"

It was a running joke between them. Aaron wanted modern amenities here at Bayou Rose Plantation, like a rain forest shower (which he'd gotten) and a keg fridge (which he did not), while Dan and Samantha pushed for more practical things, like a new roof (*What's a little rain, indoors?*), or furniture (*Folding chairs, anyone?*).

Bet Fleur would come over to my pool, if I had one. Bet she would look good in a bikini. Or a one-piece. Yeah, that would be better. But cut high and low, high on the hip, low on the chest. And when it was wet—

"On a day like today, I'd agree to the pool, but you know Samantha. Maintain historical integrity, preserve the past, yada, yada." Dan shrugged.

Aaron gave his brother a fake punch in the arm. "Hey, bro! I was just teasing." Actually, Samantha had done a great job in keeping the project on track, especially historically speaking, but that meant extra labor to meet her rigid specs. Which also meant ca-ching, ca-ching, ca-ching! Dan was the one who went bonkers over the money pit (thus, the "A friggin' in-ground pool costs too damn much money!" refrain), but then Samantha had put in plenty of her own cash, being an heiress to the Starr Supermarket fortunes. So, Dan couldn't complain too much. Mostly, her big-ticket purchases involved antique furniture which she explained away as "portable wealth."

To which Dan usually responded, "Bullshit!" Like last week, when he'd added, "There's nothing portable about that two-ton, five-thousand-dollar dresser thing." It had taken four men—him, Dan, and two of the workmen—to get the thing off the truck and into the dining room.

"It's a credenza, honey. A work of art."

Dan had muttered something like, "Art, my ass!"

Samantha had made the mistake of forgetting to take the price tag off that particular piece of furniture before it was delivered. She rarely made that mistake, especially after she'd noticed Dan searching for the stickers on her purchases.

"Anyway, good antiques are an investment. Good as gold."

Which was like waving a red flag in front of his brother. Because Samantha had a pigload of gold bars that she'd inherited, which she'd been selling off to finance some of her expenditures.

His brother had this pride thing going where he felt like Little Orphan Danny to her Mommy Warbucks. Not that Dan was a pauper, by any means. Nor was Aaron. Dan had made a good living as a doctor back in Alaska, and Aaron had reaped a bundle when the Alaska Air Shipping company was sold. They'd both done well in the stock market.

While Aaron's mind had been wandering, Dan had kept talking. Aaron caught the tail end. "Anyway, I thought you'd be spending the day with your new babe."

Big mistake, telling Dan about my infatuation with Fleur. Hey, I like that word. Infatuation. Makes me sound a little less pathetic. "Oh Lord! Don't refer to her as a babe."

"Why? That's how you usually refer to your women."

"Number one, she's not my woman."

"Yet."

"Yet," he conceded. "Besides, it's just an infatuation."

"Nice try, bro."

The thing about twins was that they knew each other too well.

"As I told you, she's practically a nun."

"But kicked out of the convent."

"But still in nun mode."

"Good luck with that. When are we going to meet this wonder woman?"

"*Wonder* woman?"

"The girl who finally brought Aaron LeDeux to his knees. Speaking of knees, have you bought a ring yet?"

"Go to work," Aaron said and walked his brother to his SUV. "I'm going to see a man about buying a bigass excavator to dig my pool."

"Don't you dare!"

No sooner did Dan leave than Samantha and Aunt Mel came down the wide front steps of the mansion.

Aunt Mel, dressed for the weather in shorts and a T-shirt, was above average in height, for an Inuit woman, due to a Russian grandfather, but otherwise, she had pure Aleutian features . . . a wide, flat face with almond-shaped eyes. She'd been very attractive as a young woman when his mother had first fallen in love with her, and still was, even as her black hair was threaded with silver.

Although he and Aaron called her aunt, she'd been more like a stepmother to them their entire lives. He loved the old lady, who wasn't old compared to Tante Lulu, being only in her early sixties. Her visit to Louisiana was supposed to be temporary, to help with the babies, but everyone hoped she would decide to move here for good.

At the top of the steps, Axel sat, looking sad and longing. The old German shepherd's hip problems precluded him from making the descent on his own anymore. He would wait there until his mistress returned.

Maddie, on the other hand, scooted around the dog and took the steps three at a time, racing off with cheetah speed across the lawn toward the bayou. She'd probably scented some bayou creature on the premises. Forget hunting dogs, they had their very own hunting cat. Once she'd even brought home a small wild boar.

Emily, Samantha's potbellied pig, had gotten even more depressed than usual when she'd spotted that boar. She'd taken the assault personally, as if the boar might have been a cousin or something.

The other cats, Felix and Garfield, were stretched out on the verandah, sunning themselves. They didn't even raise their heads to see what was going on.

Samantha moved carefully down the steps, holding on to a hand-carved side rail, which had been installed a few months ago. For a thousand dollars! He knew, because Dan had exploded when he got the bill, only settling down when told it was for Samantha's safety and that of his unborn children.

Samantha was looking extra hippo-ish today in a sundress the size of a circus tent. He thought about asking her how much weight she'd gained with this pregnancy, but had the good sense to zip that thought. It was too hot to be a punching bag.

"Are you sure you aren't going to pop those babies any minute now?" he asked when she got to the bottom of the steps, wheezing.

"Why? Do I look *that* fat?" she snapped.

Landmine! "No! Of course not," he lied. "You look beautiful."

Aunt Mel made a "Way to go!" fist pump gesture behind Samantha's back. This must be one of Samantha's pregnancy-induced, hormonal, moody days.

Samantha gave his shirtless body and bare legs a survey then, before pretending to fan her face with a hand and say with an exaggerated drawl, "Be still mah Southern belle heart! Ah do declare, if Ah weren't with child, Ah'd surely swoon, or invite ya inside fer a mint julep . . . or somethin'." She batted her red—auburn— eyelashes at him.

"Eew! Incest alert!"

She grinned at him.

"Where are you two going?" he asked.

"Shopping," Aunt Mel replied, tossing her handbag and Samantha's into the back seat of Samantha's BMW, where two infant car seats had already been in- stalled. "We're having gumbo tonight. Your mother's recipe. Gotta get a few ingredients at the grocery store. I told Samantha I could go myself."

"Yeah, Sammie, why don't you go relax by the pool?" Aaron said.

"Bite me!" Samantha replied, both because he'd made the pool complaint often enough for it to be old and because he'd called her Sammie, a nickname she hated.

"I could go shopping with you guys," he offered.

They both looked at him as if he'd suggested some- thing obscene, like nude chauffeuring, or bare buns biking, neither of which he'd ever actually done.

"You don't even like shopping," Aunt Mel observed.

"I like sanding twelve layers of paint off two- hundred-year-old window frames even less."

"Besides," Samantha said, "you'd probably just hit on every sales clerk in sight."

"And your point is, Mommy?"

Samantha beamed, which just highlighted the freckles

on her face, which she was always attempting to hide
or tone down with some kind of make-up, to no avail.
She loved any references to her upcoming Mommy-
hood.

He gave her a quick kiss on the cheek as he helped
her into the passenger seat of the car. Not an easy task!
If she fell on him, she'd crush him.

Another thing he chose, wisely, not to say out loud.

Instead, he said, "By the way, I thought of more
names for the twins. Tony and Cleo. You know, after
Anthony and Cleopatra."

Samantha made a tsking sound, but then she got the
last word in. "I invited Tante Lulu and her new roommate over for brunch, after church tomorrow. You better
air out your church clothes."

"Church clothes. What are they? And brunch? Since
when do we do brunch?" he muttered to no one in particular. The BMW was already halfway down the
horseshoe-shaped driveway. But what he thought was,
*Oh my God! This is either the answer to my prayers, or
it's going to be hell on wheels. Lavender wheels.*

After that, he went to find Ed Gillotte, the resident
construction foreman for their ongoing renovation
project. That sounded more impressive than it really
was. Ed was an ex-felon with impressive carpentry
skills. He lived, with his three kids and a live-in girlfriend (who was working on her doctorate in physics . . .
don't ask!) and her kid, in the restored overseer's house
near the cane fields. (Yeah, they had sugarcane
fields . . . don't ask.)

Dan had hired Ed originally because one of his
children had cancer and he had no place to stay while
she was undergoing treatment at the medical center. It

started with Ed fixing up one of the old slave cabins for himself. Before long, there were a half dozen of the cabins brought up to modern (*though mostly historically accurate, thank you very much, Samantha*) standards, housing other families of cancer patients.

Somehow, everything they did spiraled out of control that way.

Like his purchasing this rundown plantation as a means to lift Dan out of his slump (*Can anyone say pediatric oncology burnout?*) and give them a temporary place to live (*which had turned into Tara Revisited*).

Like them coming to Louisiana to make a family connection with one particular old lady (*Guess who?*), intending to stay one week max, and ending up still here years later, with about three dozen Cajun relatives.

Like his involvement with the Street Judes and the Magdas and sex trafficking. (*Do a favor for a friend and end up center stage in a somewhat illegal rescue operation.*)

Tante Lulu would say that it was all in the hands of the Powers-That-Be. *Hello, up there, P.T.B. It's me. Aaron. I'm a pilot, not some Rambo or Knight in Tarnished Armor.*

He found Ed up by the slave cabins/guest cottages. (*And wasn't that an homage to political correctness?*) He wore only shorts, as well . . . faded, cutoff jeans. Except he didn't look half as good as Aaron, in Aaron's not-so-humble opinion. In his early thirties, Ed was skinny, with a receding hairline of reddish-blond hair pulled back into a ponytail, and prison tats that were faded and not very attractive. One of his incisors was missing.

Ed was fixing the gate on Blue Willow. All of the little

buildings, with their picket-fenced yards, had been given names related to their unique colors (a suggestion from Tante Lulu, which, of course, appalled Samantha's historical accuracy standards, but who could argue with the Cajun bulldozer?). There was also Yellow Daisy, White Magnolia, Green Meadow, Peach Blossom, Rose Petal, and Purple Iris.

"What's the occupancy today?" Aaron asked, not seeing any vehicles around.

"Full house. Everyone's gone for the afternoon, though, either to the medical center or over to the gator farm. Del's putting on some kind of show today."

Del was Delilah Dugas, their neighbor. And, yes, she raised alligators which she sold to upscale restaurants for their meat, and to upscale designers for their skins, and, yes, she'd been known to wrestle the beasts on occasion. And no one thought she was weird, or anything.

Did I mention Cajuns are bat-shit crazy?

"Your family gone, too?" Aaron asked.

Ed nodded. "Except for Lily. She's studyin' for an exam, and the baby's down for a nap."

Lily Beth, a single parent to a one-year-old baby, was only a few courses away from being a full-blown physicist, while Ed was as blue collar as a man could get. She was pretty as her name, Southern to her dainty toes, and smart, really smart. A most unlikely couple. Go figure.

"You ready to tackle those windows?" Ed asked him.

"Unfortunately," Aaron said, wiping the sweat off his brow with a forearm. "But first, I want to show you something." They walked together toward the back of the mansion. There was a covered verandah outside the kitchens. Emily sat there munching on some pig kibble that must have been left by Samantha. The porcine pet was never far from the kitchen, unless Dan was around. Then she attached herself to him like a love-struck swain.

Beyond the kitchen porch was a courtyard paved with ancient bricks. On one side of the house there was a rose garden. Beyond that, an orchard of peaches, apples, plums, and cherries.

On the other side, there had once been paddocks for horses and other animals. Now it was just overgrown with weeds . . . a project for sometime in the future, one of many projects for the future.

"Picture this," he said to Ed. "A deluxe in-ground pool with cool blue water. Maybe a waterfall at one end coming from a rock garden, or fountain, or something. A diving board. Some pool floats, the kind with built-in cup holders for beer or watermelon margaritas. A slate or tile pool surround with loungers and umbrella tables and tiki torches. Jimmy Buffett music coming from the sound system. An outdoor kitchen with a keg refrigerator and a honkin' big barbecue."

"Are there any women in this picture?" Ed asked.

"Oh yeah. Clothing optional."

Ed arched a sweaty brow at that. "Are you serious?"

"Oh yeah!" Aaron walked the site for a while, then asked, "Do you think the water table would make a pool here impossible?"

"Difficult, but not impossible. Especially with this site being elevated quite a bit, compared to land closer to the bayou," Ed answered. "It would need a drainage system under the pool, of course."

"How much you figure it would cost?"

Ed shrugged. "I'm not an expert, but I'm guessing fifty to eighty thou."

Aaron winced but was not deterred.

"How you gonna convince your brother and Samantha?"

"I'm not sure. Wait. I have an idea. You know that rock garden waterfall thingee I mentioned . . . how about if it's actually a St. Jude shrine? Yeah, we could build a St. Jude swimming pool. If I get Tante Lulu on my side, this will be a done deal."

"Wouldn't that be kinda sacrilegious?"

"Ya think?"

"Actually, we could make it really dignified." Ed smiled, exposing his missing tooth.

The two of them exchanged high fives.

Aaron had another suggestion then. "What say we skip the sanding for today and see if there's any cold beer in the fridge?"

"Now, there's an idea."

As they walked back to the house, Aaron realized that he hadn't thought about Fleur for the past hour. A remarkable feat, considering his "infatuation." *See, all I needed was something to occupy my mind. A project. Swimming pool in, infatuation out.*

He glanced skyward and asked silently, *So, what do you think, Jude? A swimming pool memorial?*

The voice in his head responded immediately, *Cool!*

Chapter Three

*F*ancy is in the eye of the beholder . . .

A fuming Fleur maneuvered the big lavender convertible through the stone archway marked Bayou Rose before stopping at the tip of the horseshoe-shaped driveway. Okay, she wasn't exactly fuming. More like, very irritated. Still . . .

She left the motor running as she inhaled and exhaled several times to calm down before she said something she would later, like immediately, regret. Bad words were not an attribute of a person with aspirations to the religious life. Nor was irritability.

"Girl, you got a bad case of the grumpies," Tante Lulu observed. "I thought nuns, even almost-nuns, enjoyed church. I thought they got all holy and stuff from prayin'. Sorta like gassin' up fer another week. Dint ya like my church?"

Fleur decided then and there to get herself one of those metal hand clickers, the kind nuns used when she was back in grade school to signal certain commands. One click, genuflect. Another click, stand in line. Click to take books out. Click to put books away. Click for recess. Yeah, that's what Fleur needed—a clicker to help control her errant behavior. Every time an unkind thought came into her head, CLICK! Or worse yet, if a swear word slipped out, CLICK!

Now that she had a plan, Fleur patted Tante Lulu on the arm and said, "Our Lady of the Bayou Church is lovely. The service was lovely."

"Then what burr's wiggled under yer saddle?"

You, she thought. CLICK! With exaggerated patience, she explained, "Somehow, you failed to mention when we were getting ready for church this morning that we would be going to brunch afterward." And then not so patiently, she continued, "At some fancy mansion owned by that annoying Aaron LeDeux and his brother, a fancy doctor, and his wife, a fancy heiress of some kind. Fancy, fancy, fancy!"

Too late for a click with that one. It just slipped out. Fleur put her face in one hand and counted to ten, in Latin.

"Ya got a headache, sweetie?" Tante Lulu asked. "Is it that time of the month?"

CLICK. *Hallelujah! It worked. I didn't say what I was tempted to say.*

"I got a remedy fer that in my herb bag. Wait till we get ta the house. It's gotta be mixed with tea." Tante Lulu looked at her with sympathy.

And Fleur was touched.

Where are all these conflicting emotions coming

from? One minute, I'm annoyed by the old lady's machinations. Next, I feel like giving her a hug. Mother Jacinta must be right. I do have issues that need to be resolved before I take vows.

"Huh? You think Aaron LeDeux is fancy?" the old lady said, picking out the least important thing she'd said. "The way he dresses! I've seen hoboes with nicer duds. Not that the boy dint look handsome as all get-out this mornin' in church, but did he hafta wear cowboy boots with his suit and tie?"

Fleur nodded. "And what's with Aaron I-dress-like-a-broke-cowboy LeDeux being a part owner of a bayou McMansion?" CLICK.

"Sometimes you doan talk much like a nun."

"I'm working on it."

"Not that I'm complainin'. Sometimes, I talk like I ain't got no education, when actually I'm smarter than mos' folks."

That was probably the truth, Fleur realized.

"Anyways, if ya saw Bayou Rose Plantation when they bought it, you'd be callin' it a McDump. Stinky, the snake catcher, nabbed one hundred and eighty-seven snakes here one afternoon. Aaron about had a heart attack. He's not too fond of the creepy crawlers." She gave Fleur a long, sideways look, her gray eyebrows raised in question, probably because of Fleur's over-reaction to this visit. The gray eyebrows were a sharp contrast to Tante Lulu's cap of curls, dyed red overnight, topped by a green straw "church hat" with a bird's nest perched on one side of its wide brim. At least Fleur thought it was a bird's nest. Maybe it was a snake in a pile of grass. The hat matched, sort of, a puke green dress that might have been purchased in the children's department of Walmart to fit her petite frame. Same went for the lime green wedge sandals. And green eye shadow.

"I still say that I should just drop you off. I can pick you up later," Fleur said.

"No, that won't do. I hired ya ta be my companion, and companions stick like butter on a pig's snout."

Nice picture! "That's the first I've heard that my job description includes 'companion.' I thought I was to be your traiteur assistant and your biographer."

"Can't ya be all three?" Tante Lulu asked. "Get a grip, girl. All this grumblin' jist 'cause we're gonna be neighborly?"

Neighbors? The old lady's cottage was miles away. CLICK. But that was beside the point. As annoying as she was, Tante Lulu meant well, Fleur reminded herself. With a sigh, she tried to explain, "I don't mean to be difficult, but these are not the kind of people I mix with, not when I grew up in this very neck of bayou woods as poor white trash, and not as an adult almost-nun, who hopes—*expects*—to take a vow of poverty."

"There's nothin' wrong with workin' hard and makin' a good living. It all depends on what ya do with the money. Personally, I could buy a plantation myself if I wanted to. That doan make me bad."

Somehow, Tante Lulu had missed Fleur's point.

"Me and you need ta talk sometime 'bout that 'poor white trash' remark of yers. I'm thinkin' you have a chip the size of a boulder on yer shoulder. I'm no shrink, but I could give ya advice."

Over my dead body. CLICK! Fleur paused, then berated herself. *Another snarky response. I'm going to start a novena tonight. Maybe to St. Jude. Yeah, that would be good. The patron saint of hopeless cases.*

"Ya better hurry up, girl, or my Peachy Praline Cobbler Cake is gonna melt."

"So, that's why you were up at five a.m. baking. I thought it was for a church bake sale or something."

"No, that's next week. You kin help me make the beignets."

A baker, too. Fleur sighed her surrender and released her foot from the brake. As the car moved forward slowly, she took in her surroundings. Yes, there were signs of a renovation in progress everywhere, from the half-cleared jungle that encroached on the edges of the property with shovels and rakes and wheelbarrows left unattended, from ladders and scaffolding near the house, and a bulldozer parked to one side. But still it was a gem, unpolished yet, but its promise showing through the years of neglect.

The branches of live oak trees that were probably two hundred years old dripped hanging moss, forming a canopied *allée*, or alley, in a U-shape of the driveway. A raised, three-story plantation house sat majestically on the center curve. Between the sides of that horseshoe was a stretch of sloping lawn leading down to a road and across from that, a bayou stream.

"There are even columns!" she exclaimed. "I feel like Alice in Wonderland falling into the Tara garden hole." *That wasn't too snarky. No click needed.*

"Alice who?" Tante Lulu replied, playing dumb. As the old lady had just said, she *was* smart as a whip, and she had the memory of an elephant.

Fleur would have to be careful not to underestimate her in the future. Only twenty-four hours of living with the old lady and Fleur was becoming savvy to her manipulations. She gave away clues, sometimes subtle, sometimes not so subtle. Why else would

Fleur have picked "a little okra" this morning which
turned into a bushel basket? "Oh, did I fergit ta mention,
honey, it's fer the food bank at the church kitchen?"

Uh, okay.

Or ended up wearing an old sundress of Charmaine's that had been conveniently hanging in the
guest room closet. "It's jist till we have a chance ta go
shoppin'."

We?

Or found herself the target of the Cajun yenta's
matchmaking efforts, which was not going to happen.
"Ya never heard of the Thunderbolt of Love? Oh, honey!
Ya came ta the right place."

Ya think? It was a coincidence, of course, that it
thundered through the night.

Fleur had drawn the line at Tante Lulu's effort to
probe into her estranged Gaudet family.

"There's nothin' so strange about families that it
can't be fixed," Tante Lulu had insisted.

"I didn't say strange, I said estranged. And don't you
dare try to contact any of my brothers or sisters."

Tante Lulu had given her one of those "Who me?"
wounded puppy expressions that didn't fool anyone.

Now, acting as chauffeur, which was apparently another one of her jobs, in addition to organizing Tante
Lulu's folk recipes and writing her memoir and being a
companion, Fleur brought the car to a stop in front of a
ten-foot-wide staircase that rose from the clamshell
driveway up to the second floor, which was probably
the main living quarters. In the Southland with its
high-water table, you only had to dig a foot to reach
water; so, fearing floods, important rooms were never
on the first floor. At least for the rich.

"Smile, honey," Tante Lulu advised. "It's not that hard, y'know. Jist turn that frown upside down. Ha, ha, ha."

CLICK! Fleur felt like shoving the old lady out of the car and taking off for parts unknown. CLICK! The convent in Mexico, maybe. CLICK! But, no. Mother Jacinta would say that she hadn't given this respite a chance. She was definitely starting a novena tonight.

Besides, it was too late. Standing at the top of the steps on the wide porch, or what the upper crust would call the verandah, she supposed, was Aaron LeDeux, his twin brother Daniel LeDeux, Daniel's wife, who was hugely pregnant, and a tall, slightly foreign-looking woman, maybe Asian or Native American or Hawaiian . . . no, she must be from Alaska, where Aaron and his brother had been raised. Fleur had seen them all earlier in church and had managed to scoot Tante Lulu outside to avoid introductions, not realizing she and Tante Lulu were headed this way.

There were also a bunch of animals lined up beside the humans. A big old German shepherd, a huge amber-colored cat with black spots, two other smaller cats, and a potbellied pig. A pig!

Fleur smiled then. People who loved animals couldn't be all that bad, or too fancy. Fleur loved animals, though she hadn't had one since she was five years old. A mangy old dog named Harry—because he shed so much hair. Her older brothers Eustace and Joe Lee, who'd been eight and nine at the time, thought it great fun to see if the dog could outswim a gator in the nearby bayou. Her mother had smacked them both upside their heads, but her father just said, "The dog ate too much anyway, and it had fleas." The dog ate hardly anything at all, only that which slipped from Fleur's own plate, and as for fleas—

their whole house had been a flea bag, before and after
Harry.

But she hadn't really wanted her father to punish
Eustace and Joe Lee. She'd witnessed too many of her
father's punishments, usually accompanied by the smell
of home brew and the whiz-bam, whiz-bam, whiz-bam
of his leather belt. One time he broke Eustace's arm for
stealing apples from a neighbor's orchard. Another
time he knocked Gloria's front tooth out for sassing
back.

That was the least of the things her family had done,
and not worth thinking about now. Ironically, though,
her father and mother fashioned themselves devout
churchgoers, and on Sunday mornings they and their
nine children went to church in clean clothes and
scrubbed bodies, presenting a false impression to the
community.

And speaking, or thinking, of church clothes, she
noticed that Aaron and Daniel had already lost their
jackets and ties, and their dress shirts were unbuttoned
at the collar and rolled up at the sleeves.

Samantha's red hair, which had been down and
about her shoulders in church, was pulled back off her
face into a high ponytail. She wore a sleeveless, scoop-
necked, very full dress, which did nothing to hide her
numerous freckles, or her enormous baby bump.

The older woman with them had already changed
from a dress to shorts and a T-shirt with "Alaska Air
Shipping" on its front.

Fleur was introduced first to Melanie Yutu, or Aunt
Mel, who had come from Juneau to help with the babies
when they arrived. "I love your dress," Aunt Mel said to
Fleur. "It looks so cool and summery."

Fleur glanced down at the white sundress covered

with bright red peonies and started to say, "Oh, this belongs to—" but Tante Lulu elbowed her, and Fleur said, "Thank you."

Next up was Daniel, who looked just like Aaron, but different somehow. His hair was shorter, his demeanor more serious. He shook her hand warmly and said, "Welcome. Aaron has told me so much about you."

Fleur gave Aaron a sideways look, but for once he didn't make a crack or tease. He just nodded, apparently on his best behavior today.

She didn't trust him one bayou inch.

Samantha attempted to hug Fleur in welcome when she was introduced, and they all had to laugh because her belly got in the way.

"When is the baby due?" Fleur asked politely.

"Babies," Samantha corrected. "We're expecting twins in about a month, but it feels like it should be today." She patted her bulge, and her husband beamed beside her, looping an arm over her shoulders.

Fleur was used to big bellies. Hadn't her mother had eight babies, beside herself? Not to mention at least three miscarriages, and two infant deaths.

"Please, God, don't let it be today," Daniel said. "I still need to finish painting the nursery."

"By the way," Tante Lulu interjected, "while we were in church, I came up with two more good names."

Samantha groaned. "You've already given us several Biblical suggestions, including Cain and Abel, Abraham and Sarah, with nicknames Abe and Sari, and Isaac and Rebekah, nicknamed Ike and Becky."

"I know, I know, but these new ones are even better." Tante Lulu paused for a ta-da moment. "Boaz and Ruth."

Samantha looked stunned, while Daniel and Aaron barely suppressed chuckles. Aunt Mel just smiled.

"Really," Tante Lulu insisted. "Betcha no one else on the bayou was ever named Boaz."

"I'll think about it," Samantha said and winked at Fleur.

"Everyone is always making suggestions of famous couple names for the twins, including me and Dan," Aaron told Fleur. "Personally, I'm partial to Humphrey and Lauren."

"Nicknamed Hump, I suppose," Daniel remarked to his brother. "I like it."

They grinned and gave each other high fives.

Samantha rolled her eyes and confided to Fleur, "They think they're funny."

"Daniel, take your wife out back to the patio and make her rest on one of the lounge chairs," Aunt Mel advised. "She's been on her feet too much today. Tante Lulu and I will take care of the food."

Daniel looked suddenly alarmed, especially after glancing down at Samantha's feet, which swelled out of and over her flat-heeled shoes. "Sweetheart, why didn't you tell me?"

"I'm fine," she said, but let him lead her on a path toward the side of the house, presumably to the back patio. "Have Aaron show you around the house, Fleur," Samantha called back over her shoulder.

"I don't need a tour," Samantha protested, but no one was listening to her.

"Get that cooler in the trunk first, Aaron. Fleur, open the trunk fer him," Tante Lulu ordered. She was already engrossed in conversation with Aunt Mel about some upcoming baby shower as they walked side by side through a door on the ground floor verandah, behind the steps, where the kitchen was probably located.

Shaking her head, Fleur went over with the car key to open the trunk—no remote keyless system for this vintage vehicle—but Aaron didn't immediately lift out the cooler. Instead, he stood next to her, turned slowly to look at her, and then he smiled, which caused a dimple to emerge, on the left side only. A dimple! That was so unfair!

"Hi," he said. That was all, but there was a whole lot of meaning behind that one word.

A weaker woman, with a different history, would have surrendered right then.

A girl who still believed in love would have melted.

But a female whose body had been abused by men for more than five years remained indifferent. She may have healed in many ways these past ten years in the convent, but that part of her life was over.

Time to halt this nonsense of Aaron's.

"Why are you doing this, Aaron?" she asked.

"What?"

"Pursuing me. I don't mean physically, like stalking. But you've made your interest in me obvious from the beginning."

He didn't bother to deny her allegation. "I think . . . I think I've fallen in love with you."

"That's ridiculous. You don't even know me."

He shrugged.

Time for the big tell. "I was a prostitute."

He recoiled, almost as if she'd struck him.

"For six years."

His eyes widened.

"I doubt if I can have children anymore. I certainly have no interest in sex."

She could swear there were tears in his eyes, but he

said nothing. And so she walked away, not toward the house, but away. Away, away, away.

And Aaron didn't try to stop her.

There's Divine Intervention, then there's Tante Lulu Intervention . . .

Louise Rivard was the first to notice that Fleur and Aaron were missing. And so was her Peachy Praline Cobbler Cake. The others made half-joking remarks about Aaron and his talent for charming women, insinuating that he'd probably talked Fleur into checking out his bachelor pad in the *garçonniére,* and a lot more. She wasn't so sure.

"He better not be hitting on our guest," Samantha remarked to her husband. They half reclined on side-by-side chaise lounges, glasses of iced sweet tea in the cup holders attached to the arms. "I warned him to behave himself today."

"Yeah, but he's in luuuuuve," Daniel pointed out with a grin.

"Hah! Love to that rogue is spelled *S-E-X.*"

"It appears the boy hasn't changed a bit," Aunt Mel inserted, reminiscing. "Remember the time in high school, Dan, when Aaron had two dates for the prom, and he talked you into impersonating him with one of the girls."

"And it worked." Daniel beamed, until his wife reached over and smacked him on the arm.

"I don't want to know how well it worked," Samantha said.

"Me neither," Aunt Mel added.

Louise wasn't buying any of their theories about Fleur and Aaron being off somewhere doing naughty things. Fleur was still a "wounded bird" when it came to men. Hanky panky would be the last thing on her mind.

Sidling away unobtrusively, she went back into the kitchen and through the corridor, either side of which held storage rooms, until she got to the ground floor verandah out front. Her car trunk was open and the ice chest was still sitting there, baking in the sun. No sign of either Aaron or Fleur. She was about to stomp over to the *garçonniére* when she heard a dog bark and a male voice grumble, "Go away, Axel."

Following the sound, she discovered Aaron sitting on a bench with his face in his hands, a big old dog sitting on the ground next to his feet, staring up at him dolefully. Louise didn't know which one looked more pitiful.

Samantha had done a great job bringing the rose garden back to life, and Louise had contributed the St. Jude statue sitting atop a stone bird bath, which was perfect for the spot, if she did say so herself, despite what Samantha said about it being historically inaccurate. To which, Louise had responded, "St. Jude is lots older than this plantation. Who sez they dint have St. Judes around then?"

"Feelin' lower than a doodlebug?" she asked Aaron. "Kind of hopeless, are ya?"

"You have no idea."

"Well, ya came ta the right place. St. Jude listens ta folks who ask fer his help."

"I wasn't praying."

"Ya oughta be."

"Go away, old lady. I'm not in the mood."

Sitting down on the bench next to Aaron, she said, "Raise yer head up, boy, and answer me proper."

He did as she bid. His dark Cajun eyes were bleak with sadness.

"So you know," she concluded.

"I know."

"You doan know diddly squat, if yer sittin' here feelin' sorry fer yerself, boy."

"I'm not a boy, and I don't need any lectures."

"Well, yer not the man I thought ya were if yer judgin' that girl."

"Girl!" he scoffed. "She was a prostitute. A prostitute!"

"What did you say when she told you about her Shady Past?"

"Nothing."

"Nothing?" she practically shrieked. "A fool's tongue is long enough to cut his own throat."

"What does that mean?"

"Listen, you fool. Some women are sluts because they've seen more ceilings than Michelangelo. But some women could lie with a thousand men and still be a saint."

"You saying Fleur is a saint?"

She rolled her eyes. "In that movie *Forrest Gump*, the young man said life is like a box of chocolates. I doan know 'bout that. For some clueless men—and I ain't namin' names here—life is more like a jar of jalapeño peppers, and what they do t'day is gonna sure as shootin' burn their butt t'morrow."

"But I didn't do anything," he protested.

"That's the point, idjit." She took a deep breath, then said, "Think, boy. Just think."

"About what? You lost me back there with the bordello ceilings."

She slapped him on the arm with the folded St. Jude fan attached to her wrist with a loop of yarn.

"Sorry. Listen, Tante Lulu, I know you mean well, but this is something I have to handle myself."

"Fine, but while yer doin' all that handlin', ask yerself this question. If Fleur is almost thirty years old, and she was in the convent fer ten years, and she was a Shady Lady fer six years, when—or how—did she first cross over ta the shady side of the street?"

It took Aaron several moments to understand.

Dumber than dirt, some men were!

"Fourteen! She was fourteen years old! Oh my God! She was kidnapped, wasn't she, just like those girls she rescues now?" he guessed.

"Those are questions fer Fleur ta answer. Ya ever hear of Hosea?"

"Huh? Is he the butcher at Boudreux's General Store?"

"No, that's Jeremiah. Hosea is the dude from the Bible who was ordered to marry a fallen woman, by God. Ya could learn somethin' by checkin' him out."

Aaron made his eyes go cross-eyed. She could tell that he thought the Bible had nothing to do with his situation. He would be wrong. "By the way, where is Fleur now?"

"I don't know. Last I saw, she was walking down the driveway. Probably headed back to your cottage."

"What? It's five miles ta my cottage, and it's hotter 'n Hades t'day. Go get her and bring her back here."

"Maybe Daniel could—"

"Not Daniel. You." She waved her fan in his face, to get his attention. "You doan hafta come ta any understandin' with her. Jist bring her back here, and act like the gentleman I know you are."

He grumbled, but he stood, probably realizing, belatedly, how unkind it had been to let Fleur go off by herself. "She won't want to come back here."

"Talk her into it. I hear ya got the devil's own tongue when it comes ta women."

After Aaron left, Louise just sat, relishing the solitude, and the presence of St. Jude, of course. She looked up at the statue and said, "This one's gonna be a hard nut ta crack. Aaron, like most men, is still livin' in the time of the old double standard. He'll learn."

St. Jude answered her, in her head, clear as if he was sitting beside her, *Use me for the hammer.*

"My very own nutcracker," she joked.

A celestial nutcracker, he agreed.

Aaron didn't stand a chance.

He was click-worthy, for sure . . .

Aaron drove his pickup truck about half a mile down the two-lane road before he saw Fleur traipsing along the berm. Even with the AC blasting inside his vehicle, it was hot as hell. She must be roasting.

He felt like an ass for letting her walk off like he had. He hadn't liked what she'd told him. In fact, he'd been flat-out shocked. But that was no excuse for such rude behavior. His mother had taught him better.

He slowed down when he came even with her and rolled down the electric window on the passenger side. "Get in, Fleur."

"Click," she said, and continued walking.

He kept pace with her at about two miles per hour. She was walking really fast. "What does 'click' mean?"

"I'm trying not to swear."

"Or give me the finger?" he tried to joke.

"Click, click."

"So, you're saying I bring out the clicks in you?"

"Bingo."

Her face and shoulders were already sunburned but she walked on steadily. The soles of her feet were probably blistering in those thin-soled sandals against the hot asphalt.

"This is ridiculous. Get in the truck," he said, keeping pace with her.

"Don't you want to ask me, 'How much?' or call out, 'Hey, baby, you wanna date?' or 'Do you like it rough, sugar?' That's the usual protocol for you johns cruising along the highway."

"I am not a john, and I am not soliciting you for sex," he gritted out, even though he knew she was just taunting him.

"And my fav, in the early days, was, 'Honey, how old are you? I prefer girls under thirteen.'"

Aaron felt sick in his stomach. He drove forward about fifty feet, threw the truck in Park, and stomped back toward her.

She stopped, put her hands on her hips, and glared at him. For just a second, he saw the pain in her eyes, and he felt like a piece of shit for hurting her. Guilt and anger mixed up in him and he wasn't sure what to do. So, he just grabbed for her and tossed her over his shoulder in a fireman's carry.

She screamed and squealed and pounded his back with her fist, but he wouldn't loosen his grip on her until he got to his truck and tossed her in the passenger seat. He used the remote child lock on the key device to keep her from jumping out.

"Click, click, click," she said, staring straight ahead once he was in the driver's seat.

"Shit, shit, shit!" he said. Then, "Why don't you say what you really want to?"

She bit her bottom lip and refused to look his way.

"Listen, I'm sorry if I offended you."

"You didn't say anything to offend me."

"I know. I didn't say anything, and that in itself was offensive, but you have to realize how shocked I was."

"Poor boy!"

"I wasn't asking for pity."

"Neither am I."

"Let's discuss this rationally. I wasn't repulsed by you. I was repulsed by the things that had been done to you. I mean—"

"I don't want to talk about this with you, now or ever."

"We have to go back to the plantation. They're about to serve lunch, or brunch, or something."

"I'm not going back there."

"You have to, unless you want everyone speculating about what prompted your quick exit."

"You could always say that you made a pass at me."

"That wouldn't work. They know how successful I am when I make my move."

She didn't even crack a grin, let alone a smile.

"Look, we'll pretend you never told me anything."

"That's not the kind of thing you can wipe from your memory, like a blackboard slate."

"We'll go back and say it was just a misunderstanding, that you walked down to the bayou to pick some flowers or something."

She gave him a look that put him in the same category as idiots and morons and clueless men.

"If you can do better, go for it, but we *are* going back. Tante Lulu gave me orders."

"So, that's why you came after me?"

He could feel his face turning red, too. "I would have come, anyway."

"Click," she said.

"That click business is really starting to annoy me."

"Click, click."

"Can we talk about . . . you know?"

"No."

"Why?"

"I never talk about it, and I'm certainly not going to start with a man who wouldn't understand."

"So, this is why you persist in this nun nonsense?"

She visibly breathed in and out to calm down.

"I can't win with you, in this mood."

She made a low growling sound.

"See. You're ready to be insulted, no matter what I say."

"How about you say nothing? Take me back to Tante Lulu's cottage and go on your merry old way. I'm nothing to you, you're nothing to me. My past, your past, none of it matters."

"Now, who's being insulting?"

"Why is that insulting?"

"Because you know how I feel about you."

"Felt about me. Past tense."

"Says who?"

"Oh, Aaron, you wear me down."

He grinned at her. "That's one of my strong points."

"Don't flash that dimple at me. I'm impervious."

"You noticed my dimple," he said, touching the indentation to the left side of his mouth. "I only show it to special people."

She laughed. "You're impossible."

"I know," he said, and reached over to take her hand, assuming that her laugh signified a lessening of stress.

She flinched slightly, like she always did when he touched her, even in passing, but now he suspected it wasn't him, precisely, who brought out this reaction. She didn't like to be touched, period, because of what had happened to her.

That was an issue to be addressed later. Or not at all.

Instead of letting her draw her hand away, though, he laced their fingers and squeezed. "Let's be friends, Fleur. We're going to run into each other while you're living here, what with mutual friends and family, not to mention any possible future ops to save the girls. Even if it's over, for us, we can be friends." Sometimes he impressed even himself with his smooth talking.

She nodded, reluctantly.

But he noticed something she didn't. The zing of sexual chemistry that sparked where their two hands were joined was so powerful that he felt it ricocheting to all his extremities, and some important places in between. Like his heart, which swelled and ached for a brief blip of a second, causing him to catch his breath.

It wasn't over. Not by a bayou longshot.

Chapter Four

Just another day down on the bayou . . .

It was uncomfortable for Fleur when she first returned to the plantation, making some lame excuse for her absence, but Tante Lulu was more concerned about her cake, which had to be rescued by being placed in the freezer for a half hour. Then Aaron, bless his conniving heart, diverted attention away from her by mentioning his plan for, of all things, a St. Jude swimming pool.

"Aaron! Are you crazy?" his brother Daniel exclaimed. "Our next big project is a central AC system, not some fool hole in the ground."

"But a St. Jude pool!" Tante Lulu sighed. "It's so hot t'day, I do declare the hens must be layin' hard-boiled eggs. Wonder where Charmaine hid my bikini?"

"Imagine Lucy and Desi learning to swim in their very own swimming pool," Aaron persisted, as he probably tried to ignore the image of Tante Lulu half-naked. "Bet the little gremlins will be able to doggie paddle right from the get-go."

Axel, who had been spread-eagled on the flagstone patio, raised his head at the mention of dogs, but then went back to snoozing when nothing more was said on the subject. The three cats weren't all that interested, cats not being water lovers, at least of the immersion kind. And Emily, sitting adoringly on Daniel's lap, had no opinion at all.

Samantha was another story. "Aaah," she sighed at the image of her little ones swimming.

"Idiot!" Daniel said.

"Are you calling me an idiot, honey?" Samantha asked.

"No, I'm calling my brother, the idiot, an idiot," Daniel explained.

Aaron bowed, as if he'd been given a compliment.

"I wouldn't mind sunning myself beside a pool," Aunt Mel interjected.

"You and every gator south of New Orleans!" Daniel protested. "And snakes! They're attracted by water, aren't they?"

"Not when it's a St. Jude swimming pool," Tante Lulu claimed.

"It's too damn expensive," Daniel practically shouted.

"I might be willing to give you and Aaron a sort of early inheritance," Aunt Mel offered. "Why not enjoy the money while I'm alive, instead of after I'm gone?"

"If it's gonna be a St. Jude swimming pool, I could scrounge up some cash, too. For the cause." This from Tante Lulu.

"Holy crap! Next we'll be having pilgrimages here."
Daniel was getting red in the face with frustration.

"There's a thought. We could raise funds by sched-
uling 'Blessed Plantation Tours' with a St. Jude gift
shop in that old garden shed. Bet none of the other
plantations in the Southland have anything like that."
Aaron looked at Tante Lulu for her approval.

She gave him a high five.

Daniel put his face in his hands.

Meanwhile, they were devouring the delicious food
spread out on a long table on the covered verandah outside the kitchen. A Cajun omelet containing the holy
trinity of Cajun cooking (onions, bell peppers, and
celery), along with crawfish, mushrooms, cheese, and
Tabasco. Shrimp and andouille grits. Light as feather
biscuits, still warm from the oven, dripping butter.
Fresh fruit, diced and swimming in natural juices,
served from a silver bowl set in a bigger silver bowl
loaded with ice. Paper-thin slices of salty ham and
links of spicy boudin sausage. Fresh-squeezed orange
juice and pitchers of sweet tea, along with cups of
strong Creole coffee.

And then, Fleur's favorite. Fried green tomatoes, a
specialty dish of the South that she missed above all
others, even sweet beignets, when living in Mexico.
These served today were from Aunt Mel's recipe which
she called Alaskan Fried Green Tomatoes. They were
crunchy and tart and delicious, using flour, sweet
cream, and panko bread crumbs, instead of the traditional flour, buttermilk, and cornmeal. Plus, hers were
served "loaded," with a topping of crumbled bacon and
melted Asiago cheese. About a thousand calories per
slice and worth every bite!

And, of course, Tante Lulu's famous Peachy Praline

Cobbler Cake was the grand finale. It melted in the
mouth, but had just the right texture with its praline
crunch and juicy peaches. Everyone said it was even
better this time for having cooled in the freezer.

By the time Fleur and Tante Lulu returned to the
cottage late that afternoon, Fleur felt as if she'd been
through the wringer. And not just because of the heat-
induced sweat. After she took a shower and donned a
light robe (another Charmaine hand-off . . . scarlet
silk! Enough said!), Fleur set her laptop on the kitchen
table and inputted a number of the herbal recipes from
the old receipt book, with notes to herself for additional
info she would need to garner about each of them.
Tante Lulu sat in her bedroom reading her Bible.

As evening approached, both disdaining dinner after their heavy brunch, they moved to the back porch
with its comfy rockers and enjoyed the quiet. Well, as
quiet as the bayou could be with dusk falling over the
area like a foggy blanket.

The calm was deceptive, though. In this region, the
peace could explode on a moment's notice, either
from the attack of one animal on another, the fall of
yet another of the ancient cypress trees which rose
from the swamps like skinny old ladies with knobby
knees, or the climate itself which could go from sunshine to hurricane in an instant. In fact, the humidity
was about one hundred percent this evening, which
presaged a storm, or at least a shower, during the
night.

Fleur had been only five years old when Hurricane
Andrew ripped through the region, with a hundred-
plus miles per hour winds and flooding. She still remembered the sound of the tin roof being yanked off

their house and the bayou flooding and rising almost to the porch of their stilted shack.

But there was no threat of that kind of activity tonight, even though it was clearly a calm before the storm. Even the animals sensed the relative safety as they moved, unhurried, about their nighttime activities. A blue heron stood on one leg in the coffee-colored water, gazing about for possible prey. Crickets chirped, frogs croaked, and occasionally a large animal could be heard slipping into the stream. Could be a gator, or a huge snake, or a swamp rat. Maybe even a big turtle. Ripples appeared here and there as fish darted up to catch whatever fly was the hatch of the day. An owl hooted, seemingly close by. A cloud of bats swooped out of the trees and over the horizon, undaunted by a hawk that circled overhead.

Tante Lulu's pet alligator, Useless, replete from his snack of Cheez Doodles which were stored in a locked trash can near the garage, was snoozing down near the bank of the sluggish stream. Every once in a while, he let out a bellow, which got an answering response from somewhere in the distance.

"He's callin' his girlfriend. Prob'ly makin' a date fer a little whoopee t'night," Tante Lulu said, rocking back and forth. Her chair was lower than the others, to accommodate her shorter legs. It was probably handmade by one of her nephews or nieces, who seemed to adore her, despite her interfering ways.

"How do you know Useless is a male?" Fleur could just imagine the plucky old lady asking the gator to turn over so she could check. She smiled at the image.

"If Useless was a female, there'd be dozens of baby gators wobblin' around my lawn. Didja know that a gator pops out fifty or more eggs at one birthin'? Of course, only about ten of those hatchlings survive till a year old when they can live on their own."

"And you're not afraid of them?"

"'Course I am. Most of 'em would as soon bite yer head off as swim away. But live and let live is my philosophy. As long as they don't bother me, I don't bother them. Not that I haven't killed a few in my time."

Fleur looked to her for elaboration, but when the old lady just continued to rock, staring off in the distance, Fleur let it go, slapping at a mosquito that was buzzing around her head.

"We'll hafta go in soon. The bugs'll be swarmin' and we'll be eaten alive." Tante Lulu didn't move to get up, though. "I've thought about screenin' in this porch, but somehow I jist can't do it."

"Because it would obstruct the view?"

"That, and because I have memories of sittin' here with my Phillippe before he went off ta war for the last time."

Tante Lulu had already told her about the fiancé who died on D-Day during World War II, the beginning of her "Big Grief." Some people might think it was pathetic for a woman to pine over a man for so many years, but Fleur admired her loyalty and the depth of the love she must have felt for her young man. Fleur hadn't witnessed much of that kind of man/woman love, but she believed it was possible for a rare few.

Tante Lulu was a puzzle to her, though. An anomaly. For example, as annoying as she could be with her meddlesome ways, those closest to her—her family and friends—loved her passionately, would do anything for her. There had to be a reason for that. Her giving heart, Fleur concluded.

Another example was the way she spoke. Sometimes her speech was almost illiterate with mispronounced words and hokey proverbs, and other times, she could be articulate and certainly wise on many subjects.

And her appearance! Outrageous was the least of the adjectives used to describe her attire at times, or her changing hair color, and yet Fleur saw framed photographs around the cottage showing her looking age appropriate and almost elegant. At weddings, school graduations, and the like. One particular picture was especially appealing—a young Louise Rivard in the embrace of a World War II era soldier. Her Phillippe, Fleur surmised.

Then, there was her impressive knowledge of the bayou environment and folk medicine. She could teach a college course on either subject.

Did she feign ignorance deliberately, to fool people into thinking she was something she was not? Or was it a sort of split personality? Or was she just eccentric?

"So, did you and Aaron make up?"

That was another thing about Tante Lulu that was so annoying, and puzzling—how she could jump from one subject to another, without any apparent connection.

"There was nothing to make up, but, yes, he did apologize. He—we—agreed to be friends."

Tante Lulu nodded. "Thass a good place ta start. Besides, yer carryin' around so much baggage, it's a wonder they doan call you Samsonite. Aaron could help you with that baggage, but I kin see why you would wanna get rid of those issues first before you start anything."

There was so much wrong with what the old busybody had just said that Fleur didn't know where to start. Like, what baggage? What issues? And, most im-

portant, start what? Before she could ask, Tante Lulu
was off on another subject, or was it the same one?

"I know you hate talkin' about yer 'bad' years, but I
should tell you about what happened ta me, and maybe
it'll help you. Besides, you'll want it for my biography."

"Should I go get my notepad?"

"Ya better. This is gonna be juicy."

But night came swiftly on the bayou, changing from
dusk to dark without warning. A signal for them to go
inside for protection, from the flying insects and all the
dangers of this still wild land. The juicy parts could
wait until tomorrow.

Later, after completing Compline, or nighttime
prayers, from her breviary, Fleur lay in the crisp sheets
of her bed, listening to the rain pounding on the roof.
For a nun, this would be a time for reflection on the
past day, what had been done, what she had failed to
do, and vows to do better.

Fleur had only one thought, at this, the end of her
first full day back "home." *I survived.* And that was a
good thing.

Does anal-retentive have a hyphen? . . .

Aaron and Luc were on their way to the meeting with
FAA officials on Wednesday. As they stood side by
side in the elevator heading up to the sixth floor of the
New Orleans office building, Luc asked, "How's it going with you and the nun?"

"She's not a nun."

"Almost-nun." Luc grinned.

"Not so good."

Luc arched a brow at him.

Aaron wasn't about to tell him Fleur's secret or his lame reaction to said secret. Nor was he about to ask Luc how he'd heard about his "infatuation" with her. The bayou grapevine was amazing; it had probably been Bell's inspiration for the telephone. "I've been busy prepping for this meeting today and haven't had time to see her." *You believe that, and I have a bayou yacht to sell you.*

"Ah well, that's probably a good thing. Absence, fonder hearts, and all that crap."

"For her, not me. I'm already too fond," Aaron disclosed, before having a chance to bite his tongue. "You know, absence makes the parts grow harder."

"Aaah, so that's the way it is," Luc said.

Luckily the elevator door opened then and the conversation ended.

"You ready, pal?" Luc asked as they got to the door marked Federal Aviation Administration.

Aaron nodded. Which was true. Aunt Mel had helped with the documents he needed from Juneau, and Remy's secretary had been able to pull up all the information on flights he'd made for Bayou Aviation. Then Aaron had spent several hours with Luc in his office yesterday compiling a list of all the personal trips he'd made as a pilot over the past five years. He would explain away the trips to Mexico by saying he was delivering donated goods (clothing, toiletries, etc.) to the Sisters of Magdalene convent on behalf of Tante Lulu, one of its benefactors, which was actually true.

Both Aaron and Luc, dressed in business suits at Luc's suggestion, carried leather briefcases and looked well prepared for this interview. To tell the truth, Aaron was a bit nervous. His lists were sketchy at best and fudged in places.

His tension eased a bit, though, after they entered the office and Luc greeted the senior FAA official, Michael Laverge, who said, "Hey, Luc. How's your aunt?"

"Tante Lulu is same as always, Mike. How's your mama?"

When they sat down at the conference table, and the FAA guy had left the room to get his assistant, Aaron whispered to Luc, "You didn't tell me you knew the guy here."

"I had no idea. I thought Mike worked out of D.C."

Maybe this interview wouldn't be so bad.

When Laverge returned with his assistant, though, Aaron wasn't so relaxed. Elaine Forsyth was a not unattractive woman of about thirty, or at least she would be if her blonde hair wasn't skinned back off her face into an old lady bun at her nape, with no make-up that Aaron could detect, pale skin, and wearing a gray suit that did nothing for her slim figure. In essence, they soon found out, Ms. Forsyth had an obsessive need to question every single detail. If she were an accountant, she would be called a numbers cruncher, and not in a good way. Even Laverge appeared to be annoyed at one point.

"Why did you need to make the charity run to Tijuana at midnight on October 17?"

"Did you have a copilot on that flight to and from Dallas where you only touched down for fifteen minutes?"

"Where are the flight logs for January fifth, seventh, and eleventh?"

"Why can't these clothing and toiletry donations be shipped ground rather than flown?"

"Did you ever carry drugs?"

"Are you familiar with the Cortez Cartel?"

"These files are a mess. Have you considered cross-filing them by geography, type of cargo, time of day, and season, as well as date?"

When they took a break after two grueling hours, Aaron went into the men's room with Luc. "Can you use your famous charm on her?" Luc asked.

"My charm is highly overrated," Aaron replied.

"I still say you could soften her up a bit with a little charm. Maybe take her out to lunch and loosen her up with a cocktail or something. Get her to lose the scrunchie and let down that hair."

"What the hell's a scrunchie?" Aaron asked, picking out the least important of the ludicrous suggestions Luc had made.

"A fabric-covered rubber band for the hair." When Aaron looked at Luc with amazement, that he would know such a thing, he explained, "The father of three girls has to be in the know about fashion accessories. Ask me some time about skinny jeans and training bras."

Aaron just laughed.

As it turned out, Aaron and the woman did have some things in common. Ms. Forsyth—who finally told them to call her Elaine, which caused a raised eyebrow from Laverge—had served in the Air Force, too, and they had common acquaintances, including Snake. And, yes, he asked her if she would like to share lunch with him, and Luc, and her boss.

Unfortunately, Laverge had a flight to catch, and

Luc was scheduled for court in Baton Rouge in two
hours, and Aaron was stuck with having made the invitation. Thus, Aaron sat at Antoine's for several hours
where he was bored silly, and Elaine got stoned on
Sazeracs, never once losing her anal-retentiveness. She
actually took out a hand calculator to double check
their bill—before handing it to him.

Even worse, she didn't loosen up one bit on the
pigload of additional documentation she wanted for
their follow-up meeting next week. "This time, be a
little better organized," Elaine advised with a soft
belch. "And I'm thinking maybe I should examine that
plane you've been using."

In line with his good luck, or bad luck, on this day,
as he walked Elaine back to her hotel, his arm around
her waist, trying to keep her upright, he ran into Tante
Lulu and Fleur coming out of an upscale, secondhand
clothing shop, Calinda's Closet, carrying several shopping bags.

Their eyes went wide, especially when Elaine's head
dropped onto his shoulder. Only then did she lose the
damn scrunchie, and blonde hair billowed out all over
the place, and several buttons popped on her suit jacket,
making her look like a high-class tart. And him the
loser who had gotten her drunk.

"Hi!" he said and walked right past them. No way
was he going to attempt any introductions. Who knew
what Elaine might ask them, especially since Tante
Lulu's name had come up so many times in today's
meeting? And who knew what Tante Lulu would answer? As for Fleur, the almost-nun, she probably
wouldn't lie, and all the beans would be spilled, so to
speak.

He heard Tante Lulu say "Huh?" behind him. "That was rude."

He had no idea what Fleur's reaction was. He wasn't sticking around to find out.

Needless to say, Aaron was not in a good mood when he returned to Bayou Rose. In fact, he had such a headache that he went immediately to the medicine cabinet in the *garçonniére* bathroom. He rarely got headaches, but this one was like an axe embedded through his forehead.

After that, he immediately stripped off his clothes and jumped in the stall shower where he let the cool water wash over him. He would have much preferred the deluxe rainforest shower over at the main house, but it would take too much energy and effort to make his way over there.

What a day! he thought. First, the interrogation at the FAA office. Then, the lunch from hell with Ms. Anal-Retentive. And how was he ever going to explain to Fleur the street scene of him with a drunk blonde hanging all over him in the middle of the day? Any progress he'd made with her was shot to hell, guaranteed.

Maybe he should just go to bed and sleep. After all, this was the South, where tomorrow was another day. That way, this day couldn't get any worse.

Or could it?

When he came out of the bathroom, wearing nothing but . . . well, nothing . . . he saw his brother standing at the bedroom window, staring out. Dan looked serious, even more serious than usual.

"What's up?" Aaron asked, grabbing for a pair of sweat pants and slipping them on. "Is something wrong? Oh, my God! Is it Samantha? Did she go into labor?"

Dan turned abruptly, not having realized his brother had come into the room. In his bare feet, Aaron had made no noise on the soft carpet.

"No, Samantha's fine. Aunt Mel is teaching her how to knit booties, whatever the hell they are."

So, if it wasn't Samantha, it must be that stupid swimming pool idea Aaron had been teasing him about. "Do you still have your Jockeys in a twist over the swimming pool? Get over it. Besides, I was only half kidding."

"Only half? You idiot!" Dan nudged him with an elbow. "Half was enough to get Tante Lulu's ball rolling. She sent an engineer over here this morning to survey the site. A friend of a friend, who just happened to be passing by."

Aaron laughed and they both went down the stairs to the second floor living area. These old *garçonniéres* weren't very big. Separate from the main plantation mansion, they'd been intended as quarters for the planter's adult sons who were not yet married. Sort of nineteenth century bachelor pads. Bayou Rose's version was hexagonal-shaped with three stories. The ground floor was empty now, once used by Dan for an office. The second floor had a living room, kitchenette, and half bath. The third floor was a big bedroom with a full bath, nothing like the rainforest shower one in the mansion, but sufficient.

Aaron went into the little kitchenette off the living room to get them both a beer. His headache was almost gone. God bless Extra-Strength Tylenol!

When he came back, Dan was already sitting on one

of the side-by-side recliners. Aaron handed him a beer and sank into the other chair, taking a long swig before clicking on the remote. A *Walking Dead* marathon was playing on AMC. He decided that would be a good way to while away the evening.

"It's not the swimming pool I came to talk about," Dan said finally.

Uh-oh!

"How did your meeting go with the FAA, by the way?"

"Don't ask," Aaron said, but when he saw the worry on his brother's face, he added, "It'll work out. They're just making me jump through some pain-in-the-ass hoops. Nothing to worry about."

"I do worry, though."

"Payback is hell, isn't it? Think of all the time I worried about you, holed up in that fishing camp, licking your wounds."

"I wasn't licking anything," Dan protested, but then conceded with a bow of his head. "I was pathetic, wasn't I?"

Aaron shrugged.

Which caused Dan to say, "I was saved by Samantha. Are you going to be saved by a woman, too?"

"Not that I need to be saved—I'm not nearly as pathetic as you were—but, no, there will be no Princess Charming coming to my rescue. Not on a horse, not on a gator, and not in a lavender convertible. In fact . . ." Aaron went on to describe what had happened to him on the street in New Orleans. By the time he was done, Dan was bent over laughing.

"Oh Lord! Tante Lulu will have the story bouncing off the bayou grapevine by now." He mimicked Tante's Lulu's voice then, "Holy Sac-au-lait! That bad boy

Aaron LeDeux, snockered in the middle of the day! Right in front of God and all the folks on Royal Street in Nawleans! With an equally snockered, blonde bombshell practic'ly humpin' his leg. Whass the world comin' to?" Back to himself, he continued, "She'll be having the Our Lady of the Bayou rosary society saying a novena for you."

"It's not Tante Lulu's opinion I'm concerned about."

"Fleur will come around. They always do, for you. Use some of that sexy charm of yours."

"Why does everyone say I have charm? I don't have any more charm than the next guy."

Dan shook his head at him. "Tante Lulu is going to slice and dice you and toss you in her next batch of gumbo. Probably give it a name, like Clueless Man Gumbo."

"So, if you didn't come over to rag on me about the swimming pool, what is it?"

"I've had a job offer."

"Oh? Congratulations!"

Dan didn't look happy.

"So what's the problem?"

"The job is in Baton Rouge."

"Huh? Too far away. Just say no."

"It's not that simple."

"Ooookay. So you commute."

Dan shook his head slowly.

"Enough with the hemming and hawing. Spit it out."

"Celesta Care bought that old hospital in Baton Rouge and plans to renovate and modernize the entire complex, adding new wings so that there will be one massive unit devoted to nothing but pediatric oncology, complete with living facilities for families. They like what we've done here at Bayou Rose on a small scale and want the same kind of thing there, but bigger. A small village of cottages."

"Sounds like a big deal."

"It is. It will be."

"And you're hesitating . . . because?"

"Of you."

"What? Me? Are you crazy? What do I have to do with your accepting or not accepting a major promotion?"

"We've never been apart, except when you were in the service while I was in med school, and that was horrible. You know it was."

"Ah man! That's sweet, but we're not married or anything. And you're sure as hell not my daddy." Aaron was making light of a separation from his brother, but it *was* a big deal. His headache was back in spades, and he barely tamped down the panic that thrummed just beneath the surface of his skin. Which was ridiculous, of course. "If this is what you want, go for it, bro. I'm a big boy . . . we're big boys. Time to cut the cord."

"I'll never cut the cord," Dan said and reached over to squeeze his arm.

"Okay, give me the deets."

"Well, the timing couldn't be worse, of course, with Samantha's pregnancy, but they're willing to wait until after the babies are born for me to join their team. If I decide to join their team."

Aaron nodded. "How about Bayou Rose? Samantha loves this plantation, and look at all the work she's put into renovations so far."

"In the end, it's just a house. That's what she told me anyhow. She's willing to go wherever I go, and Baton Rouge isn't that far from New Orleans if she wants to continue working for Starr Foods. Besides, there's some historic mansion on the site that would go to me, as the director, and Samantha's already salivating with plans."

"Oh Lord! I'd be alone here in that big old house," Aaron said before he could check himself.

"Aunt Mel would probably stay, at least for a while. And who knows? Maybe you'll be marrying yourself."

Don't count on it. Not anytime soon.

"And I'm sure Tante Lulu would make sure you aren't too lonely."

"Very funny! What about the cottages? Would families of sick kids still come here? Who would manage all that? And how about the ongoing renovations that Samantha has been supervising?" Aaron really was beginning to panic now. All this on top of the FAA investigation, his continuing work for the Jude's Apostles/Magdas, his pursuit of Fleur, his job with Bayou Aviation.

"We could always sell, if it's too much for you. With all the improvements we've made so far, we should make a hefty profit, or at least break even."

For some reason, the thought of selling created more dismay. Aaron hadn't realized he'd become so attached to the place.

"Well, I'll tell you one thing," he said, downing the rest of his beer in one long swallow. "If I'm going to be here by myself, there's going to be a swimming pool. And probably a billiards table in the dining room. And mirrors on the ceiling of the master suite."

"Go for it," Dan said. "Anyhow, nothing's decided. We can talk about this again. I just wanted to give you a heads-up."

Aaron had a lot to think about after Dan left. Maybe it was time for him to make a huge turn in his own life. Buy a plane and start his own business again. Or try something different. Charter boats in the Caribbean, for example. That would be good.

On the personal front, maybe he'd been stalled in "infatuation" mode for too long, and it was time to kick it up a notch with Fleur. Stop treating her with kid (i.e. nun) gloves, and start using the tricks of the trade he'd mastered years ago with (many) other women.

Then again, maybe not. Maybe he should just look in new directions. Lots of fish in the sea, as the old expression went. Unfortunately, he'd had a taste for only one particular fish lately, but that could be changed, couldn't it?

Most immediate, what to do about this big frickin' plantation if he was going to be living here all by his lonesome? Dan's timing sucked the big one.

Decisions, decision, decisions.

But first, for some reason known only to God and St. Jude, he felt the need to talk to Fleur about all this.

Chapter Five

L one Ranger to the rescue . . .

Fleur needed to talk with Aaron.

But not about his apparent midday hookup with some blonde in New Orleans, as Tante Lulu kept harping about on the way back to her cottage.

"That boy is gettin' on my last nerve."

"Whoo-ee, he is in a heap of trouble. Wonder when he last went ta confession?"

"Didja see that floozy splattered all over him like honey on a hot rock?"

"I think she was lickin' his ear."

"Why dint you jist whack her with yer shoppin' bag fer skunkin' yer man? Oh, I know he ain't yer man yet. Give it time. Why are ya lookin' cross-eyed at me?"

"I been thinkin' that the fool needs ta put a ring on

yer finger, but mebbe you better put a ring in his nose, instead. Tee-hee-hee!"

All this chatter passed over Fleur, who had bigger troubles than Aaron LeDeux and his love life, or Chatty Cathy in a Zsa Zsa Gabor wig (*Don't ask!*) and a glittery shirt with a padded bra. Why hadn't Fleur insisted to Tante Lulu that they go into the nondescript thrift shop in Houma to buy Fleur's much-needed wardrobe? Why had Fleur succumbed to Tante Lulu's urging that they try the new consignment shop in New Orleans?

Now, it was too late.

A few moments ago, out in broad daylight, on the busy New Orleans street, she'd seen a nightmare vision from her past.

And he'd seen her, too.

Ten years might have passed since she'd been in the presence of the creep, but she'd never forget Miguel Vascone, a member of the Mexican mob who worked with the Dixie Mafia on sex trafficking. It was Miguel who'd tricked her, a fourteen-year-old runaway, into accompanying him to his "safe house," which turned out to be not safe at all.

Yes, she took risks all the time, especially when on a Magda mission. Like that time in the New Orleans strip club. But she was always part of a team, and their risks were minimal. Or so she'd thought. For the most part, she'd remained hidden in the remote convent, where she should be now.

How could this have happened to her?

Miguel had been one of her pimps during those six bad years as she'd been rotated from one Mexican city to another, and then occasionally to resort areas (the circuit sometimes referred to as the "Border Cha-Cha Pipeline"), places where Miguel's father, Santos Vascone, the leader of a powerful drug cartel, owned mansions-turned-prisons for the young prostitutes.

It had been Miguel who'd been knocked over the head with a baseball bat and left for dead in Acapulco when she'd been rescued by a team of Street Apostles and Magdas ten years ago. And she'd been the one wielding the bat left out in the hall by one of the brothel guards. The Street Apostles and Magdas didn't carry weapons.

Apparently Miguel hadn't died.

As she peeled out of the parking lot onto Royal Street in Tante Lulu's hard-to-miss lavender convertible, she'd seen in the rearview mirror that Miguel had at first run after her vehicle, but then stopped and appeared to be making note of the license plate, jotting it down on his hand with a pen or marker or something. Any chance of his not recognizing her were nil.

Oh Lord! Was her ten years of convent safety ended now? Surely, Miguel and his cohorts would have no interest in a woman her age. They much preferred young girls for their clients. But he would want her back to punish her for leaving, and for the injuries he'd incurred.

This was bad. First of all, if he was able to trace the license plate to Tante Lulu's address, not only was she in danger, but Tante Lulu would be, too. If she went back to the convent, Miguel might be able to track her there; then, the nuns would be in danger. Not just that, but the whole Magda mission in rescuing girls would be jeopardized.

She couldn't go to the police. Not without discussing it with the Street Apostles or the Magdas. Even then, she had no way of locating Miguel, other than saying he was in New Orleans. And then she would be revealing the activities of the Street Apostles and Magdas, which was a no-no, even for law enforcement.

What to do? What to do?

She needed to talk to someone, and for some reason the person who came to mind was Aaron LeDeux.

"What's the matter with you, girl?" Tante Lulu asked when they got back to the cottage. "You're as nervous as a porcupine in a balloon factory, and ya drove so fast back here that I practic'ly got whiplash." While she talked, she took off her Zsa Zsa Gabor wig and picked road bugs out of the blonde strands.

Fleur explained briefly and told a horrified Tante Lulu that she would give her more details later. She went into the bathroom where she threw up in the toilet, rinsed out her mouth, then straightened with resolve. No time for a pity party.

When she went into the living room, Fleur's eyes about bugged out when she saw what Tante Lulu was busy doing at the kitchen table, which was visible through the archway, but she would address *that* later. Instead, she went out to the porch to make her phone call.

"Aaron?"

"Fleur? I was just about to call you."

"You were?"

"Yeah. About that scene back in the city—"

"Never mind about that."

"But you should know, that the woman you saw with me wasn't a girlfriend, or anything like that. She was just a . . . business acquaintance."

Fleur laughed. "Yeah, that's what they all say."

"Seriously. She's with the FAA, the Federal Aviation Administration. Luc and I met with the agency people this morning. I had lunch with her after my meeting."

"A liquid lunch?"

"On her part, not mine."

"Aaron, I don't care about your women. I thought you understood that."

"You called me," he said, clearly offended.

"Not to berate you over your personal life."

"Anyhow, what you saw . . . that wasn't the reason I was going to call you, not the main reason. Something has come up involving my brother, and I need a second opinion."

"From me?" she asked with surprise.

"An objective outsider."

That sounded cold, but she couldn't really be offended when she'd pretty much wanted the same thing from him. "Can you come over to Tante Lulu's? I need to talk to you, too."

"You sound frightened."

"I am."

"What's the problem?"

"I'd rather discuss it in person."

He sighed, then agreed, "I'll be over in an hour. Are you okay in the meantime?"

"Yes."

"Is Tante Lulu with you?"

"Uh-huh."

"I sense something in your voice. What is the old lady doing?"

"Putting bullets in her gun."

He said the *F* word under his breath. "Do you have a weapon, too?"

"No, although I wield a great bat, if I can find one. Honestly, I feel like Annie Oakley's sidekick. A Grandma Moses version of Annie Oakley."

"What does that make me?"

"The Lone Ranger?"

He paused before saying, "Hi ho, Silver pickup truck."

Just when he thought she was out of reach, she reached out . . .

The Lone Ranger arrived in his silver pickup truck a half hour later. Aaron had probably ruined the shocks on his practically new vehicle, barreling over the rutted country road.

Jumping out to the driveway, he almost tripped over Tante Lulu's pet alligator. He gave the reptile a dirty look and said, "Don't even think about it! I'm carrying, and I'm in a bad mood." Useless opened his huge mouth, and Aaron could swear he yawned. So much for Aaron's threat! Taking no chances, Aaron unlocked the trash barrel that held about fifty-five gallons of Cheez Doodles, and tossed a few handfuls to the beast. The gator let out a little roar, as if to say, "Thanks, bozo!"

When he walked around to the back of the cottage, he saw Fleur sitting on a rocker, sipping at a glass of iced sweet tea. Through a window, he could see Tante Lulu inside, puttering around in her kitchen. The smell of some spicy food wafted out, a dish involving seafood. With everything so calm and natural, where was the danger?

"That was quick," she said.

"You made it sound urgent."

She didn't claim any different, which caused the fine hairs to rise on the back of his neck.

He sank down into a rocker and looked at her more closely. Her dark hair was in a windblown, messy ponytail, probably from riding in the convertible, and the skin of her face and arms was developing a warm suntan, also probably from riding in the open air. She was wearing the same clothes she'd had on earlier—white, stretchy, knee-length pants, along with an oversize New Orleans Saints T-shirt. She'd mentioned the other day that she had to rely on left-behind apparel at Tante Lulu's until she had a chance to replenish her almost nonexistent wardrobe. Fashion was not a priority while residing at the Magda convent. Thus the trip into New Orleans today to the used clothing shop, he supposed.

He stiffened, feeling an odd twinge of something—not anger, not pity, but something in between—that she had to borrow clothing or buy used. If she was his . . . well, never mind. That was a road he shouldn't—couldn't—go down right now.

"Thank you for coming," she said.

"You made it sound important."

"It is." She set her glass on a side table and clenched her hands together, almost like she was praying. "I saw Miguel Vascone today in New Orleans."

"Who is Miguel Vascone?"

"The most vile, evil, perverted . . ." She inhaled and exhaled to calm herself, then began to explain, "When I was fourteen years old, on my birthday, I ran away from home. Not for the first time. But on that particular day, I was hanging around with some friends near the bus station in New Orleans. It was a good place for panhandling tourists coming into town. All the kids did it. Sometimes we made enough to buy a fast-food meal. Other times, we'd hit pay dirt and make enough to party. Innocent stuff, especially compared to what kids do today."

He waited, sensing that she needed to tell this story in her own way. Questions would come later. Like what was so bad about her home life? And how had an underage girl gotten from Bayou Black to the Big Easy? Why hadn't she been in school?

"Miguel was young and good-looking. He couldn't have been more than twenty at that time. My girlfriend, Francine Fontaine, and I were contemplating whether we had enough nerve to buy bus tickets to actually leave town. We always had big dreams of running off to Nashville where we would become country music stars. Usually, we just ran away for a day or two before returning home and having our back ends blistered before trying again later. My daddy had a belt he called Big Ben. Frannie's father preferred kicking, with steel-toed boots."

He was as horrified by the coolness with which she spoke of the abuse. Sensing she wouldn't want to delve into the details of her family at this time, he homed in on something else she'd said. "You mentioned Nashville . . . do you have musical talent?"

"Not really, although Frannie was good on the guitar, and I sang sometimes. We busked for cash donations. Our best duo was to that old Patsy Cline song, 'Crazy.' Yeah, that's what we were. Crazy, and dumb as dirt." She paused, deep in some memory.

"Go on," he encouraged.

"Miguel told us that he had two motel rooms nearby, one of them empty since his buddy had to go home suddenly. He said we could stay there for the night. And guess what? He just happened to know a guy in Nashville looking for backup singers for a music video being made by Garth Brooks. I know, I know, how could we be so gullible? But Frannie and I had bad home lives, and this guy was being so nice." She shrugged. "Bottom line, we were drugged, and when we woke up a day, or maybe two, later, we were in some house in Mexico with a bunch of other kidnapped girls. At first, we didn't understand. But we soon learned. Oh, did we learn!"

"Ah, Fleur," he rasped out over the lump in his throat, reaching out a hand for hers.

"No!" She moved her arm so he couldn't touch her. "I'm not telling you this because I want your pity."

"So, you ran into a guy in New Orleans today. And you recognized him from fifteen—sixteen—years ago?" he asked skeptically.

"There's more. Miguel's father is a big honcho with a Mexican drug cartel, or he used to be before he was murdered by some other competing cartel. Miguel and his older brother Juan were in charge of the prostitution side of the business. I saw a lot of Miguel over those six years of hell." She shivered.

Aaron barely restrained himself from yanking her over and onto his lap, and hugging the fear right out of her.

Tears filled her eyes, and stung his own eyes, too.

"Testers were sent in to pretend to rescue a girl. If she was cooperative, she was punished in the most horrible ways. I can't even speak about that. Bottom line, I learned to trust no one."

Aaron had a feeling she'd fallen for the "tester" ruse. Probably more than once. No wonder she had trust issues!

"When I was rescued, along with five other girls, I hit Miguel over the head with a baseball bat. Hard! His skull was bashed in and there was so much blood. I thought he was dead. Apparently not. I've since adopted the Magda's philosophy about nonviolence, but at that time, I wasn't thinking. Just reacting. No excuse, but . . ." She shrugged.

"Did your friend, Frannie, get rescued at the same time?"

"No." Tears now streamed down Fleur's face. "She committed suicide a month after we were kidnapped."

"Oh, my God!" he whispered, but he had to keep calm, while she was not. "Was returning home, here on the bayou, not a possibility, after your rescue?"

She shook her head. "To my family, I was already dead. Besides, it was my fault for being in that situation, they claimed. They didn't say the words, but they really thought I should have killed myself, like Frannie. Otherwise, I must have been there willingly."

Rage filled him at the intolerance of ignorant people. Somehow, he would find an outlet for that rage, later, but he had to focus on what was important in the here and now. "Let's examine the facts here, Fleur. Ten years later, you think this scumbag recognized you and will somehow locate you and enact revenge. That is a stretch, sweetheart."

The endearment had just slipped out. Luckily, she didn't hear or just ignored it. "I saw him write down the license number of Tante Lulu's car on his hand. How hard is it today, with the Internet and everything, to trace a plate? He'll come. It's only a matter of time."

Okay, maybe not such a stretch, after all. He was beginning to share her distress. "You've got to get out of here then. Pronto. That's the first thing."

"I know," she said, more composed as she wiped her face with a tissue, "but I can't go back to the convent. Even if they don't find me here, eventually they would go after Tante Lulu to find out where I am."

She was probably right.

"Not only would that put Tante Lulu in danger, but the convent, too. And not just that. If they make a connection between me, my escape, and the Magdas, their mission to rescue kidnapped girls will be put to an end."

Maybe. Maybe not.

"Secrecy is essential; it's a miracle they've been able to conceal their activities for so long. If the criminals, or the police, don't stop their work, the church will."

Now that's where he drew the line. "We're going to have to contact local law enforcement, or the feds, no matter what you say." He held up a halting hand. "I'm not saying that we do anything without first consulting the Street Apostles and the Magdas, but this is bigger than just you. We'll move slowly, carefully. Agreed?"

She nodded, reluctantly.

"But first, we need to get you and Tante Lulu to a safe place. Bayou Rose makes the most sense."

"What? No!" Fleur protested.

"Yes. Perfect," Tante Lulu said, coming through the screen door by hitting the frame with her little hip. She carried two icy glasses of sweet tea, one of which she handed to him before sitting in the third rocker. "This will be jist like the time you hid Samantha and her step-brother from the Dixie Mafia. You worked up a bite . . . no, a whatchamacallit . . . a sting, that's it . . .

with the FBI and the FDA and a bunch of those other government letter agencies what no one understands, dint ya, Aaron? And yer plantation was the perfect hidin' place. Plus, Daniel got his chance ta woo Samantha inta bed while she was there. Lagniappe, so ta speak." She waggled her sparse gray eyebrows at him meaningfully. The gray brows were in contrast to the big blonde wig that sat lopsided on her head, as if she'd just yanked it on before coming outside.

He got her meaning about the lagniappe, the little something extra.

But Fleur didn't. She was still gaping at Tante Lulu's long spiel about all those government agencies on his plantation premises and some involvement with the Dixie Mob. Once she'd recovered, she said, "I can't intrude on you that way, Aaron. I know that I asked you to come and give me advice, but I wasn't expecting such a huge favor. Besides, your brother and his wife live there. You can't make that kind of offer for their home."

"It's half mine."

"Still . . ."

"Actually, that was the thing I wanted to discuss with you, Fleur. Turns out my brother and Samantha may be moving to Baton Rouge for a new job. So, I may be living there all by my lonesome."

Fleur looked puzzled as to why this was something he wanted to discuss with her. He wasn't sure he had an answer.

"What? Thass the first I've heard 'bout Daniel and Samantha movin'," Tante Lulu said, but immediately added, "See. It was meant ta be. We're movin' inta Bayou Rose. It'll be jist like a vacation. I get the bedroom next ta the bathroom."

"Don't tell anyone about Daniel moving," Aaron warned Tante Lulu. "Nothing definite has been decided."

Tante Lulu pretended to zip her lips and throw the imaginary key over her shoulder.

"If nothing is decided, they won't be moving right away. We would still be intruding," Fleur argued. "Especially at this time, with Samantha about to have a baby. Talk about impositions!"

"It ain't imposin' when it's family," Tante Lulu told her.

"But I'm not family."

"Shush yerself, girl. Yer extended family."

Fleur ignored what Tante Lulu just said, though Aaron could tell she was kind of touched. The old lady had a knack for doing that, annoying the hell out of you, then doing something wonderful. "The timing is also bad for you, Aaron. With the FAA investigation, you need to keep under the radar." Fleur looked imploringly at him, trying to get him on her side.

Not a chance! "No one's going to know that I'm involved with you." He liked the sound of that and couldn't help but grin.

"Stop flashing that dimple at me. There's nothing funny about this situation."

She noticed my dimple again. That has to be a good sign. "It's not about funny. It's about me being happy to help two lovely ladies."

Tante Lulu preened.

Fleur snorted, and he thought she muttered something under her breath, immediately followed by "Click!"

"Okay, I'm going to call my brother to alert him to the situation while you two start packing. I'll call Luc, too, and tell him to come out to Bayou Rose tomorrow."

"Why Luc? He's a lawyer. We don't need a lawyer. We need protection."

"We need Luc's skills in planning which agencies to contact. I'll provide any protection you need."

"I'll protect you, too," Tante Lulu offered, patting the pistol in her hip holster, which he'd just noticed.

Fleur groaned.

"Later, I'll call Snake, and see what they suggest from their end," Aaron said. To Tante Lulu, he explained, "Snake is an old Air Force buddy of mine. Brian Malone. Rather, Brother Brian Malone with the St. Jude's Street Apostles." It had taken Snake a long time to recuperate from his wounds last year, but he was back in action again, back at the Street Apostles' Dallas headquarters.

"Maybe I could hide out there . . . at the Street Apostles' ranch," Fleur said.

"Maybe," Aaron conceded, though he preferred her under his care.

"I have Shrimp Étouffée ready ta go in the oven fer dinner. Should we eat first?" Tante Lulu asked.

"No, just pack it up. We'll eat it back at Bayou Rose."

"What about Tante Lulu's convertible?" Fleur asked, apparently resigned, finally, to their move. At least temporarily. "I put it in the garage, but I'm not sure we should leave it here. Miguel and his grunts might see it through the garage window and decide to wait us out. If it's not here, they might think they got the wrong place."

"From your lips to God's ears," Aaron said.

"Or St. Jude's," Tante Lulu piped in.

"We'll bring the car with us," Aaron decided. "You can drive it or my truck," he told Fleur.

While Tante Lulu and Fleur went inside to prepare for their indefinite stay at the plantation, Aaron took out his phone to call his brother. But first, he listened in as Tante Lulu told Fleur, "Stop bein' so snarky with Aaron. He's tryin' ta help."

"I just don't want to be beholden to the man."

"Why? He's in love with you."

"He used to be. Not anymore."

"That's what you think. That boy wants ta jump you like a dead battery, if ya ask me."

"I am dead, that's for sure. In more ways than one."

"Ain't you jist a ray of sunshine. Give yerself a chance, girl. Sometimes happiness sneaks in through a door ya dint know was left open."

Fleur laughed. "You are nuttier than squirrel poop. Maybe when you're done with your herb remedy book, and your biography, you could write a book of Cajun proverbs. *Wacky* Cajun proverbs."

"Good idea. Here's a good one ta start with. 'People are lonely because they build walls instead of bridges.' And, missie, yer walls are so thick, it would take dynamite ta break through. By the way, make sure ya bring yer computer and all those folk remedy books of mine soz you can work on the project while we're at Bayou Rose. Ya never know how much time I have left and we gotta make use of every minute."

"Are you unwell?"

"Nah, but best ta be prepared. We kin work on my biography, too. Lordy, every time I think all my adventures are over, somethin' else comes up. Ain't this excitin'?"

"Yeah, real exciting!"

"Keep frownin' like that and yer face is gonna freeze like an old hag. Me—as old as I am—I'll never look like a hag 'cause I'm allus so cheery and positive. You could learn some things from me, girl."

Aaron grinned. Fleur was probably doing mental clicks in her head. He pressed the contact number on his cell phone and waited. Finally, Dan picked up.

"Hey, bro," Aaron said cheerily. "You ready for some company?"

"Uh."

"I'm over at Tante Lulu's. I'm bringing her and Fleur back there with me."

"Why? For how long?"

"Indefinite."

"What's this about, Aaron?"

"Remember how the plantation became a hideout for Samantha and her step-brother Angus and his girl-friend Lily Beth last year?"

"Yeeaah," Dan said, drawing the word out.

"This is kind of the same situation, except maybe worse."

"Aaron!"

"Are you okay with me bringing them there?"

"Of course. I'll tell Samantha and Aunt Mel to get some rooms ready, or do you think they would prefer one of the cottages? They're empty for the moment while work is being done on the new septic lines, but I'm sure we could make one or two of them useable by jerry-rigging the old pipes."

"Maybe. No, I think it would be better if they were inside the Money Pit." That was their name for the mansion that ate cash like a slot machine, the kind that only took big bills. "We can decide that later. For now, for tonight at least, let's plan on them being in the main house."

"Okay. Anything you want us to do from this end?"

"No. Just know that Fleur is really anxious about intruding. Make her feel welcome."

"Of course."

His heart kind of swelled with love and pride that his brother didn't insist on more details before agreeing to unexpected guests. "Thanks, bro. You're the best," Aaron choked out.

"Always," his brother said. "One last thing. Does this mean we're going to get a St. Jude swimming pool, with the bayou bulldozer, aka Tante Lulu, on the job site?"

"Probably," Aaron said with a laugh.

"You know what the old lady's going to say about all this, don't you? It's St. Jude and the Thunderbolt at work. All part of the celestial plan to get you to jump through the love hoops."

Aaron could only hope. As long as he wasn't making that jump by himself.

Chapter Six

Home, home, on the range . . . uh, plantation . . .

Everyone was being so nice, which made Fleur feel just awful.

Fleur took care of her own problems. She'd been on her own for a long time, without depending on other people for help. Even back at the convent, she'd carried her own weight, giving a hundred percent and more of herself to "pay her way," and not just through the rescue missions.

These people here at Bayou Rose wanted nothing in return for their favors, except for Aaron, maybe, who was behaving perfectly. Too perfectly. There was mischief in him, just waiting to pounce; she knew it, sure as God made sin and pretty red apples. It was like Tante Lulu had told her, when working on her biography, "Never trust a Cajun man with angel eyes and a devil's own grin." Fleur would add to that, "Especially if he has a killer dimple."

Of course, she was immune. But, still . . .

Fleur had picked a bedroom on the third floor, where she would be by herself. There, she felt safe, far removed from the recent threat posed by Miguel. Besides, she appreciated a solitary space to think and pray, which was of course the whole purpose of her respite from the convent. To contemplate her future. Which was looking dimmer and dimmer.

Actually, this level was the fourth floor, or attic, if you counted the ground level as the first floor. Bedrooms up here had been used by servants, or slaves, at one time. Everyone else was in one of the six bedrooms on the floor below, except for Aaron, who lived in that separate building, and except for Daniel and Samantha who had converted a second parlor on the main floor into a temporary bedroom so that she wouldn't have to go up and down the stairs in her advanced state of pregnancy.

Fleur's room was small and plain, with rough-cut pine boards arranged horizontally on the walls and whitewashed lightly so the wood showed through. The random plank cypress floors, worn unevenly by years of use, were covered only by a woven, mat-like area carpet. An antique block-patterned quilt in shades of faded indigo blue and white was folded back to expose crisp white cotton sheets on the single bed.

An electrified hurricane lamp atop a chest of drawers made up for the lack of overhead lighting. In addition, a modern floor lamp with its own round table surrounding the pole sat next to a comfy upholstered chair, both looking like flea market finds, but perfect for reading.

In fact, built-in shelves held a dozen or so books in several genres—mystery, romance, nonfiction, along with some magazines—*Time, Newsweek, Psychology Today, Architectural Digest, Southern Living*, and *Cosmo*. That latter drew a smile, especially the cover which proclaimed "Celibacy Is Hot!" The top shelf also held an old Bakelite radio, which still worked. She had turned it on low to a local station which played traditional Cajun ballads in twangy Acadian French. Right now, it was that favorite, *"Jolie Blon."*

It was a corner room with small windows, overlooking the sugarcane fields on one side, and on the other, a row of quaint, pastel-colored cottages surrounded by white picket-fenced, postage-stamp size yards, once the slave quarters, but now used for families of cancer patients under Dr. Daniel LeDeux's pediatric oncology care.

A ceiling fan, along with the open windows, allowed for a slight breeze, making the room, not air-conditioned cool, but comfortable. At least, at nighttime. During a summer day, the heat might be unbearable.

She'd come up to put her clothing and meager belongings away. There was no closet, but plenty of drawer space. Since there was no desk, she would have to figure out some place to work on Tante Lulu's projects. Maybe the kitchen when no one else was there.

Footsteps sounded on the stairs and Aaron soon appeared in the open doorway. He wore tan cargo shorts, a black T-shirt with the sleeves ripped off, and rubber flip-flops instead of his usual cowboy boots. His hair was wet and slicked back off his face, and a piney scent wafted into the room. He must have just showered. He hadn't shaved, though, and his face was covered with an evening stubble.

Leaning against the doorframe, he said, "Are you sure you want to be up here? There are bigger bedrooms downstairs with window AC units."

She shook her head. "This is perfect. In fact, it's the nicest room I've ever had."

"Really?"

"Really. You come from a different background than I do, Aaron. I grew up in a run-down bayou shack with eight brothers and sisters. Just having a room of my own would have been bliss. And at the convent . . . well, the rooms are more like cells, which they're intended to be. Bare bones. Utilitarian. This is"—she swept a hand to indicate the attic room—"pretty."

"If you say so." She could tell he wanted to ask more questions, probably about her family, but he restrained himself. Instead, he walked around the room, examining and touching things. The fabric of the lace-edged pillowcase. A sampler on the wall proclaiming in cross-stitch, "Home Is Where the Heart Is." A blue silk nightshirt hanging from a wall peg; she'd purchased the garment at the used clothing store this morning, which seemed like eons ago. Even the magazines with *Cosmo* left on top, to her dismay, but he just snickered under his breath and said nothing. Which was not normal for him. She was right to be on her guard where Aaron was concerned. He was up to something.

"You only have a half bath up here," he pointed out. "If you want to shower or soak in a tub, you'll have to go downstairs."

"Sounds good to me. Is there time before dinner?"

"Should be. Tante Lulu and Aunt Mel are going gangbusters in the kitchen. Mixing the shrimp dish Tante

Lulu brought along with the grilled cheeseburgers Aunt Mel had been planning. Should be interesting."

"Maybe I'll hurry up and take a shower then," she said, beginning to pull out drawers to gather clean clothes.

"Don't rush. I installed a super deluxe rainforest shower here, with all kinds of sprays and gadgets. You'll want to relish the experience. In fact, I should probably show you how it works." He batted his eyelashes at her with exaggerated innocence.

"I think I can figure it out," she said with a laugh. This was the first that Aaron had acted like his normal rascal self all day. She liked it.

They walked down the narrow staircase together, talking about the various meetings to be held tomorrow. With Luc. With Brother Malone, who was flying in from Dallas, representing the Street Apostles. Aaron said that he'd already talked with Ed Gillotte, the on-site construction foreman, to stop any workers from coming onto the plantation grounds for the time being, and with Ed's live-in girlfriend, a graduate student in physics, to make sure she and Ed's three kids made no mention of the Bayou Rose guests to anyone, not even their friends, and not to invite anyone in, either.

"I am so sorry for all this incon—"

"Enough, Fleur! Do you realize how often you say those words, 'I'm sorry, I'm sorry, I'm sorry'? It's tiresome. You know how you say 'Click!' every time you say or think a bad word . . . well, I have an idea."

"Yeah?" she said hesitantly. "What?"

"Well, I figure every time you say 'I'm sorry,' or apologize in any way, you'll owe me a penalty."

She smiled at the silliness of his game. "And what would that penalty be?"

"A kiss."

"Oh, no! I'm sorry but I don't—"

He chalked a mark in the air for her having said "I'm sorry" again. "Don't worry about me collecting on the spot, especially if you do your apologizing ad nauseam in front of other people. I wouldn't want to embarrass you. I'm considerate like that."

She laughed again, then paused, suddenly aware that he made her feel lighthearted and worry-free for the moment. That was probably his intent.

"And I won't be collecting on each of those 'debts' separately. You'd try to duck out by giving me a little peck on the cheek. Nope, I'll keep a tally of each of your transgressions, and when I call my markers in after, oh, let's say ten or fifteen apologies, it will be one super kiss. Definitely on the lips."

"Oh, you!" she said and went to slap at him with her free hand, but he danced away. Fleur went after him, not realizing that Aunt Mel had just come out of the bathroom, and Fleur almost ran into her. "I'm sorry," she said, before she realized what she'd said.

Aaron made a great show of marking two lines in the air.

"You are outrageous," Fleur said, shaking her head at him as he was backing down the hallway toward the other stairway.

"I know. That's what women love about me," he declared with a wink.

"What's that boy up to now?" Aunt Mel asked.

"Just silliness. I think he knows how worried I am, and he's trying to distract me."

Aunt Mel nodded. "He has a good heart, Aaron does. He and Daniel both." She gave Fleur a long appraisal, as if weighing up whether Fleur was worthy. Aunt Mel must know about Fleur's involvement in the rescue missions, along with Aaron, but did she know about Fleur's past? That would certainly affect her opinion on any potential relationship between Aaron and herself. She was about to tell her that she wasn't interested in Aaron that way, but Aunt Mel was already off on another subject. Just like Tante Lulu. "I came up to tell you that dinner will be ready in fifteen minutes. Were you about to take a shower?" she asked, glancing at the pile of clothing and the toiletry bag in her hand.

"Yes. I'll make it quick."

"Okay, honey. And listen. Don't you be worrying about all the trouble that's been hounding you and Aaron."

Aah, she realized then. Aunt Mel thought they were hiding out because of something related to their recent rescue missions. She didn't know about Fleur running into Miguel today.

"You'll be safe here, sweetie. I promise," Aunt Mel went on, patting her on the shoulder. "And if you're not, I'll take you back to Alaska with me when I return. You and Aaron both. The bad men who are after you will never find you there."

Tears burned Fleur's eyes. Over the years, she'd almost never cried, no matter what abuse was heaped on her. But these last few days, she'd gotten teary eyed at the least provocation, and usually it was because someone was being nice to her. Maybe later she would give Mother Jacinta a call. The nun would get a kick out of Fleur's hard shell being cracked by niceness.

Fleur laughed, again, when she entered the bathroom, not just because of the huge, ostentatious, rain forest shower stall, sitting right next to an old-fashioned claw foot bathtub. But everywhere she looked, there was evidence that Tante Lulu was in the house. A St. Jude bath mat. A St. Jude soap dispenser at the sink. A St. Jude stained glass image suction-cupped to the window.

When she was under the absolutely sybaritic shower (*It's probably a sin for something to feel this good.*), Fleur picked up a long-handled St. Jude loofah sponge, glanced upward, and said, "So, all these St. Jude reminders . . . are they a sign that I'm not as hopeless as I thought?"

With her eyes closed and her face raised to the cool spray, she thought she heard a voice in her head answer, *Oh, you're hopeless, all right, my child. But you've come to the right place.*

Beware of little old ladies with big ideas . . .

Louise was in her element. Cooking and being with family.

Oh, none of the folks sitting around this evening on the back verandah, outside the Bayou Rose kitchen, sipping at after-dinner coffees and sweet teas, were blood kin to her. Only Luc, Remy, and René were actual blood relatives through their mother, who had been married to that low-down bum Valcour LeDeux. But over the years, she'd taken into her fold all of Valcour's other children, born to so many different women. Tee-John, Daniel, Aaron, Simone, Charmaine. The list just went on and on. Tee-John, or Small John, was the name that had been given to one of the smallest of them when he was a boy, not over six feet tall like he was now.

Daniel and Samantha were sitting on a glider that Louise had gifted them for their wedding last year (with St. Jude cushions, of course). Samantha had protested at the time that a modern glider didn't fit in with the historic décor, but Louise noticed that it had become Samantha's favorite spot for resting, or a perfect place for her to cuddle with her husband.

Fleur sat on a bench under the kitchen window with Aaron on one side and Mel on the other. The three of them were leaning back, relaxed, with their legs extended.

Ed and Lily Beth sat on the grassy lawn under a tupelo tree watching Lily's toddler waddling around in a diaper and Ed's three girls playing with a dog and several cats, except for the big cat that resembled a cheetah which had a mind of its own and lay sprawled some distance away. Well, all cats were ornery sometimes, but this one much preferred its own space and was often off like a shot at the sign of a bird or some wild thing nearby. She'd like to see how Useless would respond to such a pet. Probably run off with its tail between its legs—the gator, not the cat.

And of course among all the animals here (leftovers from Samantha's pet rescue days) was that little pig, Emily, who sat between Daniel and Samantha on the glider. The pig probably thought she was their baby. Hah! Was she in for a rude awakening when a real baby—or babies—came into the picture! The pig would probably go into another depression.

Louise leaned back in the lone rocking chair on the porch. They should get more. There was nothing like a rocker to give a place homeness.

"So, Mel, were you always a less-bean?" Louise asked all of a sudden. She'd been meaning to ask for some time, and it just popped out now.

"Tante Lulu!" Daniel chided her. "Don't be insulting."

"Don't forget. Our mother was Aunt Mel's partner," Aaron added, glaring at her.

"Oh, pooh! I wasn't insultin' no one. Were you insulted, Mel?"

"Not at all," Mel said. "I know you don't have a mean bone in your body."

"See," Louise said to the twin dunces who were still glaring at her.

"Actually, I was married when I was in college. He was the one who got me involved in flying and eventually owning my own air shipping company. We divorced over religious differences."

"I didn't know you'd been married," Daniel said.

"Me neither," Aaron added. "What kind of religious differences?"

"He thought he was God. I didn't," Mel said with a chuckle.

Everyone laughed then.

"Aunt Mel and my mother were huge Barry Manilow fans," Aaron told Fleur. "They went to his concerts all over the States. You're bound to hear his music while you're here." He turned to Mel and said, "You did bring some of his CDs with you, didn't you?"

Daniel answered for her. "Are you kidding? We've heard so much of his music that the twins dance in Samantha's belly when 'Copacabana' comes on."

"Hey, I have an idea," Mel said, not at all offended at their teasing about Barry Manilow. "Maybe, if one of the twins is a girl, you could call her Mandy."

"Yeah, but what would the other twin be named?" Aaron asked with a grin. "Oh, I know. Randy."

Daniel and Samantha groaned. The others just grinned.

A companionable quiet followed. No one wanted to exert the energy to get up and prepare for bed. The dishes were already done; in fact, they'd used mostly paper plates and disposable cutlery to avoid running the dishwasher.

"That was a great dinner," Fleur remarked into the silence, "even if it was what you called a last-minute hodgepodge."

"Hodgepodge is the best kind," Louise declared. Everyone was too full to do anything other than nod their heads in agreement.

They'd combined Louise's Shrimp Étouffée with Daniel's barbecued cheeseburgers, her dirty rice with Mel's tater salad, Alaska-style. Samantha had stirred up a quick green salad made with a basket of veggies Louise had ordered a grumbling Aaron to pick from her garden before they left her cottage; it was served along with corn on the cob brought by Ed and Lily Beth, which they'd cooked in their husks on the grill, slathered with Cajun Tabasco butter.

Yum!

Aaron had also insisted that they whip up some fried green tomatoes, having recalled from the last time they'd been here that it was Fleur's favorite. Fleur had looked at him with wonder when he'd not only remembered her preference, but sliced, breaded, and fried them himself on a cast iron skillet in the overheated kitchen.

"I'm sorry I didn't do more to help," Fleur said suddenly.

Aaron gave her a nudge with his elbow and made a few chalk marks in the air.

"Tsk-tsk!" Fleur remarked, elbowing him back.

It was good to see those two getting along better. Everyone knew that elbow nudges were a first step in courtship.

Yes, things were going just the way Louise had thought they would.

"Ya know, Daniel, I got an idea . . ." Louise started to say.

"Oh, no! You and your ideas! I swear, if this is about that frickin' . . . I mean, stinkin' swimming pool, forget about it."

"No, it's not about the pool, though I 'spect there'll be one here, come hell or high water, afore long." She glanced at Aaron and gave him a wink. "No, I was jist thinkin', if you and Samantha are really gonna move up ta Baton Rouge . . ."

"What? Who's moving?" Mel asked.

Daniel gave Aaron a dirty look, which Aaron in turn flashed at Louise.

"Oops!" Louise said. "Anyways, Daniel, if you really do decide ta move, mebbe those cottages could be put to a better use . . . well, not better, but different."

She had everyone's attention now.

"How about they become nests fer fallen birds?"

Aaron and Fleur were the only ones who understood and they gaped at her, stunned. The others just looked confused.

Then everyone spoke at once.

"Have you lost your mind?" Daniel exclaimed.

"What fallen birds? Like a bird sanctuary? I don't get it," Mel said.

"If Daniel and Aaron wouldn't let me make this a dog and cat rescue sanctuary, why would they consider birds?" Samantha asked.

"I know your heart is in the right place, Tante Lulu, but I'm sorry, that is impossible," Fleur said.

Aaron grinned, made another slash in the air in front of Fleur, then said to Tante Lulu, "Tell us more."

"Nothing is impossible," Tante Lulu told Fleur, but to Aaron she said, "It was just a thought. Something you and Fleur could do together, but let's wait and see what Luc and that priest fellow have to say t'morrow."

"I am going to be a nun," Fleur told Tante Lulu through gritted teeth.

"Uh-huh," Tante Lulu agreed, but she winked at Aaron.

Another day, another click! . . .

It was déjà vu all over again, Aaron thought, as he awakened at dawn in the *garçonniére* apartment: people hiding out on the plantation while its residents went about their normal business, or seemed to.

Aaron had to wonder if this place had a history of being a refuge, maybe even back in the days of slavery and the Underground Railroad. He would have to ask Samantha how to check that out. Or ask Tante Lulu, who knew everything about the Bayou Black region.

The old biddy was always conning . . . um, talking . . . dumb outsiders into renovating some of the rundown plantations, aka money pits, which locals wouldn't touch with a bayou barge pole. Like that motorcycle riding Angel Sabato and his wife, the for-

mer Grace O'Brien, who had been a nun, come to
think of it, over at Sweetland. (*Is that a hopeful sign
for me? The nun bit, not the plantation.*) Like that
odd Viking Ivar Sigurdsson, who worked as a chap-
lain at Angola Prison and was married to Gabrielle
Sonnier, a lawyer, over at Heaven's End plantation.
Like him and Daniel with Bayou Rose.

But back to the present. Daniel planned to go into
the medical center in Houma at nine, as usual, but he
would come back at noon to take Samantha to an appointment with her obstetrician. Aunt Mel would do
the regular shopping at the Starr Supermarket. And
Aaron couldn't ignore his job at Bayou Aviation as a
pilot without being conspicuously absent; so, he had to
report for work by one at the latest.

Even though Remy had accommodated him with a
rearranged schedule, Aaron couldn't let him down.
Their flight schedule was overbooked with not enough
pilots to handle the work. At the very least, Aaron
would have to make three copter runs out to the oil
rigs, carrying workers, back and forth, as well as some
big wigs in from China. Remy would handle the morning flights of food supplies and machinery parts.

Offshore drilling was big business in the Gulf of
Mexico, and at any one time there were more than
30,000 workers on thousands of platforms, going in or
out on 14- to 21-day rotations. Called "floating cities,"
the platforms, the size of two football fields, with
colorful names like Mad Dog, Bullwinkle, Thunder
Horse, and Magnolia, had everything the workers
needed for home away from home, including good
food, which had to be transported daily. It was hard
work, but skilled hands could make more than a hundred thousand dollars a year, even in a bad economy.

Aaron showered and shaved, noting in the bathroom mirror that he needed a haircut. That would have to wait, of course. *Besides, if I end up in prison, I can get a free haircut there*, he joked with himself. *Jailhouse humor. Ha, ha, ha.*

Leaving the *garçonniére*, he relished the cool morning air. It wouldn't stay that way for long. Summer in Louisiana could be brutal. But then, he'd experienced the other extreme in Alaska. Way below zero. He preferred the heat.

He saw a flash of gold and black rustle the jungle-like brush that was always encroaching on the property and figured that Maddie was on the scent of some wild breakfast. Snakes were her fav. Snake kibble. Yuck!

Heat shimmered off the water of the bayou that could be seen across the lawn and road, some two hundred or so feet away. It was easy to forget that at one time, a couple centuries ago, barges navigated these waters, carrying sugarcane to the New Orleans markets. And maybe slaves on the run, he thought, going back to his earlier musing about this plantation having possibly been a refuge.

But mostly, it was the birdsong that caught his attention this early in the morning. As he rounded the side of the house, he saw that the St. Jude birdbath in the rose garden was especially busy. Maybe, if he actually went through with his plans for a swimming pool, and Tante Lulu got her wish for a St. Jude shrine tour, they could add bird-watching to the activities. Hell, why not just turn the whole place into a bed-and-breakfast?

When he entered the kitchen through the open back door, he wasn't surprised to see that Aunt Mel was already up and coffee was brewing. She wore a knee-length, floral robe, belted at the waist, leaving her skinny legs bare to red leather slide slippers. Her dark hair was in curlers covered with one of those stretchy sleep caps that older women wore. Her Inuit-like features—broad cheekbones, wide nose and mouth—brightened into a big smile on seeing him.

He loved her like a mother.

"Good morning, sweetie," Aunt Mel said, handing him a mug of the steaming brew as he sat down on a bench at the table. She'd already added the one spoonful of sugar and dash of cream, as he liked. "Want some breakfast, honey?"

"Not yet. Coffee will do for now. Sit down and join me."

She did, with her own cup of coffee. "I'm worried about you, Aaron," she said, right off the bat.

"Don't be. This issue with the creep threatening Fleur will be taken care of, one way or another."

"It's not just that. Your whole involvement with these missions bothers me. Sex traffickers are very dangerous people."

"No question, but how can I stand by and do nothing? You and Mom taught us well. 'Help others and God will help you.' 'Compassion without action is just observation.' 'The man who sits on his butt will just get a big butt.'"

Aunt Mel grinned at the reminder of those sayings that were always leveled at him and Daniel, usually when they'd been playing video games as teenagers, instead of going out to do volunteer work, or something constructive.

"Do you know, at this very moment, there are probably twenty thousand kids, mostly girls, under the age of eighteen who are being held in sexual captivity, in this country alone? The average age is thirteen, and their life expectancy is seven to ten years. Everyone is shocked when they hear about ISIS kidnappings, like those girls in Nigeria, but it's happening everywhere." Aaron winced. Quoting funny proverbs was one thing, but this sounded like a lecture, even to his own ears.

"Oh, Aaron, I had no idea. How did it get so bad? I mean, it's in the news occasionally, and I've seen TV documentaries, but I thought the government and law enforcement were handling it."

"Not very well. It's like the drug problem. Billions of dollars are involved; so, the incentive to stop just isn't there for the bad guys. Don't get me wrong, various agencies are trying to help, but working through regular channels is a slow process. Often, by the time they get a tip and act on it, the sex traffickers have moved on to another site."

"And operations like those run by the Street Apostles and the Sisters of Magdalene . . . do they really make a difference?"

He shrugged. "Not even a dent, but at least a few dozen, maybe a hundred girls get saved each year. Each life matters, doesn't it? And here's something else to consider. These rescued victims can't just be dumped back into society. They need therapy and life skills and mostly love, which they don't get, even when their families do accept them back, which is often not the case. The government doesn't have a clue or the resources for helping the rescued. In fact, sometimes they put them in juvie halls till they can figure out what to do with them. Imagine what message that sends." He definitely sounded like a lecturer now, or a person with a chip on his shoulder, all in answer to Aunt Mel's simple question.

"Tsk-tsk-tsk. Still, why you?"

"Why not me?"

"Because I love you and don't want you to get hurt."

He reached over and squeezed her hand. "You know me, Aunt Mel. I've been getting in trouble since I was a kid, and I always get by."

"Until you don't," she predicted with worry. "This is all about Fleur, isn't it? You're involved because she's involved."

"Don't you like Fleur?"

"I don't know her. She seems nice, and, of course, I feel sorry for the situation she's in."

And Aunt Mel didn't know the half of what Fleur's "situation" entailed!

"But that's not the point," she went on. "Did you really get involved in all this just to put another notch on your belt?"

"Aunt Mel!"

Aunt Mel's face flushed with embarrassment. "Let me correct that, although, you must admit, your belt does have a lot of notches. It's great to talk about altruism and helping those in need, but I suspect you got involved in rescuing kidnapped girls because you were *interested* in Fleur."

"It started that way, but I found it increasingly hard—impossible, really—to jump ship when I found out I was needed. Plus, I've been floundering lately, ever since Dan got married, trying to figure out what I want to do with my future. Maybe this—*she*—just came along at the right time for me."

"Or the wrong time," his aunt said.

"Anyhow, there's great satisfaction in seeing the faces on those young girls when they're rescued. They've been without hope for so long. Tante Lulu would say that St. Jude had a hand in all this. You know, the whole patron saint of hopeless cases stuff."

Aunt Mel rolled her eyes at mention of Tante Lulu. "I still have my pilot's license. Maybe I should join up."

"Don't you dare," he said with a laugh. He'd like to see Aunt Mel in disguise at a strip club, like Fleur had been. Then again, no, he would not!

"What's good for the gander is good for the goose," Aunt Mel declared, teasing.

"Not when the goose is as old as you are."

"I'm not that old!"

Which was true. Aunt Mel was only in her late fifties, not even retirement age. But he wouldn't let her get involved in something so dangerous, not if he could help it.

"Besides, I've been at loose ends, too. I've been looking for something to occupy my time since we sold the air shipping business."

"Take up bowling," he said.

She just grinned at him.

Tante Lulu came down the back stairs into the kitchen then. Her hair, which was suddenly blonde, due to an overnight dye job, he supposed, was a mass of curls. She wore a girl's size Snoopy nightshirt that hung down to her calves and read, "Don't Let Anyone Dull Your Sparkle." On her feet were big fluffy pink rabbit slippers which caught Axel's interest. The old German shepherd, who'd been splayed out on the cool slate floor, raised his head, eyed the potential chew toys, let out a woof, then lowered his head again when

Tante Lulu gave him The Look, which they'd all been subjected to at one time or another.

At first it was just her appearance that caught Aaron off guard, but then Tante Lulu said, "Did I hear ya say yer gonna work on the rescue missions, Mel? Yippee! I'm in, too."

"Absolutely not!" Aaron exclaimed. "Neither of you are getting involved in that operation. Holy crap! I thought older women were interested in bingo and yard sales and early bird dinners and arthritis creams, not putting yourselves in danger."

"I've never been to a yard sale in my life. That sounds like age bias to me, Aaron," Aunt Mel remarked, slapping him on the shoulder with a dish towel as she got up to refill his coffee mug.

"Yeah, we oughta file a lawsuit," Tante Lulu concurred. "Good thing I got a lawyer in the family."

"Like Luc would let you put your life in jeopardy that way," Aaron countered.

"Luc ain't the boss of me. No one is." Tante Lulu gave him the same look she'd given Axel.

Aunt Mel added, "And you're not the boss of me, either, young man."

Aaron put up both hands in surrender. "I'm just sayin'."

But Tante Lulu's mind had already skittered to another subject. "I'm thinkin' somethin' simple fer breakfast, like an omelet." Without waiting for a response from anyone, she went immediately to the fridge and began taking out eggs, butter, sausage, mushrooms, onion, cheese, and a bunch of other stuff. So much for simple! "Kin you slice up some of that leftover loaf I brought with me, Mel?"

"For toast or plain?" Aunt Mel asked.

"Both."

While they were working, Aaron sipped at his coffee and checked his cell phone for text messages. Fleur came in then. Her dark hair was pulled off her face, tucked behind her ears. No make-up, but her face and arms were tanned from her ride in the convertible yesterday. She wore a sleeveless mint green blouse over white capris. At least, he thought that was what those knee-length pants were called. White sandals exposed narrow, high-arched feet.

It was a sign of his "infatuation" with Fleur that he found even her feet sexy. Unadorned feet, at that. No polish. No toe rings. No "fuck me" high heels. He put a napkin on his lap to hide his reaction.

"Your new clothes look nice, Fleur," Tante Lulu observed.

"My new old clothes, you mean," Fleur said, explaining to Aunt Mel that she and Tante Lulu had visited an upscale secondhand clothing store in New Orleans yesterday.

"Next time you go, give me a call," Aunt Mel requested. "I need some summer clothes and I hate spending retail."

"Aunt Mel! You have enough money in the bank to buy a store. You don't need to buy someone else's castoffs."

"Idjit!" Tante Lulu shook her head at him.

He assumed she meant that he'd insulted Fleur with that remark. Why was everyone so touchy? First, he was accused of age bias, then clothes bias, or poverty bias. Whatever!

"Do you think I'm poor as a church mouse?" Tante Lulu was shaking a finger at him. "No, I am not."

He was right. Poverty bias.

"Do you think women go to thrift shops 'cause they can't afford new? No. Every female alive loves a bargain. And, yes, Mel, I'll call ya next time. They had some items from a Cher wardrobe auction fer charity that would look good on you. You're tall and thin enough ta wear her outfits."

Cher? Aunt Mel as Cher? Oh, my Lord!

Aaron glanced at Fleur to see if he'd insulted her by ripping on cast-off clothing, but she was just smiling, enjoying the setdown he'd just been given. "I'm sorry," he mouthed at her.

But she didn't acknowledge his apology, probably figuring he might use it as an excuse to make more chalk mark tallies in the air for kisses. He could wait.

Dan came in then, dressed for work in a brown-and-white-striped dress shirt tucked into tan belted slacks, a matching suit jacket hooked over his shoulder with a forefinger. Around his neck was a knotted, but not yet tightened Save the Children tie that Samantha had given him last Christmas, featuring bands of multi-national kids holding hands. His hair was wet from a recent shower and he'd shaved. He looked like a frickin' ad for *GQ*. "Samantha is still sleeping, but I'll bring a tray to her before I leave," he told Aunt Mel and Tante Lulu.

They nodded.

"Do you think you'll know the sex of the babies after the ultrasound today?" Aunt Mel asked.

Dan shook his head. "We don't want to know. If the test shows any little peckers, the technician will hide the pictures from us."

"I had a dream last night," Tante Lulu said. "There

were two little boys running around yer rose garden. Matt and Mark. And Samantha walked up to them, big as a house with another pregnancy. Twins again."

"Luke and John, I suppose," Daniel guessed.

"How'dja know?" Tante Lulu asked. "Mus' be an omen."

"Don't tell Samantha. She needs to get through this birth first."

They all sat around the table then, eating the simple but luscious breakfast, washed down with copious amounts of strong Creole coffee. While they ate, Tante Lulu made a grocery list for Aunt Mel, who at one point looked to Aaron and Daniel with dismay. She would need a truck to haul everything back here. Aaron decided that he would offer his pickup to her and take Aunt Mel's rented sedan to the airport.

Daniel took a breakfast tray to Samantha and then drove off. Aunt Mel went upstairs to dress for her shopping expedition, and they could hear "Can't Smile Without You" from the tape player she'd brought with her from Alaska. No downloaded music for Aunt Mel. Just good old-fashioned CDs. He caught Fleur's eye on first hearing the music blast out and said, "Bet the babies get dear old Barry songs, instead of lullabies."

"Or Cajun music," Tante Lulu piped in.

"There's probably a Cajun version of 'Copacabana' somewhere." Fleur was tapping her foot as she stood at the sink, washing the extra breakfast dishes and pans. The dishwasher was full and running.

"If there isn't, I could ask René to write one," Tante Lulu said.

René was a musician, as well as an environmentalist and teacher.

"Yeah, René probably could write a Cajun adaptation of the Manilow classic," Aaron decided. "Hey, if Bruce Springsteen could do a rock version of the Cajun classic '*Jolie Blon*,' anything is possible, right?"

Suddenly, the music stopped, and Aunt Mel, dressed for shopping in shorts, sneakers, and an "I ♥ Louisiana" T-shirt, came down to get the keys to Aaron's truck, along with Tante Lulu's *War and Peace* shopping list, and was off to the store. Shortly after that, and it was only nine a.m., Luc arrived with Brother Brian Malone, whom he'd picked up at the airport on his way out to the plantation, as prearranged. Fleur was wiping down the counters with a sponge, and Aaron was at the table, sending a text message to Remy.

Aaron stood to greet Brother Brian, a name he had trouble using without a grin, especially with him wearing Bermuda shorts, sockless loafers, and a Hawaiian shirt over a clerical collar. "How you doing, Snake?"

"It was touch and go there for a while, but I'm good as new now, and back in the game. Although I do have one fewer kidney and I get twinges in my shoulder from that one close range shot. How you hangin', Ace?" Snake replied, not at all priestly in his language. "Still a sex magnet for all the ladies?"

Fleur gave Aaron a sharp look.

Aaron gave Snake a dirty look.

Luc looked amused.

And Tante Lulu was just looking, from one to the other of them, with way too much interest.

Aaron and Snake exchanged bro hugs. Then, Aaron drew back, observing his old friend. "What's with the clerical dog collar? Do you wear one all the time?"

"Nah, but it's more than a fashion accessory when I travel commercial. I don't like to hide the fact that I'm a priest, in case the need for one comes up suddenly. I don't like pretending to be something I'm not."

Collar or not, it appeared that Snake still had a way with words. And the way he switched in and out of his Irish dialect and proverbs reminded Aaron a lot of Tante Lulu and other Cajuns, like Luc, who could appear almost illiterate one moment and highly intelligent the next.

In fact, Tante Lulu let out a hoot of laughter and said, "Ain't that the truth? Like I'm allus tellin' my dumb nephews, a peacock is jist a turkey under all them pretty feathers."

"Ah, a woman after me own heart! Are you sure there's not a bit of Irish in your blood?"

Tante Lulu preened.

Snake winked at Aaron, to show he still knew how to throw the blarney when he wanted, even when a member of the clergy.

Aaron would love to sit down with Snake sometime, preferably with a shot or two of Irish whiskey, or aged southern bourbon, and find out how his friend had arrived at the religious crossroad that prompted his turn away from the marriage and kids route he'd always planned.

Brother Brian was introduced to everyone.

Tante Lulu was clearly impressed to have a priest in the house, especially one associated with a group named for her favorite saint, even one dressed like Snake. But she couldn't get her tongue around the Brother salutation. She kept slipping and calling him "Father Malone—I mean, Brother Malone—I mean . . ." until finally an amused Snake told her, "Sweet lady, you can call me Father Brian, if you like. I answer to almost anything."

Fleur said to Luc after her introduction, "I apologize

for putting your family to this inconvenience." Then to Snake, she said, "Please tell your superiors and Mother Jacinta how sorry I am to be the cause of troubles for the missions."

Too late, she realized what she'd just said, but she definitely knew when Aaron made more slashes in the air and winked at her. Maybe he would collect tonight. Of course, he could ask for a good-bye kiss when he left for work shortly, but, no, there would be other people around. And he didn't want to rush things. To his reckoning, he had ten apologies on her tab so far, and in his dictionary—that would be the Clueless Men's Rule of Seduction book—two slashes equaled lips locked; three, open mouths; four, a kiss lasting longer than a second; five, a little tongue. He grinned.

Fleur blushed, was about to say something but just said, "Click!"

If she only knew, those clicks were starting to turn him on.

If anyone was confused by Aaron's ping-ponging emotions, he was the most confused, and it was damn irritating. He was tired of these roller coaster feelings he had where Fleur was concerned. Up, down, up, down. Should he, shouldn't he? Would she, wouldn't she? Right or wrong? Logical or illogical? Destined or downright monkey ass, tree swinging crazy?

Enough! Enough, enough, enough! Aaron was determined now. He'd decided, at about three a.m. last night, after being unable to fall asleep (sexual frustration being a bummer), that he knew what he wanted and was just going to hang on for the ride.

It was pitiful, though, that he had to go to such lengths. He was a master of seduction, a player, or had been in the past. But none of the usual rules applied here with Fleur. He wanted her, past or no past, and, oddly, despite her sordid experiences, Fleur appeared more like a virgin to him. Not that he'd experienced many of those! He would have to tread carefully. The usual "Oh, baby!" drawl was not going to hit any of her chimes, if she had any. And definitely not the more blunt, but to the point, "Wanna fuck?" And, yes, to his shame (but not much), he'd said just that on occasion.

Let fate, or the celestial Powers-That-Be, control the levers of this Blue Streak of madness (the roller coaster, not a Blue Steeler, though he was experiencing both).

"Was that thunder I heard?" Tante Lulu asked.

"Huh?" Aaron said, being called back from his mental ramblings.

Fleur looked at him like he was some kind of babbling idiot, while Luc and Snake just grinned.

He blinked and glanced around. The sun was shining, portending another scorcher of a day. But, yes, there was a rumbling sound in the distance. Aha! The Blue Streak of lightning.

The celestial powers were speaking, loud and clear.

Chapter Seven

D̶ream on . . . pray on . . . same thing . . .

Fleur explained the situation about her Miguel encounter to Luc and Brother Brian as they sat out on the back verandah with her and Aaron. Tante Lulu had gone off to water the roses around the St. Jude birdbath . . . and to scrub off some of the rude "prayer offerings" dropped by the birds.

Luc was a good-looking man. All the LeDeux men were. Even in his late forties with silver threading the edges of his dark hair, even in a conservative business suit and tie (He'd told them he had to be in court later this morning.), Luc carried himself with that typical Cajun swagger and *joie de vivre*. Of course, he wasn't as attractive as Aaron, in her opinion, who always seemed to be holding back his wild side. A woman (she, in particular) always felt like she had to be on her guard.

As for Brother Brian (or Snake, as Aaron persisted in calling him in the most irreverent way) . . . he was a priest. Enough said! An unorthodox priest (Can anyone say Hawaiian floral shirt?), but then many of the St. Jude's Street Apostles were considered rogues. Brother Brian had blondish red hair, and freckles, and a prizefighter's build. In other words, not traditionally handsome. But his teasing Irish personality made up for any physical deficiencies. Not that a pleasing appearance mattered much to the clergy, unless they were TV personalities oozing charisma and gold.

"Here's the problem in a nutshell, as I see it," Luc said. "The mission for the Street Apostles and the Magdas has never been to take down any crime syndicate, but rather to rescue the victims. Something you've been successful at because you operate below the radar. You leave the bigger issue to the bigger guys, or agencies, to handle, right?"

Fleur and Brother Brian and Aaron nodded.

"So, it makes no sense to contact the FBI ahead of time, or the Departments of Justice, Labor, Transportation, or Homeland Security, all of whom deal with some aspect of this sex trafficking, although they would be mighty interested, guaranteed."

Fleur winced at the mention of all those government entities.

"They would try to use you, Fleur," Luc went on. "There's no question in my mind that they would want you for a tool to entrap not just Miguel but some of the higher-ups in the Mexican cartel."

"But first they would want to try diplomacy. Even

with these scumbags. Always the politically correct route," Aaron opined with more cynicism than she'd heard from him so far. "What they don't realize is that sometimes the best diplomacy is being able to tell the cretins to go to hell so they'll look forward to it."

"Are you sure you're not Irish?" Brother Brian asked with a laugh. "But, even if we were willing to put this lassie at risk, which we aren't, the ensuing publicity would surely end our missions in rescuing the girls. Besides which, each of these arms of the government will be pissed off at our infringing on their territories."

"How about local police?" Luc asked. "Maybe we could set up our own sting to catch Miguel. Yeah, it would be only one guy, but an important one in the sex trafficking trade. And we could turn him over to the feds, but sort of sneaky-like."

"Sneaky-like? Is that a lawyer term?" Aaron asked Luc.

"Bite me," Luc replied with a grin.

"Again, we risk publicity," Brother Brian pointed out.

"Not if we're subtle," Luc argued. "My brother Tee-John is a police officer, and my sister Simone is an ex-cop who runs a Cheaters type detective agency. Both of them would know how to set up a sting."

"No, no, no!" Aaron protested. "We are not using Fleur as bait for some scumbag."

Fleur turned inch by inch to look at him. "I beg your pardon," she said.

"Begging pardon is the same as saying you're sorry," Aaron said, making a slash in the air, which caused her to shake her head at his foolishness.

She elbowed him and said, "Behave!"

"Don't you mean click?"

"Is this a private joke?" Brother Brian asked.

"I think they're under the spell of Tante Lulu's Thunderbolt of Love," Luc explained to the priest. "Although you would think a nun or almost-nun would be immune, wouldn't you?"

"Well, we always said that Aaron could talk the panties off a nun, back when we were flying jets. Seems he's still trying." If the twinkle in his eye was any indication, Brother Brian had as much fun teasing Aaron as Luc.

Fleur was also enjoying the blush that colored Aaron's face.

"Did Tante Lulu give you a hope chest yet, Aaron?" Luc asked.

"She's tried."

"A hope chest for a guy?" Brother Brian asked, looking first at Luc, then Aaron. "Isn't that one of those things girls get to hold sheets and towels and stuff for when they get married?"

"Yeah, but Tante Lulu makes them for the men in her family," Luc explained, as if that was a perfectly logical explanation. "She has her eye on Aaron and Fleur at the moment."

"Hello, everyone," Fleur said, waving a hand in the air. "I'm sitting right here. I can speak for myself." To Aaron, she said, "I *will* be part of any operation to get Miguel. I won't be happy until he's serving a life sentence in Angola. Do I make myself clear?"

"Loud and clear."

Now she turned to Luc and, in a much calmer voice, said, "I'm willing to talk to John and Simone, if Brother Brian will sit in on the meeting. His input from the perspective of the Street Apostles and Magdas is essential."

Aaron asked Luc, "Do you think Fleur is safe here? Maybe Remy's houseboat would be a better hiding place."

Luc pondered a moment before replying, "No, it's anchored too close to Remy's home and family. Wouldn't want to risk that."

"You're right." Aaron mused a moment, then brightened. "I know, I could take her to your fishing camp. It's remote enough that I would have trouble finding it, let alone some Mexican yahoo with killer intent."

"Me? Alone at some fishing camp?" Fleur shivered, knowing full well what some of those shacks on stilts deep in the swamps were like. Snakes, gators, and every kind of biting insect imaginable.

"I wouldn't let you go alone," Aaron said, taking her hand and linking their fingers. "I would willingly make the sacrifice to stay there with you. That's the kind of guy I am."

"Fool!" she said, realizing that he'd been teasing, and tried to tug her hand away, but Aaron held on tight. In fact, he rested their double fist on his thigh.

Both Brother Brian and Luc raised their brows at Aaron's gesture, but then Luc said, "I don't think a move will be necessary. Yet. Let's talk to Tee-John and Simone first."

Aaron nodded. "In the meantime, Snake, you're welcome to stay here at Bayou Rose. And Luc, could you set up a meeting with John and Simone? As soon as possible."

"On second thought, don't schedule that meeting . . . yet," Brother Brian said. "It may not be necessary." He took a long swallow of iced tea, then held the glass out to stare at the beverage with distaste, as if he would much prefer it be a cold beer or a strong whiskey. Setting the glass down with a loud exhale, he disclosed, "I hate to add further woe to you good folks, but there's a reason why Miguel Vascone is in New Orleans at this time."

His announcement went kerplunk into a waiting silence. Everyone stared at him.

"A reason that may prevent us from going after Miguel before certain other things take place."

The silence remained.

Fleur felt a chill of foreboding run up her spine.

"A big exchange of 'goods' is about to take place between the Dixie Mafia and the Vascone family enterprise in Mexico."

She and Aaron looked at each other. Why had Brother Brian waited until now to mention this? Why had he let them ramble on about her encounter with Miguel when there was apparently something more important going on? Didn't he trust them? Or was he wanting to hear about her issues to see how they would tie in with his?

"The Vascones have an order for twelve virgin girls under the age of thirteen, or ten girls and two prepubescent boys, to be delivered to some third world oil tycoon. If the southern mob can deliver them, the Vascones will give them two dozen underage, though experienced, prostitutes from their various brothels."

Aaron, Luc, and Fleur all sat up straighter.

"You know how the Vascones like to rotate their stables, making it appear as if they always have fresh 'goods' on hand," Brother Brian said to Fleur.

She glanced immediately to Luc, not having realized that he'd been told about her history as a prostitute. Her face flooded with heat, but she couldn't really complain. Luc wouldn't have been able to advise them without knowing why Miguel was after Fleur. To her relief, Luc didn't even look her way. He was too engrossed in what Brother Brian was saying.

"You're planning a rescue mission, then," Aaron guessed.

Brother Brian nodded. "Yes, and the more I think about it, it makes sense that Fleur saw the bastard in New Orleans." The priest didn't even apologize for his bad language, but Fleur knew from past acquaintance with the man that he often used colorful curses, especially in stressful situations. All the Street Apostles walked a different line than normal priests. A few years back, when Pope Francis chastised the Church's priests for hiding in their safe sacristies instead of mingling among the "bruised, hurting and dirty," he probably didn't have in mind what the Street Apostles did. Then again, maybe he did.

"What's your strategy?" Luc asked.

"There are still a lot of details to be worked out, but usually, the Vascones move their human cargo from Mexico in a tractor-trailer. They'll cross from Matamoros to the Brownsville border crossing and from there travel up the coast to a 24-hour truck depot outside Baton Rouge, in Lafayette. That's where the exchange will take place."

"Mon Dieu!" Luc exclaimed. "Tee-John should definitely know about this. He's on the police force in Lafayette."

"Careful . . . we have to be extra careful," Brother Brian cautioned.

"Do you plan on involving the feds in any way?" Aaron asked.

"We might have to. One possibility is that we tell them about the new kidnapees only, and at the last minute. Let them handle the operation from the New Orleans end, while we hijack the eighteen-wheeler en route or when it gets to Lafayette. Of course, we wouldn't mention that it's an exchange, or even that the truck of human cargo would be coming from Mexico. Otherwise, they would insist on taking over the whole enterprise, and risk losing some, or all, of these girls."

"Three dozen females!" Fleur exclaimed. "We've never dealt with so many rescues at one time. This will be big. Where will you take them? Is the convent equipped for that number?"

Brother Brian put his hands in the air. "All details still to be worked out. One of the Street Apostles is a former Navy SEAL with a talent for battle strategy. Brother Jake has a mind like a computer, spitting out times, routes, contingencies, all that crap. We just feed him the data and let him do the planning. Keep in mind, this all came to our attention just a few days ago. Our informants are still feeding us information."

Oh, Lord! Fleur had met Jake before, and they were in for it! He'd been her contact, usually via email, for years. An organizational genius, for sure. An overbearing dictator, as well.

"You must have some informant! If you have this intel, why doesn't the government?" Luc wanted to know.

"Maybe they do, but I doubt it," Brother Brian answered. "Some of what we learn is passed on through the confessional. Oh, I don't mean that priests reveal what has been confessed. That's privileged information, same as rules for lawyers and their clients. But often the sinners then feel the need to repent by revealing the details outside the confessional with the priests steering them in our direction. You have to realize that the Mexican people are largely Catholic, and the church grapevine is amazing."

"*Sacré bleu!* Just like the bayou grapevine!" Luc observed.

"I suppose," Brother Brian agreed.

"You can't be a part of this exchange mission, not with Miguel recognizing you," Aaron said to Fleur, back to his protector role.

Did the man ever listen to her? He was not her Prince Charming to the Rescue, not even her Cowboy Prince to the Rescue, she thought, glancing down at his boots, worn even with his pilot uniform.

Seeing the beginning glower on her face, he continued, "It would be even more dangerous than your being the lure in a sting, as we were discussing earlier." He was still holding on to her hand, even tighter now.

"I will be involved. Get that through your fool head," she told him and dug her fingernails into his skin. Unfortunately, her nails were short and filed smooth. To Brother Brian, she added, "As long as I can be of use, and as long as the Street Apostles and the Magdas approve."

The priest nodded, hesitantly, as he watched the interplay between her and Aaron.

"Would any of those women be friends—uh, acquaintances of yours?" Luc asked.

Fleur could tell he felt awkward asking her if they might be fellow prostitutes from her past. She shook her head. "Doubtful. I've been gone for ten years."

"I can see that this is going to take way more planning and expertise than I originally envisioned," Luc said. "Beyond my scope, for sure."

"I've been thinking. Let's still plan a meeting for tomorrow with your brother," Brother Brian decided, "and by then I may have more information from Jake back in Dallas."

A half hour later, after discussing minor details related to the two situations, Fleur's and the sex trafficking exchange, Aaron released her hand and stood. He was about to walk Luc to his vehicle out front while Fleur was going to introduce Brother Brian to Samantha in her bedroom. But first, Luc turned to Fleur and said, "There's a young officer on the Houma police force, Mickey Gaudet. Is he a relative of yours?"

Fleur felt her face heat. "Probably. My younger brother. Ten years younger, in fact."

"A nice kid," Luc remarked. "Do you want me to contact him for you?"

"No!" she exclaimed, way louder and with more vehemence than she'd intended. More softly, she said, "That won't be necessary. I've lost touch with all my family."

She hoped that was the end of the discussion.

But it wasn't. "Well, then, Sara Sue, a waitress over at Dilly's Diner, must be your sister. She and Mick are real close, both of them raised in foster care, I hear. I know Mick helped her and her two kids a lot when she divorced Alphonse Fontenot after one too many beatings. Alphie is in Angola presently for assault and battery, thank God."

Brother Brian bowed his head at the mention of God.

But Fleur was thinking, *Oh, no! Poor Sarie! She was a year younger than Mickey. And always so clingy, cowering in corners when Daddy went on one of his shouting rampages, but then she'd only been three when I left. Wait. Did Luc mention foster care? Fi-*

nally, CPS must have intervened. I wonder when. There were still five kids younger than me at home when I left. Did CPS take all of them?

Panic filled her at the mere mention of her family.

And there was guilt, too. Should she have come back to help those siblings still under that horrid roof when she was able? Not when she'd been first rescued, of course. She'd been in no shape to help anyone, let alone herself at first. But later?

She tried to recall who would have been still at home back then, ten years ago. Frankie, the youngest, would have been only seven, Sara Sue, nine, Mickey, ten, and Mary Elizabeth, or Lizzie, who had Down Syndrome, thirteen. Joe Lee, Eustace, Gloria, and Jimmy had already left home by then, the latter to juvie hall, at fifteen.

But, no, even if she'd been capable, her parents had rejected any overtures from the Sisters of Magdalene on her behalf at the time of her rescue. "We doan take back soiled goods," her father had declared. And her mother had been no better. "Are ya sayin' she's been a harlot fer six years? Oh, Lord! How kin I look at her and not picture . . . oh, Lord!"

Her older brothers, Eustace and Joe Lee, had been no better, even though they'd been twenty-three and twenty-four at the time of her rescue and working on the oil rigs. Joe Lee had laughed at Mother Jacinta when she'd told him of Fleur's kidnapping and rescue and said something like, "Un-be-fucking-lievable! Maybe I've run into my own sister in one of the cathouses down in Nawleans." And Eustace had been horrified, "I'm married now with two kids. What if some of the men she's been with came cattin' around our place?" Gloria, who had to have been twenty-two by then, was nowhere to be found, having run away from home at fifteen, even before Fleur's kidnapping. Jimmy, at twenty-one, was doing hard time by then, in prison.

The memories still cut deep in Fleur. She was jarred from her painful reverie by Aaron's voice.

He must have noticed Fleur's discomfort at the mention of two of her siblings because he was saying to Luc, "Never mind Fleur's family. Don't forget yours. Do you want to say good-bye to Tante Lulu before you leave?"

"I better, or she'll skin my hide," Luc said.

Fleur shot Aaron a look of thanks.

He just stared at her, then leaned down and kissed her on the cheek before she could draw back.

It wasn't an intimate kiss, more like a butterfly brush of the skin, but Fleur felt it deep down in her hardened core. If Aaron had grinned at her then, or made some teasing remark, she would have been safe. But he just turned and walked away.

Fleur was shaken.

But that was nothing compared to what happened later that night when she was in her bed in the attic room.

For the first time ever, Fleur had an erotic dream. No raunchy, slam-bam sex like that depicted in porno films, and, yes, she'd been forced to watch more than a few of those. Teaching tools, the pimps and madams told new recruits before turning their first tricks. No, this was a gentle loving. Coaxing. And, oh, my God, she was aroused, like she'd never been before. Oh, maybe she'd been a little excited when she'd been fourteen and running wild, before her kidnapping, but that had been different, tame, naïve, nothing like this.

Playing a starring role, of course, was Aaron.

They were naked, lying on a bed, she on her back, he on his side leaning over her. Not her small single bed here in the plantation house or in Tante Lulu's cottage, and certainly not her cot back at the convent. No, it was a double bed covered with silk-soft, pale blue sheets.

The lapping of water could be heard through the open windows where sheer curtains ruffled in the nighttime breeze. The metallic scent of bayou water teased the senses, along with the lemony floral essence of magnolia that grew so abundantly in the humid south.

Maybe it was that fishing camp of Luc's that Aaron had mentioned earlier. Maybe it was some new place. Maybe it wasn't a building at all, but a boat. Aaron had mentioned that, too. A houseboat. Hah! More like a love boat. She had to smile at that. But not for long.

"At last," he whispers, leaning over me as I lie flat on my back. "Finally, you are mine."

I should be affronted at his possessiveness. I'm not.

"I never thought . . ." I arch my neck, giving him further access to that vulnerable spot at the curve where my neck meets my shoulder.

He wets my neck with his tongue, blows on it, then nips the spot with his teeth.

I moan and arch higher, causing my breasts to rise, as if begging for attention. "More," I urge.

At this point, most men would take my reaction as a cue to plow right in, getting to the "good stuff." Slam, slam, slam, and they'd be satisfied in a minute. Services rendered.

But not Aaron.

He stares at my body for a long moment, then sighs. "Ah, Fleur. My flower. My love." Then he proceeds to adore my body with skimming fingertips and breathy kisses. He lifts my arms and rests them above my head on the pillow. His palm brushes over my flat midriff, waist, and stomach. The light furring on his forearm catches briefly on my hair down below as he reaches for one of my limbs. He raises the knee and tugs it up and to the side so I am exposed to him.

I gasp. Not in shock, but wonder at the almost-pleasure that ripples low in my belly.

There is no hurtful squeezing as he explores my bareness. No bites. No deep, gagging throat kisses. No demand for graphically outlined delights, which are not so delightful for me. At least they hadn't been before. But now? I don't know.

I'm not yet ready to touch his body, but I certainly look. And I admire what I see. Broad shoulders, narrow waist and hips, muscles, but not too bulky. He is more lean than muscle-bound.

His dark hair, which is overlong, matches the dark hairs on his arms, and legs, and chest. I don't need to look below to know how excited he is. Perspiration dots his brow as he restrains his impulses. His brown Cajun eyes are half-lidded, and his full lips part as he breathes heavily.

Oddly, I like that I have such an effect on him. For some reason, I want to please him.

This is all new to me, but, instead of being alarmed, I purr with a sheer joy of discovery. I am almost thirty years old, but I feel like a virgin.

When he moves back up to my breasts, I think, Here

it comes. Men think women like to be kneaded like dough, or plucked like cow udders. Personally, it just seems silly to me to make such a fuss over . . .

My thoughts trail off as Aaron licks one nipple, then the other. That's all. One lick each.

Okay, that isn't so bad.

Then he kisses them. So featherlight and quick, I'm not sure if I imagine the kisses there, or not. Before I have a chance to register what he is about, he places his mouth on one of the nipples.

Instantly, a swelling develops between my legs and begins to pulse, like a heartbeat. I am alarmed, but he says, "Shhh," and lays a calming hand on my belly. "Let me love you. Let your body speak for you."

And it did.

As he lightly suckles me, my body explodes. From the throbbing beat in my nest of curls, a spark ignites and streams of erotic fire ricochet out to all my extremities, causing me to moan and thrash and beg him to never stop.

I lose consciousness, and when I awaken, slumberous and sated, I see that he is above me now, his hardness pressing against the vee of my widespread legs. I smile at him and say, "Thank you for loving me."

He smiles back at me and says, "Now the real loving begins."

But then his head shoots up and he seems to be listening to something. Voices. From down below. Loud voices.

Footsteps pounding on stairs.

A knocking on the door.

Fleur emerged from her deep sleep to the sound of knocking on her door and Aaron calling out, "Fleur? Are you awake?"

She reached over and turned on the bedside lamp, then half sat up, propped on her elbows. It was dark outside, and she saw by her watch that it was three a.m. She wasn't naked like in her dream, but covered by the blue silk nightshirt she'd bought in that secondhand shop. Still, she was dazed by her dream. It had seemed so real.

"Can I come in?" Aaron asked. "Are you decent?"

That was debatable, Fleur thought, but said, "Yes."

Aaron opened the door and walked in. His hair was mussed as if he'd just gotten out of bed. He wore low-riding jeans that exposed the beginning of a vee of hair below his belly button, and flip-flops. That was all. Her dream had been accurate, she thought irrelevantly. He was lean and muscular and more sexy than any man had a right to be. No wonder he was so successful with women. No wonder he had been so successful with her . . . in her dream.

For just a moment, he leaned against the doorjamb and studied her. "Was it as good for you as it was for me, Fleur?"

"What?"

He repeated her words back at her by saying, "Thank you for loving me."

She stared at him in horror. They'd had the same dream! "Do you think Tante Lulu put a spell on me . . . us?"

He shrugged. "Before Daniel and Samantha got married, they claimed that Tante Lulu cursed them with mutual sexual fantasies. Daniel's not nearly as imaginative as I am, though, or experienced. My fantasies are way more . . . you know?" He waggled his eyebrows at her.

No, she did not know. "What are you doing here, at this time of night?"

The humor disappeared from his face. "I just got a phone call from Luc, who got a call from one of Tante Lulu's neighbors. It appears some men broke in and trashed her place."

"Oh, no! Miguel?"

"Probably. I'm going over now. Luc will meet me there, along with Tee-John."

She sat up straighter and prepared to get up and out of bed. "I'll go with you."

"No. There's always the possibility the cottage is being watched," he said, sitting down on the edge of the mattress, forcing her to stay put. "I just wanted you to know where I was if I'm not here when you get up this morning. Even Snake can't go with me, for fear of being recognized. We don't want any connection between Tante Lulu and you or the Magdas or the Street Apostles. And of course Daniel will stay here."

"How about you? Isn't there a danger of your being associated with all this?"

"I don't think so. I'm technically Tante Lulu's nephew. I've been there lots of times in the past."

"Tante Lulu will be livid. She'll want to go right over there, guns blazing."

He smiled, flashing that adorable dimple. It was a sign of her distress, or her deteriorating defenses, that she would notice such a thing at a time like this.

"Don't tell her anything. And make sure she stays here and out of sight until we know more."

She nodded. "I'm trying to remember if we left anything behind that would hint at my having been there, but I don't think so. Oh, Aaron, this is all my fault. Tante Lulu doesn't deserve this. Nor do all of you here at the plantation."

"Hush! It's our choice." He grinned then. "Aren't you going to say you're sorry . . . for all the trouble you're causing?"

She knew he was teasing to calm her fears. "No, I've learned my lesson."

"Notice that there were no kisses in our dream. Not mouth kisses anyhow. I must be saving up your markers for those, big-time. Bet they're going to be super good for having been postponed. Hope there is tongue involved. Hope they're wet ones."

"Click, click," she said, surprised that she was engaging in his silly game. Must be some kind of post erotic dream, middle of the night madness.

"Go back to sleep, Fleur. I'll call when I know more. And don't worry. I have your back, sweetheart."

In truth, she didn't know what she would do without him. She was coming to rely on him way too much. A scary thought!

Sleep was impossible, of course. So, she did what she should have been doing more of these past weeks. She knelt on the floor beside the bed and prayed. In the end, she decided to just trust in God, but she tossed in a prayer to St. Jude, too, just to be sure.

A voice in her head said, *About time!*

She was probably channeling Tante Lulu. Now that was the scariest thought of all.

The posse arrived, but the bad guys were gone . . .

Aaron arrived at Tante Lulu's place a half hour later, and John pulled in right behind him. Luc's Mercedes sedan and a police car were already there, and the lights were on inside. He could tell that John, a cop, was wearing a shoulder holster under his denim shirt, which was unbuttoned over a tank top and cargo shorts. Aaron was carrying, as well, but his pistol was tucked into the back waistband of his jeans under a T-shirt.

They nodded at each other, but said nothing as they emerged from their vehicles, their expressions grim. This had to be the first time, ever, that anyone had dared to attack the revered old lady of the bayou. They scanned the perimeter, but the sky was black as coal, no stars out tonight. The only light came from the windows.

They had to laugh, though, at what they saw when they walked together around the side of the cottage. It was the neighbor who'd notified Luc of the break-in. Jackson Dufrene, probably as old as Tante Lulu, sat in one of the rocking chairs. He had a lion's mane of unruly white hair which matched the white curls that adorned his bare arms and chest and back in a pair of bib overalls, minus a shirt, with rubber shrimp boots on his big feet. A long-ashed cigarette dangled from one hand, a rifle powerful enough to take down an elephant in the other, and the pet alligator, Useless, was splatted out at his feet munching on a pile of Cheez Doodles.

"Took ya long enough," Jackson remarked, taking a drag on his cigarette and then blowing smoke rings in the air. "Did ya stop fer donuts on the way? Or mebbe ya gave yer wives a good-bye boink before ya hit the road?"

"I don't have a wife," Aaron pointed out.

"My wife's about twelve months pregnant and boinking is the last thing on her mind these days," John said.

Neither of them were offended by the old man, whom they knew well. Especially when he flashed his false teeth at them in a big smile.

"What happened?" Aaron asked.

"Heard a ruckus 'bout two a.m. Know it was two a.m. 'cause I got up ta piss. Us old men gotta piss a lot. It's the prostate, or sumpin'. A damn nuisance is what it is. Betcha it's a curse God put on Adam fer eatin' that damn apple, or stickin' his pisser where he hadn't oughta. In fact, I tol'—"

"About the ruckus," John interrupted. "Did you come over here? Did you see anything?"

"I dint come over right away, but I saw plenty. Two fellas rode up in a van. They parked out on the road, not the driveway. Had flashlights. Saw 'em over by the garage, then around the house, lookin' in the windows. When they figgered out no one was home and the doors was locked, they broke a window and climbed in. Heard a lot of noise coming from inside, bangin' doors, glass breakin', cursin'. I tol' mahself, time ta call the po-lice, and Luc, too. Yer brother gave me his number a long time ago in case there was ever a problem, but he was prob'ly thinkin' more along the lines of Tante Lulu fallin' and not being able ta get up. Lak that TV commercial. Lordy! I laugh every time I see that thing."

"What happened next?" Aaron prodded.

"I saw they was comin' outside and I dint want them ta make a getaway before the law got here. So, I went out and fired a couple shots up in the air. Scared the shit outta them, I'll tell ya that. Tee-hee-hee! And by then, Useless sauntered onta the scene. Tore a hunk outta the one guy's leg."

"I assume they left before the police arrived," John said.

"Yep. They went one way, the cops came the other."

"Did you get a license number?" John was examining the broken window, probably planning how to cover it until the glass could be replaced.

Jackson shook his head. "Couldn't find mah glasses. Left 'em on mah bedside table."

Aaron gave him a quick look. He must have gone back for both the glasses and his dentures. "Would you recognize either of them?"

He shook his head again. "Too dark."

"Well, thanks for calling Luc and the police," John said.

"Thass what neighbors are for," Jackson said, dropping his cigarette to the porch floor and grinding it out with his boot. Tante Lulu would pitch a hissy fit if she saw that. "I wonder what them fellas were lookin' for. I allus thought Tante Lulu was poorer than Job's turkey, but mebbe she has hidden treasures." He looked to him and John for a clue. When neither of them answered, he got up and said, "Well, I'm off ta bed again. Good luck."

Aaron and John were about to go inside when Aaron put a hand on his arm. "Uh, John. Don't mention Fleur to the police."

"What? Who?"

"Fleur Gaudet. Tante Lulu's guest."

John frowned. "The nun?"

"Almost-nun."

"Huh?"

"She hasn't taken vows yet. Probably won't."

John shook his head, as if to clear it of cobwebs. "Why would it matter if the cops know about an 'almost-nun' livin' here? Tante Lulu is always takin' in strays. And why the hell are they stayin' at your place? Not that it didn't turn out to be a good thing they weren't here."

"Later. We'll explain it all later."

"We? Does Luc know what's goin' on?" When Aaron's silence gave him a resounding answer, John said, "Shiiit!"

Two cops came out then, and when neither he nor John were able to add to what Luc had already told them, one of them said, "It was probably teenagers. You know how that is, John. Kids with the brains of a flea, too much time on their hands. Looking for booze or prescription meds. Hell, everyone knows Tante Lulu lives here. Old lady like that is bound to have a medicine cabinet full of pills."

The older cop shifted the belt of his uniform over a big belly and said, "What they needed was a good paddlin' on their be-hinds when they were youngins. But that would be considered child abuse t'day. Pfff! What we got instead is eleven-year-olds smokin' pot and fifteen-year-old girls on welfare with two kids."

The cops left soon after that, promising to be back in the morning when they could better assess the damages, in daylight, and see if anything was missing. In other words, this would end up an insurance claim, with not much done to catch the culprits.

It was a shock, nonetheless, when Aaron and John entered the cottage. The place had been trashed. Drawers pulled out and contents scattered on the floor. Furniture turned over. Worst of all was Tante Lulu's traiteur pantry. The perps must have thought the hanging herbs were weed because they'd been yanked off the ceiling and crushed on the floor. Jars and containers were broken, their contents spilled and mixed all over the place. A god-awful mess.

Thank God, Fleur had gathered up all the old receipt books containing the folk remedies. Those would be irreplaceable. Maybe most of this stuff would be, too.

They found Luc in Tante Lulu's bedroom, sitting on her tiny bed, more the size of a cot, his elbows on his knees, his face in his hands. A quilt had been ripped apart and tossed on the floor. The sheets and mattress had been slashed with a knife.

"*Merde!* Tante Lulu is going to be devastated," Luc said, raising his head. There were tears in his eyes. "That quilt there . . . when I was ten years old, I ran away from home. Home being that rusted out trailer over where Cypress Oil has its headquarters now. Wasn't the first time I ran away, of course, but the beating Daddy gave me that night was especially bad. He'd been on a bender for days and was all boozed up. I remember Tante Lulu washing me up and wrapping me in that quilt and tucking me in this very bed. 'Have faith, sweetie. Things will get better,' she always said."

John sank down to the bed and put his arm around Luc's shoulders. "Hell, she was there for all of us when Dad went on a rampage. This cottage, though, it stayed the same through all those years. A refuge. And look at it now."

"Stop with the pity party," Aaron told them from where he stood in the open doorway. The door was hanging lopsided on its broken hinges. "No one was hurt, and we can clean up this mess in no time at all. We'll make it good as new. No, we'll make it good as old. You know your . . . our family. They'll make a party out of the cleanup."

The three of them contemplated that idea and nodded.

"I'm gonna kill the bastard who did this, though," Luc said.

"No! Miguel is mine." Aaron had no doubt that the creep was the one responsible for this destruction. One more sin to add to the tally for the man who'd hurt Fleur so badly.

"You two wanna tell me what the hell's going on here?" John demanded then.

Aaron decided that they had no choice but to fill him in. Still he warned, "You can't tell anyone."

"And you can't go off half-cocked when you know what's coming down," Luc added.

John narrowed his eyes at Luc. "What kind of shit did you involve Tante in?"

"Me? I didn't start this thing," Luc said, glancing toward Aaron.

Aaron flinched. "No one's to blame. I'm the one who got sucked in when I got called to the Silver Stud strip club last year where I first met Fleur."

John's eyes widened.

Luc was a little surprised at that detail, too. But then Luc said, "And I got sucked in when Aaron asked me to help him with the FAA, which is investigating him for illegal flights in and out of Mexico. But then, he took one of the FAA agents out to lunch, got her snockered, and ran into Tante Lulu and Fleur who were in the Big Easy buyin' other people's old clothes. That's when Fleur ran into that pimp Miguel."

Which was no explanation at all if John's tsk of disgust was any indication. "And Tante Lulu . . . how did she get sucked in?" John asked with not a little sarcasm.

"She sucked herself in," Aaron said. "Like always."

"It's a long story, Tee-John," Luc sighed. "Let's just say, what do sex traffickers, prostitutes, street apostles, nuns, a huge upcoming caper in a Lafayette parking lot, and a pimp with a plan for revenge in motion have in common?" Luc glanced at Aaron and added, "And a Cajun with a hard-on for a nun?"

John looked at the two of them, shook his head, and said, "What else is new?"

Chapter Eight

Blarney, BS, same thing . . .

It was not yet dawn, and Fleur was sitting at the kitchen table working on her laptop, as she had been for more than an hour, a way to occupy her nervous mind. What was taking Aaron so long? And why hadn't he called to give her a report on what was happening? Maybe he was hurt. Maybe he was dead. *Oh God, please, no!* She forced herself to be positive. No news was good news. For now.

Tante Lulu's receipt books were spread out before her, and she had to marvel at the richness of the material. It really would make a good book, and not just for the LeDeux family. What made the written words so interesting was not just the uniqueness of the ingredients (Possum gizzards, anyone?), or the bizarreness of some of the maladies (Hot Tongue, Swamp Boils, Tick Fits, for example), but the little side notes that Tante Lulu or her ancestors had made in the margins. Sometimes the remarks were simple, like, "Rubbish!" Others were more detailed, like "Dbl dose Susie L's lazy eye, worked, but now she blinks like a lighthouse." And some told a story, "Love potion given Rufus the Trapper by Patsy Mellot, he threatens shoot me, she has watermelon belly." Or the colorful "P.U. This stinks!" In fact, one of the recipes was for "Stinky Salve," which apparently cured everything from poison ivy to yeast infections.

Fleur heard footsteps on the floor above her, followed by a squawky "Holy shit! Holy shit! Holy shit!" as whoever it was passed by the parlor where Samantha's foul-mouthed cockatoo held residence.

She heard a voice with a decided Irish lilt say, "Shut up, ye filthy bird. I'm no St. Francis of Assisi. They ate fowl like you in Ireland during the famines, y'know?"

To which an unintimidated Clarence replied, "Holy shit! Holy shit! Holy shit!"

"At least you speak in triads," Brother Brian muttered. Fleur knew from her brief interactions with him over the years that the Irish loved not just their proverbs, but their triads, as well. Such as, "Three best friends and three worst enemies: fire, wind, and rain." Or "Three good things: a wooden sword in a coward's hand, an ugly wife married to a blind man, and poor clothes on a drunken man." He and Tante Lulu should write a book together. They could call it *Irish Cajun Wisdom*. Or *Irish Wisdom on the Bayou*.

She was smiling when Brother Brian came down the back stairs into the kitchen.

"What has you grinnin' like the wee fairies drunk on dew in a field of shamrocks?"

"I heard you speaking to Clarence about triads," she said.

"You could hear me all the way down here?"

"Sound travels in a quiet house."

He nodded and walked over to the coffee maker on the counter. He set down the small Bible in his hand before pouring himself a mug of the strong brew. Coming back to the table, he asked, "Mind if I join you for a bit?"

"Not at all." She shoved some of her papers aside so that he could sit opposite her. It was a huge table, four inches thick and ten feet long, probably a primitive antique from antebellum days, that could seat at least twelve, with long benches on either side and straight-back chairs at the ends.

"You're up early," he remarked, sighing as he took a long sip of the hot coffee.

"I couldn't sleep."

"Me neither. What is all this?" he asked, waving a hand at her paperwork.

She explained the project she was working on for Tante Lulu.

"A fascinating woman! And you're writing her biography, too? There's a good story there, I wager."

"I suppose. I've only gotten bits and pieces so far. She keeps referring to her Big Grief."

"Ah! Don't we all have one of those?" She would have liked to question him more about that enigmatic comment but he'd opened his Bible, made the sign of the cross, and began to read silently.

She had no choice but to continue her work, the

quiet broken only by the tapping of her keys or when he rose to refill his mug, then return to his Bible reading. She'd already said her morning prayers up in her room, a habit she'd developed living in the convent. Despite his unconventional priestly attire (Today it was a ratty Air Force T-shirt and jogging shorts with rubber flip-flops, but a crucifix on a chain around his neck.), she could tell that Brother Brian was a spiritual man. Maybe that's what the clergy needed to be in a modern world, part of it and yet apart.

Suddenly, the sound of a vehicle could be heard out front. At first, she looked up with alarm. It was five a.m. but still dark outside.

"It's only Aaron, returning," Brother Brian said.

How he could be sure of that she did not know, but she trusted his assurance. And he was right. Aaron soon walked into the kitchen, coming through the ground floor hallway from the front. "I saw the light—so, I headed over here before hitting the sack for another hour or two of sleep."

He did look exhausted. Wearing a faded Air Force T-shirt, similar to Brother Brian's, with the jeans he'd had on earlier, and a pair of athletic shoes, he should have looked grungy, but, instead, he exuded male virility. And she was reminded of their shared dream. The blush on her face must have revealed her thoughts because Aaron sank down next to her and whispered in her ear, "Miss me?"

She would have made a snarky, click-worthy remark, except that the expression in his eyes gave him away. Something bad had happened.

"Oh, my God! Did you run into Miguel?"

"No. Nothing like that."

"What is it?" Brother Brian asked, also aware of Aaron's silent message of bad news to come.

"Let's wait until Dan and Tante Lulu come down so I can spill it all in one telling."

Fleur got up and gave him a mug of coffee, which he mostly ignored. "You two been praying together?" Aaron asked, eyeing the Bible on the table. For some reason, he asked his question in a negative manner. He probably figured it was a sign of her leaning more toward the religious life than toward him.

They were saved from answering by the arrival of Dan and Tante Lulu, together. To Aaron's shock, and her own surprise, Fleur reached under the table and squeezed Aaron's hand, as if communicating that she was not yet a nun and might never be. Where that thought came from, she had no idea. She would have been distressed, except that his gaze at her held such thankfulness that she just nodded. And she didn't draw her hand away when he linked their fingers and squeezed back.

Something had changed between them. Whether it was the dream, or some woo-woo curse of Tante Lulu's or celestial matchmaking that had caused the dream, she was softening toward the man. She was so confused.

But for now, Aaron began describing what he had found at the cottage, and the real shocker was that Tante Lulu was so calm about the destruction. She always said that people underestimated her, and she was right.

"Look, no one was hurt. There ain't nothin' there that can't be replaced. Will I clobber that Miguel fella if I ever run inta him? You betcha. First thing this mornin', I'll go over and clean up. And if the bum shows up, well, I got a Luger in my bread box."

"No, you will not go back there today," Aaron declared. "Luc and John agree with me that you need to stay hidden. For now. As for the Luger, John took it with him."

"Does she mean a pistol?" Brother Brian asked with shock.

The old lady was about to protest the order (Not about the gun, though. She probably had others hidden around the place), but then she shrugged. "Well, leave the pantry alone then till I can work on it myself. Fleur already made an inventory fer me, dint ya, honey? So, we'll be able ta tell what's still useable and what needs replacin'."

"I had a text message from Brother Jake during the night," Brother Brian said then. "I'll inform him about this break-in, but I doubt it will affect the mission one way or another. We can discuss the new details on the 'exchange' later this morning. By then, the police might have some info for you, Aaron, though I doubt they'll be able to trace Miguel's whereabouts. He'll lie low now."

"I have some news," Dan said. "At our appointment yesterday, Samantha's doctor advised her to go into the hospital for bed rest the next six weeks, until the babies are born."

"Oh, man! I never asked about your appointment. Are the babies okay?" This from Aaron who stared at his brother with dismay.

"The babies are fine. It's just a precaution. Twins at Samantha's age . . . it's best to be careful."

"Oh, my!" Tante Lulu exclaimed. "What kin we do ta help? Can't she rest here?"

"No, a hospital setting is better. Monitors, nurses, that kind of thing. Plus, the stairs are an issue, which she needs to use if she wants to take a shower or bath. This isn't an emergency order, just a recommendation," Daniel emphasized.

"It's all the stress I've brought here, isn't it?" Fleur asked. "I'll leave. I can go back to the convent."

She felt Aaron stiffen next to her, and his hold on her hand tightened at the prospect of her leaving.

"Your being here is not a problem, Fleur. In fact, it's been a distraction for both of us so we don't obsess over the babies," Daniel told her. "Besides, my brother would probably go into chronic depression if you left. Bet he'd start playing sad Barry Manilow songs. Might even drown himself in that imaginary pool he's planning." Daniel winked at her and made a face at Aaron, who just shook his head at him.

"That's settled then," Tante Lulu said as she handed Daniel a cup of coffee and prepared to start a fresh pot.

Hardly, Fleur thought, yanking her hand out of Aaron's grip as she stood to gather up her papers and close her laptop. But then, Tante Lulu probably just meant that there was nothing more that could be done *for now*.

"You know, Tante Lulu," Father Brian said, "Fleur has been telling me about your folk medicine."

I have?

"We have folk remedies passed on through Irish families, too." His blue eyes twinkled and Fleur recognized that the priest was about to tell one of his "tall tales" as a means of further distracting them all. "In fact, one of my favorites is for increasing male virility. A pinch each of dried and ground bitterroot, snakeroot, wormwood, saffron, and the rind of oranges, all steeped in a jar of whiskey . . . uh, tea."

"Seems to me that it's the whiskey tea that does the trick," Fleur remarked with a laugh.

"Or the wormwood. That's the main ingredient in absinthe, the psychedelic drink that turned many a Southern planter's brain to mush," Daniel explained.

"Sounds like a load of BS to me," Aaron observed. "Or is it blarney to you Irish bullshitters?"

Tante Lulu slapped Aaron on the shoulder with a dish towel. "What is blarney, anyhow?" Tante Lulu asked the priest. "I've heard of kissin' that blarney stone but I never knew what it was."

"Ah, well, 'tis a lovely story," Father Brian began. "No one knows for sure if the rock which is now located at Blarney Castle near Cork originated in Ireland and was moved elsewhere, then returned, or if it was always there. Legends claim it to have been the rock Moses struck with his staff to supply water to the Israelites fleeing Egypt, or it was Jacob's pillow, or David hid behind the boulder when running from King Saul. Some say it was returned to Ireland from Scotland by the Crusaders. Whatever its history, those who kiss it are blessed with the gift of gab. An eloquence in speaking."

"You must have kissed it a bunch of times if your talent for BSing is any indication," Aaron remarked to Brother Brian. "You would not believe the stories this fool used to tell us when out on Air Force maneuvers," he told the others.

"Aaron! Ya cain't call a priest a fool." Tante Lulu gave him another swat with her dish towel.

"Can't priests ever be fools?" Aaron asked Brother Brian with exaggerated innocence.

"Only rarely," Brother Brian replied and gave Tante Lulu a sweet smile.

Samantha came lumbering into the kitchen then, huffing for breath. She wore a loose, voluminous, calf-length nightgown. Well, calf-length in front, ankle-length in back. Fleur could swear the poor woman's non-existent waistline had grown another two inches over-night.

"Samantha!" Daniel exclaimed, rushing over to her. "You're not supposed to come down those stairs."

"I called, but no one heard me, except for Clarence. Didn't you all hear him?"

They all glanced at each other. Mostly, the bird chirped so much, the same expletive over and over, that it had become easy to tune him out. Had Samantha been calling for them, maybe even screaming, and no one had heard over Clarence's squawking?

"Oh, sweetheart," Daniel said, leading her toward a chair, which she eased into carefully. "What did you need?"

"I need . . . I think I need to go to the hospital. Now!"

All pandemonium broke out then.

The fates were working against him . . . or was that for him? . . .

"It's a false alarm," Aaron told Tante Lulu and Aunt Mel after ending his phone call with Dan.

"Thank God!" Tante Lulu said from where she sat on a stool by the kitchen counter, dicing vegetables for gumbo or jambalaya or something massive that was going into a canning pot (*Who knew we had a canning pot at Bayou Rose!*) to simmer all day for dinner. No one had been much interested in eating breakfast, ex-cept for coffee and toast after Dan rushed Samantha off to the hospital.

"Ahhh! I was looking forward to holding those babies today," Aunt Mel said, looking up at him. She was on the floor, on her knees which were covered with special pads, scrubbing the slates with a soapy brush. (*A tension reliever, she claimed! The hard work, not the pads or the brush.*) "But I guess it's too soon."

Way too soon! Even Aaron knew that babies born at seven and a half months, and twins at that, would be at risk. Probably rushed into incubators. *Isn't that what they call those glassed-in baby things, or am I thinking of chicks? Whatever!*

"Dan says they're going to keep her in the hospital, though. He cancelled his appointments for the day so he can stay with her."

"Is there anything we can do?" Aunt Mel asked.

"She'd like a nightgown and robe so she doesn't have to expose her butt in a johnny coat, and make-up and stuff, but she'll call you this afternoon to give you a list."

"Good." Mel turned to Tante Lulu. "That throws a wrench into our plans for a baby shower, though, doesn't it?"

"Mebbe they would let us hold a shower in the waiting room on her floor," Tante Lulu mused. "I still say, it would be a lot easier to have a theme, with colors, if we knew the sex of those little ones. Betcha I could find out."

Aaron did not want to know what she meant by themes and colors. When guys threw a party, all they needed was beer . . . and sometimes strippers. But that was a taboo subject now that he'd met Fleur.

"How?" Aunt Mel asked. "How could you find out the sex?"

Whoa! I must have missed that. "What sex?"

"Get yer mind outta the gutter, boy," Tante Lulu said.

"Oh."

Tante Lulu grinned, knowing perfectly well what he'd thought. Then, she told Aunt Mel, "I have ways and means fer findin' things out."

She probably did. A friend of a friend, or the second cousin of a third aunt in the ultrasound department. But he needed to nip this thought in the bud. "No!" Aaron declared, realizing what she might be planning and that she might very well be successful. "If Dan and Samantha don't want to know the sex ahead of time, they certainly don't want anyone else to know, either."

"Party pooper!" Tante Lulu muttered. "I was only kiddin'. Anyways, how bad are things back at my house?"

Aaron had just returned from Tante Lulu's cottage when he'd received Dan's phone call. "Your great-nephews and nieces, Remy and Luc and René's kids, are hard at work, rock music blasting in their ears, cleaning up the mess, and making an inventory for you of items to be replaced. Window glass, picture frames, new kitchen faucet, shower curtain, that kind of stuff. And, yes, they're following strict orders not to go into the pantry."

"Kitchen faucet! Why would those dopes wanna break my kitchen faucet? Did they think I was hiding clues ta Fleur's whereabouts in the pipes?"

He shrugged. "Who knows! Probably just random vandalism."

"Hmphfh! Just meanness, if ya ask me."

Knowing she was antsy to go see for herself, Aaron gave Tante Lulu a more detailed description of the conditions at her cottage, and he told her what the police had to report this morning, which was nothing. Other than her neighbor, Jackson Dufrene, no one had seen anything.

He saved for last what he knew would outrage the old lady the most. "They also kicked over your St. Jude birdbath statue in the backyard, and stomped over some of your flowers in the process."

"Whaaat? Thass the las' straw." The old lady slammed her knife on the counter, causing veggies to fly. "Someone's gonna pay fer that. God doan like people foolin' with his saints. Nosirree."

If Miguel or one of his cohorts were around right now, Tante Lulu probably would have sliced and diced them with her paring knife. He and Aunt Mel exchanged grins.

"There's one saving grace in all this," Aaron continued. "When the perps were desecrating your St. Jude, Useless must have sauntered by. By the looks of a scrap of bloodied denim on the ground, it appears the gator took a hunk out of someone's leg."

"Serves 'im right!"

"Some people have guard dogs. You have a guard gator."

"And why not? If ya live on the bayou, ya make do. Us Cajuns learned that a long time ago. I'll hafta give Useless some extra Cheez Doodles."

Aaron answered a bunch of other questions then before he had a chance to ask, "Where are Fleur and Snake?"

"I wish ya wouldn't keep callin' a priest a snake. It's a sacrilege or sumpin'," Tante Lulu said.

"I'm not calling him *a* snake. Snake is his nickname."

"Not anymore," Tante Lulu insisted, pointing her knife at him . . . to make a point.

He laughed. "Okay, where are Brother Brian and Fleur?"

"They went fer a walk. The two of them and every animal within a mile of this place."

Aunt Mel laughed and added, "For a man who claims to be no St. Francis of Assisi, those animals sure do love him."

Aaron saw what she meant when he located Fleur and Snake walking up the roadway—actually a wide path—toward the old slave cottages. The priest and Fleur were in front, trailed by the ancient (in dog years) German shepherd, Axel, who limped along; by Emily, the pig, who was having trouble keeping up as well, on her stubby legs; by two cats, Garfield and Felix; and even by Maddie, who kept rubbing against Snake's bare legs. Maddie didn't like anyone, not even her mistress, Samantha—not very much anyhow. The only creature missing was Clarence sitting on Snake's shoulder, and the bird probably would have been, if his cage had been opened.

Good ol' Snake! he thought with a laugh. *Some things never change.* He remembered a time in Kabul when the mangiest, ugliest dog in the world adopted Snake, who claimed to have no love for animals, having grown up on a hardscrabble farm in Michigan. Ironically, the same mutt had saved Snake's skin on one occasion, alerting him to a kid with a bomb strapped on his back.

At a slow jog, Aaron soon caught up with them. "A priest with a following," he joked. "And not a church in sight."

"I don't know, Ace," Snake replied. "This setting feels rather blessed to me."

"Huh?"

"It's beautiful, man. The sun coming through these ancient trees and those flowering bushes are nature's own stained glass windows. The hanging moss creates an illusion of a roof in some places, forming arches, like a cathedral. The pretty cottages along here are jewel-toned colors, floral offerings at the altar. And the birdsong . . . well, what better choir could there be? I suspect the Garden of Eden was much like this. It would make a great painting."

"Bullshit!" Aaron replied, but he had to admit that he'd been looking at Bayou Rose as a pain-in-the-butt money sink of one renovation after another for so long he'd failed to remember why he was attracted to the rundown plantation to begin with. "Who turned you into the Picasso of the South?"

Snake just shrugged.

"How about you, Fleur?" Aaron asked, taking her hand in his, not unaware that she didn't pull away. *Mark that up as another point in my favor.* The progress he was making with Fleur came in the tiniest of bites, and he was discovering they were the sweeter for being so hard won. *I'm as bad as Snake with all these cornball thoughts.*

Fleur looked around slowly, pausing before she answered, "If I had a home like this, I would never leave."

Snake looked at Aaron for his response.

Aaron barely restrained himself from doing a fist pump in the air. "It's yours, then," he told her. And he meant it.

"The things you say!" She shook her head at Aaron.

To Snake, she said, "Aaron pretends to be madly in love with me only because he knows I'll rebuff such overt advances. A reverse psychology."

Aaron arched his brows at her, and Snake just laughed.

"He would be playing hard to get if he really wanted me," she explained to the priest. "This way, he figures, his compliments and bribes are so outrageous that I'm bound to just laugh. It's a game."

"You have me all figured out, do you?" Aaron asked, not really offended. More like intrigued by her mind's workings.

"You could always accept, and call his bluff," Snake suggested.

Aaron flashed his old buddy a wink of thanks.

Fortunately, or unfortunately, further discussion halted with the arrival of Ed, the resident carpenter/plumber/contractor, who asked about Samantha. Aaron gave him, along with Fleur and Snake, the update. Ed then told him that the new septic lines were almost completed, connecting all the cottages. The units should be available soon for the families of Dan's cancer patients to return, as they had been for the past year.

"Do you mind if we look around?" Snake asked Aaron. At his nod, the priest and Fleur went through a gate, across a small yard, and into one of the cottages, the purple one named Pansy, to explore while Aaron continued talking to Ed. The cottages had been given colors and names by none other than Tante Lulu: Bluebird/blue, Sunshine/yellow, Meadow/green, Rose/red, much to Samantha's dismay over historical accuracy. *Guess who won that battle?*

"I'm not sure what Dan will want to do with the

cottages, short-term," Aaron told Ed, "what with Samantha's being in the hospital and the situation here with Fleur and Tante Lulu. Maybe you should just finish up, fill in the trenches, reseed, and move on to some other project. We might have to leave them empty until the dust settles. I know, why don't you start on the St. Jude swimming pool."

"Are you serious?"

"Halfway."

Snake came out then, and after asking some pointed questions about the cottages (how many there were; maximum occupancy, etc.), went off for a tour with Ed while Fleur sank down onto the porch swing. Each of the cottages had either an old-fashioned swing, or a glider, or sets of rocking chairs.

Aaron went up and sat beside her on the swing. For several long moments, they just swung, saying nothing. She smelled like Samantha's Jessica McClintock body wash, which sat on a shelf in the mansion's rain forest shower. It smelled like lilies of the valley. He knew because he'd asked Samantha one time.

"It's peaceful here," Fleur remarked.

"Sometimes."

"I was kidding about living on a place like this." When he didn't say anything, she went on, "I mean, with my background, I would be satisfied with a little cottage like this. I would never fit into some fancy mansion."

When he still said nothing, she continued, "And I would never be accepted, either. People talk about forgiveness and all that, but they never forget. I could be eighty years old, and they would still be thinking *prostitute* when I walk down the street."

They rocked for several more moments. He could see Ed and Snake talking companionably as they left Rose Cottage and entered Meadow.

"Well, aren't you going to say anything?" she finally asked.

"I'm too busy remembering our mutual dream from last night, and wondering how soon we can pick up where we left off." He put his arm around her shoulders and tugged her closer. He even dared to kiss the top of her hair.

She tried to squirm out of his embrace but he wouldn't let go.

"You had your say, darlin'. Now let me have mine." Aaron may have been born Cajun, but he'd lived in Alaska most of his life. It wasn't until he'd moved here that he learned the value of a slowly drawled out Cajun "darlin'." More than one Southern belle had allowed her bells to be tolled with that trick—rather talent, according to Tee-John, who had a reputation for Cajun charm. Not that Aaron was looking to ring Fleur's bells. Yet.

"Go on," she said.

"I'm in love with you. Don't ask me why, or when it happened, or how. It just did. Tante Lulu thinks I'm channeling some Hosea dude from the Bible, or else St. Jude got me in his crosshairs, and bam! The Thunderbolt of Love!"

"Hosea! What? Are you supposed to rehabilitate me?"

"I think Tante Lulu was thinking more along the lines of you rehabilitating me. Bottom line, I've fallen for you. Hook, line, and bayou sinker."

"You don't even know me."

"You don't know me, either . . . darlin'," he said and stifled a chuckle at his own foolishness. "If you did, you'd know how out of character my behavior with you is. I like women. I've been liking women, or girls, for a long time." Fleur stared at him, intrigued, despite herself.

Meanwhile, he was running the fingertips of his hand, the one on the far side of her shoulders, over the bare skin of her arm. She was wearing a sleeveless blouse today and Bermuda shorts. For the brief time she'd been back on the bayou, the semitropical sun had already had an effect on her appearance. Blonde streaks lightened her brown hair which was pulled back into a ponytail, and the slight bronzing of her flawless skin had caused a few freckles to emerge on her nose and cheeks. Just a few, not like Samantha with her twenty gazillion. Her caramel-colored Cajun eyes sparkled with honesty and, yes, a sort of innocence. She could have passed for nineteen, instead of her twenty-nine-plus years. She wasn't beautiful, like some of the women he'd known, but she was pretty.

"Go on. You were telling me about your sexual prowess, starting at a young age."

That wasn't quite what he'd been doing, but if she wanted to hone in on that, who was he to argue? "My point about starting early was this. I've been around the block, sex-wise, a lot. In fact, I've been around the state, the country, the . . . wherever." He shrugged. "I have finely perfected techniques, but I don't even have to employ them anymore. Women recognize a man who knows things. I can walk into a room and cull out the prospects without saying a word. They come to me."

"So, you're attracted to me because I'm hard to get."

"I don't think that's it. If I was looking for a one-night stand, or even a series of meaningful two-night stands, it would be different. I want more from you."

"What exactly do you want?"

"I want to make love with you. I know that."

"Aaron, I don't even like sex."

"You did in our dream."

She blushed, and he knew he'd made a point.

"Give us a chance, Fleur. I can take it slowly . . . for a while. I won't push you."

"You're already pushing me." She glanced to the right, to her upper arm where Aaron's fingertips were drawing circles . . . and raising the fine hairs.

"Well, a little pushing." He leaned in and kissed her lightly on the mouth. When she didn't back away or slap him silly, he deepened the kiss, moving his mouth back and forth over her closed lips until they fit together perfectly.

She didn't kiss him back, but he noticed that her breathing accelerated.

It took all his will power to draw away and just look at her.

He'd like to think she was a bit dazed, but she was probably just wondering if he was crazy. Maybe he was. Crazy in love.

"I'll tell you another thing. I'm tired of walking on eggshells around you regarding your past life. Afraid that any little thing I say might offend you. Bad things happen to good people. It's a fact of life. Maybe it's time to find the humor in some of it."

"Humor?" she said, as if he'd suggested something perverted.

"Yeah, it's one of the best things about human beings, that we can laugh at ourselves, even in the worst of times."

"For example?"

"Well, with respect to myself, I think it's damn funny that I'm walking around all the time with a half hard-on for an almost-nun. See. You're going all prissy stiff on me just because I used a vulgar word. Live with it! And notice that I said almost-nun, not an actual nun because, darlin', I am gonna do everything in my power to prevent that from happening."

"You are not helping your cause," she pointed out. "I can't find anything funny about what happened to me over the past sixteen years."

"Oh, please! How about a bunch of nuns staked out in a strip club? How funny is it that you're living with the Dingbat of the South? And here's a good one . . ."

She put up a halting hand and laughed. "You've made your point."

"Good," he said and kissed her quick before she could push him away.

Just then, Snake returned, and he was smiling in the oddest way. At first, Aaron thought it was because he'd seen the kiss. But it was something else, he soon found out.

"Ace, m'boy, God does work in mysterious ways," the priest pronounced right off, sinking down onto the top of the porch steps and leaning against the rail post.

"Okaaay," Aaron said.

"These cottages, you know what they would be perfect for, don't you?"

Aaron looked over to Fleur. She looked as confused as he did.

"A haven for rescued girls," Snake announced in a ta-da fashion.

When neither he nor Fleur enthused, he went on, "I was talking to Brother Jake this morning about plans for the exchange, and he told me that the biggest problem we have is the large number of victims to be rescued, from both ends. Remember, there are going to be two dozen brought in from Mexico for the exchange for one dozen of the new girls from New Orleans. A total of maybe thirty-six bodies to be transported somewhere." Brother Brian glanced at Aaron and Fleur, waiting for them to understand.

When they were still confused, he continued, "Those newbies will be turned over immediately to the local police in some secret negotiations being handled by John LeDeux."

That was news to Aaron.

"I can fly a half dozen of the rescued girls to the convent in Mexico, and you could handle another six, flying into the Street Apostles ranch in Dallas."

Aaron nodded.

"But that leaves a dozen more of those poor girls. We need a place for them to hide. A temporary place, until they can be doled out to other places in the US or elsewhere. In the meantime, voilà!" He held both arms out to indicate the cottages.

"Oh, I don't know," Fleur began.

"Aaron can help when he gets back from Mexico."

I can?

"Surely you're not thinking that Aaron and I alone could handle them."

"Whoa, back up a bit. I'm still back at my plantation being offered as a way station for a dozen ex-prostitutes." Another thing occurred to him. *A pairing . . . Snake is pairing us off, like a couple. Holy freakin' crap! Is this some kind of predestined thing?*

"Neither Aaron nor I have the expertise for dealing with the physical and emotional needs of newly rescued girls. I know from past experience that some will need medical attention, others will need psychological attention if not lifelong therapy, and some will even want to run back to what they were doing, a Stockholm syndrome kind of thing. A job of this magnitude is not taken on lightly."

Aaron shot a glance at her with alarm. He hadn't even thought about all the complications that Snake's suggestion would entail.

"Details!" Snake said, waving a hand dismissively. "First of all, Aaron's brother might be willing to help with initial medical exams."

"What? Dan will shit a brick before he gets dragged into such illegal activity."

As if Aaron hadn't even spoken, Snake turned to Fleur and said, "Bet if we asked Mother Jacinta, she would send a nun or two here to help out. Maybe she'd even come herself."

"Oh, Lord!" Fleur said, as if it was a prayer. "Mother Jacinta and Tante Lulu together? The South would never recover."

"I hadn't even considered Tante Lulu," Snake said, tapping his closed lips thoughtfully. "See what happens when good people put their heads together? That old lady could gather a team of professionals to handle a temporary situation like this quicker than you could say St. Jude or Richard Simmons." Snake grinned then. Apparently he'd been around Tante Lulu enough already to get the picture. When she wasn't proselytizing about the saint, she was swooning over the aging exercise guru. "And your Aunt Mel looks like she has the organizational skills of a military commander, Aaron. Didn't she run her own air shipping company before you were old enough to think about airplanes? Come to think on it, maybe . . ."

Snake went on and on while Fleur gazed at him with horror and Aaron put his face in his hands.

What had he gotten himself into?

Chapter Nine

*C*ompany's coming . . .

Fleur was pretty much alone at Bayou Rose with Brother Brian that afternoon. He was upstairs in the study, working out plans, via a conference call, with his fellow Apostle, Jake, Mother Jacinta, and some others. Fleur had declined to participate, feeling like one of the soldiers, not a leader, in the missions, as it should be, the only way she'd want it. Instead, she worked once again at the kitchen table on Tante Lulu's herbal book.

Grace O'Brien, the ex-nun whom she'd yet to meet, had done some preliminary work organizing Tante Lulu's folk medicine recipes a few years back, and she'd been better qualified than Fleur was, having studied alternative medicine while she was a practicing nun. Grace's work formed a base from which Fleur worked now, making it easier to organize all the data into separate folders.

The ceiling fan whirred overhead. The pot of jambalaya on the stove simmered softly, and two loaves of homemade bread were rising on the counter, both exuding wonderful aromas of the dinner to come.

Aaron had gone to work before noon; three flights to the oil rigs, and one bayou air tour, he'd told them all. Afterward, he would meet with Luc to discuss some continuing issue he had with the FAA. Plus, he planned to stop by the hospital to see how Samantha was doing. Before leaving, he'd leaned in and given Fleur a good-bye kiss. A quick one, which he'd laughingly called a fly-by kiss.

She'd threatened to smack him for taking liberties. Where she'd come up with such an old-fashioned word, she had no idea. Well, yes, she did. Too much hanging around Tante Lulu.

"Oh, baby, if you only knew the liberties I'd like to take!" Aaron had declared.

Tante Lulu had shaken her folded Richard Simmons fan at the two of them. "No drinkin' wine before the gospel."

Fleur had been afraid to ask what that meant.

"We have a saying about wine back in the Old Country," Brother Brian had begun.

Everyone groaned at his continual spouting of proverbs, triads, and whatnot, except Tante Lulu, who had developed a kindred spirit with the priest.

Undeterred by the groans, Brother Brian had told them, "Wine makes good women wenches." But then he added, "Actually, I think many countries have claimed that proverb, in one form or another."

Aaron had put up his hands in surrender. "Hey, I've been on the wagon since I met Fleur."

"Huh? What wagon?" She wasn't sure if he was referring to alcohol or women. "I never asked you to go on any wagon."

On the way out, Aaron had confided to Brother Brian in an overloud whisper, "I think she's starting to like me."

Everyone was amused by the thrust and parry wordplay between the two of them. That was all she needed, to be the source of entertainment for a madcap group of people forced to hide out together in a bayou mansion! And she was feeling the most madcap of them all. Or maybe she was just going mad.

She was still reeling from Brother Brian's suggestion that she and Aaron might run some temporary shelter for a dozen rescued girls right here at Bayou Rose. That assumed a relationship, or some kind of tie, between her and Aaron. And it certainly meant a longer stay here than she'd imagined.

Really, though, the man was getting totally out of hand. Not just the fly-by kiss, or the kiss on the swing, but every time he passed by he felt the need to touch her. Nothing too personal, but alarming nonetheless. When she'd asked why he kept doing it, he said, "I can't help myself," followed by a wink and a laugh, and a comment/warning: "I've got you in my carnal crosshairs, darlin'."

Having no filter, Aaron made such outrageous statements in front of everyone. Like watching a ping-pong match, their heads kept swinging back and forth as they followed the banter.

And since when did Aaron get all Cajuny with the

exaggerated "darlin'" nonsense? He was right about one thing. He was a master at this seduction game.

Once Aaron left, Aunt Mel decided to go grocery shopping, again, after she dropped off an overnight bag of requested items for Samantha at the hospital. Fleur offered to pay for some of the food from the dwindling fund she'd been given by Mother Jacinta, not having yet received her first pay from Tante Lulu.

Aunt Mel had declined, saying guests did not pay for their meals.

"Guests" was a misnomer, in Fleur's opinion, and she'd pointed out that visitors and fish start to smell real quick, as the old saying went.

"I got a sayin' fer you," Tante Lulu had shot right back. "Doan look a gift horse in the mouth, or a saint offerin' a plenary indulgence."

"What saint?" Fleur asked.

"What's a plenty indulge hands?" Aunt Mel wanted to know.

Neither of them got an answer.

Turned out, Tante Lulu had also offered Aunt Mel money to help with the groceries . . . five crisp one-hundred-dollar bills. Which Aunt Mel had refused to take, as well.

Daniel was long gone, of course, having decided to put in a few hours at the medical center. He would visit Samantha later and stay through the dinner and visiting hours.

Tante Lulu went up to take a nap, telling Fleur to make sure she woke her if something unusual happened.

Fleur wasn't about to ask her, "Like what?" Everything that had happened to her since her return to the bayou had been unusual, to say the least.

Even Ed, the contractor guy, drove off with Lily Beth and their respective kids for a day at the beach. It was hot enough. Eighty-five in the shade, last time Fleur had checked. That dimwitted pool idea of Aaron's was beginning to sound not so dimwitted.

Fleur worked diligently on the old receipt books for more than an hour, getting up occasionally to stir the pot and check on the rising bread. There was a small TV on the counter, but she had no desire to learn what was going on in the world or to watch one of the day-time soaps. Her life was becoming too much of a soap opera all on its own. The silence was soothing.

But not for long.

"Looks like we're alone, Fleur. People are wonder-ful, but solitude is a blessing," Brother Brian pro-nounced, as if he'd read her mind. He was coming down the back stairs, followed by his tribe of animals, who were surprisingly silent. He must have put some celestial spell on them. *The priest whisperer*, she thought with a smile. They immediately settled near the open doorway, probably in wait for him to take them outside.

Instead, he walked over to the fridge, his flip-flops slapping on the slate floor, and took out the pitcher of sweet tea. He poured himself a glass which he drank, leaning back against the counter. His only concession to the heat was the removal of the clerical collar from under his Hawaiian shirt. "It's moments like this, the quiet in the midst of a storm, that I feel the presence of God most. Don't you agree?"

She thought for a moment. "I guess. Life is so hec-tic, and downright sordid at times, that we forget what's important."

Brother Brian nodded and took another sip before adding, "And sordid it is, at times."

She didn't know if he referred to her past, the present sex trafficking business, or his own history, of which she knew almost nothing.

"So many times since I've become a priest, I've run into people who have no faith, no belief in the existence of God. They want proof. To me the proof is all around us. Sunshine on a new day. Rain to replenish the soil. A baby's first smile. The love between a man and a woman."

She didn't know if that last was a prod at her regarding herself and Aaron, but maybe not. "I see the proof in the human spirit being able to survive some of the most horrendous experiences, like soldiers coming back from war, or children rising out of extreme poverty to become lawyers or doctors or scientists," she told him, adding, "The complexity of the body with all its working parts is more than science, in my opinion. And, yes, babies are too miraculous to be mere bits of scientific particles. Hey, I even get a shiver when I see a rainbow."

"Me, too," Brother Brian said with a smile. Then out of the blue, he asked, "Would you like me to hear your confession?"

When her head shot up and heat flushed her face, he said, "Just kidding. I always get a kick out of people's reaction when I ask that question. Not that I couldn't offer you the Sacrament of Penance if you're so inclined." He tilted his head in question.

"I'm not inclined," she blurted out, so vehemently that she immediately had to add, "Not that I've committed any big sins lately. It's just, well, awkward to bare your soul to a friend, or acquaintance."

His eyes twinkled at her. He *had* been teasing. Maybe.

"So, have you made a decision about taking vows?" he asked, throwing her with another unexpected question.

"No. Not yet."

"Don't do it, lassie."

She inhaled sharply. "What? Now you've really surprised me. Isn't it a priest's duty to encourage everyone possible to fill all the religious orders?"

"Not always," he said. "I know, it's intrusive of me to butt in where I haven't been invited for an opinion, but if you haven't made a decision by now, it was not meant to be, my girl."

"You think this is about Aaron, don't you?"

"You mentioned him, not me."

"I gave up on a man in my life—a normal family—a long time ago."

"Ah, child, have you not yet learned? God moves slowly, watching while we stumble through treacherous fields, but eventually His grace comes to us."

She frowned, not sure what he meant. "Are you saying that my kidnapping, the rescue, my work with the sex trafficking missions, meeting Aaron . . . all this was meant to happen?"

Brother Brian shrugged. "Who can say? I do believe that everything happens for a reason. Sometimes, after a tragic event, we say, 'Ah, so that's why it happened.' More often, we have to wait until after death to discover the hidden truths."

"And, you, Brother Brian, has nothing happened to you that made you question everything?"

His blue eyes that were so often warm and mischievous turned suddenly grim and glazed with pain. "Yes, it has." He seemed to be deep in some memory for several moments, but then he said, "Back to you and taking final vows . . . if you have a true vocation, there'll be no doubt in your mind. Please, do not enter the convent as payment for your rescue, or as a safety net from a sinful world. That will only lead to unhappiness, whether you stay in the order the rest of your life, or leave eventually. It's a spoon that soon sups sorrow for many a priest or nun."

More proverbs! "Wow! You don't paint a very inviting picture of religious life."

"Sorry if I've done that. It's a wonderful path for those who are chosen."

She noticed his emphasis on "being chosen," rather than making a choice.

"I've already exceeded my limit for unasked for advice, but I'm Irish and my tongue has a mind of its own. So, I'll go one step further. The biggest boulder in your recovery is lack of forgiveness."

"For Miguel and his crowd? I suspect that I'll eventually forgive those who kidnapped me and the abuse I suffered under their hands. That doesn't mean I'll stop trying to rescue the girls, or put the slimeballs out of business."

"As it should be, but I was thinking more of your family."

She stiffened. The priest had gone too far.

And he knew it, as evidenced by his immediate apology. "I did not mean to offend you, Fleur. Even priests can be fools. I'm reminded of that old adage that the silent mouth is musical. Obviously, I'm tone deaf."

At first, she considered going back to her work without a response, but then she said, "That's all right. Your intentions are pure. But I have to tell you, I don't hate my parents for refusing to let me come home. Not any-more. Mostly they just disappointed me. And Mama died soon after that of uterine cancer. Last I heard, Daddy was on disability with back problems from all those years of shrimping. He's in constant pain."

"Are there any of your brothers and sisters still at home?"

"I don't know. The youngest would be Frankie, who is seventeen by now. There might have been more children born after I left." She shrugged.

Brother Brian just stared at her. Not in an accusing manner. More like understanding. And that hurt more because it ate away at her defenses. If she didn't think about her family, they couldn't hurt her.

Thankfully, he decided to change the subject. Or rather the subject was changed for him by the ringing of his cell phone. He glanced down and said, "Ah. Mother Jacinta again."

He spoke to the mother superior for several moments, mostly saying, "Yes," or "I understand," or "Good," or the ominous "Oh, no!" After a few moments of this, he handed the phone to her and said, "She wants to speak with you."

"Me?" Fleur furrowed her brows at him, then put the phone to her ear. "Mother?"

"Fleur! I have been hearing so many good things about your progress."

Really? From whom? Probably Tante Lulu, the old busybody! "I'm trying," she said.

"I'll be able to judge for myself when I get there. With Sister Carlotta."

"You're coming here?"

"Yes. With Jacob."

"Jacob?"

"Yes, Jake, the Street Apostle. Didn't Brother Brian tell you about that?"

Ah, Jake the ex–Navy SEAL. But what did she say? They were all coming here? "No, Brother Brian didn't tell me." She shot the priest an accusing glare. "You're all coming here?"

"The plantation sounds like the perfect spot for our planning headquarters . . . and a temporary refuge for some of the girls we rescue."

Brother Brian had made a similar suggestion this morning, but Fleur wasn't aware that any decision had been made. Even then, the only thing mentioned had been the possibility of a landing place for the girls until something better could be arranged. This was the first she'd heard about a planning headquarters. *Oh, my!* "Did Aaron agree to this? Or Daniel?"

"We—Brother Brian and I—figured you would be the best one to convince them."

Fleur shot Brother Brian a dirty look, but he was pretending to be reading Tante Lulu's receipt books. "Me?"

"Of course, I'll have to return to the convent before the exchange takes place, to handle those wounded birds who land here. But Sister Carlotta can stay with you until you get the right professionals in place there. Perhaps a social worker, maybe a nurse. A psychiatrist would be wonderful, or else a psychologist. I leave it up to you, dear one, for offering to do this."

I offered to do this? When?

"Tante Lulu says that her niece Charmaine could even come in to help the girls with self-esteem issues.

You know, advice on grooming and clothing before they return to a normal world."

I should have known the old biddy was involved in this scheme. And Charmaine? Good heavens! Charmaine relishes her self-proclaimed title of "Bimbo with a Brain." A bimbo teaching ex-prostitutes how to be normal? I have landed in bizarroland.

After ending the call, Fleur chastised Brother Brian for his rash actions involving her and Aaron in his plans, without first seeking permission. He wasn't at all apologetic and quoted some hogwash, "Needs must when the devil rides."

Click, Click, Click! she said to herself. Otherwise, she would have blistered the priest's ears with a few choice swear words.

She was overwhelmed with all the decisions that must be made. She needed a shoulder to lay her head upon, just for a moment till she could regroup. It was no surprise that the broad shoulder she envisioned was on a man who wore size twelve cowboy boots, footwear better suited to a rodeo than the hot Cajun sun or the bayou skies he flew over. She decided to wait for the cowboy in his apartment out in that separate *garçonniére*, or bachelor quarters.

It was only later—too much later—that she wondered, "What was I thinking?"

Which one of the three bears was he? . . .

Aaron didn't arrive home until after six p.m., what with his flying schedule running late, followed by his meeting with Luc regarding the FAA. Then, he'd been

forced to ooh and aah with Dan and Samantha in front
of the nursery window at the hospital. No, not to check
out their babies, which were still nestled—rather playing
football, according to Samantha—in her ever-growing,
big belly.

"Does that mean they're boys?" he'd immediately
asked, figuring they must have decided to look at their
ultrasounds after all.

Dan had shot that idea down. "No. We don't know.
Samantha just means that it feels as if they're kicking a
ball around in there. Right, honey?" He'd gazed at his
wife like she invented football.

She'd gazed right back at him, as if he invented
something equally fabulous. Like maybe sex. No, for
women, it would probably be designer shoes, or in Samantha's case, a spiffy method for refinishing antique
furniture. Different strokes!

On more than one occasion, observing their sappi-
ness, Aaron had been nauseated, but then he felt the
warm fuzzies just knowing his brother was happy after
all of those years of being . . . well, not happy. The
bond between twins was powerful; they cared a lot
about each other. He hoped Dan and Samantha's twins
would share the same connection.

"Do you want to feel them move?" Samantha had
asked him, arching her belly out even farther. To his
amazement, he'd actually seen a ripple of movement
where the fabric of her thin robe strained against her
breadth. Holy crap! It had been like pec bounces on a
steroid-loaded bodybuilder.

Eew! "Um. I'll pass," he'd demurred, not because he
was repulsed by a woman's gut, not even a big blimpy
one, but to touch his sister-in-law *there* while she was
in Madonna mode seemed kind of incestuous.

Dan had laughed at his discomfort. "Now, honey, don't tease Aaron. You know he's afraid he'll catch the baby bug."

What? He hadn't even thought about that. But suddenly the image of Fleur with a baby growing inside her—his baby—posed a certain allure. Yeah, she'd told him that she probably couldn't have kids, but then he wasn't sure he wanted any himself.

He'd blinked several times to clear his head. *Must be that damn sun melting my brain*, he'd thought.

In any case, they hadn't been standing at that nursery window gawking at Dan and Samantha's twins, but at every other squaller born at the hospital the last day or two. Everything from scary puffballs of hair à la Don King to shiny cue ball heads, even a Donald Trump do. Big, little, fat, puny, black, white, and some so pitifully homely with squashed faces that they were cute.

But now, he was home. Or almost home.

As he drove up the horseshoe-shaped driveway to the mansion, he had to admit that it did feel like home, and not just because Bayou Rose was growing on him. Fleur was here.

He had it bad.

But he couldn't rush right in. He was a bit ripe. His smell alone would turn her off, if his overenthusiasm didn't. He'd only been gone for eight hours, and the buildings he'd been in, along with the copter, had been air conditioned, but going in and out of the scorching hot sun today had worked up a sweat which he needed to shower off before being in anyone's company. *If a Southern belle glistens (rather than sweats), then this Southern beau is one big, oiled-up diamond in the rough.* He smiled at his fancifulness. Once again, he blamed the sun, which was still hot as hell as he emerged from his pickup truck. *Or maybe it's the prospect of see-ing my girl.* He smiled some more, knowing what Fleur would say if he referred to her, out loud, as "my girl."

He took the steps two at a time up to his apartment, which was on the upper floors of the *garçonniére*. Dan had lived here when they first bought the plantation, while Aaron had stayed over at the mansion. Later, af-ter the marriage, they'd exchanged places. This smaller pad suited Aaron, for now.

He almost bypassed the second floor living area and was about to climb the stairs to the third-floor bedroom and bathroom. But then he did a double take and stopped.

What the fuck!

The air here was blessedly cool, or at least not hot, thanks to a window air conditioner. That must be what had attracted Fleur.

Yes, Fleur!

In my man cave!

Be still my racing heart!

She was lying on one of the side-by-side recliners, in the way-back position so that it was almost horizon-tal. The nightly news was playing on the television, low volume, but she was fast asleep. The faded peach sleeveless dress she was wearing had ridden up to midthigh, and one of her leather thong sandals had fallen to the floor.

The dress had tiny buttons running from the neck to the waist. He did a quick count. Fifteen. He couldn't help but smile. He was real good at counting . . . and other things. Like buttoning. And unbuttoning. A skill he'd learned in kindergarten and perfected over the years.

One of her arms was thrown above her head, showing a clean-shaven armpit. A vulnerable position and female body part that caused the testosterone in his body to amp up about a thousand percent. (Can anyone say hair-trigger arousal?)

Was this how the three little bears felt on first seeing Goldilocks in their bed? Nope, they were too young for hard-ons that could drill concrete. But, really, he'd just been thinking "man cave," and now it was "bear cave."

Is there some kind of woo-woo synchronicity or something going on here?

Nah, it's probably sunstroke.

For a brief blip of an insane moment, he considered going over and arranging himself atop her body and waking her with a slowly drawn drawl of "Honey, I'm home." Better yet, a growly, "Who's been sleeping in my bed . . . uh, recliner?"

But no, he couldn't shock her awake like that. Besides—he paused to take a whiff of one of his own pits—time to shower first.

He practically tiptoed up the stairs to his bedroom, removing his clothes as he went and dropping them wherever. Then he almost had a heart attack when his cell phone rang, sounding as loud as an explosion in the silence. He quickly checked the ID. Tante Lulu. That was just great. He clicked on the phone before the second ring.

"Yeah?" he said in a soft voice, but ruder than he intended.

"It's Tante Lulu."

He rolled his eyes. "I know."

"Ya doan hafta be snarly jist 'cause yer frustrated."

The woman knew too much! "What can I do for you?"

"Where are you?"

"In the closet." And that was actually a partial truth. He was in front of his closet, with the door half-closed to muffle his voice.

"I knew it! I allus thought it was Daniel who might be gay, but it was you all along. Not that I have anything against homo sapiens."

He gritted his teeth before saying, "I am not gay."

"Jist kiddin'."

"And, by the way, it's homosexuals, not homo sapiens."

"I know that, idjit."

"You're getting on my nerves, old lady. What do you want?"

"Are you callin' me old? I'm not so old I can't whup yer be-hind fer bad manners."

He rolled his eyes again. This must be how Luc, Remy, René, and John felt when they were ten years old and were caught misbehaving. "Sorry."

"Anyways, I jist wanted ta alert you. Fleur fell asleep up in yer apartment. Yer Aunt Mel went over ta call her fer dinner, but she was zonked out. Mel decided ta let her sleep. Poor chile is wiped out from all the stress . . ." She paused, before adding, ". . . and frustration."

"I can only hope," he murmured.

"Whadja say?"

"She's still asleep."

"Well, dinner's in the warmin' oven when you two are ready ta eat. I'll prob'ly be asleep by then."

He glanced at his watch. "It's only six thirty."

"A gal's gotta get her beauty sleep. Besides, tomorrow's gonna be a busy day."

He wasn't going to ask what she meant by that. She'd no doubt tell him. In detail. There was a long silence. Finally, he asked, "Is there anything else?"

"I fergot what I was gonna say. I hate when that happens. Oh, I know. Are ya gonna do yer thing now?"

"What thing?"

"Yer moves, boy. Everyone up and down the bayou knows you got moves."

Oh, good Lord! Is she asking if I intend to have sex with Fleur? "That's kind of a personal question, isn't it?"

"At my age—and, no, I'm not callin' myself old—nothin' is too personal. Anyways, you been draggin' yer feet, boy. Time fer some action."

He put his free hand up to his forehead and counted to five. "Is that all?" he asked, and immediately realized that he should have counted to ten because, of course, she always had something else to say.

"I could give ya pointers. Time was, I knew a lot about hanky panky, way more than I've ever admitted to. Not jist with my fiancé, either. And I keep up ta date, too. I read *Cosmo* in Charmaine's beauty shop. And whoo-boy, the things I learn. In fact, didja know . . ."

Way too much information! "You have got to be the most interfering busybody in all creation."

"You say that as if it's a bad thing ta care about people. Back ta that *Cosmo* article. If a man has veins bulgin' out of his you-know-what durin' the slip 'n' slide—that means sex ta young folks—it can be real interestin'. Do you ever get veins? If ya don't, I could ask Tee-John ta teach ya. He knows stuff like that."

For the first time since he'd met Tante Lulu, he hung up on her. He was still shaking his head with amazement at the things that came out of her mouth as he took the fastest shower in history. Not bothering to shave, although his nighttime stubble could use some work, he brushed his teeth, donned a pair of black running shorts and a plain gray T-shirt, and headed back down the stairs, barefooted.

Fleur was still asleep, thank God, and Tante Lulu was right about one thing. She was probably exhausted from all the stress of what had been happening.

He leaned over her and was about to whisper something super sexy in her ear. He had no idea what, but it was gonna be good. That was when he accidentally hit the vibrator button on the side of the recliner, and it immediately began to do its thing.

He jerked back, not wanting to be accused of doing it deliberately. That would be perverted. Wouldn't it? Like taking advantage of a woman when she was sleeping or blitzed.

But she didn't even wake up. Instead, she smiled in her sleep and jiggled her body around a little to better fit into the dips in the leather caused by his own body.

Praise the Lord and pass the gumbo! Even that unconsciously sexy realignment revved his engine, which was already humming along nicely.

Her movement caused her dress to ride up higher, and the buttons to strain across her chest. He could swear he saw the outline of her nipples.

And, oh, man, did I just get a peek at white panty?

No, it was the flicker of light from the TV.

I am pathetic.

He noticed some beads of sweat . . . um, glistening . . . on her forehead. And she was breathing kind of heavy through her parted lips.

Maybe she's having a wet dream. Do women have wet dreams?

Well, she's definitely hot. Yep, it's warmer in here than I thought.

I could turn up the AC.

Or, I bet she'd appreciate it if I unbuttoned one, or two, or three buttons.

I am losing my freakin' mind.

He patted the bulge between his legs and thought, *Down, boy, down!* It was losing its freakin' mind, too.

But then, as the vibrations continued, she raised her other arm, to join the one already above her head, and she arched her back slightly. The final nail in his coffin was the soft moan that escaped her lips.

He moaned, too, and forced himself to say, "Hey, Fleur."

Her eyes opened slowly and she smiled. She smiled! *That's it! No more Mr. Nice Guy!* "Move over, darlin'," he said and eased himself onto the recliner beside her. It was a tight fit, but with them both almost on their sides, facing each other, they fit. Real nice.

He waited a moment for her to shriek and shove him off, or to say "CLICK!" real loud, but instead she just stared at him, rather dazed. Whether from being still half-asleep or by his magnetic charisma or some other bullshit, he didn't care. He was where he wanted to be, where he had wanted to be for a long, long time.

And, just FYI, the sweet vibrations under his hip weren't too bad, either.

"This is a bad idea," she murmured as he nuzzled her neck and inhaled a light lily of the valley scent. Samantha's body wash. Despite her words, she tilted her head slightly to give him better access to her neck.

"Uh-huh," he agreed—*or the best bad idea I ever had*—and licked the skin to see if it tasted as good as it smelled. It did. Moving up to her ear, he took the tiny lobe between his teeth and tugged. Then he deep-

kissed the ear itself using the tip of his tongue and his
lips. Afterward he softly blew the inner whorls dry.

She melted against him. Really, that was how it felt to
him. And somehow—he swore he didn't know how—
eight of her fifteen buttons were undone and he was
kissing the bare skin of her chest right down to the
center panel of her bra. Forget the damn buttons. He
leaned down and took as much of one breast into his
mouth as he could, dress and bra and all, and began to
draw outward until he had the hardened nub between
his teeth. Then he flicked it with his tongue repeatedly
like a bleepin' snake.

She let out a tiny shriek, which caused him to pause.
He wanted to make sure she was awake and willing.
No way would he force himself on her. But then, she
sealed the deal by putting her hands on his head, holding him in place. "Glorious, glorious!" she said.

Her eyes were closed and for a moment he wondered
if she was praying. After all, she *was* an almost-nun.
Which should have stopped him in his tracks.

Not a chance! Instead, he pulled out his entire arse-
nal of tricks for breast play. Alternating between one
and the other, he palmed them, pinched them, licked
and suckled until she was keening in one continuous,
"Ohohoh, oh, oh, oh . . . !"

He could feel her tense and then relax in a soft climax. Her eyes got wider and wider as her lower body
spasmed. "What was that?" she asked with wonder
afterward.

Huh? She had to know perfectly well what that was.
It wasn't her first orgasm.

Or was it?

No, that had to be impossible.

But he couldn't think about that now. He had his own situation to take care of. While she was still in a sexual euphoria, he arranged himself atop her body, spread her thighs with his legs, and managed to get his hands on her buttocks under her dress to rub the silky fabric, the whole time pressing his erection against the cleft of her panties. One, two, three times, he thrust and shot his wad.

Man, it was the best dry fuck he'd had since he was a teenager. Good thing he'd thought to put on briefs under his shorts. He wondered how soon he could try again, this time inside her body, maybe up on his bed. A little wine, before or after, would be nice. And food. He could bring the warmed-up dinner over here, and they would eat it in bed. Afterward, they'd tiptoe over to the mansion and try out the rainforest shower. Happy times!

His fantasy—and, yes, it was a fantasy, apparently—was interrupted by Fleur shoving his shoulders and knocking him over and onto the floor. "Guess this was how the three bears felt when Goldy gave them the old heave-ho."

"Huh?"

"Have you lost your mind?" he asked as he got up from the floor and shot a glower at her.

"I must have. To let you manhandle me."

"Manhandle? Is that a nunly word for making love?" He was rubbing his behind as if he'd hurt himself, which he hadn't, of course. It was only his pride that was bruised.

"Making love? Hah!" She was sitting up but having trouble getting the vibrator device to turn off.

He almost smiled. Her dress was hiked up to her

thighs, and it was still half unbuttoned, with two wet spots dead center on her boobs. He was probably in no better condition, except his shorts were dark, and he didn't give a damn. "Oh no! You are not going to lay this on me. Although, yes, I almost got laid."

"Very funny! Not!"

"Hey, you wanted me as much as I wanted you."

"You tricked me." She'd finally turned the vibrator off and was working steadily to reclose the gaping dress.

"I wasn't the one all splatted out like a sexual buffet in the apartment of a member of the opposite sex who has a raging hunger."

She gasped.

That *was* crude. "Not that I didn't appreciate the buffet."

"CLICK!"

He grinned.

"I was asleep, for heaven's sake!"

"Only at first. You know what this is, don't you? Morning after regret. Typical! Females hook up with a guy, then get all embarrassed the next day, or afterward. The only way to save their pride is to blame the fool who banged them. If they could, they would demand an un-bang. Well, darlin', there is no unbanging this." He waved a hand before the half-hard-on that still bulged at his crotch. Almost immediately, he regretted his words which had to sound chauvinistic and crude. He had to remind himself that Fleur was different from other women. He had to watch his language.

Her mouth had dropped open with amazement, whether at the crudeness of his gesture, or his ramble, he wasn't sure.

He was pretty amazed himself.

"Did you learn that from Dr. Phil?"

"No, an old *Playboy* magazine. Dan and I used to collect them." He paused. "When we were ten years old."

Not even a twitch of a grin. "You took advantage," she said in a small voice, realizing that she was losing the argument.

But he wasn't giving an inch. "Maybe you took advantage of me."

That gave her more food for thought.

Which made him think of *food* food. "Why don't I go get the dinner Aunt Mel and Tante Lulu saved for us and bring it back here? We can talk." Before she started to protest, which she was obviously going to do, he added, "You must have come over here for a reason." He wasn't delusional enough, yet, to believe she'd come deliberately looking for sex. It had to be something else.

"You're right," she admitted. "Have you talked to Brother Brian today?"

He shook his head. "He left several voice mails, but I haven't had a chance to return his calls yet. It didn't sound urgent."

"That figures, that he would leave it to me," she said with disgust. "I need to tell you about today's happenings and what's about to happen tomorrow. For some reason, he and Mother Jacinta think I can convince you to—"

He put up a halting hand. "Wait. I'll get the food and be back in a sec." He thought about adding an apology for upsetting her with their little make-out session, but decided he wasn't sorry. Not one bit.

Grabbing a pair of flip-flops that were under the

coffee table, he was headed toward the stairs when he heard Fleur go into the bathroom, close the door, and then let loose with a loud shriek. He figured the mirror on the back of the door must have given her a floor-length look at herself, especially the wet spots on her dress that were like carnal headlights. To her, they would appear like neon Scarlet Letters of shame.

He should feel sorry for her, and he did, but he would bet his bottom dollar that he looked even worse, like "a horny goat caught in a barbed wire fence," as Tante Lulu was wont to say. He laughed at his thinking of the old lady at a time like this.

She must have heard him and misinterpreted the laugh because, instead of her usual click nonsense, she said, "FUCK!"

Oh, yeah!

Chapter Ten

Z apped again! . . .

Fleur was embarrassed. Of course she was. And it had nothing to do with Aaron's ridiculous philosophy about morning after regrets or about unbanging the bell, or some such nonsense he expounded. It had more to do with her being an almost-nun. Bottom line: She had really screwed up on her road to becoming a nun. Or almost screwed, she decided with a vulgar streak she hadn't known she had.

This is just great. The almost-nun who almost screwed. Sounds like the title of a tabloid magazine article.

"What's so funny?" Aaron asked. He was sitting across from her at the small table in his apartment, finishing off his second helping of jambalaya and rice, not

to mention four slices of buttered homemade bread.
All washed down by a bottle of cold beer.

"What did you say?" she asked.

"You were smiling. I asked you to share the joke."

"No joke. I was just laughing at myself for behaving
like a fool."

"You're a fool for getting your rocks off?"

She flinched. "Crude much? Why are you behaving
like this?"

"How? Like a normal guy? I'm not a kid, and neither are you. Men and women enjoy each other. It's a
fact of life. In fact, God made us that way."

"Are you saying God made you do it? Tante Lulu
would have something to say about that."

He smiled, and flashed that silly/sexy dimple. Probably deliberately. "No, sweetheart, I didn't get a call
from Above. I didn't need any push in that direction."

"This is not like you, Aaron."

"Maybe this is the real me. Maybe I've been behaving like a wuss this past year, sniffing after you like a
hungry dog. Asking 'Can I?' or 'May I?' when I should
have just jumped your bones like I wanted to."

"That's disgusting." Which it wasn't. She felt herself
weirdly attracted to this more aggressive Aaron. A part
of her, deep down, felt zapped, like an electric current,
at his mention of wanting her in that way.

"If you think that's disgusting, ponder this, darlin'. I'm
almost positive that I gave you your first ever orgasm.
You should be saying thank you, instead of knocking
my good work."

"Good work? Good work?" She couldn't help herself.
She had to smile at his outrageousness. Another zap!

He reached across the table and took her hands in

each of his. She tried to tug out of his grip, but he held tight. "Listen, Fleur, I love you. Don't know why. Don't know when it started. Don't even know if I like it all that much. But it's a fact, and I'm going to stop playing games and pretending otherwise. Okay?"

"No, it is not okay," she said, "but will that change anything?"

"Nope." He drew both hands up to his mouth and kissed the knuckles, one set, then the other, before releasing her.

Double zap!

He got up to get himself another beer from the fridge and asked, "What was so important that you braved the bear cave?"

She had no idea what he meant by bear cave. Some stupid man joke, she supposed. "Brother Brian has invited Jake, the ex–Navy SEAL priest, and Mother Jacinta to come here. Tomorrow! To help set up your cottages as a way station for the rescued girls."

"Whoa, whoa, whoa! I haven't even had a chance to discuss that proposal with Dan yet. He's been kind of distracted."

"I know."

"What's the rush?"

"Things are moving faster than they expected, and apparently it will take some planning for us to be ready to house the girls here."

"Dan is going to have a bird. And, good Lord! What if Samantha has her babies before this all comes down? How can she bring babies into this . . . chaos, or even danger?"

"That's why I wanted to talk to you. They're mentioning doctor exams, therapists, social workers, even

Charmaine giving them beauty treatments. All to be done on the hush-hush. I'm not qualified to set that all up."

"And you think I am? I suppose that's why Snake has been trying to contact me."

"Probably not." She felt her face heat.

"What?"

"That's why he sent me. To convince you."

Aaron's eyes went wide with astonishment. "Ouch! Talk about pricking the balloon of a guy's ego. You being all hot and oooh-oooh-oooh for me was just an act to convince me to participate in more crap."

She winced at his words. *Can a zap be unzapped?* She was about to correct his misimpression, but he was off on another tangent.

"I just can't believe that Snake—a priest—sent you to seduce me into agreeing to his cockeyed plan. He's usually a straight shooter." He gave her a disgusted look. "And here I thought I was the one seducing you. Was your orgasm an act, too? No, I know the signs, and you had the signs, cupcake."

Here's a news flash, Lover Boy. I am now officially zapped out. "Don't be an ass. You know very well that Brother Brian meant that I should convince you with words . . . verbal arguments."

"I don't know about that. Snake and I go way back. I wouldn't put it past him, not in a priestly minute. Especially now that he's on the God team. He must figure the end justifies the means."

Fleur was stunned that Aaron could be so far off base. "You think I would agree to have sex for the mission?"

He suddenly seemed unsure. "Maybe."

She would have tossed ice water in his face if her glass wasn't empty, and he knew it, too, as his eyes followed her hand reaching, then slapping down on the table. "I did not use sex as a tool," she said through gritted teeth.

He studied her closely, looking for signs, she supposed. Different kinds of signs now. "Well, then, I'm sorry if I offended you," he offered grudgingly.

It would take a lot more than a reluctant "I'm sorry" to wipe away his vile accusation. Just like a man, he thought his slate was wiped clean with a few casually thrown words of apology. If Aaron only knew! The shelf life on what he had just said was, like, forever.

The angry expression on his face had relaxed. Of course it had. But then, perhaps sensing that all wasn't forgiven, he added, "You must admit, I had cause to be suspicious. It was a complete turnaround for you to transform into a sex kitten on me when you've rejected my every move in the past."

She had no answer for that, and the most alarming thing was that the term "sex kitten" didn't immediately raise her hackles. She should be mortified. She wasn't. Was she finally, finally, finally healing? Had she reached the point where any simple remark about sex wasn't taken as a personal slur on her past?

Well, these were questions for later. She had other, more pressing issues. Now that Aaron had voiced his misgivings about Brother Brian's methods, a seed of doubt was planted. Fleur had to wonder.

Could the monk be so devious?

No.

But Aaron is right on one point. The cause is extremely important to Brother Brian. It is to us all.

Darn it, Aaron! You're turning my mind upside down.

"That's nothing compared to what you're doing to my mind," Aaron replied. "Mine is upside down, inside out, and twirling like a helicopter prop."

Fleur felt her face heat. She hadn't realized that she'd spoken her thoughts aloud.

"Since I first saw you asleep on my recliner tonight, I swear my brain has been on a one-track muddle of erotic fantasies, Miss Goldilocks," he continued.

"What's with the Goldilocks stuff? You turning into a pedophile now?"

He gave her a look of mock horror. "This is a grown-up Goldy fantasy." He was probably teasing her to relieve the tense mood she was in, that they'd both been in since her blowup.

"Ah, well, scrap that fantasy," he said, smiling.

Forget apologies. Aaron could melt the hardest heart with that smile of his, dimple and all. "Gladly," she replied.

"I was leaning more toward a striptease in a nun outfit, anyway."

Zapped again!

Busybody, busy bee . . . same thing! . . .

Louise was unable to sleep. She had cabin fever. Well, mansion fever.

She hated being cooped up here at Bayou Rose. She missed her family . . . her other LeDeux family. Not just Daniel and Aaron. Her garden needed tending. She itched to see the damage at her cottage and to dig in cleaning up. And her *traiteur* clients—Holy Crawfish!—

they must be banging on her door, looking for their usual remedies. A person couldn't just bop down to Walmart and buy gator snot salve or JuJu tea.

But then, after dinner tonight, Brother Brian gave her the news. They were having company. The ex–Navy SEAL priest, and Louise's friend, Mother Jacinta, and maybe a few other nuns. After that, the girls—those poor girls that had been kidnapped and prostitutin' for years—were to be brought here for a short stay, and they would be needing all kinds of help.

"Did Daniel and Aaron agree ta all this?" she had asked.

"They will," Brother Brian had promised.

She was doubtful, especially about Daniel who was a stick in the mud at the best of times, not like now when he was nervous as a long-tailed cat in a room full of rocking chairs. But then, she reminded herself, Brother Brian was a priest, even if he didn't look like one. It must be true. She brightened, no longer bored and antsy. So much work to be done! Even though it was ten o'clock, she called Tee-John. "I have a list," she said right off.

He groaned.

"Are you asleep?"

"Not anymore."

"I need two dozen of them St. Jude statues, the little plastic ones. And medals . . . a bunch of them, too. On chains."

"Where are they?"

"The storage shed."

"The last time I went in there, about fifty boxes fell on my head. And a black snake scared the shit out of me."

Yeah, and if you only knew what was in some of them, you'd have a heart attack. Note to self: Hide the box of condoms. "Stop yer complainin'. Yer fool head needs a few thumps."

"Can't someone else go? I should be stickin' close to home in case Celine decides to pop her baby out real quick-like."

Pff! Isn't that just like a man, to think that childbirth was an easy-peasy, painless popping procedure? Like bread from a toaster? "Far as I know, yer wife won't be poppin' nothin' fer another six or eight weeks, jist like the other preggers women in this family." And wasn't that a miracle that Samantha, Charmaine, Luc's wife Sylvie, Remy's wife Rachel, René's wife Val, and Celine all got bit by the baby bug at about the same time? They blamed her, as if she had that kind of hoo-doo power. Now, St. Jude . . . that was another story. *Note to self: Work on baby shower with Mel. Time's a-wastin'. Babies don't wait.*

"Are you still there?"

"'Course I am. My mind was jist wanderin'."

He muttered something about "What else is new?"

So much it boggles even my mind! "Speakin' of babies . . . go inta my pantry and see if the jar marked 'Love Potion' is still there. If it is, bring me a handful. Ya kin put it in a zippy bag."

"Uh-oh! A love potion. Who's yer target, *chère*?"

If the boy was in front of her, she'd give him a good wallop fer disrespectin' her skills. "Target? I'll give ya a target. I've gotta *help* Aaron and Fleur."

"Isn't Fleur a nun or somethin'? But wait. That wouldn't stop you. As I recall, you worked your magic on Grace O'Brien at one time, and she was an ex-nun?"

Note to self: Call Gracie and introduce her to Fleur. Lots in common. "Thass right, and Fleur isn't even a full-fledged nun yet; so, I ain't interferin' with God's work."

"Un-huh," Tee-John said, disbelieving. "Maybe those two aren't meant to be together."

"Bite yer tongue, boy. Aaron is already head over hiney in love with Fleur, and she's halfway there. She jist needs a little push."

"We could always resurrect the Cajun Village People act."

Her family put on a wonderful (some folks called it outrageous) Cajun version of the old Village People music revue to serenade someone who was dragging his or her feet in the love department. It almost always worked, probably because the person was too embarrassed not to give in. They'd even done one at Angola Prison. *Talk about! Note to self: Dry clean Red-Hot Mama dress in case needed.*

"I only order that when things get desperate. They ain't desperate yet. While yer at my cottage, grab that picture of me and Phillippe that's next ta my bed. And pick me a bushel of okra. Plus, I must have tomatoes ripe on the vine. Bring those, too. Make sure that Useless gets a bucket of Cheez Doodles fer all his good work chasin' away them bad guys. Oh, and look in the purple douche bag in the bathroom closet and grab me some bullets fer my pistol. Never know when those bad guys might show up here, and I only have a few rounds. On the way back, ya might stop at Boudreaux's General Store fer some of their spicy-dicey pickles. Ya cain't find them nowhere else. Samantha has a cravin', and they're the best thing on dressed po-boys, although they do give a body wind." Into the silence that followed, she asked, "Didja fall asleep, Tee-John?"

"No, I'm awake. Unfortunately."

"Yer a good boy, Tee-John."

"Now you're butterin' me up."

"Love ya, sweetie."

"Love ya back, you old bat."

After that, Louise called Charmaine and said right off, "I have a list."

Brotherly love, a cure for almost everything . . .

It was almost midnight, and Aaron was about to call it a day and head for the sack, when he heard footsteps coming up toward the living room. His mood lightened. She'd come back. After three hours! But she came back!

Man, she owed him for the past three hours of frustration. She was going to rake his coals, big-time. And he didn't care if that sounded crude, or not.

Okay, he could compromise. He would be nice, despite the royal kiss-off he'd been given, and he didn't mean kiss in the usual, lip-lock manner. So, he would tend her coals first. Yeah, then she could tend his fire.

He smiled, but only for a moment.

"Damn!" When he saw his brother emerge from the stairwell, his mood immediately deflated back to its previous condition. "Oh, it's you," he said.

"Thanks for the welcome."

"Sorry."

Dan had obviously not shaved since this morning, and his nighttime stubble was not designer attractive. (Charmaine had taught Aaron about designer stubble.)

His dress shirt was unbuttoned at the top and wrinkled, not the norm for his usually well-groomed brother. There were some dark stains on his khakis.

"Dan! Is that blood?"

"Nah! Just kid barf. I stopped at the clinic after visiting with Samantha, and one of the toddlers was having a bad reaction to chemo."

That his brother, a pediatric oncologist who had been burned out for years, could say that without cursing or going into a deep depression was an indication of just how far he'd come in healing since they moved to Louisiana. A lot of that was due to Samantha.

"How's the soon-to-be mommy?"

"Hanging in there."

He sensed something wrong with Dan, though. Twins had a way of feeling each other's emotions. So, he knew what to ask next. "And the daddy?"

"Not so good. It's hard being so positive and calm around Samantha when, in fact, I'm scared shitless."

"Oh, man!"

"I see every day in my practice all the bad things that can happen to babies. What if . . . ?" His voice choked off.

Aaron walked over and gave his brother a hug. "Stop torturing yourself, Dan. The babies are fine."

"I guess." Dan glanced over at the empty bottles on the counter, then looked pointedly at him. "Got any beer left?"

"A few," he said, grabbing a cold one out of the fridge but deciding not to have any more himself. He'd had several after Fleur left, and instead of getting high, he was feeling low.

Dan stared at the almost fully level recliner and

plopped down into the other one. He took a long draw on his beer, then said, out of the blue, "Remember that kid who died back in Alaska, Deke Watson?"

"Yeah. The one who finally pushed you over the edge."

"I don't know about that. My burnout was more a cumulative . . . well, that's not important anymore. Here's the thing. I was thinking . . . if one of the babies is a boy, we could name him Deke."

"Hmm. And if the other baby is a boy, he could be Zeke. Deke and Zeke. Has a ring to it."

Dan choked midswig. "The names don't have to rhyme, you know. Ours don't."

"Yeah, but it's more fun that way. You do know that other kids will call him Deke the Geek."

"You think? I wouldn't mind if my kid was a geek, but I wouldn't want him to be teased . . . or bullied."

"On the other hand, if the other baby is a girl, she could be Monique." Aaron waggled his eyebrows at his brother. "Hubba hubba, as Tante Lulu would say."

"Good Lord!"

Aaron put the other recliner into an upright position and sank into it with a sigh.

They sat in silence for several moments, watching the *Tonight Show* on low volume. Jimmy Fallon and Adam Sandler were engaged in some half-ass comedy routine that had the audience howling.

"Have you made any decision about taking that job in Baton Rouge?" Aaron asked.

"Yes. It's a golden opportunity I can't pass up, and Samantha is with me, either way. I haven't officially accepted yet."

"Congratulations, and I think you're making the right decision."

"Are you sure you're going to be all right here, alone? I feel like I'm abandoning you."

"We're not conjoined twins, you know. We can live apart. Besides, Baton Rouge isn't that far away. We'll see each other all the time." Aaron was trying his best to be upbeat, but he felt like hell. This break with his brother would be huge, and they both knew it.

"Maybe you won't be alone here," Dan offered, raising his eyebrows in question.

Aaron made a snorting sound.

"What's got you in a mood? Things not going well with Mother Teresa?"

"Actually, I made some inroads tonight, but it is slooow going."

"And you're not used to that," Dan said with a grin. "Are you sure she's worth the trouble?"

"Was Samantha worth the trouble?"

"Hell, yes!"

"Ditto."

"Anything I can do to help?"

"Nah. Well, actually . . ." He stared at his brother. "Houston, we have a problem."

"Uh-oh."

"I hope you don't have any immediate plans to fill those cottages."

"Let me guess. You're moving in some nuns, and you're going to turn the mansion into a convent."

"Not nuns," he said. "Prostitutes."

Dan put his face in his hands, then raised his head to look at him. He was grinning. "You're opening a brothel?"

"Very funny. We need a place to temporarily house some of the rescued girls. About a dozen of them." He explained what that would entail. With each thing Aaron mentioned, Dan's mouth gaped wider.

Finally, Dan said, "I'm not going to tell Samantha about this."

"Good idea."

"And, if I were you, I wouldn't tell Tante Lulu, either. Move her out somewhere else until this is over."

"Too late," Aaron said. "She's probably planning a welcome party as we speak."

"Can I move in with you?"

"No. And here's another thing. Tomorrow, an ex–Navy SEAL rogue monk and a couple of nuns will be arriving."

"Well, that settles it. I'm moving over to the doctors' quarters at the medical center until this blows over."

"Aren't you afraid I'll install a swimming pool while you're gone?"

"Go for it. That would be the least of the outrageous things you've done lately. In fact, maybe you can have all these visitors digging the hole for you."

"There's a thought." Aaron paused. "On the other hand, are you allowed to have roomies at the medical center?"

Well, fiddle-dee-dee! . . .

Fleur had no trouble sleeping that night. In fact, she overslept. It must be true what they said about . . . well, never mind!

When her alarm went off at seven a.m., she stretched and got up, reluctantly. She caught herself smiling.

Smiling?

What is that about?

No, I don't want to know.

A vague memory of an erotic dream tugged at her, but she couldn't recall the details. No, her memories this time were of the make-out session with Aaron last night. It hadn't even been real sex, and yet she'd had her first ever orgasm. How embarrassing was that?

She was the last one up, or one of the last ones, she realized, when she went into the bathroom and saw a number of damp towels hung on the racks. She took a quick shower, which was a sacrifice, the high-tech sprays being a hedonistic invitation to dwell overlong. Then, she donned clean clothes. White capri pants; a black spandex, racerback tank top; and white athletic shoes. Her damp hair was piled atop her head, twisted, and held in place with a claw comb.

She knew that Tante Lulu or Aunt Mel, or both, were already down in the kitchen by the smells wafting upstairs. Bacon, for sure. Maybe sausage, as well. But a sweet smell, as well. Homemade beignets?

Aunt Mel was the only one in the kitchen, wearing an ankle-length, brightly floral, muumuu-style house dress and red slides. Her gray-threaded dark hair framed attractive Aleutian features, and, yes, she was still attractive at fifty-something.

The older woman glanced up and smiled from where she was sprinkling powdered sugar on the warm fried pastries, which had been draining on paper towels. "Good morning," she said warmly in welcome.

"Good morning. Sorry I overslept. I should have been down here helping out."

"No problem, sweetie."

Getting closer, Fleur saw that she had been correct at guessing beignets, the absolutely delicious New Orleans specialty, served for breakfast, dessert, or anytime a sweet tooth addict needed a fix. But not for the diet conscious. Which Fleur hadn't been. Until now.

Oh, well, maybe next week she would think about cutting back. For now, she took a huge bite out of one of the beignets, washed it down with a sip of strong Creole coffee, and almost swooned.

Mel watched her reaction. "They're that good, aren't they?"

"Yeees! Did you make them?"

"Tante Lulu made them, but I fried them."

"Where is she?"

"Off with Daniel and Brother Brian, checking out the cottages to see what needs to be done before our 'guests' arrive." She arched her eyebrows at Fleur, as if warning her about what was to come.

"Uh-oh. I take it Daniel is not a happy camper."

"You could say that."

"And Aaron?"

"He went to the airport to pick up Brother Jake . . . I know, it's hard saying that, isn't it? Somehow, priest and the name Jake just don't jive together. Oh, well. Aaron will also be bringing a couple of nuns, and heaven only knows who else."

Fleur winced. "This really is an imposition, isn't it?"

Mel put her hands up in a "Not my problem!" manner. "Not for me to say. I can always go back to Juneau if it gets too crowded here."

Fleur sat down at the table and motioned for Mel to join her with her own cup of coffee. And, yes, Fleur was eating another beignet. *So, sue me,* she said to her nagging conscience. To which, the voice replied, *They* are *heavenly.*

"Aaron wanted to go up and wake you before he left, but I wouldn't let him," Mel said with a twinkle in her eyes. "He had that mischievous look on his face."

Fleur felt herself blush and decided a change of subject was called for. "Tell me about yourself, Mel, and how you're connected to Aaron and Daniel."

"Well, you know I'm gay, right?" She paused, probably wondering how a nun, or almost-nun, would react to that revelation.

Not my business to judge! "Yes, I knew that. But you met Claire Doucet when she already had the twins, right?"

Mel took a sip of coffee and nodded. "And I was married. Turns out we were both latent homosexuals. When we met, she was a premed student and I had just bought a fledgling air shipping business from the proceeds of a divorce from my husband, best known as The Asshole. Oops, forgive my language."

"That's okay. I've heard worse."

"Barry Manilow first brought us together, we liked to say." Mel smiled. "In fact, I met Claire in a music store where we both reached, at the same time, for Barry's second studio album that featured the song 'Mandy.' We were never apart after that, until the day she died." Mel's voice went husky with emotion at those last words.

Fleur reached across and squeezed her hand. "I'm sorry. I didn't mean to stir up bad memories."

"No, no! Those were good memories."

"Tell me about Claire."

"She was a remarkable woman. I know, I'm prejudiced, but she really was. Her family kicked her out when she got pregnant as a teenager by that horndog

Valcour LeDeux. Luckily, he gave her some money,
just to get rid of her, probably figuring she'd get rid
of the babies, though she didn't know then that she'd
have twins. Not that it would have made any difference.
Anyhow, she moved as far away from Louisiana as
she could get, and that was Alaska. Almost immediately, she decided that she was going to become a
doctor, and she did. Lots of skimping and ramen noo-
dle dinners and tiny little low-income apartments. But
she made it, and she raised two fine boys."

"You were a close family," she guessed.

"Very. And the boys were especially close, being
twins and all. I don't know how they're going to deal
with the separation."

"What separation?" She had a vague memory of Aaron
mentioning something about Daniel and Samantha
moving, but she couldn't recall the details.

"It's not official, but Daniel is about to accept a new
job in Baton Rouge. They won't move until after the
babies are born, of course."

"You mean, Aaron will be alone here on this plantation?"

"Maybe," Mel said, eyeing her speculatively.

"That man!" Fleur exclaimed, knowing what Mel
was thinking. "Can you honestly see me acting like
some mistress of a plantation?" She assumed that Mel
now knew about her background. "Face it: A modern
day Scarlett O'Hara I am not, nor could I ever be."

"I doubt that's what Aaron would want you to be.
And this is no Tara, for darn sure."

"People would condemn Aaron."

Mel shrugged. "They already condemn him for some
of his wild ways—well, former wild ways. Frankly, my

dear," Mel said with a grin, "you need to stop dwelling on the past, and worrying about other people's opinions. What do you really want?"

Fleur's eyes misted, and a lump formed in her throat. "Why are you being so nice to me?" she choked out.

Mel got up and came around the table to sit on the bench beside her. Putting an arm around her shoulder, Mel kissed the top of her head and said, "Child, it's time to forgive yourself."

"In these few moments, you've acted more like a mother to me than my mother ever did." Fleur proceeded to explain the rejection by her parents when she'd been rescued by the Magdas.

"Honey, do you know what my mother said when she found out I was gay?" Mel said. "She said I was sickening and destined for hell. That was before she told me to get out and never come back."

Thus it was that when Aaron returned, he found Fleur crying on Mel's shoulder, and the older woman leaking tears, as well, and intermittently, both of them giggling. Along with Aaron were an equally shocked, or at least surprised, hunky priest, with salt-and-pepper hair cut short in a high-and-tight style, his military-buff body encased in a short-sleeve black shirt with clerical collar and belted black slacks, and three nuns in religious street garb—short-sleeve, calf-length, black dresses and short white veils, no wimple or half-circular breast cloths, but there were huge wooden crucifixes hanging from long chains around their necks, and big rosary beads dangling on the side from twisted rope belts. They all would have provided an attraction out in public, clearly being of religious orders, especially the big-bodied Sister Mary Michael, who matched Brother Jake in height and looked as if she could carry all their luggage, by herself.

And, boy, is there a lot of it! Fleur noticed with alarm. *Are they planning a long stay?*

After blinking several times in disbelief at Fleur and his aunt, who were no longer sobbing, but dabbing at their eyes with Tante Lulu's St. Jude paper napkins, Aaron asked, "What's going on here? Have you two been hitting the bourbon? For breakfast?"

"No, Mr. Sensitivity," Mel told him. "Fleur and I just decided"—she glanced at Fleur and winked—"we decided that tomorrow is another day."

Chapter Eleven

He and Rhett had a lot in common . . .

Aaron was in the dining room, which had been converted into a war room by the Bayou Commander, the name soon given to Brother Jake by both Aaron and Daniel after watching with amazement as he ordered everyone about like an Army drill sergeant. Well, not Army since he was a former Navy SEAL. Still, he had taken over Bayou Rose like Patton storming Normandy.

"Aaron, put those computers over there."

"Somebody, go put a cover over that bird cage. If I hear 'Holy shit!' one more time, I'm gonna duct tape its beak."

"Hey, hey, hey! That's my wife's pet, Clarence," Dan said, although everyone knew she couldn't stand the cockatoo, either, and would give it away to a good home, if only someone would offer.

Brother Jake didn't even apologize. He just grunted

and continued with his orders. "MM, where's that black suitcase that holds all my maps?" MM was his nickname for Sister Mary Michael, whose name he deemed too much of a mouthful.

"Snake, my man! Where you been hiding? Did you get the latest intel from the ranch? No, you better go check. I don't do blind dates. The exchange date has been moved up, again, you know."

Luckily, Snake had locked up all of Samantha's other pets, who continued to follow him around like the Pied Piper. He could hear the unhappy cats, and pig, and dog barking and meowing and oinking below in a storage room. Otherwise, Brother Jake might commandeer them into some job or other, too.

"Can you find some extension cords, Mel? Preferably heavy duty."

"Holy hell! The wireless here is weak as piss. You better call your cable company, Dan, and see what you can do about amping up the speed."

Needless to say, he didn't hesitate to use a few curse words, which caused Tante Lulu to wince and reprimand him, "Jist 'cause ya look like a fallen angel, doan mean ya kin swear like the devil. Watch yer potty mouth, or I'll show ya some ampin' up."

Taken aback for a second, Brother Jake then laughed and picked up Tante Lulu, lifting her high in the air and giving her a big kiss on the cheek. "Sweetheart, if I weren't a priest, I'd be chasin' your tail like Roger Rabbit on Jessica Rabbit. You got any more of those ben-yays? You're surely a saint in the kitchen. Some coffee, too. Blonde and sweet, like before. But more sugar this time."

Tante Lulu made a harrumphing sound, but she was

obviously pleased as she went off to bring the dictator more of the pastries, of which he'd already wolfed down at least a half dozen. That was all he needed! More sugar and caffeine to hype him up!

"Aaron, see if you can contact that brother or half brother or whatever he is of yours, the one that's a cop."

"John LeDeux?"

"Yeah. He needs to know that New Orleans police spotted Miguel Vascone at the Silver Stud last night."

Maybe I should go there myself tonight, and kill the bastard, Aaron thought.

"I know what you're thinking, LeDeux," the Dictator said.

Does everybody know I have the hots for Fleur?

"Don't you dare go off half-cocked on your own," Brother Jake ordered. "No weapons!"

Aaron bristled. As Tante Lulu was wont to say, *This guy is getting on my last nerve*. Instead, he responded with, "They have a saying here in the South. 'Some men need killin'.'" He wasn't sure if he meant Miguel or the bossy priest.

The bossy priest assumed he meant Miguel. "I can't argue with that, but the Street Apostles are a nonviolent group. No killing, unless in defense or unless absolutely necessary. You already know this."

Yeah, I do. Dammit! "I'll do it later, then," Aaron said with a grumble.

"They lost track of the tango in the French Quarter, anyway." Tango was a Navy SEAL term for a bad guy. "Oh, and tell your brother John that some Mexican dudes have been asking questions about Tante Lulu around Bayou Black. Some lady at Boudreaux's General Store chased them out with a broom."

How did this guy, who'd just arrived in Louisiana, know so much? He must have contacts all over the place. That was good, for the mission, Aaron supposed. But it didn't stop him from being a major asshole.

Aaron was glad that Tante Lulu had left the room. If she'd heard the news about Boudreaux's, one of her favorite haunts, she'd be storming down the bayou with her own broom . . . or an AK-47. And she wouldn't give a damn about any nonviolence rule.

When Brother Jake began tacking maps on the wall, Dan yanked Aaron outside. "Oh, my God! Good thing we're moving, or Samantha would be chasing that guy with a measuring stick, priest or no priest. Do you have any idea how much that wallpaper cost? Two hundred dollars a roll!"

Personally, Aaron didn't think anyone had any business spending that much money on wallpaper, but he wasn't about to tell that to Dan . . . or Samantha. "Your mistake was coming back to the house," Aaron pointed out.

"I needed some more clothes, but I'm outta here now. I have a consult in a half hour. You're on your own, bro."

"Lucky you! Actually, I need to go to work, too. Remy's swamped."

Aaron walked Dan to his car.

"Where's Fleur, by the way?" Dan asked.

"Helping Mother Jacinta up at the cottages. Call me later and let me know how Samantha's doing."

"Will do."

On the way back around the side of the house, Aaron noticed Mother Jacinta and Sister Carlotta walking down the narrow roadway from the cottages toward the mansion. Fleur must still be up at the cottages. Alone.

The two nuns were talking animatedly and didn't

even notice him. Not that he was hiding from them. He just didn't have time to chat before leaving for work . . . and doing some other things.

He waited until they'd entered the kitchen before he headed up toward Magnolia, the last cottage refurbished so far. It was the most traditional of them all, being painted a creamy white.

Fleur was bending over the sofa, fluffing the cushions and arranging some throw pillows. For a moment, he just leaned against the doorjamb, enjoying the view. Idly, he made a mental note to call Ed before he left and remind him to hang a screen door ASAP, or whoever stayed here would be bitten alive by mosquitoes or those blasted no-see-ums once dusk hit the bayou.

When Fleur straightened, she noticed him. "How long you been standing there?"

"Just long enough to admire your heart-shaped ass in those tight pants."

"In crude mode again, Aaron? Tsk, tsk! Back to the New Raunchy You, I see," she said.

"Nah. Back to the old raunchy me."

"My pants aren't tight."

"They are when you bend over. Do it again, and I'll show you."

"Not a chance." She laughed.

At least she was laughing.

And, man, what was she was wearing on top? It looked like a black bra, but it was probably one of those running things. Was she planning on jogging? Regardless, her top was made of some stretchy material that molded her breasts and lifted them. Which, of course, reminded him of how sensitive her breasts had been under his hands and mouth last night, so sensitive she'd climaxed.

She knew what he was thinking, too, he could tell,

and not just because his eyes were latched on the twin
mounds. She was looking at his hands, and his mouth.
Under his perusal, the nipples pearled against the tight
fabric.

Good sign!

She backed up a step and asked, "Did you want
something, Aaron?"

"Oh, yeah." He stepped inside and closed the door
behind him.

She blushed and backed up another step. "I mean,
did you come here for some particular purpose?"

"Oh, yeah," he repeated. *One more step backward,
sweetie*, he urged silently. It wouldn't take many steps
for her to reach his goal. The cottage was small, an
advantage in his present ulterior calculations.

She backed into the counter of the kitchenette, right
where he wanted her. He barely stifled a grin of satisfaction.

"I've come to collect my apology kisses," he said.

"Oh, that!"

"Yes, that," he said, moving in closer. "Remember
what Aunt Mel said earlier today?"

"Huh?" She tried to laugh, but she was nervous.

Good! Nervous is good.

"Are you saying your aunt gave you the idea for
kissing?"

"I got that idea all on my own, darlin'." He put a
hand on either side of her on the counter, which was
just a bar separating the tiny living room from the tiny
kitchen. She was trapped now. "It's about that line that
Aunt Mel tossed out from *Gone with the Wind*. The
'Tomorrow is another day' one."

She tilted her head at him. "You're a *Gone with the
Wind* fan?"

"Not exactly. Next to Barry Manilow, Mom and Aunt Mel loved that movie. Dan and I couldn't help but watch it sometimes."

"And that has what to do with—"

He lifted her to set her butt on the bar so he could step between her legs. The counter was just the right height.

"—this?" she squeaked out.

"Her quote reminded me of my favorite line in the film. Rhett tells Scarlett, 'You should be kissed by someone who knows how.'"

She made an exaggerated tsking sound. "Your humility knows no bounds. Now you're saying that you're an expert kisser."

"It's one of my top three talents. In fact, you could say I'm a world-class kisser." He had a sudden idea. And those were the best kind, by the way. If he was able to make Fleur come by touching her breasts, what if he could do the same by just kissing?

Now there was a challenge!

He smiled.

She pretended to sigh and said, "Oh, Rhett." Then she burst out laughing. She probably thought she could deflect him with mockery.

He was not to be deflected.

And she wasn't laughing for long.

THIS was his idea of kissing? . . .

After the meltdown Fleur and Mel had engaged in this morning, Fleur made a decision. No more fighting this attraction to Aaron LeDeux. She was going to let the chips fall where they may. It was a gamble, but she was hoping that the fire would fizzle out of its own accord. And, if it didn't, well, then, she'd know for sure that she wasn't destined for the religious life.

That decision was all well and good until faced with the irresistible rogue and his claims of world-class kissing. He was so adorably outrageous and irritatingly outrageous that she could only shake her head in wonder, both at him and at herself.

"Go for it," she challenged with more bravado than she was feeling.

"I thought you'd never ask," he replied with a smile which, of course, caused his dimple to emerge, which, of course, made her even more susceptible to his charms.

"Don't expect much from me, Aaron. I mean, despite my past, this is all new to me."

"This is new to me, too."

"Puh-leeze! That's like Houdini saying he's new to knots."

"Who? Never mind. Seriously, babe, I haven't been this nervous about kissing a girl since we played spin the bottle at Kirima Askim's tenth birthday party. Kiri was the hottest girl in fifth grade, but she had braces, and I hadn't figured out that maneuver yet."

One never knew when Aaron was kidding or not. She would have to ask his Aunt Mel if there was such a girl. Or maybe not, if she'd have to explain why she asked.

Meanwhile, as her mind was wandering, his hands were wandering. Before she could say "Slow down, Rhett," he'd put his hands under her knees and tugged her forward until her butt barely rested on the edge of the counter, belying his nervousness. He pushed aside a paint can and an assortment of various size brushes to give her more room. Still, her precarious position, teetering on the edge, forced her to put her hands on his shoulders for support. Was that his intent? Then he yanked her knees wider and stepped up even closer. Definitely not the move of an insecure man.

When his hardness pressed against her, she gasped, and blinked, and saw stars for a moment behind her closed lids. "This doesn't feel like kissing."

"It's prep work."

"Like a professional chef?" she joked.

He didn't laugh, just shook his head.

Good Lord! He's watching me like a hawk, studying its prey. The slightest opening, and I am bird kibble. Maybe if I keep talking, he'll stop and give me a chance to think, to reconsider. "Don't you mean foreplay?" she stammered out.

"No, that comes later."

Oh, boy! I am officially out of my league! Fleur decided.

He traced her lips with a forefinger. Lightly. Then he did it again. And again. Each time he seemed to awaken more nerve endings. Until her lips parted, and her eyes closed.

But almost instantly, her eyes shot open at a new sensation.

Using the smallest of the dry paint brushes, the one for edge work, he was stroking her lips. Who knew lips were such an erotic spot on the human body? She hadn't. Oh, she knew that kisses themselves were supposed to be arousing, but the lips themselves having erogenous triggers . . . that was new to her. The pleasure he was inciting was almost painful in its intensity.

She moaned.

"Atta girl," he murmured as he dropped the brush and brought his mouth to hers, and used his lips as a brush, back and forth, gently, gently, gently, shaping. When he got the right fit, he breathed into her mouth, causing her to inhale sharply, and open for him.

After that, she couldn't keep track of what was happening. His tongue was in her mouth, and then it wasn't. Every time he did something daring, like nipping at her bottom lip with his teeth, or sucking on her tongue, or kissing her hard and deep, he alternated with little butterfly kisses or sweet licks of her lips.

New and exciting sensations unfurled in Fleur. In her "working days," Fleur had avoided kissing whenever possible, it somehow seeming more invasive and distasteful than other things, but occasionally a john would manage to trap her face and invariably it would be some big, fat tongue plundering her mouth almost to the point of suffocation. There was no comparison with this. Heaven and hell, if anything. But she wasn't going to think about the past. Not now, anyhow.

She moved her hands from his shoulders and cupped his face.

Which caused him to gasp with surprise, then murmur, "Oh, Fleur!"

She liked that she could surprise him like that, and she smiled against his mouth. Who knew that you could smile and kiss at the same time? Who knew there was anything about close contact with a man that would ever make her smile? *Who knew! . . . Who knew! . . . Who knew!* she kept thinking at every little thing he did. And then at some not so little things.

To her embarrassment, she felt an odd thrumming

begin in her lower belly and beyond, which she now knew presaged an approaching climax. Even her breasts felt fuller and achy. Surely, other women didn't have climaxes so easily. Maybe it was just that Aaron was so skilled.

But she couldn't let him see how pathetic she was. She stiffened, bracing herself against the oncoming onslaught. Maybe if she thought about something else she could halt this spiraling of sensations, like okra, a slimy vegetable she just could not like, or mustaches which made some men look kind of slimy, or slime itself, like that stuff kids bought at Halloween.

"Oh, no!" Aaron protested. "None of that stiffening up. Relax, sweetheart."

"Wait, wait . . . oh, no!"

As his tongue began a slow in-and-out movement in her mouth, his lower body undulated against her, and she crashed into an explosion of rippling spasms. This was no gentle orgasm like the previous one had been. This was sparks and a kaleidoscope of colors and pure, cascading bliss.

Aaron's forehead was pressed against hers. Was his excessive breathing a sign that he hadn't yet climaxed, or that he had, and it took his breath away?

"I'm not sure if I like this, Aaron."

He drew back to look at her. "If you're not sure, then I'm not doing it right."

"I mean, it feels like a merry-go-round, or one of those crazy amusement park rides where you start off slow in circles, and you think, *This is nice.* But then it goes faster, and faster, and you start to get a little bit frightened. You need to hang on because you're spinning out of control, and what if you fly off."

He just stared at her.

"Is that how it is for you?"

"Not quite, though your way sounds like more fun. I always did like amusement park rides, the scarier the better."

"You would!" She tried to push him away so that she could get off the counter. Now that sanity had returned, she worried that someone might walk in on them, like Mother Jacinta. Or, horror of horrors, Tante Lulu.

But of course he was continuing the discussion which by now she regretted bringing up. "No, for me, an orgasm—a good one—is a rocket taking off. There's all the preparations. Fueling up. Oiling up. Firing up. A couple practice runs. Some tweaks. And then bam. You're off to the moon!" He grinned at her.

"Well, if that was your idea of kissing, they need to put a new definition in the dictionary."

"That good, huh?"

She shook her head at his outrageousness. "Well, now that I've paid my mea culpa penalties with kisses, time for you to back off. I need to think about all this climax/orgasm/rocket/merry-go-round stuff to decide whether—"

"Oh, no, no, no! No backing off. No thinking."

"You have to realize, Aaron, that until yesterday, I was convinced that I didn't like sex." She realized her mistake immediately.

He grinned, of course. "And now you do?"

"Not necessarily."

"That's because we haven't done the deed yet. Or all the other things I have planned."

"You have plans?" Another mistake realized too late!

"You have no idea!"

"Why haven't you given up on me, Aaron? I've told you over and over that I can't live a normal life."

"Define normal."

She rolled her eyes. He was impossible.

"If you want me to stop, Fleur, I will. I would never force you. You know that, don't you?"

She nodded.

"Give me a chance, Fleur. Let's make love. Oh, not here, and not now. I want a better place and more time to do things right."

Right? That's what she was afraid of.

"I don't mean just having intercourse in fifty different positions. I want to dance naked with you to a Barry Manilow song. How's that for stupid? Or really romantic? It will probably be 'Mandy' or else 'Ready to Take a Chance' or 'Can't Smile Without You.' I haven't decided yet. Your choice."

That was so outrageous, and tantalizing, that she couldn't respond at first. "You dance?"

"Did I mention my top three talents? Dancing is number four."

"Is there anything you don't do well?"

"I'm having a helluva time winning you over."

She didn't know about that. She was sitting on a counter with her legs spread, having just enjoyed some world class kissing or whatever you wanted to call it, and he was still planted way too close for comfort. He was winning something.

"Anyhow, naked dancing is one of the things on my Fleur Bucket List." He pretended to be flicking through a notebook in his palm. "I also want to make love to you underwater in my pool."

"The nonexistent pool?"

"The St. Jude pool yet to be installed."

"And I assume we would be swimming naked."

"Of course."

"Wouldn't St. Jude disapprove?"

"Hah! I think St. Jude and Tante Lulu maneuvered this whole love spell thing on me."

On me, too.

"Wanna know what else I have in mind?"

"No."

As if she hadn't spoken, he went on, "You know that antique couch thingee that Samantha has in the front parlor? It's red velvet and has only one arm. The kind of thing Cleopatra might have reclined on."

"I think it's called a chaise lounge."

"Yeah, that's it. Can you imagine the kinky things that—"

"Enough! I get the picture."

"Of course, when it comes to furniture, I will always have fond memories of my recliner." He waggled his eyebrows at her.

"You really are hopeless."

"In a good way?"

"Is there a good way to be hopeless?"

He shrugged. "So, those are just a few of the tame fantasies I have. Wanna hear about some of the more, um, wild things I'm imagining?"

"No, I do not." Actually, she was intrigued. "Enough of your nonsense! It's time I get back to the house to see how the exchange plans are going. And you have to go to work, don't you?"

He nodded and let her slide to the floor, but not before giving one more gentle kiss to her mouth. And a pat on the rump. "Be prepared, the dictator has mapped out the whole mission, and he has assignments for all of us."

"I'm not surprised. Brother Jake is great at battle planning, and this *is* a battle of sorts. Minus the guns." She paused. "And, yes, his arrogance has rubbed more than one fellow priest the wrong way, and a few nuns, too."

Aaron laughed out loud. "That almost makes me like the guy. Almost."

As they walked back toward the mansion, Aaron took her hand in his, and she had to admit that she liked that, almost as much as all the other intimate stuff he was introducing her to. Halfway there, his cell phone rang. Without releasing her hand, he raised the phone to his ear and clicked it on with a thumb.

"Hello. Yes, this is Aaron LeDeux . . . Aah, Ms. Forsyth. Okay, Elaine. How can I help you?"

Fleur tried to pull her hand away, but he held on tight and shook his head at her.

"I can't meet today. I'm on my way to work. Yes, I'm still flying. Is there any reason why I shouldn't be? No, I can't make it for dinner tonight, either. Sorry. Another commitment." He glanced over at Fleur and gave her an air kiss.

"Okay, tomorrow would be fine. Two o'clock. Did you get the paperwork my lawyer prepared? More? What else do you need?"

Aaron was clearly annoyed with whomever he was speaking with.

"Right. We'll be there at two then. Unless Luc can't make it. He might have to be in court. Okay. All right."

When he clicked off, Aaron told her, "That was Ms. Forsyth from the Federal Aviation Agency. Once you're on their radar, they just don't let go."

"Is this the woman you got drunk in New Orleans?"

"I did not get her drunk. She did that all on her own."

"She invited you to dinner tonight. Does that mean she has the hots for you?"

"Probably. Are you jealous?"

"Hardly." Well, a little. "I thought your issues with the FAA were all cleared up."

"Not all of them."

"Are you worried?"

"Nah. One way or another, we'll work it out. I just need to be more careful."

"Maybe you should drop out of the missions. Take a break."

"Will you?"

"No!"

"Then I won't, either."

They couldn't say anything more because Tante Lulu was standing in the doorway with a pleased expression on her face. "Tee-John came by ta bring me some supplies and he dropped off yer present, Aaron." She narrowed her eyes at the two of them, then added, "And none too soon, either."

Fleur and Aaron looked at the large oak box decorated with hand-painted flowers. They both knew what it was.

"It looks like a small coffin," Aaron said. "I'd never fit."

"You know 'zackly what it is, you fool. Yer hope chest."

Fleur grinned, but only for a moment.

"And I put somethin' in there fer you, too, Fleur. A bride quilt."

The best laid plans of mice and men, and Cajun rogues . . .

When Aaron left for work late that morning, he'd had big plans for tonight. But, with one thing and another, he didn't get home until almost midnight.

Fleur was probably still waiting up for him, though, wearing a sheer negligee, or nothing at all. Wine would be chilling in an ice bucket next to his bed, on which black satin sheets had magically appeared. (*Where did one buy black satin sheets, by the way? At Walmart? Or one of those fancy bath stores? No, probably the Internet. Dumbmanideas.com or GettingLaid.com.*)

Or maybe she would be reclining like some 1940s pinup on the red velvet chaise lounge he'd mentioned to her. Yep. And Barry Manilow would be crooning something soft and sexy. A good choice would be "Looks Like We Made It." He sure as hell would like to make it. Love, that is.

In a far-off room, something delicious would be in a warming oven. For later. Maybe ribs. No, that would be messy. Oyster po' boys? Nah, they would be messy, too. Maybe some of the crawfish appetizer thingees like Samantha made for parties. Canapés, they were called. He teased her all the time, calling them can-a-peas. But, man, he could eat about two dozen of them right now. (*Did I forget to eat dinner tonight? Yeah, except for that bag of chips and a soda after I left Luc's office.*)

Most of all, Fleur would welcome him, smiling.

He couldn't wait.

To tell the truth, after the day he'd had, he doubted he would be up for anything, let alone a romp in the hay.

There had been one problem after another: some difficult customers who'd required him to circle the bayou
property they were interested in purchasing an extra
three times; a meeting with Luc about the FAA meeting
tomorrow which Aaron would, in fact, have to attend
alone; a quick stop at the hospital where Samantha got
way too much pleasure out of Aaron's description of the
mayhem at Bayou Rose (*Of course, she doesn't know
about the wallpaper yet.*); and a stop at the all-night
Starr Supermarket to purchase a few things Tante Lulu
requested, which turned into an overflowing basket after
a series of voice mails, each adding something she'd
forgotten to her list. Seriously, they needed twenty-four
double rolls of toilet paper?

He didn't intend to check in at the mansion at this
time of night, but when he saw lights on in the front
parlor, he decided to see who was still up. Maybe it was
Fleur, after all. But, no, she wouldn't be in the front
parlor. Or, at least, he didn't think so. There was that
red velvet chaise lounge, though. He grinned.

But then, he stopped grinning.

It was the Brothers Snake and Jake. *Oh, Lord! This
is the first time I realized that the two names rhyme.*
They were watching TV on a set which they must have
moved downstairs from one of the guest bedrooms.
Samantha didn't allow such modern conveniences to
mix with her antique furniture. And there was the dictator himself sprawled out, half on and half off, the red
velvet chaise lounge. There went that sexual fantasy!
They were dressed in shorts and T-shirts, presumably
sleep attire, watching *Game of Thrones* on cable. Beside each of them was an open Bible. Maybe they'd
been praying together, not watching the tube. Clarence

was quiet, for once, a shawl having been thrown over his cage.

"How's it hangin'?" Snake asked.

"That's some workday, buddy," Brother Jake remarked at the same time, glancing at his wristwatch. "Can I assume you got lucky? My door's always open for Penance. Ha, ha, ha."

"Ha, ha, ha! Back atcha!" *Did I mention these priests are like no other priests I've ever met?* That thought was reinforced with Snake's next question.

"Want a beer?" Snake asked, pointing to a cooler sitting between the chaise lounge and the Biedermeier rocking chair he was sitting on. Samantha had purchased it, the chair, not the cooler, at an auction last year for an amount she'd refused to disclose to Dan.

Aaron wondered idly if Samantha and Dan would expect him to purchase all this antique crap when they moved, or if they would take it with them? In fact, would Dan want him to buy out his half of the plantation? Man, he got a headache just thinking about all that. And, frankly, my dear (*yes, his brain was exploding with exhaustion*), if he was going to be stuck here alone, he'd prefer a swimming pool to two-hundred-year-old furniture.

On the other hand, maybe he and Dan would sell the whole kit and caboodle and divvy up the proceeds? (*Kit and caboodle? Jeesh! Hangin' around Tante Lulu much, Aaron? Next, I'll be saying, "Aw, shucks, y'all!" or "I do declare," or "Samantha looks like a giant balloon about to burst, bless her heart."*) Assuming there would be profits. A lot of their expensive improvements might not translate into a higher selling price.

"Sure," he said, belatedly, to Snake's offer of a beer, but wavered over whether he should sit on the floor, which was covered with an oriental carpet purchased at Costco, or the ratty love seat that had been a wedding gift from Aunt Mel. He opted for the floor where he sat cross-legged, and leaned back against the love seat. After taking an extended draw on the Dixie longneck, he let out a sigh. "No, I didn't get lucky," he finally answered Brother Jake. "I've been working . . . and shopping. Oh, hell! I forgot. I have to unload all those groceries Tante Lulu asked me to buy on the way home."

"I'll do it," Snake offered.

Which left Aaron alone with Father Frowny. Just great! Should he ask if it was true what they said about Navy SEALs, that they were badasses? Or he could tell him about his problems with the FAA? Then there was already the offer to hear his confession. But Aaron was saved from making some forced chitchat by Brother Jake's blunt question.

"What are your intentions toward Fleur?"

Aaron choked on the beer he'd just swallowed. "I beg your pardon. Are you for real? Not to mention, are you her long-lost father or something? Wait—I forgot. You are a father. Ha, ha, ha." Two could play at the jokey crap.

"No, I'm not her father, but I care about her. I've known Fleur since she was rescued. She's been through hell, both during her kidnapping period, and after. If she's going to jump the convent wall, I want to make sure there will be someone to catch her."

"I'll catch her," Aaron said without hesitation.

Brother Jake nodded, accepting him at his word, which surprised the hell out of Aaron.

"I love the woman, in case you hadn't noticed."

"Oh, I noticed, but the question is, does she love you?"

"Not yet."

Brother Jake nodded again. "Good luck with that. She's a strong-willed woman. Had to be to survive in those Mexican cesspits for six years. She would have made a great SEAL."

Aaron had a million questions he'd like to ask about the place where they'd found Fleur, what condition she'd been in then, had she really tried to kill Miguel with a baseball bat, what work she'd been doing with the Magdas and Street Apostles, and so on. But, he decided, it would be wrong to ask someone else. If he really wanted to know, he should ask Fleur. And if she didn't want him to know, that was that.

"How long have you been with the Street Apostles?" he asked instead.

"From the beginning, when they were formed, twelve years ago. I'd already left the teams . . . got too good at killing and my soul was turning black. So, I joined a seminary, studying to be a monk. But then, once I was ordained, I realized that the regular cloistered monk life didn't suit me."

"You weren't into making wine, or cheese, or God forbid, fruitcakes?" Aaron joked. At Brother Jake's arched brows, he explained, "I watched a Christmas special on the Food Network last year, featuring monkish gifts. That's the extent of my knowledge about the religious life."

"I'm lactose intolerant, and I would probably chug down all the booze, even the rum in the fruitcake. Hell, there was a time I would have stolen the little barrels of whiskey from the mastiffs' necks at the St. Bernard's Hospice, just to get a snort, not that those dogs ever really carried booze."

Aaron noticed then that Brother Jake was drinking Diet Coke. The beer must have been Snake's idea.

"No, I might have left the military, but I needed action. They say there are three reasons why a guy would want to become a SEAL. To prove something to himself, to prove something to someone else, or because he was bat-shit crazy. I fit all three at one time, and probably still do," Brother Jake went on, obviously enjoying his captive audience. "Anyhow, another monk and I, Sebastian Oliver, started the Street Apostles after we saw a TV special on the sex trafficking of young children in the Dallas area. I had inherited a small ranch from my grandparents, and Seb, a computer guru, had made a bundle in tech stocks. So, we were set."

Aaron hadn't realized that Brother Jake was one of the founders of the organization. "Does the Pope allow you guys to still be priests and do all the stuff you do?"

"As long as we keep it low-key and weaponless."

"Must have been difficult, though, to go from 'spray and pray' in the teams to weaponless fighting," Aaron speculated.

"In some ways, yes. In some ways, no. We've been forced to develop our own methods of covert ops, and they're always evolving. Instead of weapons, we rely on timing, skill, stealth, teamwork, creativity, and lots of prayer. Hiding in plain sight by the use of disguises. That kind of thing."

Aaron was beginning to like Brother Jake a little bit more. Not a lot. But a little.

Snake came back and asked Aaron, "You folks shit a lot around here?"

Aaron laughed.

Brother Jake asked, "What?"

"It's a private joke," Aaron said.

After that, the two men gave Aaron an update on the mission plans, and he was bowled over by how much had been done in his absence and how efficient the Street Apostles and Magdas were in planning their forays into the sex trafficking world. The situation was fluid and ever-changing, as Brother Jake had said, but they seemed able to adapt to those variations.

Aaron shouldn't have been surprised, based on past experience with these professionals. Maybe it was because this particular operation seemed more complex in terms of numbers and the trickiness of all the time elements coming together just right.

"Tell me more," Aaron encouraged Brother Jake.

"The perimeter of the truck depot in Lafayette has been secured as of this afternoon. The ETA for the big rig is twenty-three hundred on Friday night. The cargo from New Orleans should have arrived shortly before that. Everyone on our team will be boots on the ground and in place an hour earlier, no later than twenty-two hundred."

"In fact, some of the Street Apostles are already there, working at various spots around the truck depot," Snake added. "And, of course, we'll have spotters along the highway from the border crossing upward, and from New Orleans to Lafayette, notifying us of any glitches or changes in plans."

That was only two nights from now. Eleven p.m. for the exchange. Arrive an hour earlier. It was a two-hour drive to get there. All these calculations figured in Aaron's mind as his adrenaline jacked up about a hundred percent. The same way he'd felt when preparing for a bombing raid over Iraq when he was in the Air Force.

But he had mixed feelings about this particular mission. Yeah, he wanted this all to be over and successful, but he also dreaded the possible negative outcomes, especially with Fleur involved.

"So, if timing is everything," Aaron said, speaking his thoughts aloud, "there will be only that small window of opportunity when the exchange is about to take place. Are you prepared for that?"

"We are, as much as we can be, with God's help. Of course, any operation is a FUBAR waiting to happen," Brother Jake replied, a little pissed off by Aaron's questions, as indicated by the frown that furrowed his brow.

"Prepare for the worst, and hope for the best. And pray, pray, pray," Snake added with a laugh, clearly seeking to cool any rising temperatures. "We already have a rusted-out school bus, the smaller kind used to take kids on field trips or for special needs kids. It has a new logo painted on its side, 'Sisters of Mercy Day Camp.' It will hopefully carry a load of passengers back here to Bayou Rose. In addition, two vans, a Bayou Cable Co. box truck and Dick's Plumbing cargo van, will also be there to transport six girls each to the airport.

"Oh, and did I mention, we're hoping to use your pickup truck, Aaron?"

"Huh?"

"We'll put removable decals on the side, spelling out, 'Cajun Bob's Produce.' It'll be loaded with potatoes and melons, high enough to cover some of the Street Apostles hiding underneath, if that becomes necessary."

"We wanted it to be melons and peaches, but you know how the Irish are with their potatoes," Brother Jake teased Snake, who just grinned.

Aaron shook his head to clear it of confusion. "I don't see the connection between the nuns and Farmer Bob," Aaron said.

"Several nuns from the Sisters of Mercy will be there, picking up donated produce from Bob's farm. They'll provide the distraction once the perps arrive in the lot so that we can gain control of their vehicles and the 'cargo,'" Brother Jake explained.

"Nuns? Which nuns?"

"Sister Mary Michael. Sister Carlotta. Sister Fleur."

Aaron groaned. "Oh, no, no, no!"

"Oh, yes, yes, yes," Brother Jake countered. He explained in detail how the convoluted plan would play out.

"There are so many variables in this half-assed scheme that could go wrong," Aaron countered.

"And more variables that could make it work," Snake said. "Trust us, Aaron. We know what we're doing."

That was debatable, in Aaron's opinion. He decided then and there that he was going to be carrying a weapon.

"And don't be thinkin' to hide a pistol in your pocket, laddie," Snake said, as if reading Aaron's mind.

"Laddie my ass," Aaron muttered.

Brother Brian just grinned, then continued explaining the plan in more detail. "The commercial vehicles will go to the airport outside Lafayette. I've arranged for two planes to be gassed up and approved for take-off sometime between eleven p.m. and one a.m., one destined for Mexico where the girls will then be taken to the convent, the other for Dallas and ultimately the ranch."

"It's a two-hour drive from here to Lafayette, and, yes, we could have operated from a base closer to the target site," Brother Jake said, "but, in the end, the remoteness here is an advantage that overweighs that long drive to and from."

Aaron nodded, reluctantly, knowing one of those planes was designated for him. Even so, the mission seemed monumental and fraught with possibilities for screw-ups. Most dangerous of all was the fact that the bad guys would be carrying guns, and they would not.

His continued skepticism must have shown on his face because Snake went into a lengthy explanation of the day's happenings, probably to illustrate that they were not amateurs. "Mother Jacinta's crew has been busy and incredibly efficient here at the plantation, making arrangements for the late-night arrivals. As you know, the Magdas have a network of volunteers that kick into gear on a moment's notice. A medical doctor from Alabama is coming in, which means that Dan won't have to be involved, although he did offer to come in as backup, if needed."

When had that been arranged? And how come Dan had failed to mention it tonight?

"A social worker from Dallas will work with the girls, starting Saturday morning, getting family histories, notifying parents in some cases, looking for placements in others. Most will be under the age of eighteen. That's considered experienced and 'tired goods' in the prostitute business when they've started at thirteen," Snake went on. "By Sunday, the dozen girls here should be down to six or fewer. They'll all be gone by midweek."

It sounded great in theory, but would it pan out in

reality? "Exactly how many people are involved in this operation, including volunteers for the small jobs, like highway spotting?"

"Seventeen," Brother Jake replied.

"Unbelievable!" Aaron said.

"We're a well-oiled fighting machine when we have to be," Brother Jake concurred, taking Aaron's exclamation as a compliment, "even without artillery. It's all in the planning."

Aaron rose, about to depart. "One more question. Besides being a nun, what will Fleur be doing in this operation?"

"Driving the bus," both men answered with grins.

That was just great, Aaron thought, as he returned to his *garçonniére* apartment. Right in the middle of the fray. Possibly chased by gun-toting bad guys.

But that settled it. There was always a danger in any military operation, whether it be on behalf of Uncle Sam or some poor kidnapped girls, and there was always a chance that someone was going to get hurt, or killed. He needed to get up close and personal with Fleur before that happened, and tomorrow was the only time he had to do that.

The Brothers Jake and Snake weren't the only ones good at making plans. Aaron had a few strategies of his own and a skill set he hadn't yet utilized.

He smiled.

Fleur didn't stand a chance.

Chapter Twelve

God's dream team at work . . .

Brother Jake might think he was the king of the hill upstairs, and Mother Jacinta clearly ordered her nuns and volunteers about with an iron hand, but Louise ruled the kitchen. She was busier than a moth in a mitten, ordering everybody about down in the kitchen.

By ten a.m. on Thursday morning, a huge pot of gumbo was boiling away on the stove, two Peachy Praline Cobbler Cakes were baking in the oven, five loaves of bread were rising on the counter, and that was just the start. A triple batch of Alaskan Fried Green Tomatoes sat draining on paper towels for munching throughout the day. They were yummy, even at room temperature.

Of course, she had lots of helpers. Mel, Fleur, Mother

Jacinta, whom she had known for a long time, and the
Sisters Mary Michael and Carlotta. They were all preparing for the influx of girls who would arrive tomorrow
night, God and St. Jude willing. But there was work to
be done for all the folks already here, as well.

The morning had started at sunrise with Mass in the
library for those who were up. Brother Brian had cele-
brated the Sacrament, assisted by Brother Jake, both in
traditional priestly attire for once. The service had
been simple, but rejuvenating.

There had been no sermon, except for Brother Brian's
words, "Please bless our work, Lord, as we go about
Your business today. We especially ask for Your holy
assistance with the rescue of all these young women,
and keep us pure of heart so that we may forgive those
who perpetrate these evil deeds."

"Amen," Brother Jake had said.

Louise had felt compelled to interject a comment
then, even though it was not right to interrupt a priest
during Mass. "And doan fergit St. Jude. Nothin' is hopeless when he's got yer back."

Brother Jake had winked at her, right in the middle
of Mass, and said, "St. Jude, patron saint of hopeless
cases and namesake for our very own Street Apostles,
let us never lose faith. No mission is impossible if we
trust in you and our Holy Lord."

Everyone chorused, "Amen!" then.

At about one o'clock, Louise said to Fleur, who was
helping her clean up the kitchen, "Come with me upstairs to my room. I'm gonna take a little nap. Bring
yer laptop and the receipt book, too."

Fleur looked up at her with alarm. "A nap? Are you
okay?"

"I'm fine. A power snooze never hurt no one. Besides, it's good to have some alone time."

Still, Fleur was overprotective of her, helping with an arm under her elbow as they climbed the stairs. Not that Louise needed her help. She might be slow but she still got where she was going.

When they got to the guest room which she shared with Mel now that there were additional folks about, Louise lay down on one of the twin beds, propping herself against two pillows, and Fleur drew a chair up beside her, opening her computer on her lap.

"Where did we leave off las' time we talked about herbs?" Louise asked.

"Bayou plants useful with babies."

"Thass right. Oh, before I fergit. I was thinkin' las' night how I tol' ya 'bout all the trips through the swamps I took with my mother and my MawMaw, lookin' fer rare plants. Didja know, when snakes are threatened, a water moccasin smells like cucumbers and water snakes stink like rotten cabbage?"

"Is that really true?"

Louise shrugged. "All I know is, if I start getting' a sudden hankerin' fer sauerkraut or a stalk of salted celery, it's time ta skedaddle."

"Oh, my! I don't think I'll be able to eat anything with celery or cabbage in it anymore." Fleur shivered with distaste.

"Snakes ain't so bad, and I've seen my share over all the years I've traveled up and down the bayou in my pirogue. I s'pose you and me'll hafta go out and gather more plants if those lowlifes ruined some of my stock." Something occurred to Louise then and she turned on her side to look at the girl. "You are comin' back ta my cottage with me after this is over, aren't you?"

"I suppose so." Fleur sounded uncertain, though, and her face flushed with color.

"What? Did ya decide ta become a nun, after all?"

Fleur shook her head. "No. I haven't made a firm decision, but it's looking more and more like that's not the life for me."

"Because of Aaron."

"No!" Fleur said, way too fiercely, but then she amended that to, "Maybe."

Louise nodded. Things were going just as St. Jude and the Thunderbolt intended.

"It's not that Aaron and I are a couple, or anything like that. But I'm attracted to him, and if I can be drawn to a man—any man—then I must not have a true vocation."

"Doan be lookin' all guilty like. Ya kin still serve God without bein' a nun. Even if ya got married and had babies."

"Oh, I'm not thinking about that! Besides, I already told you that I probably can't have children."

"You never tol' me that, or mebbe I forgot."

"A doctor who examined me one time said I would probably never be able to conceive. Something about scar tissue." Fleur's face got even redder, and Louise knew there must be more to that story.

"You kin have children without bearin' them yerself. And, by the way, Remy and Rachel adopted a bunch of kids because he was wounded in the Iraqi war and became sterile. And guess what? He and Rachel became pregnant after all. Turns out, the doctors ain't allus right." Louise yawned behind her hand and shimmied down on the bed a bit.

"You're tired," Fleur said. "Let's put off the herb work until another time."

"All right," Louise said and yawned again.

"Don't feel like you have to get up soon. I'll keep an eye on the kitchen. I might not know how to make bread, but I can certainly bake it." As she was gathering up the laptop and the receipt book, her cell phone rang. Fleur glanced at the screen and smiled as she read something. It must be one of those text message thingies.

When Fleur put the phone in the pocket of her shorts, Louise asked, "Aaron?" The boy had been gone all day, since early this morning.

Fleur nodded. "He wants to take me out to dinner."

And what else? Finally, the boy is doin' what comes natural. Louise wanted to let out a little whoop of triumph but she held back, knowing how skittish Fleur could be on the subject. "But we already have dinner planned fer t'night," she pretended to argue. As if it was dinner Aaron had in mind!

"I don't have to go."

"Thass all right." Louise sighed. *I am such a good actress. I shoulda been in the movies.* "It will be good fer you ta get away fer a bit. Is it safe, though?"

"Aaron says it is, where we're going. Not that I know where that is."

I kin guess. "That settles it then."

Once she was alone, Louise had a little talk with St. Jude in her head, like she always did. "So far, so good!"

We make a good team, the voice said.

A boat, the bayou, and Barry . . . what else could she want? . . .

Fleur was ready for her date. The first one in her entire life! How strange was that?

She felt both apprehensive and excited at the same time. Being alone with Aaron, away from the plantation, seemed like crossing a line.

Not that she hadn't crossed that line a few times already with the bayou bad boy, but each time she'd bounced right back. Would she be able to retreat once again after tonight?

She took one last look at herself in the mirror on the back of the bathroom door. She should have never told Tante Lulu about Aaron's invitation to dinner because, of course, the interfering busybody (bless her heart), aware of Fleur's limited wardrobe, had called Charmaine and asked for help. Thus the pretty coral sundress with spaghetti straps, big white belt, and high-heeled white sandals she wore now, from Charmaine's very own bimbo closet. Not that this attire was slutty, just not Fleur's style. *Like I have a style?* Fleur even borrowed some mascara and lip gloss from Samantha's stash in the medicine cabinet. After she'd shampooed her hair, she'd blown it dry and left it loose about her shoulders.

Fleur barely recognized herself. Was she trying too hard? For a moment, embarrassment flooded her, and she would have changed her outfit, except she checked her watch and saw it was already five forty-five. Aaron had asked her to meet him out front at six.

With a sigh of surrender she headed toward the front staircase. Hopefully, everyone was still down in the kitchen lingering over dinner. No one had come looking for her; so, she assumed that Tante Lulu had made her excuses.

Luck was not with her, though, because sitting out on the front gallery was Mother Jacinta, saying her beads. A cup of after-dinner coffee steamed in a china cup and saucer on a white, wrought iron table. Mother sat on a matching, cushioned, wrought iron chair, one of a set, all of which were probably antiques that Samantha had picked up at an estate sale.

"Oh, don't you look lovely!" Mother Jacinta said. "I'm so glad I got a chance to see you before I leave in the morning."

"You're leaving?" Fleur sank down into the other chair.

"Yes, I want to be at the convent to greet the new girls when they arrive tomorrow night."

"You seem certain that the mission will work, and the girls will be rescued."

"As certain as one can be with God on our side." She raised her rosary beads in the air. "But it's always best to back up optimism with prayer."

"I've missed you, Mother."

"And I've missed you, too. But I can see that this 'retreat' has been good for you."

"You can?" Fleur wasn't so sure.

Mother nodded. "You will not be taking final vows."

Fleur froze. Was this yet another line she was crossing? And was it evident to everyone? "How can you tell?"

"You're different already. Oh, not in your inner goodness, child. Don't ever think that I'm judging you. No, I just mean that you're glowing."

"I've been out in the sun too much."

"Or perhaps you are being given a chance for a new beginning. To start all over with a clean slate."

"Hardly a clean slate!"

"Tsk-tsk-tsk! Isn't it time for you to stop wallowing in guilt? If God forgives you, how can you do any less?"

"I'm not in love," Fleur blurted out and could have bitten her tongue. Where had those words come from? A classic case of protesting too much, it must appear.

"That's too bad. It's the most important thing in the world, you know."

"Have you been talking to Tante Lulu? She's been pushing me toward Aaron from the first minute I got here."

"She means well."

"Yes, but—"

Just then they heard a door slam, and Aaron walked out of the *garçonniére*, heading toward his pickup truck in the driveway. He waved at the two of them.

And, oh, my! He had prepared for their date, too. He must have gotten a haircut this afternoon. Not overly short like his brother's but decidedly shorter and well styled. He'd shaved, as well. He wore his cowboy boots, highly polished tonight, but instead of his usual T-shirt and faded denims, he had on a light blue, long-sleeve, tapered dress shirt, worn outside a pair of black jeans.

Fleur stood, then leaned down to kiss Mother Jacinta on the cheek. "I'll call this weekend to see how everything is going at your end."

Mother squeezed her hand and said, "Be happy, my dear."

Do I even know how anymore? Do I have the right to be happy? Or is Mother right, that I need to move on from my past?

Aaron helped her into his truck, which was a little high to climb with her shoes. "You look amazing," he said before he closed the door.

"So do you."

He smiled then, dimple and all. "I've been waiting for this night for a long, long time."

"I thought your dinner invitation was a last-minute idea."

"Oh, sweetheart, I wasn't referring to dinner. I've been waiting for you and this night all my life."

Yikes! That sounded ominous.

They drove companionably along the two-lane road, chatting about the day's events, with her ducking or turning aside anytime they passed another vehicle, just in case Miguel or his thugs were still in the vicinity.

He told her about his meeting with the FAA people this afternoon. It appeared as if his problems were over for the time being, thanks to some favors Tante Lulu had apparently called in from someone in D.C. "Really, that woman gives a new name to networking," Aaron said.

She regaled him with stories about the running feud between Brother Jake and Sister Mary Michael over some lesser role he'd assigned her for the mission. And they both laughed when she told him that the animals following Brother Brian had gotten so bad that when he went to the bathroom they trotted in after him, which prompted him to shove them all in the rain forest shower and turn on the water. The barking, meowing, and oinking could be heard a mile away. And the mess when they came out took an hour to clean up.

At some point, he'd tugged her closer, across the bench seat so that they were shoulder to shoulder. When he wasn't using his right hand to shift gears, he rested it on her thigh.

They'd already traveled a couple miles along Bayou Black, in the opposite direction from Houma or any other towns where restaurants might be located. In fact, until they'd passed Tante Lulu's cottage, Fleur thought he might have been taking her there. But then, they also passed Fleur's old homestead, which looked as ramshackle and seedy as always. She was surprised that the place hadn't fallen down onto itself long ago. But there must be someone living there because there was an old truck parked in a driveway overgrown with weeds.

Aaron didn't say anything as they passed, and she wasn't about to call it to his attention. Maybe he wasn't aware that she'd lived there once.

"Where are we going?" she finally asked.

"It's a surprise," he said. "We're almost there."

They soon came to a large property where a sprawling ranch house perched on a man-built rise overlooking the bayou. "That's Remy LeDeux's place," he told her. Just beyond Remy's property, he veered his truck off onto a dirt road until they reached the same bayou, farther along, where a houseboat was anchored.

"This is where we're having dinner?"

"Uh-huh! No way Miguel would ever think to look for you here."

She slid over and was about to open her passenger door.

"No, wait," Aaron said, getting out of the truck and coming around to her side. "M'lady," he quipped as he handed her down.

"Chivalry is not dead on the bayou," she said.

"We knights do aim to please."

That's what she was afraid of.

He took her hand and led her down a path toward a small dock, then across a ramp onto the boat itself. The

sun wouldn't set for another hour or two; so, the water
and its surroundings were fairly calm and noise-free.
The craft itself was rather shabby, but clean and impos-
ing in size. It might once have been a luxury toy for
some millionaire.

"Why does Remy own a houseboat?"

"He bought it used years ago when he got out of the
service. He'd been wounded pretty bad in Desert Storm
and needed a place to stay. The house we saw back
there wasn't built yet. It was either this houseboat or
live with Tante Lulu."

They smiled at each other at that prospect.

"Anyhow, Remy rents it out occasionally. I lived here
for a while before Dan and I bought the plantation."

There was a railed porch or deck that ran around all
sides of the boat. They went toward the back, facing
the bayou, and he opened a screen door for her, letting
her enter first.

She gasped. "Oh, Aaron! This is wonderful!"

A large great room included a salon, a galley
kitchen, and an alcove office. A built-in booth beside
the kitchen held a candle centerpiece. A skylight let in
enough of the fading sun to turn the cypress walls and
floors to a golden yellow. Red fluffy pillows lined the
window seat storage units, and a huge oriental carpet,
once jewel-toned, now faded rose, sage green, black,
and ivory, covered a large portion of the floor.

"Rachel, Remy's wife, is a feng shui decorator. She
did most of the work here," Aaron explained as he
leaned back against the wall, arms folded over his
chest, watching her examine the inside of the boat with
obvious delight.

"But you've been busy here, too," she commented,

making note of the fat candle on the kitchen table, as well as the fragrant, lit candles throughout the room. She couldn't help but notice how clean the place looked, too, and that all the brass fittings gleamed. Even the narrow horizontal windows that lined the room on two sides sparkled within their frameworks of red velvet drapes. It should have looked bordello-ish, with all that red, but instead it spoke of class and old money. "You must have spent hours getting this place ready."

"I did."

"A great bachelor pad."

Aaron nodded. "It was, for Remy, at one time. But then he married Rachel, they had a bunch of kids, adopted and natural, and a boat no longer suited them."

She noticed that he hadn't mentioned himself in the context of a horny man cave. Had he brought other women here? But she wasn't about to ask that. "You've been busy with cooking, too," she remarked, sniffing the air. Overriding the scented candles and beeswax cleaners was the smell of something in the oven.

"Not cooking. Warming up. I bought take-out from a Houma restaurant. Oysters Rockefeller for appetizers, surf and turf for entrées, as in steak and lobster thermidor, a Caesar salad, and bread pudding for dessert. Are you hungry?"

"Not yet."

He walked over to the mini fridge, took out a bottle, and poured white wine into two stemmed glasses. He handed one to her and took a sip from the other before placing it on the counter. Reaching back, he flicked a switch which immediately turned on a sound system, and soft Cajun music filled the air.

Turning to her, he said, "Well, I am."

"What?"

"Hungry. In fact, ravenous." The way he looked at her, she knew he didn't mean food. "Can I kiss you now? I've wanted to ever since I first saw you coming down the front steps of Bayou Rose in that sexy dress and hot-damn high heels."

She took a huge gulp of her wine, which burned a path down her throat and settled low in her stomach, radiating shards of sweet shock out to all her extremities.

Aaron walked up to her, took the wine glass, which she'd been clutching with two hands, away from her, and set it on the table behind her. Before he laid his lips on hers, before he took her face in his palms, before he whispered, "Oh, Fleur," he closed his eyes. His dark lashes made fan shapes on his upper cheeks, and he looked so handsome that Fleur wanted to trace the outlines of his jaw, the hidden dimple, his cheekbones, even his eyebrows, but that would have to come later.

Because he kissed her.

And it was everything a kiss should be.

Fleur was reminded of some country song about a kiss—by Faith Hill, as she recalled. The song talked about a certain man's kiss being a pivotal moment, a combination of centrifugal motion and perpetual bliss. The singer mentioned sensations of floating and flying at the same time.

All of those impressions flitted through Fleur's body, hazing her mind until she became mindless.

Aaron's hands, which had been framing her face, moved to her back, tugging her closer, making wide sweeps down her back, along the bare skin of her shoulders and arms, even cupping her buttocks and pressing her against his erection.

Her hands were busy, too, running fingertips through his hair, stroking the bristles of his shaved jaw, caressing his shoulders. And, yes, she even moved her hands over his tight bottom, too.

And they were dancing.

How had that happened?

And why was she reminded of Aaron's teasing comment one time about them dancing naked? They weren't naked now. But it felt like it. And there was no Barry Manilow song playing. But wait, the stereo system clicked and a new stream of songs came on, starting with "Ready to Take a Chance." She would have smiled at Aaron's foresight, if she had a chance to think past the whirlwind of emotion flooding her mind and body.

And then, she *was* naked, wearing nothing but a plain white, strapless bra, bikini underpants, and the white high heels. *Did he do that?*

And, lo and behold, his shirt was unbuttoned, and his jeans were unsnapped and unzipped. *Did I do that?*

And still, they danced.

Aaron was right. Kissing was one of his top three talents. And dancing was right up there at number four.

Was she about to find out about his top two?

Would she survive?

Chapter Thirteen

*S**he was the ultimate prize . . .***

Aaron talked a good game when it came to sex, and, hell, yes, he was a player. In the past. This night with Fleur was a whole new ball game for him, though. The goal—or the trophy—was Fleur herself.

And that would be better than a Heisman Trophy any old day, ha, ha, ha.

Have I mentioned, I'm losing it here?

But seriously, winning Fleur would require new rules, new strategies, and maybe a Hail Mary pass or two. Bottom line: There was no playbook.

Please, God, help me do this right, he prayed. *St. Jude, you suited up yet? Okay, that has to be a new low for me. Praying for sex.*

Well, why not? the voice in his head said.

There was a time when he would have laughed at any person who said they talked to voices in their head. Looney Tunes, for sure. But that was before he'd moved to Louisiana and was introduced to the saint channeler, aka Tante Lulu. All the LeDeuxs experienced it at one time or another.

Families pray before meals. Soldiers pray before battle, El Voice-o continued. *God created sex. He wants people to do it, for heaven's sake. Within the confines of the Holy Sacrament, of course.*

I would marry Fleur in a heartbeat, if she would have me.

We'll hold you to that.

"Are you talking to yourself?" Fleur asked.

"No, I'm praying."

Instead of laughing, she said, "Me, too."

Aaron picked Fleur up and carried her, Rhett-style, into the bedroom. He hoped he wouldn't trip over his jeans. Somehow, Fleur had managed to unsnap and unzip him without his embarrassing himself. But, no, his pants were in no danger of falling down. They were being held up by his mondo erection, hereafter to be referred to as Super Dick.

How embarrassing!

On the other hand, how amazing!

He tossed her on the bed, a queen-size, not the king-size which he was accustomed to, but one of those would never fit in this small space. There were no lamps, but there was enough light from all the candles that he could see the glow of her eyes.

"It smells like a rose garden in here," she murmured.

"Or else a frickin' funeral parlor," he countered with a self-deprecating grimace.

"Are you nervous?"

"No. My hands shake like this all the time."

"You don't have to—"

"Shh." He put up a halting hand. "No talking. I need to concentrate." And he did, studying the "treat" spread out before him, wondering where to start.

Even though she wore a plain white bra and bikini underpants, nothing Victoria's Secret extreme, she looked sexy to him. In fact, he liked that she hadn't gone out of her way to sex herself up, like many females did on a date. If he never saw another set of silk tap pants, and, yes, he knew what they were, or a push-up bra that raised boobs to impossible heights, it wouldn't bother him a bit.

She looked dazed now, as she lay where he'd placed her, unmoving, just staring up at him as he undressed, almost falling over as he stood on one foot, then another, trying to get out of his damn boots. He loved his cowboy boots, usually, but at times like this, they were . . . inconvenient.

When he was full commando, she continued to study him. No "ooh baby, you are so big," or anything phony like that. But she didn't look unhappy, either. Aaron had a good body, and knew it, but he imagined that she'd seen . . .

No, no, no! I am not going there.

He went to the foot of the bed and removed her high heels, then tugged down her panties, exposing a patch of pretty dark curls. Again, no special effort made to entice. No female grooming, like a runway strip. Or glitter, which was the trend for some women today. Vajazzling, they called it. Which he personally considered a bit silly. A waste of crystals. And, man, they were a pain in the ass to get out of the sheets afterward. It was like sleeping on pebbles.

Kneeling on the edge of the mattress, he spread her legs, then moved between them, but not too high. He was still looking. A man liked to look at what he was doing. With an expertise learned as an adolescent on the dress form owned by the grandmother of his friend, Freddie Mack, he flicked his fingers just so, and voilà! The bra was off.

"You are so pretty, Fleur," he said, feasting on her breasts, in fact, all of her body.

"So are you."

He tried to smile, but he was in agony. "Fleur, honey, I can't wait." He moved up and over her, touching her between her legs. She was thankfully damp. So, without preamble, he rolled on a condom, took himself in hand, and placed the tip of Super Dick at her opening. Then, bracing himself on straightened arms, he eased inside.

She was tight, but there were no welcoming spasms from her inner folds. Damn! She was not as turned on as he'd thought she was. Either that, or her mind might be aroused, but her body was not.

He slid out and then back in again, to satisfy his own need. But then he forced himself to freeze.

She must have sensed his disappointment because she said, "I'm sorry. My body has learned to shut down. It probably can't respond anymore, not like you want." Tears filled her eyes.

"Oh, Fleur! I love you. Whatever you give me is enough." He began to kiss her then. Slow, drugging kisses that went on and on. It felt like starting over again, which was fine. He would do what he had to do to win Fleur.

She put her arms around his shoulders, which he took for a good sign. She was trying.

Still embedded in her, still kissing her, alternating with murmurs of encouragement, he played with her breasts, remembering how sensitive they'd been before. He played with her ears, too. Slowly, he was learning about her body's erotic spots. His fingers also traveled lower and gently flicked her clit.

She squirmed under his hands, and he felt a quivering spasm against his cock.

His body's inclination then was to begin the long thrusts that would bring him to completion. But he sensed they would be too soon for her.

With sweat beading his forehead, he rolled over onto his back, taking her with him so that now she sat astride his erection which he could swear was pulsing like a heartbeat. "You call the shots here, darlin'. Move or not. Touch me or not." *Or just sit there like a female Buddha, torturing me to death.*

Leaning forward, she explored his face and neck and shoulders with her fingertips.

Little did she know that her position, moving forward, gave him even greater pleasure, and in fact should be putting pressure on that bud of hers that he'd already stimulated.

She moved back to sit her rump on his thighs, and once again the movement gave his cock a jolt of pleasure. "Tell me what you want me to do," she said.

"It's not what I want. It's what you want."

"I don't want anything."

Oh, great! He closed his eyes and tried not to panic. "Does nothing with me please you, Fleur?"

"I like touching you and seeing your response. I like

your kisses and I liked when you touched my breasts, but the rest . . ." She shrugged.

Man, oh, man! This was bad. Very bad. With infinite care, he withdrew his swollen cock from her, then rolled over onto his side, tucking her face onto his chest. He kissed the top of her hair. "Do you trust me, Fleur?" he asked.

She nodded against his chest. Even her breath against his nipple was sheer agony.

"Then just let me love you," he husked out, "and I do love you, Fleur."

"But—"

"No buts. We'll work through this."

And for the next hour, they did work. Well, *he* did, harder than he'd ever worked in his life, to arouse his love. Maybe she wouldn't come from intercourse the first time, but he was going to try his best to make sex at least enjoyable for her.

If he'd been thinking clearly, he would have gone into the bathroom and taken care of business before starting on this venture into unknown territory. But he hadn't and now . . . pure torture!

He kissed, he stroked, he fluttered, he whispered soft words, he groaned and sighed. He used his mouth, his breath, his fingers and palms, even his hairy legs to excite Fleur's deadened nerves. Well, not totally deadened or she wouldn't have climaxed those two other times for him.

After an hour of this torment, more for him than her, obviously, Fleur thrashed her head from side to side and moaned, "Oh . . . please . . . now . . . oh . . ."

That was his cue.

This time when he entered her, his overstimulated

cock was met with soft spasms. *Thank you, Jesus!* he thought, then immediately amended, *Oops, sorry, that was not appropriate.*

It didn't last long. How could it, the condition he was in?

He began the long, slow strokes which almost immediately became short and hard. Not too hard, he kept telling himself, when he was able to focus even a little through the fog of his overarousal. Hard might equate to force or assault with Fleur. And God help him, he never wanted her to think of that during sex again.

Still, she seemed to welcome him. Staring up at him in wide-eyed wonder, or surprise, she tried so hard to be accommodating—to please him—when the goal was to please her.

But he couldn't keep his eyes open. When he could no longer forestall his climax, he squeezed his lids shut, arched his back till the cords in his neck about popped, and came with a wild, hot, ecstatic rush.

Fleur moaned, then cried out as her back bowed in her attempt to meet him in a mutual climax. And she did come! Not in wildly convulsing squeezes of her inner muscles, but gentle waves of spasms.

For a long moment, he lay flat on top of her, unable to breathe. A quick glance at the bedside clock showed him that it had been an hour and a half since he'd brought Fleur to the houseboat. He almost chuckled as he recalled that old song "Sixty Minute Man." Yep, Aaron had finally joined the club.

When he was able to raise his head, he saw that she was looking up at him with a shy smile on her face. "That was nice," she said.

Nice? NICE? Whaaat? Is there a man in the world who wants his bedroom skills to be called nice?

Oooh, that was a challenge if he ever heard one.

Rubber duckie, you're the one . . .

Fleur knew that Aaron was disappointed. *She* was disappointed. In herself. Not him. He'd been wonderful. Patient. Kind. Teasing. Loving. But she was less than a woman, and it showed. No matter how much she'd tried, Fleur couldn't be normal. Parts of her were too scarred over to have feelings anymore.

Not that she hadn't enjoyed his lovemaking. She had. In a mildly pleasant way. But it was not the way women should respond to expert sex play. Not the way Aaron's partners behaved, she was sure of that.

She'd warned him, but did he listen? No. He thought that love conquered all. Even her broken body. He thought he could work a miracle.

Well, now he knew.

No sense trying to slither out of bed. He had her pinned with a knee over her thighs and his head on her breast as he took a breather. Or maybe he was asleep. But no, the second she tried to push him off, he was alert and looking down at her.

"Um . . . I think you should take me back to Bayou Rose now."

"Huh? We have a good six to seven hours yet."

Since he'd raised his head, she managed to push his knee off her legs and was about to roll away from him.

He caught her with a hand on her hip and turned her on her side to face him. Which was even worse because now her body parts—her *nude* body parts—were aligned with his nude and growing (*Again!*) body parts.

"Aaron!" she chided. "I should return while everyone is asleep."

Nuzzling her neck, he murmured, "I figure if I take you back around three a.m., everyone will still be asleep. Not that we're fooling anyone, but still we can try to be discreet."

"Six to seven hours! What would we be doing for all that time?" She realized her mistake immediately. She grabbed at that hand which was wandering where it shouldn't and arched her head back to glare at him.

He grinned and tried to pull her into his embrace again. "Making love, darlin'. That's what we'll be doing."

She sighed at the hopelessness of arguing with a horny man, but still she tried. "Don't pretend that I was anything but a dud, Aaron."

"What? Are you kidding? Do you hear me complaining?"

"That's because you're too nice."

"*Nice* again? We have got to wipe that word from your vocabulary. I am not nice. I am a lean, mean . . . ouch! Stop squirming."

"Stop putting your hand there."

"Whatever you say, honey," he said, batting his eyelashes with innocence. "Fleur, I loved making love to you, and if that was only nice for you, I promise I can do better. With practice." Now he was not only batting his eyelashes, but waggling his eyebrows at her. "Besides, that was just the appetizer. And speaking of food, maybe we should refuel." He got up off the bed and disposed of the used condom in a waste basket. "But first, I have something to show you."

She rolled her eyes and attempted to pull a sheet up to cover her nudity. "I've seen it, and it's very nice."

"*Nice* again. I swear, you are going to eat those words." He yanked the sheet back down and stared at her body with deliberate intensity. "No, this is something else. Sex toys."

That was her cue to exit, fast. "I have to go to the bathroom," she lied.

"Good. We'll go together."

"We will not!"

He took her hand and yanked her off the bed, forcing her to follow him.

"Are you crazy? I do not share a bathroom. And sex toys are the last thing I—"

He opened the bathroom door and she had to laugh. Even though the room wasn't large, there was a big shower stall with a dozen or more faucets that would hit the body at different angles.

"I got the idea for the rainforest shower at Bayou Rose from this," he told her, shoving her into the stall and stepping in after her. After the door was closed, he turned on one of the faucets, and a warm spray hit her square in the face. It was probably a deliberate hit.

"So, a shower is a sex toy?" she sputtered out.

"It can be, but here's the best sex toy of all." He handed her a bar of soap. "You can play with me all you want."

Which she did.

And then he did.

At one point she remarked, "Soap as a sex toy? What next? A rubber duckie?"

"How did you know? That's one of my nicknames for . . ." He glanced downward at his erection. "When we were kids, and took baths together, Dan and I used to see these little things bobbing in the water and we called them rubber duckies."

She laughed. "So you name your . . . um, body part? Honestly, I never know when you're teasing or not."

"Swear to God," he said, making the sign of the cross on his wet chest. "He also answers to Super Dick, or just 'Hey, you!'"

"He?"

"Of course, *he*!" he answered indignantly.

Afterward, as she ate voraciously of the meal he set before her and drank the wine he continued to replenish in her glass, she began to feel a little more relaxed and womanly. He'd wanted her to sit on his lap while they ate, which she'd declined. But then, he might have been teasing again. Instead, they sat across from each other in the kitchen booth, which was cozy in the candlelight.

He was wearing only boxer shorts, and she wore his blue dress shirt, but she didn't mind too much. It was either that, or eat naked, which would be way out of her comfort zone.

Barry Manilow music played softly in the background, and to her amazement, she was becoming a fan. As they ate and listened to the music, they talked. Aaron told her of life in Alaska while his mother was still alive and how he and Daniel came to live in Louisiana. Tante Lulu, of course, had a hand in that. Fleur laughed a lot, or smiled as he told stories of the antics he and his twin indulged in growing up, and then as adults. The overly serious Daniel and the wild Aaron.

She found herself talking about her past, too. Some of it. Growing up in poverty with eight siblings in a small stilted cottage on the bayou, but somehow she was recalling some good parts. Catching crawfish, or mudbugs as they called them, with nothing but a leafy branch and a bushel basket. Playing barefoot in the pudding-like mud. Rowing a pirogue through the swamps with her older sister Gloria searching for wild Indians (her brothers Joe Lee and Eustace). Singing in the church choir.

He smiled as she talked and took one of her hands in his, as if sensing that she was giving him a rare gift. A peek into a painful past. He never asked about the day she was kidnapped or the months and years afterward. Nor did he ask what happened when she tried to go home after being rescued.

He didn't say the words, but she saw them in his eyes. The eyes did not lie. He loved her.

And she was pretty sure she was falling in love, too.

When they went back to the bedroom, they continued their soft conversation and finished off the bottle of wine. She let him caress her body, *everywhere*, while they continued to exchange memories. She knew that it was a deliberate ploy to distract her while he attempted to arouse her body for more lovemaking, but she allowed it. At first, she allowed it because she owed him. Later, she allowed it because it felt so good to go from mellow to a thrumming awareness of her skin and heightened senses. Still later, she turned the tables and worked diligently to examine his body, which was so different from hers, and remarkably alike in its erotic spots.

To her surprise, Fleur didn't find these things she did with Aaron as repugnant as she'd imagined they would be. They didn't trigger memories of other things she'd done with men because there were no similarities. This was lovemaking.

When Aaron entered her this time, it was still not wild, screaming sex, but it was good. Very good. And when she whispered, at the end, "I think I love you," there were tears in Aaron's eyes.

Family ties . . .

Aaron had no time the next day to be with Fleur, in private. Just a look exchanged, or a passing touch. Fleur had told him last night that she thought she loved him. That was enough. For now.

Soon after dawn, the Brothers Jake and Snake said Mass in the library for all those currently at Bayou Rose, including a bevy of miraculously quiet and well-behaved animals in front of the altar/library table. When it was time for Communion, Snake arched a brow at Aaron and Fleur as if questioning whether they were in a state of grace to receive the host, but he gave it to them anyway.

For some reason, Aaron couldn't think of what they'd done as sinful. Aaron knew what sex-as-sin was, the kind that made the parish priest blush and inflict a humongous penance on a randy youth. This wasn't it.

Another breakfast feast followed the services. Aaron would have to resume his jogging routine soon. They all would if they continued to eat like this.

After that, it was nothing but organized mayhem at Bayou Rose. Ed drove Mother Jacinta to the airport and took Lily Beth and the kids to one of her friends, just to keep them out of the way. A physician's assistant arrived and was up at one of the cottages setting up a makeshift examining room for the girls when they arrived.

Aaron helped Aunt Mel carry a folding table and chairs up to another cottage, along with a laptop, a phone and its charger, and some office supplies so she could work with the social worker when he arrived in processing the girl's histories.

"You seem happy," Aunt Mel commented.

"I am." *I've got to stop grinning, or everyone will know . . . if they don't already.*

"Your dinner went well?"

And what came before and after. "Perfect."

"Should I be making plans?"

If I'm lucky. But wait, I better cross my fingers, knock on wood, toss salt over my shoulder, and all that crap, just in case. "Not yet." Changing the subject, he said, "I'm sorry to have mixed you up in all this mess. And the danger."

"Pfff! What else would I be doing back in Alaska? I never was much for knitting. At least I feel useful here. And I still say you should have let me fly tonight. I keep my license up to date."

Oh, Lord! "Maybe some other time. If you decide to stick around here." The last he said with a question in his voice.

"It all depends."

"On what?"

"Whether I'm needed."

He noticed that she hadn't said "wanted." That went without saying. "We will always need you."

She nodded, with tears in her eyes.

He hugged her, and might have had a tear in his eye, too.

"Of course I could always join one of those Internet dating sites. But, no. I tried eLesbo.com one time and what showed up at my door was a sixty-year-old woman with purple hair on a Harley with so many piercings she probably ran like a sieve whenever she took a drink of water. Not that she drank water. Oh, no! She asked me if I had any vodka in the house. She liked it straight up. Preferably Smirnoff."

"You're kidding!" Aaron said, aghast.

"Of course I'm kidding," Aunt Mel said, giving him a playful punch on the arm.

Oh, Lord!

Between Aunt Mel and Tante Lulu—who was dressed today all in black, commando-style, including a black kerchief wrapped around her head and tied in the back and a kitchen knife strapped to her belt—he might very well have a heart attack . . . or attack the supply of bourbon hidden in the library closet. When he'd questioned her attire, she'd given him one of her dirty looks, aka "the stink eye," and said, "Someone's gotta protect the home front while the rest of you are gallavantin' off ta fight the tangos." She must have picked up that term from Brother Jake.

Oh, Lord!

Back in the dining room of the mansion, the two Brothers and Sister Mary Michael were busy tying up last-minute details for the mission. More maps on the wall!

Oh, Lord!

As for Fleur, last he saw her, she was in the kitchen whipping up masses of food with Tante Lulu. Unlike Tante Lulu, Fleur was dressed for the weather, another steamy late August day coming up. Demure Daisy Dukes—demure as in short, cut-off denim shorts, but not so short that her butt cheeks showed. *Shucks!* A stretchy-necked peasant blouse that begged a snap from a male finger. *Mine, in particular.* And a ponytail that bared her neck. *Wonder what she'd do if I snuck up and blew in her ear?*

She blushed whenever he looked at her. Which was often. He was about to go to the kitchen to see if he could make her blush some more when he saw Dan driving up. He met him in the front hall. "I wasn't expecting you this morning."

"Just came by to drop off laundry and pick up some clean clothes." He motioned for Aaron to follow him upstairs.

Just then, Emily came out of the bathroom (*Don't ask!*) and Dan brightened. "Hey, Em! How's my girl?"

The miniature pig, who was not so mini anymore, barely gave Dan a look as she passed them by. Aaron could tell that his brother was a little miffed, especially when he called out, "I can always give Miss Piggy a call, you know."

Emily just raised her snout and continued trotting down the hall toward her new BFF, the Irish priest.

"Is it my breath?" Dan asked with a laugh.

"Could be. Did you have bacon for breakfast?"

They headed upstairs to the master bedroom where Dan opened an empty suitcase on the king-size bed and started to pile underwear and socks (always dark blue or dark brown depending on his pants), folded shirts still in their laundry cardboards, two pairs of khakis with perfect creases (no doubt due to Aunt Mel's ironing), and a half-dozen ties from the closet rack that held another dozen. Aaron wasn't sure if he even owned six ties, probably two, maybe three max.

"How's Samantha?" Aaron asked as he arranged

himself on the bed, propped on two pillows, with his hands folded at his nape.

"I'm worried."

Uh-oh! Aaron sat up. "What?"

"It doesn't look like she'll be able to carry to term."

"Oh, my God! What happened?"

"Nothing happened. It's just that one of the babies is in the wrong position for a vaginal delivery. That on top of her age for a first baby. And some other minor complications." He shrugged. "They'll probably have to do a C-section."

Aaron didn't know much about childbirth, but he seemed to recall that a C-section was considered major surgery and a last resort. "When?"

"I don't know. We're playing it by ear."

"Soon?"

"Possibly."

"Oh, man! Please don't let it be tonight."

"Tell me about it!" Dan said, clicking the suitcase shut and sitting down on the edge of the bed. "I'm coming back here tonight to help with the rescued girls."

"You don't have to do that. There will be a doctor here, coming from Alabama, I think."

"Yeah, but I have local hospital privileges. If something critical comes up with one of the girls, I could get her admitted with the least amount of trouble."

"Well, then, you just better tell Sonny and Cher to hold on, at least until tomorrow. Better yet, next week. I have plans for tomorrow."

"Oh? Do I sense a certain glow about you today? Dare I hope you got lucky, finally?"

First, grinning. Now, glowing. I give up. "Super lucky!"

"I actually knew that. I got a tingly feeling last night."

"You did not." Twins *did* get the odd sharing of emotions, even pain, across wide distances at times, but he wasn't so sure about communal sex.

"Yeah, I did. Right here." Dan pointed at his crotch. "And believe me, I haven't been getting any tingles of my own for the past two months. So, bring 'em on."

"You are so full of it."

"Seriously, though, Aaron, I hope it all works out the way you want it to." But then he grinned. "Do I need to have Aunt Mel pull out my tux?"

"Let's not get ahead of ourselves. I don't want to jinx anything."

"Okay. Just one thing." He paused. "I better be the best man."

"You already are."

Mission Impossible . . . or Mission Possible? . . .

Finally, it was eight p.m., time to head out for the mission, and Fleur was more than ready for it all to be over. Brother Jake and Brother Brian wore uniforms with logos for a cable company and a plumbing contractor, while Aaron wore farmer bib coveralls. Fleur and Sisters Mary Michael and Carlotta were dressed in full-length, black nun habits, complete with wimples. Luckily, Mother Jacinta had left behind outfits in several different sizes just in case they might be needed. It wasn't the first time they'd used religious costumes as disguises, both the men and women.

The five of them were all packed into Mel's rental

car and Aaron's truck with its newly installed side door
logo and fake license plate.

Aaron kept glancing her way with dismay. He was
probably worried that she would grow to like this nunly
attire way too much. Not a chance. It was hot and itchy
and very uncomfortable.

Fleur and Sister Carlotta would be coming back
here in the bus, hopefully carrying a dozen girls from
Mexico, and Sister Mary Michael would follow in the
rental car. The two commercial vehicles driven by
Aaron and Brother Brian would take six girls each to
the airport. While the pilots were gone, Brother Jake,
with some help from Street Apostles on hand, would
clear the site. Then, Brother Jake would drive Aaron's
truck to the airport and wait for the pilots to come back
from their flights to Dallas and Mexico. The three of
them would return to Bayou Rose together in Aaron's
truck, by then minus the farm decals and produce and
fake license plate.

John LeDeux and Tank Woodrow, a fellow police
officer, would take the new girls from New Orleans directly to their Lafayette police station, claiming they
learned of the kidnapped girls at the last minute. They
would not be transporting into custody any of the bad
guys they could catch. Police would be called to the
scene after they were all gone to make the necessary
arrests. Luc was on standby back in Houma with Remy,
who could fly him there on a moment's notice, in case
they needed legal help with their superiors.

Originally, they had planned to have more of the
Street Apostles at the depot to help, but it was decided
that fewer was better. And, besides, they were all experienced professionals in one form or another. Fleur her-

self had been on at least forty missions for the Magdas over the years.

So, that was the plan. Fleur only hoped that everything went as prearranged. It never did.

Before they left, the priests gathered everyone into a circle and they prayed for safety and success, God willing. Then, Aaron pulled her aside and gave her disguise an exaggerated survey.

Despite his obvious panic over seeing her as a nun, Aaron commented, "Don't you look hot, sugar!"

"You consider this hot?"

"Oh, yeah. It will be added to my bucket list of sexual fantasies."

She laughed. "That's okay. I have a sudden attraction to farm boys."

"I aim to please, darlin'." He put his thumbs under the straps of his bib overalls and waggled his eyebrows at her. Then he kissed her, in front of everyone. "Don't take any chances. Be careful. I love you."

Fleur didn't have time to say anything in return. She wasn't sure what she would say, if she did. She was still confused. She did call after him, though, "You be careful, too."

"Always," he replied. "Especially now."

She wasn't sure what that meant.

"Remember, lads and lassies, caution is the key. Don't show all your teeth until you have the bone in your mouth," Brother Brian advised.

"Roger that," Brother Jake concurred. "Time to engage the enemy! Is everyone good to go?"

Frankly, Fleur thought they were both full of it, and Aaron must have shared her sentiment because he glanced her way and winked.

"Yes," they all said.

Aaron drove the truck with Brother Brian and Sister Mary Michael as passengers. Fleur went into the rental car with Brother Jake and Sister Carlotta.

On the way, Brother Jake communicated with his spotters on the highways from New Orleans and from the Mexican border crossing. All appeared to be running as expected. Adrenaline was running high for all of them.

They got to the truck depot at ten on the dot and drove to the far, darker end. There was an office with a light on inside and probably a night watchman. A small clapboard building held a restaurant that catered to truckers who brought their big rigs here for long-term parking when not on cross-country runs. It had just closed for the night a half hour ago, and people were leaving the building, calling out good-nights to each other, getting in cars and driving away.

Aaron squeezed Fleur's hand just before she went over to the school bus. She used her key to open the door and then made sure it remained open. Although she didn't turn on the engine, which might attract attention, she did put the key in the ignition, just in case she might drop it if all hell broke loose, as it sometimes did.

The two priests approached the commercial vehicles parked and ready for the trip to the airport—a red Dick's Plumbing cargo van, and a yellow Bayou Cable Company box truck. Sister Mary Michael and Sister Carlotta remained in the rental car, for now. Hopefully, John and Tank were here somewhere, waiting to come out at just the right moment. First off, the cops needed to take care of the guard. Which they must have done right now, because the light went out, then back on, and out again. A signal that all was well.

After twenty minutes, which seemed like twenty hours of waiting, a long, white, shuttle-type van, the type used by hotels and airports, pulled into the parking lot. This would be the one carrying the one dozen newly kidnapped girls from New Orleans. They'd learned last night that it would be only girls, no boys. The van drove to the far end of the lot, where they were, and just sat, its engine idling.

She saw John and Tank run at a low crouch up behind the van. While Tank remained unseen near the rear, John moved forward and rapped on the driver's window. Speaking rapidly, he claimed to be one of the advance men from Mexico for this exchange. The driver—a black man wearing a backward baseball cap, put down his electric window, but he didn't get out. The two of them exchanged angry strings of words and expletives. Something about idiots arranging a job for Friday night when they'd rather be with their women. The girls in the van could be heard crying and screaming until the man in the passenger seat yelled, telling them to shut up or he'd give them something to cry about.

Time for step two of the plan.

Sister Mary Michael and Sister Carlotta wheeled supermarket carts, which had been conveniently left in the lot for them, over to Farmer Bob's truck where the farmer, aka Aaron, and two black-clad men she recognized from the Apostles, began unloading potatoes and melons. Loudly, they discussed the donations for the convent and day camp, in case anyone was listening.

Immediately, the nuns headed toward the shuttle

van, Sister Carlotta crossing in front of the headlights, Sister Mary Michael toward the passenger door.

"Hey, hey, hey!" John hollered. "Watch where yer goin', Sister."

The driver was also shouting. "What're nuns doin' in a truck parking lot late at night?"

"Yeah, what you doin' here, Sister?" John demanded of Sister Carlotta, who was about a head shorter than John and looked very frail and helpless, in comparison.

Sister Mary Michael was being berated at the same time by the guy in the passenger seat because she'd managed to ram her cart into his door, which he was unable to open.

"We're just picking up some donations from a farmer," Sister Carlotta said, her voice quivering as she pointed to her and Sister Mary Michael's overflowing carts and the farm truck parked some distance away, then pointed to the Sisters of Mercy bus, where Fleur waved at them.

"Three nuns!" the driver complained. "This lot was supposed to be empty this time of night. You ladies better get the hell outta Dodge or someone's gonna get hurt." He was waving a gun in the air, inside the van.

"That's no way to talk to a holy woman," John told the driver. Then he turned to Sister Carlotta. "But he's right. You shouldn't be here, Sister. Why are you here so late, anyhow?"

"We got lost, and arrived three hours late. The farmer must have left, and so we are unloading the truck ourselves," Sister Carlotta said, and went wide-eyed at the weapon she'd just noticed holstered at John's hip. She began to back up, tripped, and over-turned the cart, as planned. There were potatoes and

melons rolling everywhere, some of the melons crack-
ing open and making a slippery mess.

"Sonofabitch!" John cursed and began to help Sister
Carlotta raise the cart and pick up the produce that
wasn't damaged. Also cursing was the driver who
yelled, "Holy fucking hell!" and got out of the van to
help John clear the space in front of his vehicle.

All the time this was going on, the girls in the vehicle were screaming and crying for help. Fleur would
have liked to go in and assure them that they were the
good guys, but no time for that yet.

The passenger guy finally managed to shove his
door open, causing Sister Mary Michael to go chasing
after the cart which was rolling away in the other direction. And Tank came up behind him, knocking him
over the head with a melon, which caused the man's
legs to fold. He dropped to his knees, and his rifle
slipped from his fingers.

"What the fuck!" the driver said, looking toward his
fallen buddy and Tank, who was using police plastic
cuffs to immobilize the guy, finishing with a potato
stuffed in his mouth as a gag.

John used that opportunity to grab for the driver's
gun and put him in a stranglehold.

It had all happened so fast, it had been hard to follow who did what. But then, Aaron and Brother Jake
and Brother Brian rushed forward with ropes and gags.
They quickly tied up and gagged the driver, then
dragged both men off to the bushes. Meanwhile, John
got into the driver's seat and Tank in the passenger
seat. They would be pretending to be members of the
Dixie Mafia making the exchange.

The girls in the back seats continued to scream and

pound on the windows. Perhaps that wouldn't be a bad thing. It would be expected. If they were quiet and unafraid, the bad guys would be suspicious.

The rest of them worked quickly to clean up the scene until there were no carts or fallen produce about. Aaron gave her arm a quick squeeze to assure himself that she was all right, but no words were spoken. She and the two nuns went to the bus to wait, while the others returned to their assigned vehicles. She noticed the two black-clad Street Apostles leap over the tailgate of Aaron's truck and burrow under the remaining potatoes and melons.

It seemed like forever that Fleur and the two nuns were in the bus together, remaining silent. Praying. Fleur's heart was beating so hard she could scarcely breathe. The waiting was almost painful. But then, with a swoosh of air brakes, a tractor trailer turned into the lot, followed by a dark-windowed SUV. Which meant there would probably be at least four men to deal with. Maybe more.

The driver got out of the truck and stretched, looking around. His cohort got out of the other side and went back to talk to the driver of the SUV. Two other men got out of the SUV. Okay, that meant six men had been sent to handle this mission—the two from New Orleans who had been driving the shuttle van, and the four from Mexico. Not a lot, considering the numbers on this side, but they were armed. A decided advantage.

Wait. Wait. Wait. As Brother Brian had warned, timing was everything. One of the men began walking toward the white van, and John yelled out something in Spanish. It must have sounded all right because the man continued to approach at a leisurely pace. Meanwhile, one of the men from the SUV proceeded to pee, right out in the open, and the other walked over to the semi, unlocking the back door.

The exchange had been planned so that the girls would remain in the vehicles they arrived in. Except the drivers would change, and they would be heading toward opposite destinations.

It appeared as if some final arrangements were being discussed by John and the other guy, perhaps some money changing hands. When some of the men moved to join their compadre at the shuttle van, Fleur turned on the ignition of the bus, which prompted all the men out in the open to become immediately alert, and turn her way. She drove the vehicle slowly forward, as planned, until she was right beside them. When the passenger door whooshed open, Sister Carlotta stepped down and said, "Could you gentlemen please help us? We're lost."

She was clearly visible in the headlights of the shuttle van, the SUV, and the eighteen-wheeler.

Fleur put the bus in Park and got out, too, pretending to weep. "Mother Superior is going to be so angry. We were supposed to pick up some parcels for her at the Truck 88 Shipping Depot two hours ago, but we must have made a wrong turn."

One of the men said, "Piss off! We're busy here."

Another man slapped that man on the back and chastised him, "You don't speak to a nun that way, brother. What would Mama say to you, disrespectin' one of the sisters?"

A third man volunteered, "This is the Truck 88 Repair Depot, not the Shipping Depot. Where you comin' from?"

"Baton Rouge," Sister Mary Michael said, stepping out of the bus, which caused the men's eyes to widen, whether it was at her size or yet another nun on the site, Fleur wasn't sure.

"How many of you holy wimmen in that bus?" yet a fourth man asked.

"Just us three," Fleur said.

The men were all dark-skinned and spoke with Mexican accents, including the first man who told Sister Carlotta with much politeness, "You're about five miles off course, Sister."

"Can you help us find our way?" Sister Carlotta asked.

"We don't have time for this shit!" someone said. Another slap, followed by, "Sorry, Sister."

But then, engines of three vehicles suddenly came to life and moved quickly to block the exit, the two commercial vans and the farm truck. At first, the bad guys were frozen with shock. A melee ensued in which the priests and Aaron were yelling, "Drop your guns! Drop your guns!"

At the same time, the white shuttle van driven by John LeDeux with his partner Tank in the catbird seat peeled out, up and over a berm, and out of the parking lot.

In the midst of the chaos that followed. Running, punching, random gunshots fired, someone coming up behind Fleur, yanking off her veil and wimple and putting a knife to the front of her neck. "I should have known you would be involved in this, *puta*," Miguel said against her ear in heavily accented English. In surprise, she tried to turn, but he had a pistol pressed against her back with his other hand.

He began to frog march her away from the others,

right past Sister Mary Michael, who was not yet aware of what was happening, busy as she was with hog-tying another of the Mexicans with his hands tied behind his back and then roped to his bound ankles. The whole time the man was crying out long streams of curses in Mexican. "Shush! No taking the Lord's name in vain," the nun said, and none-too-gently stuffed a huge water-melon rind in the man's mouth.

The others were busy, too, engaging and incapaci-tating the enemy. Luckily, none of the gunshots fired a few moments ago had hit anyone, far as she could tell. But unluckily, Miguel had already maneuvered her into a somewhat darker area, heading toward the open driver's door of the semi.

But then, Aaron noticed her. He handed off to Brother Jake the guy he had pinned to the ground with a knee in his back and rose, slowly.

"Take it easy. Don't give the tango an excuse to do something stupid," Brother Jake cautioned. "Let me handle this."

"Fuck off," Aaron told the priest. "Let her go," Aaron said to Miguel in a voice cold as arctic ice.

"I don't think so, gringo. Me and Fleur here have a long history, don't we, baby?" He pressed the knife tighter to her neck, drawing blood.

Aaron inhaled sharply.

She wanted to tell Aaron to be careful, that Miguel also had a gun, which he might not have seen yet, but she couldn't speak with the knife pressed against her neck.

"This sweet piece of ass is gonna take a little ride with me. In that big old semi there. Any objections, fuckface?"

"Actually, yes, and that's Mister Fuckface to you. Miguel Vascone, I take it," Aaron said, inching closer. "You have no idea how much I've been wanting to meet you."

As if sensing the connection between her and Aaron, Miguel laughed and said, "This one, she has been trouble for me ever since I first fucked her lily-white ass. But the men liked her, especially those with a taste for—"

Aaron suddenly pulled a sharp knife from his back pocket and flicked it at Miguel's crotch. A direct hit. Miguel screamed and his leg buckled. His gun and knife fell to the concrete where they both bounced away. Fleur managed to slip out of his grasp.

The danger was not over, though.

The hit must not have been as direct as she'd thought because Miguel quickly yanked it out, righted himself, and managed to tackle Aaron. He still had Aaron's knife in his hand.

The two men rolled on the ground, first one on top, then the other. Fists flying. But then, Miguel was on top, and he had his knife poised to attack.

Fleur didn't hesitate. She grabbed the gun off the concrete and raised it. At the same time, Aaron managed to grasp Miguel's wrist and, with sheer strength, pushed the hand with the blade up from his chest. In that split second, Fleur pressed the trigger, aiming for Miguel's back, and, simultaneously, the knife twisted in Miguel's hand and somehow landed in his own neck. Miguel slumped, blood gushing from both wounds.

Fleur was shaking as she walked closer. Aaron shoved Miguel off him and took Fleur into his arms. He was also shaking, but she suspected it was more from his fear for her than himself. In any case, it was clear that Miguel was dead, or close to it. What was unclear was who was responsible, her or Aaron. At this moment, it didn't matter.

Brother Brian knelt over Miguel and murmured some words, making the sign of the cross. If he was still alive, now would be the time for the sinner to repent. But, no. Miguel was gone, and Fleur had a good idea of his final destination.

"Let's get this show on the road, folks," Brother Jake yelled. "Go, go, go!"

First off, they had to get the two dozen women off the truck and into the small bus and two vans. Most were under eighteen. They'd been drugged and the truck reeked of vomit and urine. Who knows when they'd been put in the vehicle? Maybe this morning. Some were crying, but most of them were hardened after years of the life, and they probably figured they were being shuffled into some other brothel.

They randomly separated the group into three parts. A dozen in the short bus, and six each in the two vans. The bodies of the four men lay on the ground, at least one of them dead. They would be left for police to dispose of.

Just then, there was the loud honking of a horn and the screech of brakes. Another of Miguel's gang? Or some of the Dixie Mafia alerted to the aborted exchange?

But, no, it was a big lavender convertible which swerved to avoid hitting the semi, shot over the berm which John had used earlier as an exit, and then came to a screeching stop in front of Fleur, Aaron, Brothers Brian and Jake, and the two nuns, all of whom had mouths gaping open.

Inside the convertible sat two nuns, the tall one in the passenger seat clutching the dashboard with whitened fingers, and the shorter one who could barely see over the steering wheel.

Aaron released Fleur from his embrace and went over to help his Aunt Mel free her fingerhold and step out of the car on wobbly knees. "I'm sorry, Aaron. But I couldn't let her come alone."

Sister Lulu, on the other hand, wasn't at all repentant. "Oh, heck, did we get here too late?" She was carrying a rifle. The kind used by big game hunters.

"Old lady, didn't you hear me say that we're a non-violent group," Brother Jake sputtered out. "I must have said it a hundred times."

"Pff! I dint know you were talkin' ta me. Everyone knows us Cajuns doan listen to no one when it comes ta our guns."

Brother Brian burst out laughing then, and they all joined in. The perfect stress reliever to a successful mission, although the two dozen rescued girls probably thought they were all crazy.

They were. Cajun crazy.

Chapter Fourteen

A little gratitude would be welcome . . .

The two pilots made a quick turnaround to Dallas and Mexico and back, and were in the rental car with Brother Jake by three a.m. on their way back to Bayou Rose. Along the way, they got updates on the outcome, rather progress thus far, of the mission.

All hell was breaking loose in Lafayette where John LeDeux and Tank Woodrow had delivered the twelve recently kidnapped girls to their superiors. They claimed ignorance of the dead or wounded or restrained bodies in the depot parking lot. Said they'd just got an anonymous tip that there was a shuttle van full of crying girls over there, and this is what they found. They had no idea what that empty eighteen-wheeler was doing there.

The news media was all over the story, and the FBI

had been called in, too. John and Tank were being grilled like crazy. Aaron hoped they held up. He was pretty sure they would be okay. John LeDeux was notorious for pulling off crazy operations, within the confines of the law. Besides, Tante Lulu would never allow anything to happen to her favorite nephew.

Fleur was safely back at Bayou Rose with the busload of a dozen other girls. How this would all pan out, Aaron had no idea.

"I'm getting too old for this crap," Aaron said with a sigh as he hunkered down, half lying across the back seat. "I don't know how you guys do this all the time."

"Once your heart starts beating lower than the speed of sound, and you pretty up your wounds, you're ready to go again," Snake told him.

"Just like the military," Brother Jake added. "You go where you're called. Except our commander has a bit more clout."

"It's like childbirth. You forget the pain after the delivery, and feel real good about what you produced." This from Snake, who hadn't a clue about actual childbirth. At least, Aaron didn't think he did.

"Speaking of which . . . have you heard from your brother?" Brother Jake asked.

"He was at Bayou Rose when the girls arrived. So, I assume that he and Samantha are still in a holding pattern," Aaron told them.

It was five a.m. and not yet dawn when they got back to the plantation. The cottages were dark, except for some dim lights, maybe lamps, and only a few rooms were lit in the mansion, the kitchen, and one of the salons. None of the bedrooms, as far as he could tell. He didn't see Dan's car among the three or four that were there, presumably the social worker and other volunteers. Even the bus was gone.

"I'm going to see if there's any grub in the kitchen before hitting the sack for a few hours," Brother Jake said.

"You know there will be," Aaron said, "especially with Tante Lulu in the house. In fact, I wouldn't be surprised to see her waiting up for you."

Snake yawned widely. "Me . . . I need sleep more than food. See you both in a few hours."

"I'm going to check on Fleur," Aaron said, and he didn't care if the two priests objected.

They didn't.

But first, Aaron felt the need to wash away the muck of this night. He went over to his pickup truck, which was still parked in the driveway, and pulled out a clean T-shirt and a pair of boxers from a gym duffel bag. He didn't bother to go to the *garçonniére*, but instead used the rain forest shower in the mansion. Within ten minutes, he was on his way to the third floor and Fleur's bedroom. He was barefooted, so hopefully he wouldn't awaken Sister Mary Michael, who was in the other bedroom up here in the attic.

He didn't bother to knock. Again, not wanting to awaken the nun next door. Instead, he eased the door open. To his surprise, he could see by a dim nightlight that Fleur was sitting up in the bed, wide awake. She opened her arms to him and said in a whisper, "I thought you'd never come."

He could have made a joke with some double entendre, but he was too happy to be home. Yes, home. And the time for jokes was over.

The terrible trouble was over . . . or was it? . . .

Aaron was still sleeping when Fleur slipped out of bed
at seven a.m. He was lying on his stomach, nude, with
his head resting on his folded arms.

What beauty God created when he first made man!
Fleur thought as she looked down on him. *Adam could
have been no more perfect in his heavenly design.*

Aaron was long and lean with wide shoulders, a
narrow waist and hips, nicely curved buttocks, and
black-furred legs. He was muscular, but not overly so.
Frankly, she could have stood and admired him for
hours. But she was already late, and there was much
work to be done downstairs.

Not for him, though. Aaron had endured a hard
night, even harder than she had, and she didn't just
mean the already purpling bruises on his arms and ribs
and thighs, even his face. And his stress level had been
higher, too. The risk of flying those girls to Dallas and
back into Mexico had posed all kinds of dangers, especially when Miguel's group failed to report back to
their bosses. If human flesh equated with money, they'd
probably lost at least a million dollars, between the two
mafias.

As Fleur dressed quickly in capris and an oversize
tunic which she belted at the waist, she considered the
dilemma she now faced. One of many. Miguel had
been killed tonight, by one or both of them, despite all
of Brother Jake's admonitions about nonviolence.

She wasn't sorry the man was dead. It would have
been either him or Aaron in that last struggle. But the
Bible said that people had to forgive their enemies.
She wasn't sure she was ready to do that yet. If ever. And

that fact certainly put an exclamation mark on her religious aspirations.

The thing she felt most guilty about was that Aaron now bore the burden of Miguel's murder, too, and it had been almost solely on her behalf. So, either way, she was responsible for a man's death.

It was a moral question soldiers had to handle all the time. Killing for a good cause. If Brother Brian hadn't left yet, perhaps she could talk to him about it. But then, he would probably want to hear her confession, and her face heated at what she would have to disclose.

Ah, well, these were weighty issues to be resolved later.

She'd been up herself until three a.m. When she'd returned to the plantation, around one-thirty, she'd helped to process the girls that she and Sister Mary Michael had brought in, with the help of Mel, Tante Lulu, Sister Carlotta, a social worker, a St. Jude's Street Apostle volunteer, Dr. Alphonse Dorset from Alabama, his medical assistant, and Daniel LeDeux.

Surprisingly, Tante Lulu had been the one most successful in calming the girls down, all of whom were now wearing St. Jude medals on chains around their necks, whether they were Catholic or not. The energy of Tante Lulu was remarkable for a woman her age. She'd still been awake when Fleur had gone to bed, even though, in the end, it had been decided that the best thing for everyone was sleep.

It had been a restless sleep for Fleur, though, as she worried about and listened for Aaron's return. He had called earlier, when he'd returned to the airport following his flight to and from Mexico, but still she couldn't be sure of his safety. She didn't hear the sound of the rental car until five a.m.

When she'd lifted the sheet for him to come into bed with her, he'd shucked his shirt and shorts with amazing speed, the grin on his face promising big plans. But he'd cuddled up to her, spoon-style, whispered against her neck, "I love you, Fleur," then fell instantly asleep.

She couldn't complain. In fact, sleeping in Aaron's embrace had been as satisfying as his lovemaking would have been, in its own, different way. He would have scoffed at that idea. Still, there was no doubt about it, she had fallen for the man.

On that thought, she traveled downstairs to find the two priests in the hallway outside the now-cleared dining room, dressed for travel in the normal garb of their profession. Actually, Fleur had seen some of the Street Apostles in the brown hooded robes of monks on occasion, but she imagined they would be uncomfortable in this heat and for traveling. No, what they wore now were short-sleeve black shirts with white clerical collars tucked into belted black slacks. What a switch from their attire of last night! Still, these two priests would turn heads at the airport, where Ed would drive them shortly for the short jaunt to Dallas. Many a woman would sigh as they passed by and wonder why the "best ones" were always either priests or gay.

"You're leaving already?" Fleur asked.

They both nodded.

"Our work is done here," Brother Brian said.

"Others can take over now," Brother Jake added, then laughed. "I know Sister Mary Michael will be glad to see me gone. I heard her tell that other nun that

I have a Patton complex, whatever that is. I don't think it was a compliment."

Fleur smiled and said her good-byes to both men, a bit embarrassed by the background yapping of "Holy shit!" coming from that infernal bird nearby in one of the parlors.

But Brother Jake just laughed and said, "No respect for God's disciples!"

"Rather humbling, isn't it?" Brother Brian mused. "Reminds me of—"

"Spare me, Lord! The man is going to start spouting Irish proverbs again, all the way to Dallas. As silver is tried by the fire and gold by the hearth, thus the Lord trieth this monk's faith. See, I know proverbs, too. That was a proverb, wasn't it?" Brother Jake was still rambling on as they picked up their carry-ons and walked toward the front door.

Fleur noticed that all of the animals had come to say good-bye to the Irish priest, too. And, bless his heart, he leaned down to say a special word to each of them.

The kitchen was empty when Fleur got there, but she could hear Tante Lulu and Lily Beth talking, back in the laundry room. Fleur was able to get a mug of coffee and grab a sweet beignet before going outside and up the lane toward the cottages.

It was hard to imagine that these twelve girls were the same ones she and Sister Mary Michael had transported last night. Scrubbed clean, wearing normal teenage clothes (shorts or yoga pants with T-shirts), they looked almost normal. Which they would never be again, not quite, Fleur knew.

Fleur found Mel in the first cottage with the social worker, both of whom were on phones, whether to parents or agencies that might help them, she wasn't sure. In one of the cottages, she found two of the girls lying in beds, needing medical attention from the doctor who was still there with his assistant. Daniel had left last night—rather, early this morning—when it appeared that none would need hospital admissions.

Sister Carlotta had arranged several girls in a circle in another cottage, and they appeared to be praying. Fleur noticed that one of the rescuees was clutching a plastic St. Jude statue.

Fleur found out from Lily Beth, as she was passing, that Sister Mary Michael and Ed were returning the bus and the rental vehicle this morning. They should be back soon with a friend of Ed's.

In the last cottage, there was a young girl sitting on a glider on the front porch. She was older than the others. Probably closer to seventeen. Her pale blonde hair framed a delicate face that would have been pretty if it weren't for the hardness of her blue eyes and a scar which caused one side of her mouth to lift slightly.

"Do you mind if I sit with you?" Fleur asked.

The girl shrugged.

Fleur just sat and they rocked forward and backward for several minutes. It was pleasant this time of day, sunny but not too warm yet. And the surroundings were beautiful. Not that this wounded bird would care about any of that. Not yet.

"My name is Fleur Gaudet," she said.

At first the girl said nothing. But then, she reluctantly told her. "Annette Tyler. From Louisville, Kentucky."

They rocked some more in silence.

But then, Fleur sighed and began to disclose her story. "I was fourteen years old when I was kidnapped by Miguel Vascone from a bus station in New Orleans.

My best friend Frannie was taken with me. She died a month later. But me . . . me, I died slowly over the next six years in one brothel after another in Mexico and other places."

The girl turned slowly to look at her. "Six years?"

Fleur nodded.

"Three years for me," the girl whispered. Then, "My friends used to call me Annie."

"Well, Annie, I can only say that things will get better. I know, hard to believe now, but they will. I'm proof of that."

There were tears in the girl's eyes now, and hope.

This is what I am meant to do, Fleur recognized, and began to relate the story of her rescue and the long years of healing. When she was done, both of them were weeping. Fleur took her hand and led her down to the cottage where Mel was still working. She told the older lady, "Annie would like to talk to you about her grandmother who might be willing to take her in."

To Fleur's surprise, Annie turned abruptly and hugged her tightly. "Thank you. You are an angel."

Hardly, Fleur thought, but she was pleased as she turned to walk away. That was when she saw Aaron walking toward her.

He was fully dressed in jeans, a Swamp Rats band T-shirt, and his usual cowboy boots. His face, white and bloodless, caused her to freeze and gasp.

"What's the matter?"

"They've taken Samantha into surgery. I'm leaving now for the hospital."

"Oh, Aaron!" she said, stepping into his arms and hugging him. "What can I do?"

"Pray."

Oh, baby! . . .

Aaron arrived at the hospital in record time. An atten-
dant was waiting for him by the emergency room door
and escorted him up a private elevator to the surgical
wing. That was ominous.

"Have the babies been born yet?" Aaron asked ur-
gently.

"Nah. I think they're waiting for you."

They who? "What? No way!"

But they were, the whole surgical team, and some
were not too happy about the delay. They would only
do this as a favor to a fellow doctor. "Can we get this
show on the road now, Doctor LeDeux?" a man in full
surgical scrubs asked sarcastically of Dan, who was
also suited up in blue doctor attire, complete with cap
and mouth mask and paper boot thingees over his
shoes.

"Hurry!" Dan urged Aaron, after tugging down the
mask to speak. "Nurse, can you help him scrub up and
get him in here pronto?"

"Are you crazy? I can't go in there," he told Dan. "I
mean, I'm here for you, bro, but you don't really want
me seeing your wife's coochie parts."

Dan laughed. "You won't be seeing her coochie
parts. This is a C-section. All you'll be seeing is her
belly when they slit it open."

"Oh, that's better."

"I need you," Dan said. And that was all he needed
to say.

The nurse scrubbed his hands and arms practically
raw before suiting him up like a blue space man, then
led him into the icy cold surgery room where Samantha

was laid out, surrounded by a group of doctors and nurses, including Dan, who was leaning over talking to her at the head of the table. Machines hummed and tubes connected her to various monitors.

"She's awake?" he asked the closest nurse.

Dan nodded. "She's had a Duramorph spinal, but we need her awake during the birth."

"Oh, boy!" he said and moved up to stand beside his brother.

"Hello, Aaron," Samantha said through a voice which was surprisingly calm. Her head was covered by what looked like a shower cap, leaving only her face exposed. And, man, were the freckles standing out on her white skin today! Had she already lost a lot of blood or was this how she always looked without make-up? As if any of that mattered! Dan was looking at her like she was the most beautiful woman alive.

But then, they bared Samantha's huge belly, which seemed to be rippling with activity. And Holy Craw-fish! Talk about freckles! And big ones, too! Some of them were the size of dimes. Probably because of her expanded skin, he decided with hysterical irrelevance.

After swiping her belly with some kind of disinfectant, the surgeon immediately made a slit across the bulge (*Whoa! How about a little warning, doc?*), raising a strip of red which got wider and gushier as the cut was spread. Aaron heard an oomphy sound beside him and watched with horror as Dan slid to the floor in a dead faint. Almost immediately, Samantha grabbed Aaron's hand in a death grip and ordered, "Don't you dare fall on me, too."

Thus it was that Aaron got to watch the whole bloody, gory, wonderful process up close and personal while his brother was being revived somewhere in the background. When the two slimy masses, covered with some white crap resembling lard, were removed from Samantha's belly, a nurse announced, "Here you go, Mommy," and placed them briefly on her belly where she touched them with reverent fingers. Then, the babies were handed over to a nurse for immediate suctioning and cleansing and medical tests.

When the infants made little squeaking sounds that passed for crying, Aaron couldn't help but exclaim, "Would you look at the peckers on those big boys?" Unfortunately, there had been a momentary lull and his words echoed in the silent room before laughter burst out.

"They're both boys," Dan said with awe, gazing at the newborns. Apparently, he'd risen just in time and he now took Samantha's hand in his to kiss the knuckles through his mask. The look they exchanged, then cast toward their newborns, which were being raised above her belly again for their inspection, now that they were clean, was pure love.

Although certainly of a viable size at three pounds five ounces each, as announced by one of the nurses, they were still premature and had to be taken away in small preemie carts to the neonatal care unit. This was all as expected, as Dan had warned him earlier when he first mentioned a C-section days ago.

The surgeons shooed them out then as they stitched Samantha up. She was already dozing off. Aaron went into a private waiting room with Dan where the two brothers stared at each other with amazement over what they'd just witnessed, then hugged each other tightly.

"Thank you for having me here," Aaron choked out.

"I wouldn't have it any other way. Maybe I can do the same for you someday."

"From your mouth to God's ears."

Whose ears? the voice in his head said.

It was a miracle, all right . . .

Everyone was excited back at the plantation over the birth of the twins, not least of whom was the babies' honorary grandmother, Aunt Mel. In fact, she burst out bawling at the news when Aaron called her a little after noon.

When Mel was told that the newborns, both boys, would be named David and Andrew, following on the *D* and *A* names of Daniel and Aaron, she burst out crying again. And then she laughed when Aaron told her that forever after the twins would probably be referred to as the DNA boys, which he had to explain, "You know, *D* and *A*." For some reason, that word association had never been made with Daniel and Aaron.

But then, he sent photos of the babies, and Mel wasn't the only one crying. They were adorable, even as preemies with their eyes closed and little caps on their heads, wrapped tightly in swaddling blankets. He also sent a selfie of himself and Daniel in hospital scrubs with their arms looped over each other's shoulders with loopy grins on their identical faces (more identical now in the same attire). The tagline read: "Proud Father and Proud Godfather-to-be."

Almost immediately after that, Aaron left Fleur a private voice mail message:

"Meet me in one hour in the garçonniére. *Man!*
Try saying that real fast. I'll bring champagne.
Wait till I tell you how I practically delivered these
babies by myself. Just kidding.
Did I mention, Dan fainted? WTF! He will never
live that down.
Anyhow, I'm on my way.
Be there.
Please.
Love you."

Aaron sounded higher than a kite, and Fleur had to
smile at that. But she also felt a tugging of her heartstrings at how excited he was over the babies, knowing
he could never duplicate that with her.

Fleur first checked with Mel to see if she needed her
help with the girls.

"No, we're managing here. We've already arranged for
five of the girls to be picked up by family. No, not here at
the plantation. We don't want there to be any connection
between us here and the rescues. A restaurant parking lot
outside Houma will do for the drop-offs."

"And the others?"

"There are some group homes for troubled teens
that have openings. The social worker and her assis-
tants will take them when they leave."

"It's amazing how fast it goes."

"Isn't it? But then, the longer it takes, the greater the
chance of the authorities or the news media showing
up. Not that we're doing anything wrong, but there
would be so many questions. I keep forgetting, you've
been through all this before, on previous missions."

"Yes, but they're never the same. Often there is no
family willing to take any of them."

"That happened with two of the girls today. So sad! To be rejected by one's own family!"

Fleur nodded, knowing how that felt. "Then, there are some girls who want to go back to the life."

"In any case, chances are that there will only be two or three girls here by tonight," Aunt Mel told her. "By tomorrow, those left will probably go back to the convent with the two sisters."

After that, Fleur went into the kitchen where Tante Lulu was cooking, again.

"Do you mind if I put together a tray for Aaron?" Fleur asked. "He'll be back soon, and I don't think he's eaten since yesterday afternoon."

"Sure, honey. There's ham and cheese and bread jist warm from the oven fer sandwiches. Sweet and sour pickles. Some of them leftover Alaskan Fried Green Tomatoes you like so much. A slice of my Peachy Praline Cobbler Cake. One of them fruit tarts from Starr Bakery. Canned pears."

"Enough!" Fleur said with a laugh. While she was preparing the tray, she mentioned, "Now that Miguel is out of the picture, you'll be wanting to go back to your cottage, I suppose."

"Yep. Can't wait ta get started on the cleanup."

Fleur was filled with sudden dismay. Would she be leaving Bayou Rose and Aaron so soon? Surely, Tante Lulu would expect her to go with her. After all, she had a job to fulfill, compiling her herbal remedies and writing her biography. "Did you want to go back today?"

The old lady shook her head. "Not yet. Still work ta be done here. Mebbe t'morrow. Tee-John took my car ta be gassed up, but he's bringin' it back any minute now, jist soz it's on hand."

"Speaking of John, is he okay? With his superiors, I mean?"

"Oh, that boy could wiggle outta anything. Allus could."

"And the news media?"

"Thass another story. The New Orleans TV station reported this mornin' on a bunch of kidnapped girls bein' suddenly rescued by some off duty cops in La-fayette. And they said the FBI was investigatin' that empty tractor trailer left in the parking lot. Thass all. Still, it's a worry, 'specially with the newspaper folks. Those journalists gotta dig and dig till they get some dirt. I figger it's best fer everyone ta lie low fer awhile. And say nothin'."

Hah! Tante Lulu had nerve warning others to keep quiet. But Fleur said nothing in that regard.

"Of course, now that the babies are born, and all those other babies are about ta be born, we gotta hurry and arrange a baby shower."

Fleur didn't like the sound of that "we."

"It'll be the biggest baby shower the South has ever seen. Has ta be when we're celebratin' at least seven little ones comin' inta this world, mebbe more. Not jist Samantha and Daniel's twins, but comin' up real soon are Luc and Sylvie, René and Val, Remy and Rachel, Tee-John and Celine, Rusty and Charmaine. You should start lookin' inta a place ta hold the shindig. Mebbe the veterans hall, or the convention center, or mebbe ya could talk Aaron inta hostin' it here. Yeah, that would be good. And games . . . do ya know any good games? They don't have strippers at baby showers, do they? No, I think that's jist bridal showers. But what the hey! Mebbe we kin start a new tradition. Then, there's the food. Oh, Lordy! So much work ta do! Ya better get started soon."

Fleur felt like putting her face in her hands. First she was to be a recorder of folk medicine history, then a biographer, a chauffeur, a companion, now a party planner. But she knew enough to keep her lips zipped. Arguing with the old lady was comparable to hitting a brick wall.

After she'd put the tray together and carried it over to the *garçonniére*, up to the second floor living area, she looked around at the disarray. Aaron had left in a hurry this morning, and there were bits of clothing about, a dirty coffee cup, an opened jar of instant coffee. She straightened up a bit and put a CD into an old-fashioned player when she heard Aaron come bounding up the steps.

"It's a miracle," Barry belted out, just as Aaron came swooping in, lifted her in his arms, spun them both around, and said, "It was. A miracle. I can't wait to tell you about it." But then he kissed her and added, "Later."

Happy birthday (or something) to me! . . .

Aaron was so happy he couldn't contain himself. On the way back to Bayou Rose, he found himself alternately laughing and crying, and even singing along with some country song on the radio, something about all of a guy's ex's living in Texas, and that's why he lived in Tennessee. He'd never imagined in a million years that he'd feel this way. About babies! And somehow it was all mixed up with how he felt about Fleur, too.

Crazy!
Crazy good!

And then, the icing on his personal cake of happiness was waiting for him in his apartment. Thank God she'd heeded his voice mail. She might not have. She might have been too busy. Or she just might not have wanted to. He hadn't been sure. But here she was!

Happy, happy, happy, crazy, crazy, crazy.

He felt higher than a kite, and drunker than a skunk. And he hadn't had a drop to drink for days. Maybe weeks. No, he'd had those beers a few days ago. Whatever.

With a joyous rebel yell, he picked her up, swung her around, and kissed her soundly. Which wasn't nearly enough.

Picking her up, he carried her up the stairs to his bedroom and set her in the middle of the room. "I'm going to take a quick shower to wash off the hospital cooties. When I get back, I expect you to be in my bed, bare-assed naked, ready to screw my brains out. Or if you're not so inclined, I might be willing to screw your brains out. Oh, man, was that too crude?"

"Go!" she said with a laugh.

When he returned, he found it was a day for miracles. Not only was she in his bed, bare-assed naked, but she was beckoning him with the fingers of both hands. "You know what I told you the other night, that I think I love you?"

"Uh-huh," he replied, hesitantly, as he crawled onto the bed and over her.

"Now I know. I do. Love you."

He was pretty sure the candles on his cake just burst into flames, like sparklers. Joy was a wonderful thing.

Then he found his joy in other ways.

Instead of tiptoeing around like he usually did with Fleur, worried that this or that might offend her or remind her of other times or other men, he let himself go. He just loved her. Loved her and loved her and loved her until she softened and began to respond in a like manner. With hands, and fingers, and lips, and tongues, and softly spoken words, he showed how he felt.

He couldn't be gentle this time. His emotions were too high and too raw. He was rough in his need for her. But she didn't seem to mind.

And he was done with coaxing, too. His kisses and caresses were insistent. "Show me," he demanded.

To his surprise, and elation, she gave back as good as she got.

When he entered her, he could have cried with the sheer pleasure of her body's reception. When he began his long, slow strokes, she was the one who cried . . . for more. When his thrusts became harder and shorter, and he made his final thrust into her spasming folds, they both shouted out their mutual elation.

"Tell me again," he whispered afterward.

"I love you."

"I love you, too. Oh, Fleur, what a day this has been!" He tucked her into his side, kissed the top of her mussed hair, and related what had happened at the hospital. He couldn't stop marveling over every little detail.

She didn't ask many questions, but then, he didn't give her much chance to speak.

"Wait until you see the little buggers. They already have a personality. Dave is more serious. He looks at you like he's trying to figure out how he got here. Oh, I know newborns can't really see. Then, Andy, oh, he is a wild one. Flailing his arms and legs, ready to skip this joint and go out into the world. Do you think they make cowboy boots for infants? Of course, these little guys will be in the hospital for a few weeks until they're bigger, but they're okay. Dan swears they are. Honestly, they are so teeny, their hands are no bigger than a half dollar." He noticed the little smile on her face. "I'm going overboard, aren't I?"

"No, you've just fallen in love with two little miracles."

"I have, haven't I? But then, that's not the only miracle I've fallen for." He leaned down and pressed his lips softly to hers. Her lips looked raw and kiss-swollen from his earlier roughness. He should feel guilty, but he didn't.

"Oh, Aaron, don't refer to me as a miracle," she said, putting a hand to his face and rubbing her cheek against his chin.

"Us, then."

"*We* are definitely not a miracle. Men and women have been doing what we just did from the beginning of time."

"Someone's in an argumentative mood. Okay. What say we create some miracles then?" He rolled over on his back so that she was on top.

He was teasing. He meant more sex. But she got an odd look on her face, as if he'd hurt her.

What is that about?

But then she made love to him, with a fervor that was powerful because of its tenderness. Afterward, she had tears in her eyes.

And he had to wonder, again, *What is that about?*

Some bucket lists are heartbreakers . . .

Fleur managed to get an appointment that afternoon with a gynecologist in Houma, a last-minute cancellation. She needed to get some conclusive answers before things went any further with Aaron.

Unfortunately, Fleur had to use Tante Lulu's lavender tank of a car. Talk about being conspicuous! Not that she was being secretive, exactly.

Dr. Georgette Vincent sat down with Fleur after her examination, and her question was blunt. "What happened to you?"

Fleur told her.

Dr. Vincent didn't seem shocked by Fleur's words, and she was compassionate listening to her story. At the end, Fleur asked, "Can I ever have children?"

"No. The damage is too great. In fact, I would suggest you have a D&C. Oh, miracles happen sometimes, but your chances of ever conceiving are about one half of one percent, if that."

"That's what I thought," Fleur said. "I just needed to make sure."

After that, Fleur didn't allow herself any time to wallow in self-pity, she had other equally important items on her to-do list today. She'd left Aaron sleeping back at his apartment. He wouldn't miss her for several hours.

She stopped by the admissions office of the branch campus of Pelican University and got brochures related to social work majors and financial aid.

After that, she plugged a certain address into the mapping app on her iPhone and within fifteen minutes found herself on a little side street in Houma. She parked in front of a small ranch house which was neat but shabby in a neighborhood that would be considered low income. In front, there was a tricycle, and on the door, a neighborhood watch sign.

Fleur inhaled and exhaled several times before getting out of her car and walking up the sidewalk. She rang the bell, and it was several moments before a young woman, no more than nineteen or so, wearing a waitress uniform, answered. She carried a toddler in her arms, and a little boy sucking on his thumb clung to her knees. The poor girl must have had her first child when she was only sixteen.

"Oh, I thought you were the babysitter. Can I help you?" the girl/woman asked.

The last time Fleur had seen her she'd been three years old.

"Hi, Sarie." Fleur gulped several times. "I'm your sister. Fleur."

Chapter Fifteen

*H*ope for the hopeless . . .

"What do you mean, you don't know where she is? You know where everyone is." Aaron paced Tante Lulu's little kitchen while she continued to stir something on the stove.

"Stop yellin'. My ears are ringin'."

"I'll wring something if you don't tell me where the hell Fleur is."

"Now, he's swearin' at me." She looked up at the St. Jude picture on the wall, as if she was talking to the saint. Then she swatted Aaron with her wooden spoon. "Sit down and have a bowl of gumbo. Then we kin talk things over."

"I don't want any damn . . ." He inhaled and exhaled to calm himself down. Fleur had been gone for more than a day, and even her cell phone service had been disconnected. He was frantic. Not because he feared for her safety. She had disappeared willingly. Still . . . "I don't want any food. Just information."

"Sit," she ordered.

He sat.

After placing the bowl of gumbo and a slice of buttered lazy bread on a St. Jude placemat in front of him, along with a tall glass of iced sweet tea, she sat down across from him. "Tell me 'zackly what the problem is."

"She loves me. She told me so. Just a few hours before she left Bayou Rose. I fell asleep, and then I had to run out to the airport to take a crew out to the oil rigs for Remy. When I got back, she was gone. She left a note."

"What did it say?"

"Not much. After thinking things over, she decided that we have no future. So long, it's been nice seeing you. Blah, blah, blah."

"She did not!"

"Not in those exact words, but that's the gist of it. Did she say anything to you?"

"Not really. She apologized fer not comin' back here ta help me clean up and asked if she could work on my folk remedies somewhere else for a while. Said she'd come back some other time ta help replenish my stock."

"And you didn't ask where she was going?"

"Sure I asked, but she dint tell me. Said I would be tempted ta tell you if you tortured me or somethin'."

He rolled his eyes at the torture notion. "I love her. I don't know what I'll do without her." He couldn't stop the tears that filled his eyes. It had been a day and a half filled with emotion, highs and lows, starting with the hospital yesterday morning. That seemed like eons ago.

Tante Lulu reached out and squeezed his forearm. "I do have one clue. I found it on the floor of my car." She got up and went over to the counter where she picked up a folded piece of paper, then placed it in front of him.

He shoved the food aside and unfolded the paper. It was a receipt from a gynecologist's office in Houma, dated yesterday. He frowned. "Why would Fleur have felt the need to go to a gynecologist yesterday?"

"Mebbe she wanted ta get some of them birth control pills."

"Yesterday? In the midst of all the chaos at Bayou Rose?"

Tante Lulu shrugged. "There wasn't so much chaos by then."

Suddenly, he understood. "It's because of the babies born yesterday morning. She told me a while ago that she probably couldn't have children. I bet she went to a doctor to find out for sure."

Tante Lulu nodded. "And the verdict musta been bad."

"Oh, man! I can see it all now. I went on and on about the babies and how wonderful the experience was. I must have made her feel awful."

The old lady narrowed her eyes at him. "Is that a deal breaker fer you? Havin' yer own kiddies."

"Of course not. Yeah, it would have been nice. But I'd rather have Fleur and no babies than another woman with a bunch of rug rats." He ran his fingers through his hair. "This is a mess. A total hopeless godawful mess."

"Hah!" Tante Lulu said.

"Now what?"

"You came ta the right place if yer feelin' hopeless."
I'll second that, the voice in Aaron's head said.

Beware of old ladies with plans . . .

It had been two weeks since Fleur left Bayou Rose, and
she was miserable. It had been the right decision, she
was convinced of that. But, oh, how she missed Aaron!

In fact, she missed Tante Lulu, too. And Aunt Mel.
And all those people she had come to know so well in
such a short time. Funny how sixteen years away from
Bayou Black and she hadn't missed her family, but a
few weeks with those LeDeuxs and she'd been en-
folded in their circle of love and friendship.

Fleur was staying with Sara Sue, babysitting while
her sister worked a double shift at an area restaurant.
Fleur had sworn to secrecy her whereabouts to both
Sarie and her brother Mickey, the cop, whom she'd also
reconnected with. Not that Aaron would think to look
for her with them, but still, she wasn't ready to meet
him face-to-face. Her emotions were still too raw, and,
frankly, she wasn't strong enough to resist the man.
Not yet. She would be later, though, she vowed. If
nothing else, Fleur was a survivor.

It was true what they said about love meaning sometimes walking away. Real love had to be unselfish.
Aaron was better off without her. Eventually he would
find another woman to love, who could bear his children. It was for the best.

Even so, it was hard.

During the past two weeks, Fleur had learned that
her youngest brother, Frankie, now seventeen, had

joined the Navy. Another child, born after she'd left home sixteen years ago, had died of a drowning. Her sister Lizzie, the one with Down Syndrome, had also died of some congenital heart condition; she would have been twenty-three by now. That left her older siblings, Joe Lee, Eustace, Gloria, and Jimmy.

Why was it that some people could pop out babies so indiscriminately, and then others couldn't have even one? She swiped at her eyes and stared at the notepad in front of her. She'd jotted down a few questions related to the folk remedy book she was working on. After finally getting both Jason, the toddler, and Miriam, the baby, down for a nap, she was preparing to call Tante Lulu. Fleur hadn't even given Tante Lulu her phone number, but she did promise to call every day at two p.m. to check in. It was that time now.

She scrolled down the contact list on her new phone and tapped Tante Lulu's number.

"Hallo!"

"Tante Lulu? It's me. Fleur."

"I know that, sweetie. How are you?"

"Okay. I have a few questions for you. It's hard for me to read some of the writing on these pages."

Tante Lulu laughed. "MawMaw had terrible penmanship and she couldn't spell worth a darn." She proceeded to answer all of Fleur's questions, then added, "I need ta pay you fer yer work so far. Where kin I send a check?"

Fleur had to smile at the blatant deviousness of the old lady. She hadn't told Tante Lulu where she was staying, although she might have suspicions. "You can pay me next time I see you, and I'll print out all the pages I have so far for you to proofread." Actually,

Fleur really could use the money. The five hundred dollars Mother Jacinta had given her when she left the convent was almost gone. She would need to find a job, even if she did go to college, as she planned.

"Well, see, you kin do that real soon. The baby shower is this Saturday at two o'clock, and yer gonna be there. I mean it, girl, I expect you ta come."

Fleur felt bad that she hadn't been there to help the old lady clean up her cottage following the break-in or to help her plan her big bash. And it would be big. A shower for multiple women in her family: Samantha, who had already had her twins, and Charmaine, Sylvie, Val, Rachel, and Celine, who were due to deliver in a few weeks.

"I've never even met most of these women. They won't expect me to be there."

"Oh, they're expectin' you, all right."

That sounded ominous. "Why?"

"'Cause yer my associate. Besides, me and Mel need you ta come early ta help set everything up. You doan expect women the size of whales with swollen feet ta do any hard work, do ya?"

The guilt trip now! "Where's this shindig going to be held?"

Tante Lulu paused before answering, "Bayou Rose."

"Oh, no. No, no, no!"

"Now, girl, it's jist gonna be us wimmen there. The men are gonna get t'gether over at the Swamp Shack. If yer worried about Aaron bein' there, doan be frettin'. If he ain't drunk outta his mind, or cussin', or cryin', he's off ta Dallas helpin' them Street Apostles."

"Crying?"

"Mebbe not cryin', but he's sorta sad. Mostly mad."

"What's he doing with the Street Apostles?"

"I doan know. Mebbe he's gonna become a priest, fer all I know. He stopped talkin' ta me after I called him a cranky ass. Yer makin' a mistake, y'know."

"About what?"

"'Bout everything. I keep tellin' people they gotta stop thinkin' they kin plan their futures without help from Above. You know what they say? Let Go, Let God. Thass what you need ta do, girl."

"Oh, Tante Lulu! You don't understand."

"I understand more than you think I do. Do you still have that St. Jude statue I gave you fer yer purse?"

"I do, along with the medal, and the prayer card, and—"

"Anyways, come over 'bout one o'clock. That'll give us plenty of time ta talk and help Mel with the decorations and such."

"I am not ready for this."

"Yer ready if I say yer ready."

After Fleur ended the call, she just stared into space. Maybe she *was* ready. Connecting with Tante Lulu and the women would be a first step. Maybe later, much later, she would be able to talk to Aaron. But by then, it might not be necessary. He would probably have moved on by then.

Yes, she would do this. And it would be fun.

She could swear she heard laughter in her head.

It wasn't the God squad . . . it was the LeDeux squad . . . almost the same! . . .

Louise Rivard had called for a pow-wow of all the Le-Deux family for Saturday morning at Bayou Rose. Oh, they would be long gone by the time Fleur arrived, but there was much to be planned before that.

Sitting at either end of the huge kitchen table were her and Aaron. Along either side were Luc, René, Remy, Tee-John, Daniel, Charmaine, Sylvie, Val, Rachel, Celine, and Mel. Rusty was outside playing ball with some of the kids and the animals. Samantha was at the hospital visiting the twins who hadn't been released yet.

"First off, wear a nice suit, and ditch the cowboy boots," Louise advised Aaron.

"What's wrong with my boots?" Aaron asked.

"I think he should wear a T-shirt and jeans," Charmaine said. "*Tight* jeans. You have a nice butt, Aaron."

"I heard that," Rusty yelled from outside.

"Better yet, wear nothing at all," Tee-John said.

"Works for me," Luc agreed.

Sylvie elbowed Luc in the side.

"What?" Luc asked.

"Behave," she warned.

"Maybe Aaron didn't misbehave enough," Daniel remarked.

"Like you're an expert on misbehavior!" Aaron scoffed at his brother. "Some people say you invented uptightness."

"Who?" Daniel pretended to appear offended.

"Everyone!" was the communal response from all present, except for Louise. She didn't see anything wrong with a little uptightness. "I still say we should have planned a Cajun Village People act out front for when Fleur arrives, and Aaron could be coming down the front steps—"

"—wearing nothing but his boots," Tee-John finished for her.

Louise rapped Tee-John on the knuckles with her notepad. She'd been making a list of everything that needed to be done for the "Fleur Seduction Project," her name for today's event.

"Now for the food. Did you bring the raw oysters, Charmaine?"

Charmaine nodded.

"How do I know if Fleur even likes raw oysters?" Aaron remarked.

"For a man who's bein' helped by his family, you sure are soundin' ungrateful," Louise remarked.

"I should be doing this myself."

"How's that workin' fer you so far, boy?" Tante Lulu inquired sweetly.

Aaron blushed and ducked his head.

"Well, if she does like raw oysters, I suggest a batch of oyster shooters. You got any bourbon in this house?" This from René, whose band played in enough bars on the bayou that specialized in that potent drink. A raw oyster with tabasco sauce in one shot glass which was downed in one long swallow followed by another shot glass filled with one hundred proof bourbon. Yum!

"Or you could offer her some of Sylvie's love potion jelly beans. They worked on me." Luc waggled his eyebrows at his wife.

"You said that you fell for me long before you scarfed off my chemical experiment," Sylvie said. Sylvie was a chemist who once invented an honest-to-God love potion that she put in jelly beans.

"It was a combination of both, darlin'," Luc said diplomatically.

"I brought the bouquet of white roses," Val interjected.

"I fixed the sound system so Fleur will be able to hear Barry Manilow songs playing the minute she gets out of her car," René said, "though why anyone would want to listen to that crap is beyond me."

"Hey!" Mel said.

"Oops! I meant to say that Barry would be serenading Fleur with sweet music in case Aaron doesn't have the words to say how he really feels," René amended.

"How *do* you really feel?" Daniel asked his brother.

"Bite me," Aaron replied. Under his breath, Aaron muttered, "This is a goat fuck waiting to happen."

Louise overheard. "Yer not so big I cain't soap out yer mouth."

After that, conversation swirled around recent and upcoming events. Yes, there would be an actual baby shower for the six women. Next week.

Mel reported that all of the rescued girls had been taken care of in one way or another, and that included the ones who had been taken to the convent in Mexico, according to Mother Jacinta. There was still some flak over local and federal authorities investigating the circumstances surrounding the rescues, but thus far no connection had been made with the Magdas or the Street Apostles. No one seemed too concerned.

Aaron said that Brother Brian and Brother Jake were already talking about a new mission, this time in the Philippines, of all places. He wasn't sure if he would be involved or not because of the distance and pilot licensing issues.

Daniel told them that he and Samantha would be bringing the babies home next week. With the help of Aunt Mel and a daytime nanny, they figured they could handle the boys themselves. Louise had seen the little critters at the hospital and they were adorable. She was already thinking ahead to the day when they would need their own hope chests. She might not be around that long, but she would make sure they got them anyhow, in her will, maybe.

She couldn't wait for all the other babies to be born, too. It was a glorious time. A blessed time.

Daniel also informed them that he and Samantha would be moving to Baton Rouge in two months. After that, Aaron would be on his own here. Or not, depending on today's events.

Finally, everyone had gone, except for Charmaine and Rusty, who were waiting for her in the driveway out front, and Aaron, of course. All the vehicles were gone, even Aaron's truck which had been parked out near the sugarcane fields, out of view.

"So, are you ready?" she asked Aaron.

"I will be."

"I have somethin' fer you."

"What?" he asked suspiciously as she reached a hand into her big carry bag. He backed up a step.

What did he think, that she was going to pull out a snake or something? Instead, she handed him a velvet box.

"What's this?"

"Remember how I allus tol' you boys, when you were back in Alaska, that I had a gift fer you from yer grandmother."

Aaron nodded. "You gave Daniel a ring from Grandmother Doucet before he married Samantha."

"And this one is from yer Great-Grandmother Chaussin, from the other side of yer fam'ly. It's not the usual kind of engagement ring, and the stone is small, and the setting's kinda old-fashioned, but I think it's nice."

Aaron opened the box to see a pale blue stone in a filigreed silver setting, maybe platinum. A few tiny diamonds circled the stone. Aaron didn't know much about jewelry, but he liked this ring. He thought it would suit Fleur. If she would accept it.

He hugged Tante Lulu and said, through a choked voice, "I love you, you old bat. You know that, don't you?"

"Of course," she answered matter-of-factly. "Now, go say a quick prayer ta St. Jude and get ready."

Then Aaron was alone.

And he did pray.

Sometimes being punk'd isn't all that bad ...

Fleur was driving Sarie's twenty-year-old Volvo, which was on its last legs, when it gave up the fight. At the bottom of the horseshoe-shaped driveway leading to Bayou Rose. So much for horseshoes and good luck!

At least she hadn't broken down some distance away and at least it was a balmy day, not too hot. And at least she was dressed for the weather in the same white sundress of Charmaine's, the one covered with bright red peonies that had been hanging in Tante Lulu's closet, not the coral one she'd borrowed later. And at least she wore flat-heeled white sandals, no stockings, for her short trek to the house.

She would have to call a towing service. Fortunately, she should be getting some money from Tante Lulu today, in payment for her work. Otherwise, she probably couldn't afford even the tow, let alone any repairs.

She took out the reusable grocery bag that held her wallet and the paperwork for Tante Lulu's project, along with a bunch of wrapped gifts for the shower. Nothing expensive, of course. Just hand-painted enamel Christmas ornaments for babies that she'd found in a boutique. They could be monogrammed with a marker later with the babies' names and birth dates. She'd already filled them in for David and Andrew LeDeux.

As she walked up the driveway toward the mansion, she noticed something strange. There were no cars. None at all.

Did I get the date wrong?

No, I'm sure Tante Lulu said Saturday. Come early at one, she'd said. The shower will be at two.

Oh, well, maybe Tante Lulu and Mel had run to the store for some last-minute necessity.

She walked through the ground-floor corridor leading past the storage rooms, the laundry, and then into the kitchen, which was spotless, and empty. That was odd. Where was all the food for a party? She peeked into the fridge and saw a platter of raw oysters on ice and some picky-type sandwiches, both covered with plastic wrap, but nothing that would do for a large gathering.

They must be having the event catered, and were forced to go pick up the food themselves for some reason, she concluded.

But why didn't they leave a note for me?

Because I'm not that important to this party, that's why. They would have had other things, and people, on their minds.

Then she noticed something else. No animals. Even the bird was quiet. Hmmm.

Fleur walked out the back door. All quiet. Too quiet. Walking around the side toward the St. Jude bird-feeder shrine thingee, she stopped in her tracks.

Oh. My. God! And that was a prayer on her part.

Aaron was sitting on a bench, facing the statue. He was wearing a dark suit with a white dress shirt and a red tie. And those ridiculous cowboy boots. Which looked new. And they were red! He was sitting with his legs spread, elbows on his knees, chin propped on his fists, deep in thought, or prayer, or something.

"Aaron?" she exclaimed before she had a chance to catch herself and perhaps sidle away without his knowing she was even here. But then, she had no car for a getaway. Hard to make a quick exit when hoofing it.

He stood abruptly, almost knocking over the stone statue pedestal of the bird feeder. "Fleur! I didn't hear your car."

"It broke down at the end of the driveway." She cocked her head to the side. "What's going on, Aaron? Where is everyone?"

Aaron shifted from foot to foot.

"You look nice, Fleur," he remarked. "Is that a new dress?"

Pfff! How like a man! This was the second time he'd seen her in this dress. But she didn't bother to point that out. She was too busy trying not to notice how handsome he looked . . . even with red boots.

What kind of man wears red boots? she asked herself.

One who's up to no good, she decided.

"Oh, hell! I'm not good at playing games," he told her when she didn't respond to his compliment. "Not this kind of game anyhow."

"Games?" *Definitely no good!*

"Yeah, you've been punked. Sort of."

"What do you mean?"

"This was a setup."

She wasn't so much angry or even surprised as she was panicked by this news. "By you?"

"By everyone. Masterminded by you-know-who, but everyone in the family got involved. Butted in, actually," he revealed, with disgust.

She didn't want to ask what he meant by "everyone," but she suspected that she was going to be embarrassed around a whole lot of people, most of them with the surname LeDeux.

"Why?"

"Isn't it obvious? So you and I could be alone." He dropped down to one knee and took a small box out of his pocket.

"Oh no! Get up, Aaron." She took a hold of his arm, trying to make him stand, to no avail.

He wouldn't budge. "Hear me out, Fleur. C'mon, sit down here and just listen."

What choice did she have? The image came to her, again, of her trotting, conspicuously, down the driveway, and along the several miles of lonesome road to the nearest gas station, where she could use her last five dollars to call a cab. She sank down to the bench.

But Aaron remained on one knee before her.

"What if I found out that you had cancer, Fleur? Do you think I would leave you?"

"I don't have cancer, Aaron. And I'm not about to die," she answered with exasperation.

"Precisely," he countered, as if he'd just scored a point.

When she didn't concede, his shoulders slumped and he went on, "Here's a hypothetical for you. Suppose you and I were a couple—don't interrupt—I need to get this out, my way. Suppose we were in love—a couple—and you found out that I was sterile. Sit down or I'm gonna tie you down. Anyhow, suppose I was sterile from some holdover from childhood mumps, which I incidentally never had. Just sayin'. Or suppose my sterility was the result of some battle injury, like it was with Remy. Would you have dumped me because I couldn't give you any kids?"

Fleur closed her eyes for a moment as pain struck her heart. He knew. Somehow, Aaron knew. "Of course not," she answered, "but this is different."

"How, Fleur? How is this different?"

"Will you get up? I can't talk to you when you're kneeling."

"It's only a one-leg drop down, not a kneel, and I'm not getting up until I get my answer."

"What answer? To why it's different?"

"No, to the *other* question. The big one."

She blinked away the tears that burned her eyes. "Don't do this, Aaron," she whispered on a moan.

"Will you marry me, Fleur? Will you be my wife and share your life with me? For better or for worse, and believe me, I would be getting the better end of the bargain, please, please, say yes."

She went down on her knees in front of him. "But—"

"No buts." He took the ring out of the box and slid the ring on her finger. "There isn't anything we can't work through if we love each other enough. I'll love you through your baby issues. You'll love me through my issues. Have I mentioned that I snore, and I'm really stubborn sometimes, and my boots stink when I wear them without socks, and I'm inordinately attached to my twin brother, so if you take me, you get him, too, and, boy, if you think I'm a pain in the ass, you should see—"

"Yes."

Is it as simple as that? All this grief and angst these past two weeks, and a mere mention of reversed roles, and I succumb?

"—how much he interferes in my life. To be honest, I butt into his affairs, too. But . . . yes? Did you say yes?"

She looked down at the beautiful ring on her finger, then nodded.

He said nothing.

At first, she didn't want to look up because he would see how tears were streaming from her eyes. She felt like such a fool.

When she finally raised her head to look at him she saw why he was remaining quiet. Tears filled his eyes, too, and he was gulping to hold them back.

"Oh, Fleur, I love you so much."

"I love you, too, Aaron. I tried not to, but I couldn't help myself."

"Good thing you gave in because I'm pretty sure Tante Lulu was going to bring the entire gang back to serenade you with a Cajun Village People act until you agreed."

"What?"

"Oh, I forgot to turn on the sound system. You were supposed to hear Barry Manilow bellowing over the bayou when you got out of your car. Some romantic I am! Should I go turn it on now? No? Did you notice my boots? I bought them just for you. Well, for me, to seduce you. That's the name of the boots. Yeah, some boots have names. These are 'Seducible You' by Sexy Leather Goods. I'm sorry. I'm talking too much. I am just too damn happy!"

Which caused her to burst out crying, again.

And then he was kissing her tears away, looking at her in wonder, then hugging her tight, as if he wouldn't ever let her go, then kissing and hugging her some more. Not surprisingly, they fell over onto the grassy plot.

But then, Aaron sat up abruptly and pulled her up beside him. "I'm sorry, darlin', but I can't make love to you in front of St. Jude. It just seems perverted."

"And perverted bothers you all of a sudden?"

"Well, yeah."

"Aaron, perverted would be if I dressed up like a nun and did a strip tease in front of the statue."

"Hmm," he said with a laugh.

"Do you think St. Jude had anything to do with us getting back together?"

Aaron took her hand and was about to lead her toward the house. "I wouldn't be surprised. I was getting pretty hopeless."

"So was I."

It might have been a flicker of sunlight, but it looked as if the statue winked at them.

Epilogue

It was a family affair . . .

Fleur and Aaron were married one month later at Our Lady of the Bayou Church by a visiting priest, Father Brian Malone, with a reception to follow at Bayou Rose Plantation. Everyone came. All two hundred of the invited guests! The weather cooperated with a beautiful fall day for the outdoor event, held under various tents.

Tante Lulu gave the bride away, telling one and all that she was responsible for this match. As if everyone didn't already know that!

Daniel, the best man, had tears in his eyes as he stood at the altar next to his brother. The groomsmen were all named LeDeux: Luc, René, Remy, and John, except for Raoul "Rusty" Lanier, Charmaine's husband.

All the men wore tuxes and looked "hotter than a goat's behind in a pepper patch," according to Tante Lulu.

Fleur's sister, Sara Sue, was her matron of honor, looking pretty in a rose-colored sheath gown. Many of the LeDeux men, the single ones, were giving her the eye. Fleur's attendants were all women born or married to LeDeuxs or were former LeDeuxs: Samantha, Sylvie, Rachel, Val, Celine, and Charmaine, and all hugely pregnant in their pastel-colored maternity gowns, except for Samantha. "Like a flower garden," Tante Lulu declared. Needless to say, the old lady had a hand in selecting the wedding attire. And the venue. And the food. And the music. The only thing she didn't plan was the wedding night, but that was another story.

But no, that wasn't quite correct. Tante Lulu hadn't chosen Fleur's gown. That had been her personal choice. From a New Orleans thrift shop, despite Aaron's protest. It was a vintage ivory lace cocktail dress that reached all the way to her ankles where she wore matching open-toed ivory pumps. On her head was an antique veil Tante Lulu had dug up from one of her trunks. She wouldn't tell anyone where it came from.

The flower boys were David and Andrew LeDeux in tuxedo onesies complete with tiny boutonnieres. They were being pushed up the aisle in a double stroller by their already slim-again mother, Samantha, in a bridesmaid's gown of pale green "to match her eyes," said her adoring husband. Samantha was the one tossing rose petals, not the boys, of course.

Mother Jacinta sent a pair of pearl rosary beads for Fleur to carry with her bouquet. The gift carried a note, "All according to God's plan. Be happy!" One of the recently rescued girls was serving as Mother's assistant these days and working out very nicely.

Fleur's brother, Seaman Frank Gaudet, was able to get a liberty to attend the wedding. He was seen in close conversations with another wedding guest, Justin "Cage" LeBlanc, a Navy SEAL, who was somehow connected to the family of Tante Lulu's long deceased fiancé Phillippe Prudhomme. Folks speculated that there might be another Navy SEAL someday in the LeDeux extended family.

A platform had been erected on the front lawn of Bayou Rose for dancing with the music provided by René LeDeux's band, the Swamp Rats, which played a mixture of classic rock and traditional Cajun. René, playing the frottoir, or washboard instrument, was a favorite with the crowd, and he even had his little son Jude come up and sing with him at one point.

Tante Lulu preened, dressed to the nines today in pink. Lots of pink. Even her hair. Enough said! Tante Lulu's gift to the pair was a huge—really huge—statue of St. Jude, which would eventually grace the St. Jude swimming pool/shrine at Bayou Rose. Enough said!

Daniel and Samantha would be moving soon with their family to Baton Rouge. Aaron and Fleur would stay on at Bayou Rose. No definite plans had been announced yet, but there were rumors about some sort of a retreat or haven or some such thing called "Wounded Birds" to be established in the cottages. Aunt Mel was involved in some way, and, of course, Tante Lulu.

Tante Lulu sat on a folding chair next to Tee-John, staring out at all her family and friends. So many of them! So many memories! So many good people!

"Y'know, Tee-John, if ya listen ta the news, there's

nothin' but bad people and evil deeds in the world. What them newsmen doan recognize is that at heart we are a world of families, whether blood kin or not, and thass the most important thing. Family."

"Amen," Tee-John agreed, raising his bottle of Dixie beer. "So, I guess you've about run out of matchmaking prospects. Time to retire the hope chests, right?"

She smacked him on the arm. "Bite yer tongue, boy. There's lots ta take care of yet. Jist look around you. I kin name a dozen right off the bat."

Tee-John smiled. He'd been teasing, of course.

"Even yer son Etienne."

"What? He's just a kid."

Tante Lulu just shrugged.

René announced a song for the bride and groom to dance to. An old blues favorite in the South that pretty much said, "If you don't like my peaches, stop shaking my tree."

When Aaron took Fleur into his arms, he kissed her softly and said, "Happy?"

"Happier than I've ever been. Thank you."

"Thank me later," he said, waggling his eyebrows at her.

"I intend to."

And she did.

And the (Southern) beat goes on . . .

Later that night, the maternity wing at the local hospital was busy with five—FIVE—women from the same family giving birth, almost all at the same time. Overseeing the whole enterprise was . . . guess who? A little old lady with pink hair passing out St. Jude statues and waving a Richard Simmons fan!

Nurses were said to have come from all the wings to get a look at the good-looking men pacing the floors and offering encouraging words to their wives. One nurse asked, "Who are they? I haven't seen so many hot men in one place outside of a Chippendales bar."

"They're LeDeuxs," another nurse replied.

"Enough said!" someone else remarked.

To everyone's surprise, all the babies were male.

Could the South survive five more LeDeux men . . . seven, if you counted the twins born last month?

"*Laissez les bon temps rouler,*" as Tante Lulu always said. "Let the good times roll."

Reader Letter

Dear Readers,

Did you like Aaron's story in *Cajun Persuasion*? I must admit this was a hard one to write.

Rule of thumb for writers: Never make a secondary character compelling if you don't plan to give him a separate story. And, boy, did Aaron turn out compelling in *The Cajun Doctor*! Who wouldn't love a hot pilot with a wicked sense of humor! Especially one who had such a poignant love for his twin brother and his new, extended bayou family. Why else would he have bought a rundown plantation?

Second rule of thumb for writers: Never write a character into a corner, unless you have an escape plan. Previously, I described Aaron as mysteriously disappearing every night and no one knew where he went. Here's a bit of gossip. I didn't know either.

Most of all, you have to admit that Tante Lulu was in her usual outrageous form. She had a great pal with Aunt Mel.

Hard to believe that *Cajun Persuasion* marks the twelfth book in my Cajun series. It all started with *The Love Potion* (Luc's story) and has come all the way to the most recent *The Cajun Doctor* and *Cajun Crazy*. What a colorful life the old lady has lived! What else could she possibly have in mind? <grin>

And, by the way, did you notice recent news stories about the Cajun Navy? You all know how much I love Cajuns, but now I like them even more. Google them. You might be surprised.

On a more serious note . . . although I placed this story of sexual exploitation as a back story to this novel, it is a horrendously real fact of life, even in the United States. Currently, there are more than 20 million victims of human trafficking worldwide, more than 4 million of those for sexual purposes. In the United States alone, there are 1.5 million victims, and 300,000 more added each year. The average age of the victims is 11–14 years old, and their life spans are seven years, once they are taken into the sex trade. Shocking, right?

I love to hear from readers and can be reached at shill733@aol.com or my website at www.sandrahill.net or on Facebook at Sandra Hill Author. As always, I wish you smiles in your reading.

Sandra Hill

Aunt Mel's Alaskan Fried Green Tomatoes

Fried Tomato Ingredients

2–3 green tomatoes
1/2 cup (or more) heavy cream
1 egg (beaten and mixed with a tsp of water)
1/2 cup (or more) flour
1/2 cup (or more) panko
1/2 cup (or more) cornmeal
Salt
Pepper
Sugar
Cayenne pepper (optional)
Oil (canola, preferably, but bacon fat works, too, if you
  have it)

Directions:

Slice and salt the tomatoes, then set them aside.
Mix the panko and cornmeal together in equal parts.
Set up four bowls containing, in this order, the heavy
cream, flour, beaten eggs, and panko/cornmeal mixture.

Note that directions call for one half cup to start. This is to accommodate however many tomatoes you choose. More can always be added.

Get the oil in a frying pan to sizzling, but not so hot that it would burn the breading on the tomatoes.

Drain any excess water off the tomato slices and now sprinkle lightly with sugar to cut the tartness.

Now carefully dredge each slice, both sides, in the cream, flour, egg, then panko/cornmeal mix. Fry on one side to a golden brown, turn, fry on other side. Try not to turn more than once to preserve the breading. Salt and pepper to taste. If you like spicy, you can also sprinkle with cayenne, or add a dash to the flour or panko/cornmeal mix.

Serve hot or cold with dipping sauce.

Dipping Sauce

$1/2$ cup mayonnaise
3 tbsp catsup
2 tbsp (more or less to taste) horseradish
1 tsp paprika
Tabasco (a dash if you like extra spicy)

Directions:

Mix thoroughly and refrigerate. If you have extra, it works great with fish or onion rings, too.

Continue reading for an excerpt from
the book that started it all—the first book in
Sandra Hill's sizzling Cajuns series,

THE LOVE POTION!

And don't miss the first book in
Sandra Hill's new Bell Sound Series,

THE FOREVER
CHRISTMAS TREE,

On-sale October 2018.

Chapter One

Forceful seduction, for sure . . .

Samson was a stud, no doubt about it.

With his usual raw animal magnetism, he stepped through the low doorway, then reared up, bracing a shoulder against the glass wall. Nostrils flaring and body quivering with tension, he surveyed the far corner where his "harem" huddled together in fear.

Or was it anticipation?

Immediately, his beady eyes honed in on one female . . . Delilah. She was nibbling on a tiny red jelly bean. It mattered not that her mousy brown hair stood up in spikes, unlike the renowned beauty of her namesake. Or that she darted her head this way and that,

seeking escape . . . a clear contradiction to the famed
Biblical siren who supposedly craved sexual attention.
At the same time, her timid glance kept returning
to Samson. Clearly, she was attracted, despite herself.

Samson was not so shy. His widespread stance and
outthrust pelvis sent a message as old as time. *I am
male. I am aroused. And I want you.* There would be
no escape for Delilah. Not from this glass-walled
prison. Not from the scurvy rat who would have his
way with her.

But Samson was a cool dude. He didn't force his at-
tentions on any female. He didn't have to. Snagging her
gaze, Samson held his prey transfixed . . . the first step
in eroding her defenses. Then he waited.

Delilah made a little squealing sound of protest,
but couldn't seem to break the eye contact. It was as if
she were under some spell. Nervously, she gulped
down her jelly bean, followed by two more, a yellow
and a green. Gradually her body relaxed, and her eyes
dilated with some strong emotion. The only thing
missing from her surrender was the white flag.

Samson moved forward slowly, cutting Delilah from
the pack. Every movement he made, from narrowed
eyes to self-assured body movements, bespoke a fever
pitch of sexual arousal. Delilah was becoming equally
affected, a shivering mass of excitement, the closer
he got.

Acting swiftly, Samson pounced on Delilah, giving
her no chance for second thoughts. Without foreplay,
he mounted her and was soon thrusting frantically, as
if he had not done this a hundred times before. As if
they would get no other chance to repeat the ecstasy.

Then, when they were both exhausted with sexual
satiety and the door to Delilah's "prison" swung open

providing a means of escape, Delilah did the strangest
thing. Instead of darting for freedom, she cuddled next
to Samson and nuzzled his neck. The victim was staying with her seducer, *by choice,* even after the fever
had passed. It was almost as if Delilah loved Samson.
Amazing!

Amazing . . . because Samson really was a rat.

Success is sweet . . .

"I did it! I did it!" Dr. Sylvie Fontaine shrieked with ex-
hilaration. "Move over, Viagra. Here comes JBX . . . 'The
Jelly Bean Fix.' "

Her best friend, Blanche Broussard, stood with her
arms crossed over her chest, shaking her head at what
she must consider an overexuberant reaction on Sylvie's part to a mere scientific experiment. *Mere?* There
was nothing *mere* about this. It was so much more . . .
the breakthrough of the century!

Sylvie had just run the hundredth trial run on her
JBX project . . . the hundredth *successful* trial run.
Despite her methodical, time-consuming analyses, she
was still stunned at the fact staring her in the face . . .
through two sets of beady, sex-glazed eyes.

"I have invented an honest-to-God, legitimate love
potion," she said in an awe-filled whisper. "In two
weeks the human experiments will begin, but there's
no doubt as to the outcome."

Unable to contain her elation, Sylvie boogied a little
victory dance around her research lab, witnessed only
by a bunch of unimpressed rats and the equally unimpressed Blanche.

"Yech!" Blanche had a profound dislike for rodents

of any type, even the cute, miniature variety of rats that
Sylvie used, which were more like large mice, and she
stood tentatively on the far side of the room, away from
the animal cages. She brushed a hand with perfectly
manicured lavender nails over the front of her long,
gauzy dress, as if she might be contaminated, even
from that distance.

In her white lab coat, plain linen shirt, and jeans,
Sylvie felt frumpy and staid next to Blanche, but after
more than thirty years of friendship—thirty-three, if
you counted the time they'd spent lying next to each
other in high-wheeled, designer carriages while their
nannies strolled them to Magnolia Park as babies—
she'd long ago given up on competing with Blanche's
beauty or flair for style.

"Really, Sylv, you've gotta get a personal life.
Watching rats have sex is not . . . well, normal."

"Is that a professional opinion? From 'The Love Astrologer'?" Sylvie asked with a grin. Blanche was a
self-trained astrologer, a local radio celebrity whose
"love horoscopes" were must-listening every morning
across Louisiana—a combination star chart analysis
and philosophy for daily living.

"I develop horoscopes for all aspects of life, not just
love charts," Blanche corrected her with a little harrumphing sound of consternation. "But you're changing
the subject, Sylv." She let out a whoosh of exasperation.
"You've been cooped up in this dreary place for too
long, hon."

"Do you think this is dreary?" Sylvie was so used to
the dim light lab rats preferred that she no longer noticed. "You just don't get it, Blanche. I have invented a
love potion . . . *a love potion!*"

"Well, big whoop! A potion to reduce thighs . . . now *that* I could get excited about."

"As if you have to worry about your thighs!" Sylvie made several more notes on her clipboard before casting a sidelong glance of disgust at Blanche's perfect figure. At five-foot-ten, Blanche didn't carry an ounce of excess fat. Sylvie, a good four inches shorter, didn't either, but she had to work at it every single day. Darn it!

"Every woman in the world has to worry about her thighs, honey. Especially after she passes the big Three-Oh. Forget cellulite. *Everything* starts to swell up or slip down then."

"That's precisely why my discovery is so important. It moves the emphasis away from physical appearance."

"With rat aphrodisiacs? Disgusting!"

Blanche just didn't understand.

In this spare room, off the main laboratories of Terrebonne Pharmaceuticals, Inc., a company that dealt almost exclusively with birth control and hormone replacement products, Sylvie had been conducting her experiments for the past year on dozens of rodent couples in their glass-walled cages. It hadn't started out that way. She'd been immersed in her regular work involving progesterone when she noticed an elevation in pheromone levels as different ingredients were manipulated. Out of that had grown her JBX Project, which would be of special interest to any for-profit company, especially after the way Pfizer stock had almost doubled in price following the announcement in mid-'98 of its little blue pill.

Of course, there was a world of difference between Viagra and JBX, but they were both drugs that could enhance a person's love life. The public would love it . . . there was no doubt about that fact in Sylvie's mind.

She'd given her chemical formula to just the male rat, the male and female, just the female, two males, two females, every combination possible. She'd adjusted the proportions, measured heart rates and blood pressure, tested blood samples, studied changes in physical characteristics. Samson and Delilah were the standard against which all the other "guinea pigs" were studied, and they'd proven in more than a hundred encounters that physical and emotional attraction could be directed *on a short-term basis*.

Oh, the idea of inciting or heightening lust had been around since the beginning of time. Everything from amulets to oysters. And, of course, Viagra. But being able to orchestrate the emotions, perhaps even love itself, through chemistry, now that was a big-time breakthrough.

"Isn't this illegal or something, hon? Drugging someone without their permission?"

"Well, in the wrong hands it could be problematic, but that will never happen . . . well, any more than Viagra, or any other substance, is misused. Besides, it will be at least a year before we're ready to go public with this . . . lots of time to iron out those little wrinkles."

"But it sounds sort of like that date rape drug, GHB . . . you know, the one they call 'Easy Lay.' "

"Absolutely not! Gamma-hydroxybutyric acid knocks a person out; my love potion turns them on . . . *emotionally*. Well, physically, too, but the most important part is that the receiving party is attracted temporarily, on an emotional level, lasting anywhere from a few days to several weeks."

"I just don't know, Sylvie."

"Think about it, Blanche . . . How many times have you and I said that the mating game is based too much on youth and physical appearance . . . that men and women often overlook the perfect partner? This potion gives that perfect person an opportunity to be with the mate they want, to have that person get to know the *real* individual. Hopefully, when the potion wears off, the lovin' feelings will remain."

"But the ethics of it all! The manipulation!"

"Hah! How is this any more unethical than following the advice of that popular book *The Rules*? Or wearing a push-up bra? Or seductive perfume? Health food stores are loaded with bottled love aids. Heck, women have been manipulating men, and vice versa, for centuries, ever since Eve gave Adam the apple."

"I know you've worked hard to conquer your shyness, Sylvie, but I still can't visualize you setting yourself up for the publicity this would engender. *You* would be the spokesperson for this potion when it hits the market, right?"

"No! Never!" She shivered with distaste at the notion of making a spectacle of herself, not having come that far in her shyness therapy. But she did want credit for her work. She came from a family of overachievers, and it was her turn to get some much-overdue credit. Fame and fortune, without being the deer in the headlights, that was what she wanted.

"Your company might feel differently."

She shook her head. "I may be working in Terrebonne facilities, but this is my project. All the project data is stored in my safety-deposit box, and the essentials of my everyday work are kept in that locked briefcase," she said, pointing to the desk, "which I carry home with me every day. I have no interest in being personally associated with this product in the public eye, but I do expect recognition behind the scenes and in the professional scientific community."

"This is all about your boss, isn't it, Sylv?" Blanche walked over to the coffeemaker in the corner, the multi-colored bands of purple in her skirt shimmering in the thin stream of sunlight coming through the single window.

"Partly," Sylvie admitted, taking one of the cups her friend handed to her. Before she continued, she took a sip, savoring as always the pungent scent of the thick, black Creole coffee, with enough caffeine to revive a corpse. In fact, it was one of the secret ingredients in her love potion formula—an idea she'd gotten from the voodoo ritual handbook that had once belonged to her great-grandmother many times removed, Marie Baptiste, the demented antebellum mistress of a sugar plantation out on Bayou Noir. "I mean, I didn't start this experiment with Charles in mind, but once I saw the implications, I knew that I would volunteer to be one of the dozen female guinea pigs when the human experiments began, and Charles would be one of the dozen male targets. It took a little convincing, but eventually he agreed . . . for the sake of the company. We're starting in two weeks."

"Charles Henderson is a middle-aged dweeb . . . an executive stick-in-the-mud. Bo-o-o-ring, with a capital B," Blanche asserted. "You can do ten times better than him. Besides, you're approaching this whole seduction business wrong. You zap a man with a love potion and it takes all the mystery out of romance. What's wrong with the old-fashioned way of falling in love?"

"Ah, but that's why I've been thinking that I would be better off with a man like Charles."

"Honey, you've been dating the wrong men if you think that. I wonder if you realize what you're doing here."

"I know exactly what I'm doing. No more handsome men with overinflated egos. No more BMW-driving, bottled-water-drinking, exercise-addicted, vitamin-conscious, suntanned hunks of testosterone in Gucci loafers. No more boring nights of deep discussions on the lofty subjects of golf handicaps or 401K portfolios or mega-amp woofers. It's time for a 180-degree turn in my life. All I want now is a quiet, scholarly type, like Charles . . . or a reasonable facsimile. A companion. A husband. A man to make a home with me and give me children. Lots of them." She sighed with frustration, knowing she was failing miserably in explaining her motives, especially since tears of concern were welling in Blanche's eyes.

"Where's the sizzle in that picture, my friend?" Blanche asked.

"I don't need sizzle." Sylvie raised her chin defensively.

"Sylvie Marie Fontaine!" Blanche declared, setting down her coffee and planting her hands on her hips. "Everyone needs sizzle. Are you sure there's Creole blood flowing through your veins? Every Creole woman has passion in her soul."

Oh, there was Creole blood in her veins, all right. Some families prided themselves on having ancestors who'd come over on the Mayflower. Sylvie's family took great pride in being one of the original white Creole families of French or Spanish descent who settled in the Louisiana colony centuries ago.

Sylvie laughed at the notion of anyone questioning

her Creole bloodlines. Meanwhile, Blanche swiped at her tears with a tissue, careful not to mar her makeup. "Do you really believe my mother or my grandmother have experienced a lustful day in their lives?" Sylvie asked. "Or Aunt Margo or Aunt Madeline? Even my cousin, Valerie?" She made an exaggerated shiver of distaste. Valerie was the perfect example of Breaux womanhood, held up to her as a role model from the time Sylvie first demonstrated her profound shyness as a young girl. Shyness and timidity in any form were considered a weakness in the Breaux family.

"Well, in every family there's an aberration," Blanche conceded.

"Aberration about says it all," Sylvie said with a sigh. In Sylvie's matriarchal family, there were no men. Mostly, they just gave up and died under all that feminine domination. In her family, the women didn't divorce their men; they buried them. The Breaux women were known throughout Louisiana as the Ice Breaux, in recognition of their cold ruthlessness in pursuing their goals. Her mother, Inez Breaux-Fontaine, was a state legislator with aspirations of being elected to the U.S. Congress. Her grandmother, Dixie Breaux, was a hard-as-nails oil lobbyist. Her aunts, Margo and Madeline Breaux, had stopped at nothing in setting up their mail-order-tea dynasty. Valerie Breaux, daughter of her deceased Uncle Henri, made no apologies for her roughshod, fast-track career path from jury consultant to Court TV anchor.

The look of compassion in Blanche's eyes said without words that she understood perfectly how many of Sylvie's present actions were based, deep down, on lifelong insecurities stemming from her family. With a shrug of resignation, Blanche asked, "So, when are you going to do the deed?"

"Soon. Two weeks . . . a month, at most. We're still synchronizing schedules for all the test candidates." Sylvie pointed to a petri dish filled with dozens of jelly beans.

"Jelly beans?" Blanche raised an eyebrow in question.

"Yep. My lab rats like them, and . . . oh, I might as well tell you. Charles has a passion for jelly beans, too."

Blanche snorted with disgust. "It's about the only thing he's ever demonstrated a passion for."

Sylvie shot her a glance of condemnation for that snide remark, even though it was true that Charles hadn't succumbed to any of the normal hints and downright obvious seduction techniques she'd tried the past year.

"Would they work for anyone?" Blanche picked up a handful and let them slip through her fingers. "I mean, if I give them to some guy, would they work for me?"

"Not those. They contain my enzymes. In order for them to work for you, your enzymes . . . in fact, putting your simple saliva, or a drop of blood, even a hair, inside a neutral set of jelly beans, like those over there . . . would work for you. Along with my secret ingredients, of course." She pointed to her briefcase, where a plastic ziplock bag held dozens of the multi-colored candies.

"Be careful, honey," Blanche warned as she picked up her purse and prepared to leave. "Sometimes the worst thing that can happen in life is we get what we wish for."

Sylvie refused to let Blanche's admonition dampen her spirits. Nothing could ruin her good mood today.

Man on a mission . . .

Lucien LeDeux was in a lousy mood.

He was supposed to be on a two-week vacation. The crawfish were fat and sluggish this summer, and he'd much rather be down in the bayou checking his nets than cruising into the sweltering city at rush hour. But duty called in the form of entrapment . . . by his own conniving brother.

"You are in some kind of wild-ass-lousy mood," his brother René griped from the passenger seat of the jeep where he was holding onto the crash bar with white knuckles. The right door had fallen off two months ago, and Luc hadn't bothered to replace it. "I think it's Sylvie Fontaine that has the steam risin' from your ears."

Sometimes René had a death wish.

"I think you've had the hots for her since we were kids," René went on. "I think your testiness is just a cover-up for deeper feelings. I think you're afraid of—"

"I think you better shut up, René. I only do one good thing a year, and your tab is runnin' out fast."

"Cool your jets, man. I was just pointin' out that you and Sylvie are—"

"Knock off the love-connection talk, René, or I'm outta here."

"*Dieu*, if you don't wanna help, I can get another lawyer."

"I should be so lucky."

"Maybe F. Lee Bailey is available. Or Roy Black. How about that guy with the fringed leather jacket . . . Jerry whatshisname?"

"Hah! You and I both know there isn't another attorney who'd take on your case."

"*Mais oui*, but then I am fortunate to get 'The Swamp Solicitor.' " René smirked at him.

Luc gritted his teeth and refused to rise to that particular bait, but he took great delight in pressing his foot to the accelerator and speeding down the highway, hitting every pothole the parish road crew had missed in the past few years. He got grim satisfaction from the surreptitious sign of the cross René made on his chest.

"I shouldn't have put you in this spot, Luc."

René's sudden contrition surprised Luc. "You had no choice," he admitted. "*C'est ein affair à pus fi nir.*" It was a much-used Cajun saying, but particularly applicable in this case. "It's a thing that has no end."

René nodded. "Perhaps we can finally put an end to it."

The hopeful note in his brother's voice tore at Luc's heart. It didn't matter if it was a seven-year-old René looking up to a ten-year-old Luc for answers, or a thirty-year-old René and a thirty-three-year-old Luc. Their father's misdeeds were never-ending. The scars never got a chance to heal.

Luc's stereo suddenly kicked on, and René's static-y voice belted out:

Bayou man is a woman' delight.
Catch fish all the day
And make love all the night.
Don' matter if he rough
Like a scaly red snapper.
Long as he give his baby enough
Good hot Cajun lovin' . . .

Even René's raucous demo tape couldn't raise Luc's spirits now. His brother was an excellent small-time commercial fisherman, a fair singer and accordionist on the side, and a horrible lyricist. But he fancied himself the next Garth Brooks of the Bayou with his combination of country, zydeco, and Cajun music, which he played on off nights going from one dive to another across Louisiana.

Swerving his jeep off the highway, Luc ignored the sounds of a half-dozen horns blasting behind him. His turn signal hadn't been working for the past year.

He took a quick look at the crowded parking lot of Terrebonne Pharmaceuticals and muttered, "That figures!" Without hesitation, he pulled his jeep into the "No Parking" slot reserved for the company president. The car continued to rumble even after he turned off the ignition, finally coming to a halt with a loud belch from its rear end.

"Your car needs a tune-up," René advised, unwisely.

"My life needs a tune-up."

"Yep."

Luc glanced over at his brother to see what that terse remark implied.

"You're a pain in the ass. A royal *chew rouge*." René was grinning at him.

"I know." Luc couldn't help grinning back.

"Let's hope Sylvie Fontaine has a taste for pain-in-the-ass, over-the-hill Cajuns."

"Oh, yeah! Ab-so-loot-ly!" Luc shook his head at the futility of this whole mission. "René, my agreeing to come here today isn't about impressing Sylvie. As if I could!"

"It wouldn't hurt you to try. You don't have to nail her, or nothin'. Just be nice."

Pour l'amour de Dieu! Where does René get these ideas? "Nail her? Where did that brain-blip come from anyhow? Me and Bunsen Burner Barbie? Ha, ha, ha." He shivered with exaggerated distaste.

Come to think of it, he always felt kind of shivery when he was around Sylvie . . . nauseous, actually. He couldn't stand the woman. Never could. Without a word—just a toss of her aristocratic head—she always managed to reduce him to the small, ill-clothed, bad boy from the bayous, anxious for a favor from an uptown Creole girl. Not that he ever showed it. Instead, he played down to her expectations.

"I still can't see why I have to be the one to approach her, René. You know her, too. I remember her greeting you at the Crawfish Festival last summer. Seems to me she gave you a big hug of welcome. 'Oooh, René, it was so sweet of your band to come play for us.' " The last he mimicked in a high falsetto voice. Then he added in a grumble, "All I got was her usual frown."

René laughed. "Sylvie likes you, deep down."

"It must be real deep."

"Here," René said, offering him the rearview mirror, which he picked up off the floor. "Your hair looks like a bayou hurricane just swept through."

Luc raked his fingers through his windblown hair, then gave up. Was he seriously buying into René's warped idea of impressing Sylvie?

"I still say you should have worn a suit."

"A suit! What, you don't like the way I'm dressed now?" He looked down at his jeans and the black T-shirt emblazoned with the logo "Proud to be a Coonass." He lifted his chin defensively. "My clothes are clean."

In truth, his clothes were always clean. Rumpled,

yeah. But always, *always* clean. One time Sylvie had
looked kinda funny at his muddy jeans and sniffed, as
if he smelled. It didn't matter that he was only eight
years old at the time. His clothes were never dirty
again, even when he'd had to wash them in cold bayou
stream water in an enamel basin at night, along with
those of his younger brothers Remy and René, and
wear them damp to school in the morning. A slap or
two from his father would be thrown in there somewhere. By mid-morning his head would often droop
with exhaustion, and Sister Colette would rap him
awake with a ruler to the head, deriding, "You bad boy,
you! You're never going to amount to anything but a
gougut . . . a slovenly, stupid person."

Lordy, he hadn't thought of that in years. No wonder
it rankled like hell that he had to go to Ms. Goody
Two-Shoes for a favor today.

"Well, come on," he urged as he climbed over the
driver's door, which was rusted shut. "Time to put our
pirogue in the water and see if we float or sink."

"Uh, me, I think I'll stay here. Better you should
dazzle Sylvie with your moves in private."

Moves? What moves? Watching his brother squirm
uncomfortably in the seat, avoiding his eyes, Luc realized that he'd been set up good and proper. René had
never intended to go in with him. Whatever. He might
as well get it over with. Maybe he'd still get in an hour
or two of fishing to night.

"Bonne chance," René called after him as he
headed for the front entrance of the pharmaceutical research company, where workers were beginning to
stream out, ending their workday.

Yep, it is a thing without end, he decided. *Sa fini pas.*

At Avon Books, we know your passion for romance—once you finish one of our novels, you find yourself wanting more.

May we tempt you with . . .

- **Excerpts** from our upcoming releases.

- Entertaining **extras**, including authors' personal photo albums and book lists.

- Behind-the-scenes **scoop** on your favorite characters and series.

- **Sweepstakes** for the chance to win free books, romantic getaways, and other fun prizes.

- Writing **tips** from our authors and editors.

- **Blog** with our authors and find out why they love to write romance.

- **Exclusive content** that's not contained within the pages of our novels.

Join us at
www.avonbooks.com

AVON
An Imprint of HarperCollins*Publishers*
www.avonromance.com